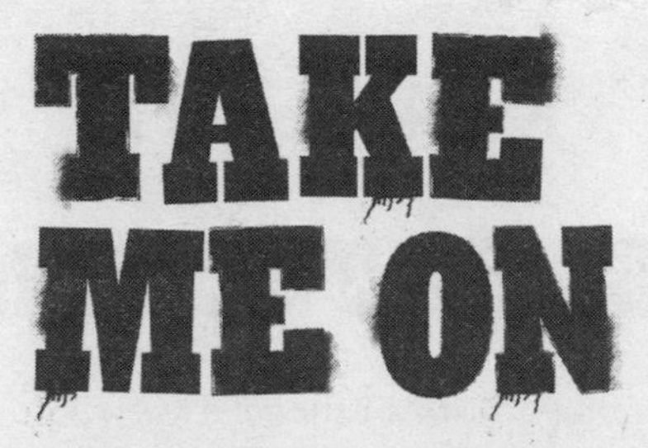

His lips press against my shoulder and I allow myself to melt into him.

Goose bumps rise on the back of my neck and I shouldn't, but I angle my head so more of my neck is exposed. He kissed me. I should tell West to stop, that he's crossed lines, but his lips against my skin created a feeling of togetherness, a closeness I've been longing for.

In quiet acceptance of my invitation, West skims his nose along the sensitive skin near my hairline.

'What did home feel like?' he whispers into my ear.

'Warm,' I whisper back.

Praise for

Katie McGarry

bestselling author of

PUSHING THE LIMITS

'The love story of the year' —*Teen Now*

'A real page-turner' —*Mizz*

'A romance with a difference' —*Bliss*

'McGarry details the sexy highs, the devastating lows and the real work it takes to build true love.'
—Jennifer Echols

'A riveting and emotional ride'
—Simone Elkeles

'Highly recommend to fans of hard-hitting, edgy, contemporary and to anyone who loves a smouldering, sexy, consuming love story to boot!'
—*Jess Hearts Books* blog

'McGarry is definitely a YA author to keep an eye out for.'
—*ChooseYA* blog

Also available

PUSHING THE LIMITS

CROSSING THE LINE (eBook novella)

DARE YOU TO

CRASH INTO YOU

Find out more about Katie McGarry at www.miraink.co.uk and join the conversation on Twitter @MIRAInk or on Facebook at www.facebook.com/MIRAInk

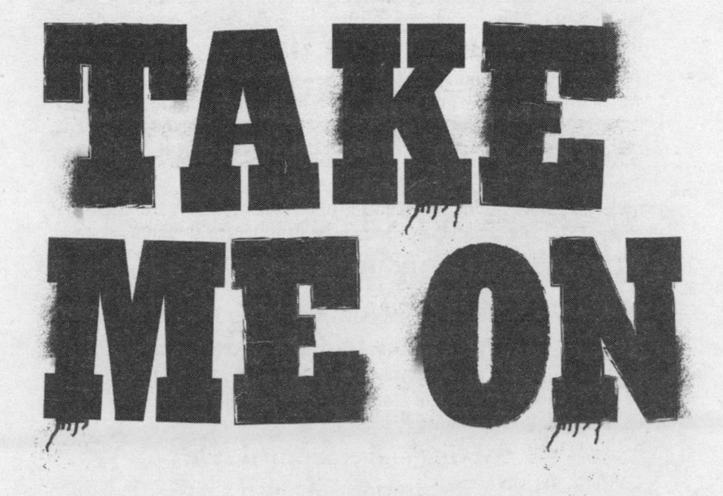

Katie McGarry

Published in Great Britain 2014
by MIRA Ink, an imprint of Harlequin (UK) Limited,
Eton House, 18-24 Paradise Road,
Richmond, Surrey, TW9 1SR

ISBN 978-1-848-45290-9
eBook ISBN: 978-1-472-05505-7

47-0614

Harlequin (UK) Limited's policy is to use papers that are natural, renewable and recyclable products and made from wood grown in sustainable forests. The logging and manufacturing processes conform to the legal environmental regulations of the country of origin.

Printed and bound by
CPI Group (UK) Ltd, Croydon, CR0 4YY

Katie McGarry

was a teenager during the age of grunge and boy bands and remembers those years as the best and worst of her life. She is a lover of music, happy endings and reality television and is a secret University of Kentucky basketball fan. She is also the author of *Pushing the Limits*, *Dare You To*, *Crash Into You* and the novella *Crossing the Line*.

Katie would love to hear from her readers. Contact her via her website, katielmcgarry.com, follow her on Twitter @KatieMcGarry, or become a fan on Facebook and Goodreads.

Haley

A DOOR SQUEAKS OPEN at the far end of the barren hallway and the clicking of high heels echoes off the row of metal post-office boxes. I attempt to appear casual as I flip through the mail. All of it leftovers from our previous life: my brother's mixed martial arts magazine, an American Girl doll catalog for my sister, another seed and gardening catalog for my mother.

Collection notices for my father.

There are more demands for payment. I wonder if I should give them to Dad or hand them off to my mother or grandfather. Maybe I should save us all from the reminder and set them on fire. It's not like there won't be a fresh batch tomorrow.

I juggle a few pieces to keep all of it from falling onto the floor. Beyond the windows, the sky darkens into dusk. I inhale deeply to calm the nervous adrenaline flooding my veins. Too much to do, not enough time: the mail, the grocery list from my aunt, convince the grandfather who hates me to write me a letter of recommendation, dropping off and picking up my father's antianxiety medication. It's Friday night and I've got two hours to make my uncle's curfew or I'll be spending the night on the streets.

The woman with the noisy heels continues down the hallway and doesn't acknowledge my existence as she heads to the employee entrance. Unlike me, she's dressed in a thick winter coat. Her hair is the same light brown as mine, but my hair is longer. I imagine my cheeks are painted red, like hers, from the February wind.

This building is normal for her. Nothing about this is normal for me. My family and I, we no longer have a brick-and-mortar mailing address in Louisville. We no longer have a home.

I pause at the last letter in the stack, and not in an enlightening way. No, this is the same pause I had when my father announced he'd lost his job. The same pause I had the day the county sheriff taped the eviction notice on our front door. It's a thin white envelope. Its appearance wouldn't cause anyone else's heart to sink to their toes. For me, it does. It's from the University of Notre Dame, and it's obviously not an acceptance.

I slam the door of the mailbox shut. Today sucks.

Walking into my grandfather's gym, I feel a little drunk on hope and a little like I'm marching to the gallows. Getting the rejection from Notre Dame left an emptiness and the thought of scoring a letter of recommendation for a scholarship to anywhere is definitely a potent wine. Alcohol and an empty stomach shouldn't mix, but, at the moment, I'm feeling bold.

"My, oh my, the flies are drawing in the shit." From the inside of an octagon cage, my cousin Jax shouts at me. Beads of sweat blanket him from head to toe. He wears boxing gloves on his hands and protective gear on his head. I say nothing as I'm fresh out of comebacks.

A group of newer fighters warms up by jumping rope to the pissed-off voice of Dr. Dre booming from the speakers. Returning here, I feel younger than eighteen, older than six, and, for a few seconds, like I'm home.

The gym is a metal building, a step above a warehouse and several steps below those fancy chain gyms. Black punching bags hang from metal framework, and pictures of my grandfather's various award-winning fighters cover the wall. A sweet combination of bleach and a tropical plug-in overwhelms my senses.

In one corner, two guys go at it in a boxing ring, and in the other corner some guys, including Jax, watch a demonstration of a takedown in a caged-in octagon.

The rustling of nylon athletic pants gains my attention as my grandfather cocks a hip against the doorframe of his office. His name is John, and he requires us to call him that. As usual, he wears a white T-shirt with the black logo of his gym: Freedom Fighters. Like every guy here, John is toned and a fighting machine. Sixty-two years hasn't slowed him down. In fact, the death of my grandmother a couple of years ago has driven him harder.

"It's a bit chilly," he says. "But not cold enough for hell to have frozen over."

My chin lifts in response. "You said I was always welcome."

"Thought you said you'd rather drink poison then step in here again."

I did. And he has me exactly where he wants me, but I refuse to break eye contact. We stare at each other for what seems like a year. My grandfather has a weathered look: a firm face set in stone, crow's-feet stamped near his eyes and lines creating parentheses around his mouth. Occasionally, my grandfather smiles, but he hasn't shown me that feature since I left his gym a year ago.

"Is your uncle bothering you?" he asks.

My uncle. Jax's dad. My father's half brother. The guy whose house we've been living in since the bank repossessed our home and we moved out of the shelter. I'm sure a few terrorist organizations refer to him as The Dictator. The answer to John's question is yes, but I say, "No."

"Is it your mom?"

His daughter. "She's fine." Sort of.

"Is something wrong at school?"

Everything is wrong at school. "No."

"Haley," he says with an overabundance of exasperation. "I've got fighters to train. Whatever it is, spit it out."

I glance away and focus on the fighters warming up, unsure what to do. They stare at me as the ropes go over their heads, then under their feet. Snap. Snap. Snap. It's as if they jump in unison now. Some guys I know from school. Others I don't. My older brother, the one who's leading them, is the only one who looks away.

My grandfather sighs and pushes off the doorframe to head toward the fighters.

"I can't give him the collection notices again," I whisper in a rush. "I...can't..."

It's not what I meant to say. I meant to ask for a recommendation, but somehow the intention became a traitorous ninja. Now that the spillway of the dam's been opened, the words cascade like a long drop from a mountain.

"I don't know what to do. Mom constantly works and she's

tired and she doesn't know how to handle Dad and when I bring the notices home..." I hesitate. Not home. That hellhole is not a home. "To the house and—" that low-life slimeball of an uncle "—*he* sees them, then it gets worse and I can't do it, okay? Not today."

Not when I lost my dream. Not when everything inside me is so twisted it hurts to breathe. Not when I don't know if I'll ever get accepted to college or, if I do, whether I'll have a way to pay for it.

The stone expression slides off John's face and his dark eyes soften. Mom has his eyes. So do I. My grandmother loved our eyes. In two strides my grandfather reaches me and angles himself to hide me from the fighters. The moment I'm out of view, my shoulders sag and I close my eyes.

"It's okay," he says under his breath.

It's not. It's never going to be okay again. He places his hand on my arm, squeezes, and that one show of emotion, show of support, jostles the fragile foundation on which I stand. Tears form behind my closed lids. I shake my head, wishing he'd go back to being an asshole.

"Give them to me," he says. "I'll take care of it."

I swing the pack around and hand him the new notices. "What are you going to do with them?"

"Something." John barely has the money to keep his gym open. "Don't worry."

I tuck my hair behind my ear and rub the back of my neck. Jax has stopped watching the demonstration and leans against the cage with his gloved hands resting on the fence over his head. He whistles at my brother, Kaden, and nods his chin at me.

Jax isn't related to John, but after the first few years of family gatherings and witnessing how Jax's father treats him like garbage, John became Jax's surrogate grandfather. My grandfather does his best to counteract the evil that is Jax's father.

Now not only do I have my grandfather's full attention, but that of my cousin and brother. The fact that I'm here after a yearlong hiatus—six months when I left to train with the competing gym, Black Fire, and the past six months spent protesting the sport of kickboxing altogether—is reason enough for Jax and Kaden to be nosy. The fact that my grandfather and I have spoken without ripping each other into dog food is enough for them to be dying of curiosity.

"Is there something else, Haley?" And the warm, fuzzy moment we shared vanishes.

I pull out the scholarship application I found this morning in the guidance counselor's office. It offers to pay for books for four years. It's not huge, but it's something, and sometimes in life you just need something, no matter how small it is.

"I thought you could help me with this."

He snatches the papers out of my hand quick enough to cause a paper cut on my finger. My breathing hitches with the sting, and a discontented sigh escapes his lips. How easily I forgot he has no room for weakness.

His eyes roam the page before settling on me. "I don't get it."

"It's a scholarship application."

"I can read."

"For kinesiology."

Not big on repeating himself, he tilts his head with enough annoyance that I have to work on not shrinking.

"I have all the requirements." I *was* a student athlete who showed leadership potential, my GPA is high and I'll major in kinesiology if they grant me a scholarship. I'll major in dinosaur dentistry if someone will give me money. "I need a letter of recommendation from someone who knows what I'm capable of, and no one knows what I can do better than you."

Not true. My father was the complete expert when it came to me. He's the one who taught me how to fight. He's the reason I loved kickboxing, but a recommendation from a trainer of my grandfather's caliber is what's required. Not a letter from my father. Not a letter from someone who hasn't fought or trained in years.

"Did the trainer from Black Fire turn you away?"

Even though I knew it would be coming, the mention of my ex-boyfriend Matt's gym wrings me of energy like water from a sponge. "I won't go to them."

"So you're saying you need a recommendation for betraying your teammates? Your family? For being a quitter?"

I honestly flinch, because that dagger stabbed into my heart hurt like hell.

John flips through the paperwork. "Kinesiology. Study of human movement. A study for people interested in physical therapy or becoming trainers. A degree for sports people." John slams the papers back into my hand. "Not you."

He leaves. His back turned to me like I don't matter. No. This isn't how it's going down. An insane flash of anger propels me forward. "I hold a national title."

"Held." John weaves through the punching bags and I follow. Twice I have to jump out of the way of a bag kicked too hard.

"That's right," I say. "Held." A bag flies in front of me and I push it back.

"Out of the way!" the fighter behind it shouts.

“Screw you,” I snap, and then I say to John, “That’s a hell of a lot more than most of the people training here.”

John rounds on me so fast I stumble into a bag. “The people in here are dedicated. They didn’t walk away. They didn’t forsake everything and everyone who loved them.”

I try one more time through gritted teeth. “I need this.”

“I only write letters for people who earn them. You want it, then get your ass in that locker room and start sweating on my floor. Or are you still a runner?”

His face is in mine and it’s a testament to my stubbornness that I haven’t broken into tears. A wave of nausea disorients me. John’s not going to help me, and, to protect the two people I love the most in life, I can’t work out in this gym again.

With all eyes on me, I pivot away from my grandfather and walk out the door.

West

I ASK WHY MORE THAN I SHOULD, some days I regret the decisions I make and most mornings I wake up on edge. The three don't often combine, but today I hit the shit trifecta.

Leaning against an aging telephone booth, I withdraw the envelope from my coat pocket and ignore the chill of the evening wind. The University of Louisville logo stands out in red across the top. I snagged the envelope yesterday before my parents figured out it had arrived. They've been stalking the mailbox, desperate for news that isn't bad.

My bruised and cut knuckles scream in protest as I unfold the paper. Each joint in my fingers pounds in time with the muscles in my jaw. A few hours ago, I got expelled from school for fighting.

Mom and Dad should know better than to expect good news from me. Mom holds on to hope. Dad, on the other hand...

I'm not a rocket scientist and don't need to be to know thin letters aren't good. My head literally throbs reading the words. I silently swear and slouch farther against the glass. It's only February and the rest of spring is going to bring more rejections.

I crumple the paper and toss it into the ashtray sitting outside the doors of the Laundromat. The remains of a smoldering cigarette char the edges of the letter. Ironic. The rest of my life is also going up in smoke.

My cell rings and I snatch it out of my coat pocket. "Yeah."

"Your father said you haven't come to the hospital." It's Mom and my eyes narrow at the entrance of the shit-hole bar at the end of this decrepit strip mall. She steps out of the bar and onto the sidewalk, a black scarf hiding her blond hair. Huge designer sunglasses disguise her face, and she sports a tailored coat that costs more than every car parked in this dump.

Mom is high-end, high-style and high-maintenance. And this landfill? I glance around the gray lot. Not a car made in this decade in sight. A Laundromat, a dollar store, a grocery store, a pharmacy with bars over the windows and, down toward the end, the bar.

She stands out here. I blend in better with my sagging jeans and hat on backward, which is good because she doesn't know I'm here. Mom's a petite thing, and I tower over her at my six feet. I inherited Mom's looks with the blond hair and blue eyes. If I need to, I can defend myself, but Mom has no business being here. Yet she shows once a month. Same damn time. Same damn day. Even with her youngest daughter, Rachel, in the hospital in intensive care.

"You're not staying with Rachel?" I ask. Mom has no idea I've been following her for the past ten months. I came to this hellhole last spring to buy pot from a potential new dealer, someone cheaper than the guys at my school. Private school equates to marked-up.

"No," she answers.

Shocked doesn't describe the reaction I had when I saw my mother walking into the bar the first time. After that near encounter, I keep a tight watch on her. It's my job to protect my family. I failed with Rachel and don't plan on failing again.

"Your father arrived," Mom continues. "He told me to take a break and eat."

Take a break. Eat. Screw the guy she's been meeting.

A year ago, I would have laughed if anyone suggested my mother would have an affair, but what else could be the explanation for the wife of one of the wealthiest men in the state to be hanging out in the armpit of the city? I can't say I blame her. My father has a habit of ignoring his family.

Mom freezes by the door to her car and I silently urge her to get in. A guy a few steps from me has become too interested in her, her Mercedes or both.

"West." She sighs into the phone and her shoulders slump. "You need to visit Rachel. When she's awake, she's asked for you. Her condition is serious, and you need to come."

I inch the speaker away from my mouth. My insides ache as if the blows I took today at school created internal damage. Rachel's legs were trashed in the accident and no one needs to tell me that she may never walk again. Her accident is my fault and I can't face her.

"Your principal said the fight you had today was over a joke about her."

Joke, my ass. Some asshole junior called my sister a gimp. No one talks shit about Rachel. But even though I was defending Rachel, the school still threw me out. As the pasty head of our school explained, there have been too many detentions, too many warnings, and, though he regretted the situation with my sister, I had left him with no choice—I just wasn't Worthington Private material.

"How is she?" I ask, changing the subject.

"Come to the hospital and ask her yourself."

Not going to happen. When I say nothing, Mom continues, "She's in pain and she needs you."

"She has Ethan." Her twin. "And Jack." Our older brother. Gavin, the oldest of our brood of five, has also been there, but I don't mention his name. Mom is still having a hard time dealing with his gambling issues. The entire world thinks the Youngs are perfect, but our family is a damn mess.

"Rachel wants you."

She doesn't. Our last words were spoken in anger. Hell, our last month of words were spoken in anger. How can she forgive me when I can't?

Mom allows the silence as she slides into her car and starts the engine. The muscles in my neck relax the moment she backs out of her spot. She transfers me to her Bluetooth and switches me to speaker. "Your father is upset. In fact, this is the angriest I've seen him. He told you to go straight from school to the hospital."

That would have left Mom defenseless; plus I'm done with Dad ordering me around. Playing Dad between meetings doesn't make him my father. "I'll talk to him at home."

She pulls out of the lot and softens her tone. "After what's happened with Rachel and with Gavin..."

I readjust my stance. I tried to prevent all of this with

Gavin, but then Rachel told me she needed the money I took from her to help Gavin and... I can't continue the thought.

"This isn't the time to antagonize your father. He made it clear months ago he wouldn't help you if the school expelled you. I've tried talking with him, telling him you were defending your sister, but he isn't moving on this. He wants you at the hospital tonight. He means it. This isn't the time to push boundaries."

Dad and I have been a gasoline fire nearing a tanker for months. He doesn't understand the problems facing this family. He doesn't understand everything I've done to protect them all. His entire focus belongs solely to his business, then on Mom. In the end, my father doesn't respect my brothers or sister or me.

"It'll work out," I say. Because there's no way he'd permit his son to fail out his senior year. Dad's expectations of me may be low, but he won't let anyone else think poorly of his family. The bastard has always been about reputation. "I'll be up there later tonight."

"Make it sooner—as in now." She pauses. "And visit Rachel."

"I'll see Dad." I hang up and head for my car. I told Mom it would work out, but a restless thought inside me wonders if Dad's serious.

Haley

AN HOUR BUS RIDE to my uncle's, forty minutes waiting for Dad's prescription and, as I walk out of the pharmacy, I still haven't thought of a witty enough comeback for when Jax looks at me from across the dinner table and mouths John's last word to me: "Runner."

"Am not" won't do the job.

Especially since Jax will ignore his actual age of seventeen and revel in his maturity level of six with the response of, "Are too."

Short of kicking him in the balls from underneath the table, there's no way to win once someone says, "Are too." Besides, Jax has learned to cover himself when he sits across from me.

On top of it all, I've been rejected by the University of Notre Dame. My eyes sting and I blink. I could say it's the wind burning my eyes, but that's a lie. I'm awesome at lying to everyone else but have yet to perfect lying to myself.

Trying to ignore the cold, I shove my hands in my jeans pockets and weave through the crowd huddled underneath the covered sidewalk. The plastic bags from the pharmacy and grocery store crackle as they swing from my wrist. Between the darkness of the winter night and the faces buried under hats and coats, the people I pass become nothing more than expressionless ghosts.

The sun set a half hour ago and I've got a little less than fifteen minutes till curfew. The Dictator is strict about the comings and goings of anyone living in his household.

We're having squirrel tonight for dinner.

Squirrel.

As in the rodent with the fuzzy tail that gets zapped on power lines.

Squirrel.

And it's my turn to say grace. On top of not securing a comeback, I've also failed to find a way to thank God for the bounty that is squirrel. I'm sure, "Dear God, thank you for the fuzzy rat you gave us to eat and please don't let me die of the plague after I digest it. Is that gristle? Amen," will meet my uncle's approval.

With ten people in one two-bedroom house, there are bound to be some personality clashes or, in my and my uncle's case, a revisit of the Cold War. Actually, Russia and the U.S. liked each other a tiny bit more. He has a problem with girls who think, and I'm a fan of using my brain.

The moment I round the corner of the strip mall, two hulking silhouettes emerge from behind the back of the building. More male muscle reeking of ominous threat than friendly passerby. Instincts flare. Senses go on alert. I wouldn't be the first girl jumped in this neighborhood.

I freeze and glance over my shoulder. Behind me, the ghosts fade into the stores, leaving me alone and with limited options. Going forward forces me to pass the two shadows, but it's also the lone path into the neighborhood. Heading back toward the shops will make me late, and I promised Mom I'd never break curfew. My breath billows out in a cloud, a reminder that sleeping outside can mean frostbite.

Six months ago, I would have met the shadowy threat with no fear. In fact, I probably would have taunted them, but being hit until you break causes courage to disappear.

"I don't have any money," I call out. It's not a lie.

A voice carries from the dark blobs. "Just give us the pills."

My head shakes back and forth. Mom saved for two months to buy this medication. We lost our insurance. We've lost everything and Dad's suffering. We've all been suffering. And Dad needs to get better. He needs to find a job. We have to get out of this awful place.

The shadows descend and I stumble backward off the curb. My heart pounds as I free my hands from my pockets and the bags slide farther up my wrist. It's not my hands that I'm lethal with. It's my legs. My feet. I've been trained to kick. The instinct to run battles my instinct to fight.

A horn blares. My head jerks to the right. Lights blind me. My hand flies to my face to act as a shield as my stomach shoots up. A scream tears out of my throat.

West

"JESUS CHRIST!" I slam on the breaks and practically push the pedal through the floor as I will my SUV to stop. My tires squeal and my body whiplashes as the car jerks to a halt. The headlights spotlight a girl. Her arms protect her face and I try to process that she's still standing.

Standing. As in not on the ground.

Not dead.

One thing went right today.

The relief flooding through my body is quickly chased by a strong helping of anger. She jumped out in front of me, not taking one look. Jumped.

She lowers her arms and I'm met by the sight of wide dark eyes. Her wild mane of light brown hair whips across her face as the wind picks up. She blinks and so do I.

She glances over her shoulder and I follow her line of sight into the shadows. Panic sweeps over her face and she stumbles, acting disoriented. Shit on it all damn day, what if I did hit her?

I throw the SUV in Park and, as I open the door, she points at me. "Watch it!"

Watch it? She's the one who stepped out in front of me, then froze like a damn deer. I launch myself out of the car. "Sidewalks, chick. That's where you stop. Not in the middle of a street!"

With a shake of her head, she tosses her hair over her shoulder and actually steps into me. If it were anyone else, such a movement would send rage from the tip of my toes to my fists, but instead I smirk and cross my arms over my chest. She may be tall, but compared to me she's a tiny thing, and for the first time today, I find amusement. I've seen that type of fire burning in people's eyes a million times in my life. Just never from a girl, and never in eyes so hauntingly gorgeous.

"You were the one not paying attention!" the girl shouts. "And besides, this is a parking lot, you moron. Not a dragway. You were going, what? Fifty?"

The word *moron* slips underneath my skin and my muscles tighten. But she has me. I was speeding. "Are you hurt?" I ask.

"What?"

"Did my car hit you?"

The fire within her wavers and she peers into the dark again. "No."

Two huddled forms skulk near the back of the building. I refocus on the walking, talking inferno in front of me and, despite my Calc teacher's opinion on my intelligence, I'm able to do the math. "Is that trouble for you?"

Her eyes shoot to mine and in them is a blaring yes, but because girls make no sense she answers, "No."

A crackling sound draws my attention. The edges of a small white paper bag poke from a plastic bag. It's a prescription. I give her the once–over, then turn to the guys hiding by the building. Dammit. Even the book geeks at my school who've never seen the outside of their PlayStation basement shrines are aware of the urban legends surrounding this neighborhood. She can deny it all she wants, but she has problems. "Get in my car."

The fire returns. "Hell no." She inspects the bruises forming along my jawline, then surveys my scraped and swollen knuckles.

"Look, it's me or them." I motion toward the thugs with my chin. "And I'm telling you, I'm not the bad guy in this scenario."

She laughs. And if it wasn't such a beautiful sound, I'd be insulted.

"Because a guy driving an Escalade in this neighborhood is the equivalent of a Boy Scout."

The right side of my mouth tips up. Did she call me a drug dealer?

"From the looks of you—" she glances at my knuckles again "—well, let's just say you must have your own baggage and I'm not a baggage-claim type of girl."

"No, you're the type that runs into traffic."

She smiles and I like it. The anger racing through me moments before vanishes. I rub my jaw, then lean my hand against my open car door. Long light brown hair with waves, dark eyes that sure as hell suck me in as they sparkle, a tight body and a kick-ass attitude. Truth be told, I like more than her smile. Too bad I almost killed her by running her over. It'll make asking her out awkward.

"Get into my car and I'll drive you home." I hold up both my palms. "I swear. No drive-bys on the way."

The smile fades when I say the word *home* and her eyes lose the sparkle. Something deep within me hollows out.

She slides close, very close—as in her clothes brush mine. She angles herself so that she's between me and my car door. The heat of her body rolls onto me and my fingers itch to touch. I suck in air and I'm overwhelmed by the sweet scent of wildflowers.

She lifts her face to look at me and whispers, "Getting into that car with you is as big a risk as walking down that viaduct. If you're bent on helping me, do me a favor."

"What?" I breathe out.

"Stand here and act like you're talking to me. Convincingly enough that it'll buy me time."

And before I can process a word, she cuts past me, crouches against the Escalade, ducks behind the vehicle and escapes into the night. "Hey!"

The shadows emerge from behind the building. Two guys bolt into the beams of my headlights and in the direction of the neighborhood. Their feet pound the concrete.

In the distance, instead of two dark forms running into the night, there are three—and the first one doesn't have a decent head start. I jump into my Escalade and tear off after them.

Haley

MY LUNGS BURN and my arms and legs pump quickly. The graffiti on the concrete walls of the freeway viaduct blend into a colored blur. I'm out of shape. Six months ago, I could have outrun them, but not now. Not today. My feet smack against the blacktop and the sound echoes in the tunnel. The stench of mold and decay fills my nose.

There's a splash as someone stomps into a puddle, followed by the sound of more shoes against the street. My breath comes out in gasps and I will my muscles to move faster.

Heat rises off my body and into the cold night and my nose begins to run. I don't want them to hurt me, and the thought of a man's hand colliding with my body causes my heart to clench. My fist tightens around Dad's medication. I don't want to lose it. The answer is to be faster, but, if they catch me, I'll be left with no other choice than to fight.

Their footsteps ring closer in my ears and my old training floods into my brain. I need to turn, face them and form a defensive stance. I can't be dragged to the ground by my hair.

Lights from behind create a beacon of hope. My pursuers' footfalls continue in their hunt but fall off near the walls of the tunnel, out of sight of the approaching car. I put on a burst of speed. Two more blocks and I'll be inside. Safe from this.

Brakes squeal and a door snaps open. Voices. Shouting. The sound of a fist smacking into flesh. Continuing, I peek over my shoulder and air slams out of me when I notice the Escalade.

No.

Please, God, no.

My body rocks forward as my feet become concrete. It's the guy from the shopping plaza. He's fighting them. Three shadows spar against the headlights; a hellish dogfight of arms, fists, legs, grunts and growls. They're all the same height, but I know which one's him. He's thicker. More muscular. He's a scrapper, but he's going to lose.

Two against one.

My chest rises and falls and I glance down the street, toward my uncle's house, toward relative safety. I'm minutes away from curfew, I've got my father's prescription in my grasp, but leaving a guy behind—it's not how I was raised.

Knowing this has the potential to end extremely badly for me, I switch directions to join the fight.

West

SON OF A BITCH.

My head turns as the bastard with the black hoodie sucker punches me in the jaw. Blood pours from my lip, but I ignore it and the pain as I ram my fist into his stomach. He goes down, but it's not him that has me worried.

I spin to the left, but I'm too late. The asshole with the winter coat, the guy who's schooled on how to fight, he's back on his feet after I busted him in the nuts. The psychopath grins as he nears me. He rubs a spot on his forehead and widens his stance, just like I've seen pay-per-view fighters do in the ring.

My fists go up, but my muscles are heavy. Two fights in one day and taking on two guys at once. I could almost laugh. Guess I've learned my hard limit. We round each other and I try to keep an eye on the guy still on the ground.

We circle.

Slowly.

Shit. This kid's a fighter. A real one. And something tells me he's not going to make the mistake of letting me kick him in the balls again.

He flashes toward me at lightning speed. Two rapid-fire punches from the left. My body sways and my vision becomes fuzzy. I swing out, sensing he's close, but I miss.

A hit from the right—mind-shattering, blinding pain—and I fall to the ground. Rocks dig into my knees and warmth rushes to the area near my eye. Everything wavers. My thoughts. My sight. A metallic taste floods my mouth and I grab on to one thought.

"Is she gone?" I ask. "Did she get away?"

This can't be in vain.

I couldn't protect Rachel. I couldn't stop Gavin from pursuing his addiction. I couldn't stop Dad from placing everything else first. I couldn't stop Mom from having an affair, from finding a way out. But I can do this. I can protect her. I need redemption.

He stands over me, and through one eye I see yellowish hair and dark eyes fixed on me. "Don't worry," he says. "I know where to find Haley."

Haley. Pretty name for a pretty girl. I try to breathe, but my lungs cramp up. I glance at him one last time, knowing there's no mercy rule with this kid. "Mind leaving the car?"

"Sure."

Yeah. It'll be gone before I peel myself off the concrete. I plant my foot on the ground and the world rotates. Fuck, I'm screwed. I lift my head and chuckle when I notice blood trickling near his mouth. "I nailed the fighter."

He pulls his arm back and the world goes black.

"Please be breathing!" A familiar voice calls me from the darkness. A feminine voice. A beautiful voice. Soft fingers brush against my forehead and I suck in air. Pain slices through my chest—breathing is bad.

"Please wake up. I didn't go through this for you to be dead."

"It's okay, Rachel," I mumble. Her tone, a mixture of torture and agony, scrapes at my soul. It's the same tone Rachel had when she felt I had betrayed her. "I'm sorry."

The cold fingers touching my head pause. Why isn't she warm?

"Oh, thank God. You're alive."

The voice is familiar, but not Rachel's. I fight the fog and force consciousness and every muscle screams as I stretch.

"I'm awake." Not what I meant to say. I meant to ask if she was okay. At the moment, brain and mouth aren't connected. My mind's jumbled; a scattered mess as I try to sort out why I fell asleep, why I'm in pain, why it's cold, why my bed's hard—

"You scared the crap out of me. I thought you were dead."

—why there's a girl in my bed wondering if I'm dead. I pry my eyes open and successfully free one. There's three of her at first and, through blinking, she slowly evolves into one. "I know you."

On her knees, Haley hovers near me. Behind her, my car sits, still running. The headlights highlight a couple of blond strands in her light brown hair.

"Why did you follow me?" she demands. "All you had to do was act like we were still talking. But no, you call out after me, then look to where I was heading. Why not skywrite I had bolted for the neighborhood?"

She's trembling. I reach out and rest my hand on her wrist. The skin beneath my own is ice. "You're cold."

"So are you. You're probably in shock."

My thumb swipes across her skin, as if that one movement could warm her. Protect her. "It's all right."

"No, it's not. None of this is all right." She removes her arm and I suddenly feel empty.

There's a tear on her face. Just one. And she quickly wipes it away. The action causes an ache beyond the pulsating of my skin and head. Something's wrong. My eyes dart around and I quickly catch up on events. I'm not in bed. I almost hit her with my car, we fought, I discovered she had trouble, I followed her here and then I got my ass kicked. I lift my head and immediately regret the movement with a groan. "Are you okay?"

"You should have listened!"

Not an answer, and I left my patience back at the shopping plaza. "Are. You. Okay?"

"I'm fine," she snaps. "Just fine. Freaking fantastic fine. Meeting you is the pinnacle of my existence."

"Some people say thank you when a complete stranger jumps two guys for them."

Haley slumps against the bumper of my car and a rush of air leaves her body. "Sorry and thank you. It's—" she waves her hand in the air "—messed up, but that's not your fault. It's mine."

A car slowly drives around us. I expect it to stop, but it keeps going. Great neighborhood. "They left my car."

"Yeah." She glances away. "They're gone."

My eyes narrow on her face, but she flips her hair so it's hiding her cheek and jaw. I blink as my sight blurs. Something's off. They would have stolen the car... "I need to get up." But not a single cell in my body responds. "They could come back."

"They won't." Haley nurses her right hand. "Trust me—they won't. At least not tonight. Tomorrow maybe, but not tonight."

Tomorrow? What? I rise onto my elbows and the nauseating spinning convinces me to ease my head back to the ground. Driving is going to be a bitch.

"Stop it. You need to stay still. In fact, you need an ambulance."

"No hospitals." Showing at an E.R. like this will cause Dad to go Chernobyl.

"Your friend told me the same thing. It's why I haven't called 911. Possibly a stupid decision on my part."

The pounding stills. "What friend?"

"Haley called Isaiah," says a female voice to the left. Haley and I jerk our heads toward the darkness. Haley bolts up and jumps over me, acting as if she's my protector.

I'm dreaming. This is all a bad dream. I'm going to wake tomorrow and think how crazy real this whole thing felt because there is no way my little sister's best friend would be here.

"I'm Abby," the voice says to Haley, closer now. "You and I go to Eastwick together."

Like a stunning yet sadistic version of the grim reaper with long dark hair, Abby walks into the light wearing a black hoodie and skintight blue jeans.

"No, you don't," I mumble. "Eastwick is a public school. Abby goes to private school. Not mine—one of those religious ones." Saint Mary's. Saint Martha's. Saint who-the-fuck-knows. It's what Rachel told my mother. This is a dream. Just a dream.

Haley's eyes flicker from me to Abby, then back again. She never relaxes her position and my mind stops and starts like it's stuttering. Fuck me—Haley's in the same stance as fighter guy.

"I've seen you around," Haley says to Abby. "Do you know him?"

"Yeah. Do you?"

"We sort of ran into each other."

I laugh and they both stare at me like I'm insane.

"That's West." Abby slurs my name. "He's been causing problems for a friend of mine."

Haley edges herself between me and Abby like she's willing to box this girl for me.

Abby chuckles. "Relax. You called Isaiah and Isaiah called me. For the moment, I'm playing guardian angel."

Isaiah? "Hell no." I shove off the ground like I'm doing a sit-up and only get far enough to prop my arms on my knees. I've never liked rides that went in circles and I haven't recently changed my mind. My eyes shut tight. "I don't want that bastard's help."

"Well, you're getting it," says Abby. When I reopen my eyes, Abby smirks. "And it looks like you need it."

"Screw that," I mutter and spit out new blood that's trickled from the cut on my lip.

Isaiah is Rachel's boyfriend and he's the reason why she's in the hospital. Dad found Rachel with him at a dragway and that's where Dad and Rachel had their accident. I'll roast in hell and haul Isaiah there with me before I accept his help. "How does he know about this?"

Haley drops beside me. “You were out. Cold. I found your cell and I was desperate to find someone who knew you to see what hospital you should go to, so I dialed the first number I found—”

“And *he* answered,” I cut her off. Haley must have called Rachel. My brother told me that except for a few hours here and there Isaiah’s been chained to Rachel’s bedside at the hospital. Night and day. And that he carries her phone because he discovered it in the wreckage the day after the Jaws of Life pulled her out of the car. We assumed it was broken. Who would have guessed a phone would make it when Rachel barely survived?

“West.” Haley surveys the damage to my face, my hands, my body. “I really am sorry.”

God, I’m jacked up because everything pounds like a bitch and I can only think about her beautiful dark eyes. “It’s all right.”

She grabs a bag off the ground and stands. “I’ve got to go. I’m late.”

Abby tilts her head as she assesses Haley. “You know who I am?”

Haley straightens like she’s greeting an ax murderer. “Yes.”

I’m missing entire puzzle pieces here, as in everything except for the one corner piece I hold. Nothing here is as it seems, and I hate being the odd man out.

Abby thrusts her chin in my direction. “His younger sister is my best friend. I can help you...with whatever situation this is.”

“No,” says Haley quickly. “I’m fine. Look, I’ve really got to go.” She takes a step into the darkness.

"What the hell are you two talking about?" They ignore me, and why shouldn't they? It's not like I could get up and force them to listen.

Abby shrugs. "If you change your mind..."

"I won't." Haley finally turns her attention to me. "Thanks, West. But the next time a girl tells you to do something, do it, okay?"

I'd call her nothing but attitude if it weren't for the defeat in her tone. "Haley..."

She doesn't wait for me to talk; instead she races down the street. Fucked. Up. Dream. I rub my eyes and consider standing.

Abby's tennis shoes crunch against the crumbling blacktop and halt at my feet. "Your choice—home, hospital or a place to lay low until you're ready for one of the first two options. The prize behind curtain C comes with a shower and a change of clothes."

I dismiss my original answer of no when I notice the blood on my shirt. I can't go home or to the hospital like this. I can't do that to my mother.

Using the bumper of my car, I struggle up and hobble to the passenger side as I eye Abby sliding into the driver's seat. I'm slow getting in, but I'll be damned if I ask for help.

The interior light dims when I shut the door. Abby fastens her seat belt and wraps her fingers around the steering wheel. "I don't have my driver's license."

"Can you drive?"

"Sure."

That didn't sound reassuring. "Just go."

She doesn't. "You should buy goldfish."

"What?"

"For your car. Like build a tank in between your front and back seats. It'd be different and I like different."

If it will get me to a shower faster... "Okay."

She smiles. "Really?"

"Sure."

Abby shifts the car into gear. "And, West?"

I roll my head to look at her.

"I know your mother's secret."

Haley

I'M LATE.

My feet pound rhythmically against the pavement. Is my uncle standing by the door waiting? Will he grant me mercy since it's my first offense? I have no idea how he'll react, and, I'll admit, my uncle terrifies me.

I'm in shock. I know it. I'm calm. Too calm. And nothing hurts. After what happened...I round the corner and light shines through the cracks of the closed curtains, but the porch is completely dark. At night, the small vinyl house radiates an eerie white glow. My legs slow as I approach. I am so screwed.

"Pssst. Haley!" It's a whispered shout from above. My cousin Jax leans out the attic window. His whitish-blond hair shines in the moonlight. "Through here."

Wary of spying eyes, I cut across the neighbor's yard and approach the side of the house through the shadows. My brother Kaden paces behind Jax. Mom must be a nervous wreck and Dad... Dad needs this medication.

Before stepping closer to the house, I peer at the living room window again. If the two of them get caught helping me, they'll also be kicked out for the night. Because he's seventeen and their arguments have moved from heated to toxic, Jax's dad would possibly throw him out for good.

"Come on, girl, move," says Jax. "It's cold."

"Catch!" I launch the bag up to Jax. The first indication I had been in a fight reveals itself as my biceps convulse and the bag hardly makes it two feet. I catch it and panic flickers in my bloodstream. If I can't toss a bag, how am I climbing up?

"Again!" commands Jax.

I fling the bag again. My heart tears past my rib cage when Jax falls out the window to grasp the bag. I stifle the scream when I notice Kaden holding on to his legs. Jax fires the bag through the window, then dangles headfirst and waves his hands. "Let's go."

Taking two burning cold gulps of air, I stumble backward into the darkness. The frozen ground crunches beneath my feet. I swallow, lick my lips and narrow my eyes. I can do this. I'm a champion kickboxer. If I did that, I can do this. If I could do what I did a few minutes ago...

I derail that train of thought. I don't want to think about that now.

Or ever.

Again.

I'm not a fighter. Not anymore.

With one last deep inhalation, I run straight toward the house, kick off against the vinyl and fumble with the old trellis. I climb until my palm smacks into Jax's. His other hand grabs on to my flailing wrist and, seconds later, both he and Kaden pull me through the window.

The moment my butt hits the floor, Jax shuts the pane and Kaden drops a blanket over me. "What happened?"

"I'm late." Yes, I'm definitely in shock.

"Noticed." Kaden ducks his head under the beams of the vaulted ceiling as he crosses the compact attic space. This is my room. Better yet, it's what my life has been reduced to: a blow-up mattress among boxes of old clothes, picture frames, spiderwebs and the smell of mildew.

Kaden cracks open the attic door and stares through the one-inch space. Sounds from the television mingle with the voices of my mother and aunt. There's a thud followed by a grunt. Probably Jax's brothers wrestling in the room below us.

"Haley," says Kaden. My brother and I used to be close. Like everything else in my life, I miss him. When I say nothing, he rattles the bag in his hands. "Where's Dad's meds?"

"In the bag."

"No, they're not."

"What?"

"There's lettuce in there and no meds."

My lungs collapse and my fingers tug at the neckline of my shirt. "No, they're in there. They have to be."

"Not here." Kaden shakes the bag again so that it crackles. "It took Mom two months to earn enough for the pills. How could you lose them? Dad needs them."

"I know," I snap and throw my hands over my eyes. "I know."

I bang the back of my head against the wall. I lost Dad's medication. My family's only hope of getting out of this god-forsaken place. That's why the guys left. I didn't lose the meds. They stole them. The muscles beneath my right cheek begin to pulsate. Tears burn my eyes and my chest becomes heavy. I swore I'd never fight again and I did. I swore I'd never be hit again. And I have. This is the penance for breaking that promise. God, I'm worthless.

"Go, Kaden," says Jax. "It's happened and can't be undone."

Kaden disappears down the stairs and Jax crouches next to me. My cheeks feel numb against the warmth of the house. The skin there tingles and so do my fingers. Jax grabs them and begins to rub. "We need to find you a jacket."

"You don't have one," I mumble blankly and flinch when regret cuts deep. Jax's hands pause against mine and we make fleeting eye contact.

"I'm sorry." I broke a cardinal rule. Kaden and I never mention what Jax doesn't have.

"It's okay." He massages warmth back into my fingers. "I can take frostbite. You can't."

I offer a weak smile. "I'm tougher than I look."

"Yeah," he says under his breath then releases my hands. "You are."

"I lost the meds," I announce as if he wasn't part of the earlier conversation. "I lost Dad's pills." Why do I keep screwing up?

"You had a shit ton of errands and not enough time. You ran home and they probably fell out of the bag. It could have happened to any of us. If you're going to live here, you've got to learn to let stuff go. Otherwise, you'll go insane."

I meet his green eyes at the word *insane*. What if I'm already there? What if I can't take much more? I don't ask those questions because I see the same ones forming in his eyes.

My cousin glances away. "We covered for you. Said you came in through the back door and came straight here."

"Thanks. Why did he buy it?" Typically we have to present ourselves to The Dictator like soldiers in his make-believe war.

Jax scratches at the thin three-inch scar streaking across his forehead. He's chosen a skater look today, and his hair lies flat against his head. "We told him you had an accident."

My stomach drops. I'm not going to like this. "An accident?"

He avoids eye contact as he absently gestures with his hand. "Girl problems. Blood…in spots…on clothes." Jax bolts up. "We're not discussing this anymore. We covered for you. He bought it. That's all you need to know."

Heat finally races to my cheeks. Freaking kill me now. "Thanks."

"No problem." Jax looks at me again; then he's really looking at me. Like pissed-off looking at me. "What the fuck?"

Instinctively, my fingers go to my cheek and I regret it the moment Jax's fists clench.

"Did you get jumped?" he demands. "Is that how you lost the meds?"

"Jax!" his dad bellows from the bottom of the stairs. "Come here!"

"Haley," Jax says, ignoring his father.

"Jax!" This time the glass of the old window shakes with his voice and I shudder.

"Go!" I say to him, preferring not to be the reason the two of them get into a screaming match. "Please."

He points at me. "This ain't over." Jax turns and, like Kaden, bends as he crosses the room.

I brush my fingers against my sensitive cheek. "Jax."

He hesitates near the door.

"I can't go down to dinner like this and my makeup's downstairs. Can you help?"

Jax nods. "Consider it done."

West

"I THINK YOU'RE DEAD."

My eyes flash open and I scramble up when I come face-to-face with hazel eyes and long dark hair. A quick scan of the room and I discover I'm on a couch in a gray concrete unfinished basement. A single bulb lights the area. Behind me are a washer and dryer. In front of me is a bed and to the side, a TV. Last night, I took a hot shower and crashed.

I scrub my hands over my face. This is bad. Last night happened. It wasn't a nightmare.

"Damn, I guessed wrong. You're alive." Near where my head had been, Abby falls back from her knees to her butt. "I can't decide if that's good or bad news."

"Screw you." My muscles are stiff. Sore. I hesitantly stretch to see if anything's broken.

Abby presses a hand over her mouth and mock gasps. "Your mother would be appalled by your manners. Tsk. Tsk. I believe pleases and thank-yous are in order." She loses the fake sweetness. "Even if you are slumming it, Rich Boy."

She kicks my shin as she stands. "Get up. I've got work to do and babysitting is not on the list."

Memories of last night crash into my mind. More importantly of the girl who possibly rescued me from dying of exposure on the street. "Is Haley okay?"

Being a damned loser last night, I couldn't muster enough energy or self-respect to drive her home.

"She was the last time I saw her. Are you dating her?"

"No."

"Fucking her?"

I glare at Abby, but I can't throw too much anger into it. She also saved my ass. I pop my neck to the side, hoping to expel the annoying insecurity over Haley's safety.

"Good. Rumor has it she's decent. She deserves better."

She probably does. Haley's probably one of those dinner, a movie, roses type of girls who take a month to work up to the first kiss. Me—not my style. "What time is it?"

"Too early for my clients to be awake, but they will be soon." Abby pulls a cell phone out of her back pocket. "Get your ass moving. This isn't the Holiday Inn."

I'm 30 percent curious over the word *clients,* then realize I don't give a shit. "No continental breakfast?"

"How about you bite me?"

I actually chuckle; then I roll my neck and circle my arms. How the hell did my sister get involved with her? The nonmedical assessment says I'm bruised. Nothing more. "Where am I?"

"Isaiah's foster parents' house."

Damn. I reassess the room, searching for the bastard.

"Don't worry," she says as she scrolls down the screen. "He stayed with Rachel at the hospital last night since he doesn't have school today."

That's right. Today's Saturday. "We."

"What?"

"You said 'he' as if you don't go to school, or did you lie about being a junior?"

"Meh, I consider school optional, but I am a junior."

"So everything you told Rachel, besides what grade you're in, was a lie?"

Abby's lips form a smirk. "I don't lie to Rachel. But yeah, you can assume anything that comes out of my mouth to anyone but her or Isaiah is a different rendition of the truth. Maybe also to Isaiah's friend Logan. I like Logan. He reminds me of hot queso and I like queso."

The veins beneath my scalp begin to pulse. "So you lied about my mother."

"No, that was the truth. I do know why she goes to the bar once a month. Third Friday of the month to be exact. Comes around seven in the evening. Sound familiar?"

My shoulders slump forward. Shit, Abby does know. "Why does she go there?"

"They sell awesome snow cones. The red one won a blue ribbon in the state fair last year."

The pounding intensifies. This girl is like one of those damned flies that swarm your head and your food. "Let me guess—you're lying."

She winks. "You're catching on fast, and here I pegged you for stupid."

A muscle in my jaw twitches. I can't stand this girl, but she did give me a place to crash, so I watch my manners and change the subject. "Did *he* tell you to bring me here?"

Figures the asshole would want something to hold over me: help with a bad situation, then he'll squeeze me for something. Money, drugs. It's gotta be the type of angle he used to snare Rachel. Why else would she have been around a guy like him?

"Isaiah's initial response was to let you bleed out in the street, but then he got sentimental and thought Rachel would be sad if you died, so he called and asked me to take care of you. I told him Rachel would've gotten over you and that we could make her happy if we bought her a bunny, but he was so damned insistent. See, Isaiah and I have this past. I've known him forever because we met each other in a Dumpster—"

"Why here?" I cut her off, not caring about their tragic backstory. Everyone has a tale to sob over. Rich or poor.

Abby looks at me with wide eyes. "Because if I took you to my house that would start rumors. Really, West. I'm a single girl. I've gotta protect my image. We wouldn't want people to think we've been doing something indecent."

Talking to her is like watching a cat chase its tail. "Another lie."

"I can pretend that's my answer. I like pretending. You can create anything you want out of the world."

"You're possibly the most fucked-up person I've met."

"That's not news." Abby slides her phone back into her pocket. "Now, if we're done 'pretending' to have a conversation, I'd like to go see my best friend. And, no, that's not a lie."

She turns on her heel and heads for the stairs.

"Abby," I call out as I shove my feet into my sneakers. She hesitates at the landing and waits for me to reach her. "Tell me why my mom's going to the bar."

A wicked grin spreads across her face. "I could tell you, but there would be absolutely no fun in doing that." And she walks up the stairs.

Haley

EVERY BREATH TASTES OF DUST, spilled gasoline and oil. Layers of grime coat the cold concrete floor of the garage and my cheek has become numb against it. How long has it been since Matt abandoned me? Seconds, hours, days? At first I assumed he left to get help—to find sanity in the insane, but no...he left. He just left.

"Haley!" The voice is far away, yet a nagging inside me says it's near.

Blood soaks my hands. It's Matt's blood—I think. Maybe mine. I don't know. We argued. That's all we do anymore... argue. It's what we're good at, but now it seems wrong. He hit me. I hit him back. And somehow neither of us stopped.

"She's cold," Jax says. "And look at her eyes. I think she's in shock."

It's an effort to turn my head toward Jax. His whitish-blond hair is spiked into a Mohawk. His shirt goes up and over his head and he lays it on my arms and chest, but not my hands. No, he wouldn't let it touch my hands. The blood would ruin his white T-shirt.

"Haley!" Jax poises his hands near me, not touching, just

there...moving as if he doesn't know what to fix first or worried that if he did make contact he'd become diseased, cursed like me. "What happened?"

"I don't know." I don't recognize my voice. I'm different now. Changed.

I'm up like I've done a sit-up and my older brother, Kaden, supports my weight with his chest. He lifts my wrists. "Are you bleeding?"

I shake my head. "No." I don't think so.

The room spins and so do I. Kaden drops my hands to grip my shoulders. "Easy, Haley. Is she hurt?"

I tilt my head and thoughtfully look at Jax. Am I? Matt slapped my face. It's how the fight started. Is there a permanent bruise there? My own personal scarlet letter branding me as defeated?

Jax's eyes dart everywhere. "She looks okay, but she ain't acting right. Her knuckles are bruised. She's definitely been in a fight."

"There was blood." That seems important to tell. "Matt and I have been together for a year." Because that also feels important. One month after the end of my sophomore year, Matt and I began. Now, it's the end of my junior year and Matt and I are over.

I nod. Yes, we're over. There's no coming back from this.

"Yes," I repeat. "There was blood."

"Who did you make bleed?" asks Jax. "Matt?"

Matt and I argued and he was mad, so mad. He slapped me, punched my stomach, then went for the head, and I intercepted him. I was a few hits in when he took advantage of my dropped guard and I absorbed the blow behind the ear. I collapsed to the floor and then he left. "I hit him."

I stopped his initial attack and I made him bleed.

"Matt did this to you?" Kaden's voice is pitched low yet hard, a promise of violence.

I shiver at the unsaid warning. They can't go after Matt. They can't. I've already created too much destruction.

"I saw her leave the party with him," Kaden continues.

Jax launches off the floor. "He's fucking dead."

"You can't." Ignoring the pressure of Kaden's hands, I press my feet hard against the concrete while swatting at my brother. He lets me go and Jax grabs my arm when I sway.

Jax leans into me as he holds me up. "What the fuck happened?"

My eyes flash open and Jax's shouted words echo in my head.

I've never been so relieved to see the roofing nails sticking through my uncle's roof. I suck in a breath to calm the rush of blood pounding my temples. I used to have this nightmare frequently after things ended between me and Matt this past summer and it figures I'd have it again after what happened last night. Especially since it was his younger brother who jumped me.

What sucks is it's not just a nightmare. It's the past reliving itself in my dreams.

I sit up and shiver against the cold air of the attic. No, it's not the cold air flowing from the cracked window causing the chill. It's the fact that life has become complicated. I gather my long hair at the base of my neck. Complicated. When is life going to be easy?

This past summer, I lied to Jax and Kaden. I told them that Matt and I got into a verbal argument and broke up and that after Matt left, someone I didn't see attacked me from behind.

My family hates me now because of what I've done, but I'm lying to protect them. I've walked away from everything to protect them.

If I'd told Jax and Kaden the truth about what happened with Matt, they would have gone after him and then Matt and his friends would have retaliated. All of it on the streets. All of it in pure hatred. The fighting would never end.

And last night…I might have destroyed everything I've built in order to protect Jax and Kaden. I broke a rule. I got involved. I hit Matt's little brother and Matt will want payback.

Even though I miss Jax and Kaden, I made the right decision. I blow out a long breath. It is. It's the right decision and I've lived with this lie for too long to let Matt's brother ruin it.

My eyes fall to my shoes on the floor and I silently curse. If my uncle finds out that I wore shoes in the house, he'll throw a fit.

Snatching them up, I tiptoe down the wooden stairs in my socks. Twice the material snags on an exposed nail. At the bottom, I relish the fact that I descended without a loud groan betraying my existence.

I pause, then strain to hear the light breathing of the nine other people sleeping in the house. Straight in front of me is the bathroom. To the right of the bathroom, my uncle's loud snores can be heard past the shut wooden door, and in the room to the left of the bathroom, my sister strangles her American Girl doll as she rolls over on the floor in her sleep. With her eyes still closed, my mother reaches down and touches Maggie's head full of tight brown curls.

I take an immediate right and carefully maneuver over Jax, whose bed has become the carpet of the living room. Kaden's long arms and legs fall off the couch. Even before we moved here, the living room was Jax's home. My parents displaced his younger brothers by taking over their room. The Dictator banished them to sleep in the unfinished basement. I offered to let them have the attic. Jax threatened to kick the crap out of them if they accepted.

In painfully slow movements, I leave my shoes near the front door. I'm assuming Jax and Kaden's lie accounted for my missing shoes, but just in case...

The light glowing at the back of the house catches me off guard and I weave through blankets, pillows, T-shirts, socks, arms and legs to gain access to the lime-green kitchen that's large enough for a stove, fridge, sink and a few cabinets. What doesn't fit is the large oval table that seats ten people. It consumes the entire kitchen, and, even with the mismatched wooden seats and folding metal chairs pushed in, it's difficult to walk around.

I'm hesitant as I poke my head in, then I smile.

Dad: dishwater-blond hair, tall like Kaden. He sits at the end of the table, reading the paper while jotting something into a notebook. The joy bubbling inside me is like running downstairs on Christmas morning. I can't remember the last time I spent time with him alone.

"Hi." I lean against the doorframe, nervous to enter. Sticking with what Jax originally assumed, I told my parents that I was late for curfew, ran home and Dad's medicine rolled out of the bag without my realizing it. Regardless of how it happened, I lost his medication. Am I welcome anymore?

His eyes shine as he lifts his head. "Haley—what are you doing up?"

"Just up." We speak barely above a whisper. It's rare when

this house is quiet; rarer are the moments when anyone can find peace. "How about you?"

The dark circles under his eyes indicate he's battling insomnia again. Mom said his mind races with everything that's happened, trying to figure out where it went wrong or scrambling to discover a way to fix it. "Same as you. Just up."

"What are you doing?" I ask.

Dad motions at the paper. "Job hunting."

I nod, not sure what to say. Talking to Dad used to be easy. Very easy.

Back when he was younger, he used to train with my grandfather. It's how Mom and Dad met. It's all very romantic and love-storyish, and I adore every second of the gooey-eyed tale. He was a kickboxer, like me, and swept Mom, the trainer's daughter, off her feet.

Dad practically raised Kaden and me in the gym. Kaden fell in love with boxing, then wrestling, then mixed martial arts. Me? I stuck with kickboxing and Dad admired that and me until I left my grandfather's gym. Then he lost more respect for me when I gave it up altogether.

I bite the inside of my lip and slip into the kitchen, focusing on the scratched brown linoleum floor as I progress toward my father. "Any luck?"

He shakes his head and closes the paper. "Most everything is online now."

I drop into the chair next to his and hug my knees to my chest. "Library then?" My uncle doesn't believe in internet access.

"Yep." Dad taps a beat onto the table. Eventually it loses the rhythm and spirals into a persistent drone. Is conversation with me painful for him or is it conversation in general?

"Kaden's got a fight in three months," I say. "He's going pro."

My brother will stare holes through me for a week because I told Dad this. I wasn't supposed to know. I overheard him and Jax discussing it on the bus. For some reason, he wanted to keep it private, but I'm desperate to end the silence. "Odds are he'll end up fighting one of the guys from Black Fire and you know they dominate in a stand-up fight." But Kaden is a force of nature on the mat.

"He's going to start fighting for money?"

"Yeah." It would have been better if Kaden could have fought amateur for a few more years, gained some experience, but with money tight the lure of a prize is too strong.

Unable to stay still, Dad rolls the pencil on the table under his palm and never glances at me. "In other words, he'll be fighting Matt?"

I flush—everywhere. Heat rises off my cheeks and the back of my neck. Will I ever be forgiven? By anybody? "Maybe. If Matt's gone pro."

"We both know he did the moment he turned eighteen."

He's probably right, so I say nothing.

"It's too bad you taught him how to defeat Kaden."

A knot forms in my windpipe and I pick at a hole in my jeans right above the knee, ripping it wider. "I know." I'm well aware of the rotten choices I made. I clear my throat and try again. "I was thinking maybe you could help Kaden train."

I was thinking Dad could get out of this house. I read once that exercising causes a rush of endorphins. Maybe if he did something he enjoyed, something he was good at, he'd get better.

"I'm sure your grandfather has that covered." Dad manages

a half smile when he looks at me. "What about you? Have you thought about going back?"

I have that heavy sinking sensation as I shake my head—the type that feels like cold maple syrup running from my heart to my intestines. Would it make him happy if I did return? I've dug my grave so deep at the gym it may be impossible to go back even if I wanted to.

The refrigerator kicks on, a loud hum signifying something is on the verge of breaking.

"Your mom talked to her great-aunt in California. She's offered to let us live with her."

I raise an eyebrow. "She lives in a retirement community. As in no one over sixty-five."

"She's gotten permission to let us stay."

I assess the kitchen. This house is the dirty dark secret of hell on earth, but the thought of leaving Kentucky cuts my soul. Leaving the state means we've given up hope and it wasn't until this very moment that I realize I've held on to a shred. No matter how battered and bruised the shred is, it's still faintly alive, praying that Dad will land a job and take us home. "Are we leaving?"

"We're going to try to hold on until you and Kaden graduate. We'll go if things haven't improved by then."

"You'll find something. I know you will."

"How's the college search going?" Dad rushes out.

I freeze, unsure how to respond. I've kept the rejection private, though I crave to tell Dad. Once upon a time, he would have been the first person I approached with any problem because he always had the right words. He'd place an arm around my shoulder, kiss my temple and tell me, "Bad luck, kid. We'll get 'em next time."

The hurt inside, knowing I've let him down with the gym and kickboxing and now college, it's like being gutted open by a serrated blade. "The college search is going great."

"Do you have any scholarship leads?"

No. "Yeah. Plenty."

"Good." A pause. "Good. At least Kaden has the gym." His voice cracks as his skin fades into the color of ash. The expression is off when all my memories of him are of a courageous fighter. I've watched my dad battle in the ring against opponents who were stronger than him and win. How did he become this broken?

Dread causes my hands to jerk because I itch to stick them over my eyes. It's awful to watch his undoing, knowing I'm partly responsible. If I had gotten the meds, he wouldn't obsess over his mistakes and he could start sleeping at night.

"Kaden will continue on at the gym, but I thought I'd have something to offer you for college. I had some money tucked away, not a lot, but enough to help, but then we needed it for the mortgage..."

A strange noise leaves Dad's throat as he slides his chair back. "Library."

Though it's not open for a few more hours. Dad squeezes between the wall and the table and as he's on the verge of leaving the kitchen, I open my mouth. "Daddy..."

My father presses a hand against the doorframe, his knuckles shifting as he tightens his grip. I haven't called him that in years. He peers at me from over his shoulder. "Yeah?"

"I'm sorry."

"I know, Hays. I know."

West

THE INTENSIVE CARE UNIT of the hospital has that slasher-movie quiet to it. That moment right before the psycho jumps out from behind a counter and hacks the people to bits. From the family waiting room, I can hear the occasional monitor beeping, the rustle of paper and the low murmur of conversation between the nurses. I loathe this place. It's cold, sterile, smells of rubbing alcohol and is filled with death.

Rachel shouldn't be here. This place is the opposite of her. Unable to sit anymore, I jerk out of my seat. The guy on the other side of the room tugs his head up to look at me. We stare at each other. His wife is dying. I overheard him tell someone a few minutes ago.

Dying.

As I said, Rachel doesn't belong here.

I glance away and walk to the windows. My jaw hurts. The knuckles on both my hands are scratched to hell and throb like a bitch. I drove here hours ago. Abby visited Rachel and left. I texted Dad and told him I was here.

Silence—from my entire family. From my way older brothers, Jack and Gavin, to Rachel's twin, Ethan, to Mom and Dad. They want me to visit Rachel, but I can't. Not with her here, not with her surrounded by people who are dying.

I failed her. My heart pounds hard and the sharp ache creates an edginess. I shut my eyes, wishing I could leave.

"West."

I turn to the sound of my mother's voice. Tears have dug grooves into her makeup and her black mascara smudges in clumps near her eyes.

Nausea slams into my gut. "Is it Rachel?"

"We talked to the hospital's specialist. The damage to her legs is severe and—" Mom chokes on her words, then clamps a hand over her mouth. She exhales and regains composure. "It was unexpected news."

I harden into a statue, yet her words sink in past my shock. More surgeries. More time in the hospital. "Is she going to walk again?"

"I don't know."

I rub my eyes to readjust my equilibrium. This is my fault. If I had found another way to handle things, Rachel wouldn't be in this hospital. She wouldn't be fighting for her life.

Mom's heels click across the wooden floor toward me. When she raises her hand, I tilt my head away. I don't deserve Mom's forgiveness or her comfort. Persistent, Mom gently lays her hand on my jaw and moves her thumb as if her touch could erase the bruises. "Why do you do this to yourself? Why must you always fight?"

"I don't know." I step back, forcing her to drop her hand.

Mom puts distance between us and pours herself a cup of coffee. "Have you visited with Rachel?"

"No." A sweep of the room confirms the guy with the

dying wife vacated. No wonder Mom's being open about family business.

A gruff clearing of a throat draws our attention to the doorway. Dad stretches to his full six feet and sets his pissed-off dark eyes on me.

"Miriam." He softens his tone when he addresses Mom. "The nurses need you."

Mom nods, and as she hurries out, Dad gently wraps his fingers around her wrist. She lifts her gaze to his and he bends down to kiss her lips. They do this. My parents love each other. Dad worships her, and it's why he's a control freak with us. If everything isn't about business, it's about Mom's happiness.

When Dad releases her, she leaves. Not once peeking in my direction.

I stand taller when Dad enters, as if preparing for a physical fight. We've yet to come to blows during an argument, but the fire in his eyes says that day will happen. Sooner now than later, and I hate it. When I was a kid, Dad and I used to be close.

"You didn't come here last night like I asked."

I stay silent. The truth won't help my case. I've been in detention more than any kid at my school and have been suspended more days than we've had off. Dad, in his own way, takes my shit, but he made it clear months ago that he'd be done with me at expulsion.

"Did you go home or did you pass out at a party?" he asks.

"Does it matter?" I've seen that expression before. He's already made up his mind on me.

"No," he answers. "They've expelled you."

I utter something I've never said to him. "I'm sorry." I am.

For Rachel. For the fight at school. For making this horrible situation more complicated.

His face remains emotionless. "I don't care."

I blink and my shoulders fall a half inch. "I mean it. I'm sorry. I'll apologize to the principal, to the guy I hurt, his family, whatever. I screwed up this time."

He points at me. "Damn right you screwed up. But not just this time. This is one of many mistakes, and I'm done with it. I told you months ago that I drew the line at expulsion. All you had to do was stay out of fights and stay out of trouble until you graduate and you couldn't even do that. What's worse is that you chose to cross this line with your sister in the hospital. What is this? A cry for attention? You don't think that your mother has enough to deal with?"

"Fine. Tell me what you want me to do and I'll do it."

"Your sister is in agony and from what I understand you had a hand in this nightmare."

My eyes snap to his. "I tried to keep her from Isaiah." That's where I failed, and I don't care for the reminder.

"You never bothered telling me she was seeing him in the first place! I'm her father, not you. I'm the one who makes those decisions."

I throw my arms out to my sides. "That would have required you to be home and not on your goddamn phone!"

A muscle in his jaw jumps. I drew blood and I don't fucking care.

"Care to tell me about the money you took from your sister?" I don't like the way his eyes slice through me, as if he shoved a blade into my chest and he's enjoying watching me bleed.

"I told Rachel I'd pay her back."

"Tell me about the money you took from your sister."

"I told you already. Gavin owed money to a bookie and I came up with the amount needed."

"You never told me you stole that money from Rachel."

"I didn't steal it. I borrowed it." Without her prior knowledge or consent, but I swear I promised to pay her back.

This is old news from days before Rachel's accident. Not knowing I had the situation under control, Jack broke down and told Dad everything: how Ethan, Jack and I had been covering up Gavin's gambling issues because Mom couldn't handle the truth that her firstborn son was a gambling addict.

But when Jack cried to Daddy, he neglected to bring up how Gavin tried to discuss his problems with Dad on three separate occasions and how each time Dad blew him off over a business meeting or Mom. So when Dad wouldn't give him the time of day, Gavin did what needed to be done: he came to me.

"Did you know Rachel was in trouble?" Dad demands. "That she lost some street race and owed money to a criminal? That it was your friends who took her to the race? That they introduced her to that life?"

"Rachel doesn't hang out with my friends." And I'd kick their asses if Rachel crossed their minds.

"She was at the dragway the night of the crash because you stole the money she earned to pay off the debt. She was there because you, for the millionth time, took matters into your own hands and instead of thinking for thirty seconds about the outcome of your decisions, you acted on instinct. This accident is on you."

"It's a lie." Everyone knows Dad was driving from the

dragway with Rachel in the passenger seat when he stalled out the engine of her car. Everyone knows the tractor trailer that struck them had lost control. "Who told you this?"

Dad steps in my direction, and if he were anybody else, I'd swear he was itching to take a swing. "Isaiah."

The name causes my insides to boil. "He's a liar."

"If he's a liar, then he's a better one than you," Dad snaps. "But I don't think Isaiah is lying. He's the one who's been standing by your sister while you're out getting into fights."

I step back, the near crazy making the room spin. Yeah, I thought I failed by not keeping Rachel from Isaiah, but then my last conversation with Rachel crashes around in my brain. Fuck me. This could be true. "You don't understand. Rachel doesn't want to see me."

She doesn't, because if what Dad's saying is true...if the last words Rachel said to me the night of the accident are true...I stole money she needed and because of that, I left her in danger.

"You don't want to see her!" Dad's forehead crumples as if he's exasperated. "All she asks is to see her family. When are you going to stop thinking of yourself? It's time for you to grow up and become a man!"

Fear and chaos claw from my gut into my windpipe. I shake my head, trying to make his words wrong. No—this isn't all on me. It can't be. "You're the selfish bastard of the family."

Not me. Dad's the one who hurts the people I love. That's his role. Not mine.

Dad rushes into my space, his breath hot on my face. "What did you say?"

"You heard me." Adrenaline pumps into my bloodstream. I

crave to hit him. He's jonesing to hit me. The air is thick and tense with violence. It's practically crackling with the shit.

"I'm tired of dealing with you and your temper." Dad pulls back, his face flushed red. "I've enrolled you at Eastwick. You start there on Monday and you'll finish your senior year there. After that, I don't care what you do. It's time you learn how to clean up your own messes."

That's right. Dad's great at playing this game. Get pissed at me, mess with me, then my anger explodes and I'm the one still in trouble, but not this time. If he's pushing me, I'm pushing back. "Did you find something you couldn't fix with your money? Could you not pay off the board of trustees at school to keep me from being expelled? Or did you decide to finally put out the trash?"

A vein on his forehead pulsates. "Do you have any idea how many chances that school has given you? How many chances I've given you? Your sister is here and she's in pain, and you go out and party and fight and get expelled from school! I don't understand you! I don't get you at all."

"No," I shout. "You don't."

He hasn't seen who I am in years. But I see the line. Hell, I'm stomping on it and because I hate the man in front of me, I cross it. "I'm impressed to see you here. Was this the afternoon you usually spend golfing or did your business partners take pity on Rachel and cancel the meetings themselves?"

His lips thin out. "Don't do this, West."

The warning is out and I should listen, but I get a strange high seeing him squirm. "You missed Little League games, middle school graduations, fuck...you don't even have a clue if I'm home most the time. Who knew in order to get your attention we'd have to wrap our car around a semitruck?"

Dad rakes a hand through his hair and angles his foot toward the door, but I'm not done with him yet. "When you stalled out Rachel's car, were you on your cell? Because, let's face it, your business has always come first."

The ice-cold glare he shoots me kills a portion of my soul. I struck a nerve that's real. Too real. I meant it to needle him. I meant to rub against that constant I'm-better-than-you bravado. I had no idea I'd be right.

"Dad," I start. "I didn't mean—"

"Go home, pack a bag and get out of my house." Spit flies out of his mouth as he points out the door. "Get out of my sight. Get out of my life. If you're there in two hours, I'll call the police and tell them to drag your ass out and send you to a group home."

Dad leaves and I follow him past the first couple of ICU rooms. He can't throw me out. There's no way he meant what he said. My vision tunnels and a low buzzing noise fills my ears. He's not serious—he can't be. "Funny. So what, I'm grounded? Two weeks? Three?"

Dad keeps walking straight ahead. "This isn't a joke. Get out of here. It's obvious you don't feel like you belong."

Fuck me, he's serious. "Where do I go?"

He doesn't even look at me as he responds, "I don't care. That's what happens with trash, West. Once you toss it on the curb, you don't care what happens to it."

My body grows cold and I can't think clearly. Every thought I have splits apart and drifts into nowhere.

"Isaiah!"

I flinch at the terrified sound of my sister's voice and my

hand rises as if to block the sight of the room to my right. Rachel. She's worse than they described: black-and-blue bruises over her face and arms, her exposed skin scraped and cut, her legs completely immobilized. Like in a bad sci-fi movie, wires and tubes run from my sister to beeping machines.

My mind wavers and the floor trembles beneath my feet. Since entering the hospital, I've never made it past the waiting room. Never. Because I can't handle this. I can't handle seeing Rachel broken.

The bastard that led Rachel astray leaps from his chair and catches her hand. He wipes her tears away and murmurs to her. Tattoos mark his arms. The guy hasn't even shaved. He hovers over her, one hand grasping her fingers, the other smoothing back her hair. My fists curl at my sides. He's touching my sister.

"She has nightmares," says Ethan from behind me.

I glance at my brother, then slide away from the window, not wanting Rachel to spot me. Who the fuck am I kidding? I can't stomach witnessing her like this.

My mind can't process what's happening. It's too much: seeing Rachel, my dad kicking my ass to the street, being within feet of the bastard who's responsible for all of this destruction. "Why is he in there?"

"She wants him, and Mom and Dad aren't in the arguing mood." Ethan sags against the wall. "Isaiah can convince her to sleep and she'll force herself to stay awake if he's not there."

Ethan resembles Dad with dark hair and eyes, which means we appear nothing alike except for our height. If I ever wondered what hell on earth looked like, Ethan would be the prime example. Days without sleep can turn anyone into a zombie. At least he's not sobbing like he was the other night. Hell I can deal with; crying I can't.

I can't hug him again and tell him it's going to be okay. That would require me to be stable, and stable isn't my strong suit. There's a disconnection of emotion inside me as I step back...step away. It's a dream. All of this is a bad dream.

Feet shuffle behind me, footsteps of people walking into Rachel's room. I can't go in there. I can't. Gravity draws me and it's not in the direction my family prefers. I move toward the pull and Ethan slams a hand onto my shoulder. "She wants to see you."

I yank my shoulder out of Ethan's grasp. "No, she doesn't." It's safe to say no one here wants me.

My brother says nothing more as I head for the elevator. As I said before, Rachel deserves better...including better than me.

Haley

"HALEY WILLIAMS CHOOSES, once again, another form. Could this be the one, ladies and gentlemen?" Jax mock whispers beside me. "A hush rolls over the crowd as Miss Williams glances over the wording. Her eyebrows furrow. Is this it? Will this be the one?"

My cousin spiked his whitish-blond hair into a Mohawk this morning, meaning he's feeling ornery. If he keeps up the running commentary, he'll discover how ornery I can be.

From over the open bottom drawer of the filing cabinet, I glare at Jax. "Don't you have something better to do?"

Jax and I sit on the floor, tucked away in the corner of the main office. We've been here for an hour and the receptionists forgot we exist, so they gossip freely. The stench of cafeteria coffee transforms into a film over my clothing. I shudder with the knowledge that I'll smell like this for the rest of the day.

He cracks a wide grin. "Yeah. If you tell me what's doing then I can go do my thing."

The ghetto to English translation of "what's doing": what am I hiding about Friday night. I didn't spill this weekend and I don't plan on spilling now.

It's Monday morning and I woke early and took the city bus to school so I can, once again, peruse the filing cabinet full of scholarship applications. I use the internet at the library, but trying to find applicable scholarships on there is like trying to search for a lost ring in a sand dune.

"Nothing's doing, so go do your *thang*." I waggle my eyebrows and give him a sly smile. "There's got to be a girl around here who hasn't been done wrong by you."

"You'd think, but evidently girls talk to each other. Damn shame."

"Damn shame," I echo. I cram another useless application back into a folder and yank yet another out. "Do you think I could pass for Alaska Native?"

"Sure." He bites into an apple he five-finger discounted from the cafeteria and dangles a piece of paper in the air. "Bet you could pass for a guy who's ranked in tennis, too."

I snatch the application from his hands and shove it back into the cabinet. "Funny. Just wait until next year and you'll be doing the desperate dance."

"No, I won't. High school is as far as I'm going." Jax is a year younger than me, seventeen, and a junior. When we were younger, we were inseparable, but then he grew up, I grew breasts, he became interested in girls and I became interested in anything other than what I liked at ten.

"I'm getting a job," he says. "And as far from Dad as possible."

Amen to that. Guess we're more alike than I originally thought.

A knock on the window that overlooks the main hallway grabs our attention. Kaden flips us off and mouths, "You suck!"

Jax laughs and flips the finger back. I giggle when Kaden shakes his head and stalks off. "You didn't tell Kaden you were becoming my shadow today?"

"Nah, he knows, but I didn't wake him when I heard you getting ready upstairs. He trained hard yesterday and needed the sleep. Kaden's pissed he had to ride the bus by himself and I wasn't there to act as shield with that freshman puppy dogging him."

Kaden's a year older than me, but he was held back in first grade. Because of that, we're both seniors at Eastwick High. It's hard on Kaden with the whole world knowing he's in the same grade as his younger sister. At least I know it is. Back at a time when we were close, he confided in me. Repeating a grade, it's why he fights hard in the gym, why he's quiet in public.

"There's still some time left before class," I say. "Why don't you go pester him?"

"Because I'm pestering you." Another crunch of the apple.

Why didn't I play an instrument in band? There's an entire scholarship section devoted to that. "I'm not changing my story."

"Don't expect you to, but if I'm right—which, come on, it's me and I'm not wrong—I expect the truth to reveal itself. Today. At school."

My head jerks in his direction. Jax watches me with thoughtful green eyes. He reminds me of an owl when he does this and it makes me feel like a mouse, which isn't a good thing. Jax's family does kill things for sport.

"I've been living in this neighborhood a lot longer than you have," he adds. "That drug addict little brother of your ex-boyfriend jumped you Friday night and you're covering for him, aren't you?"

"No." Yes.

Jax leans into me, his playful demeanor evaporating. "I thought you were over Matt."

"I am." The most truthful thing I've said to Jax in six months. What happened between Matt and me was unspeakable.

"Then why are you covering for his brother?"

Because they don't play fair. The words tumble in my head, crashing into one another. Even when I was dating Matt, his younger brother carried a knife. It's been six months. I cringe to think what Conner has graduated to. Jax and Kaden hate Matt and Conner. They've been enemies since I can remember.

"I kicked Conner's ass at the last tournament, Hays, but you wouldn't know because you weren't there. I can take care of myself, Kaden can take care of himself and our job is to take care of you. If Conner thinks you're weak prey, he'll come after you again. You aren't living in the middle class anymore. This is the streets and there are rules."

And I'm the one who got jumped. "You don't think I know that?"

"Is there a problem here?" I flinch when I notice our school's in-house social worker, Mrs. Collins, standing next to me and Jax. She's all blond and thin and middle-aged hip and, except for this moment, typically has a smile on her face. My grandfather attended the parent–teacher conference in lieu of my parents last month and he talked to her for way too long about his gym.

"Haley and I are arguing," says Jax.

My stomach twists like a dishrag. *Shut up, moron.*

"Can I help?" she asks in a cheerful voice. "Maybe mediate?"

"No," I answer while Jax says, "Yes."

I whip my head to him and slam my hands against the carpet. "Really?"

"Why not?" He crunches into the apple again. "If anyone needs therapy, it's our family." He winks at me, then redirects himself at Mrs. Collins. "I'm yanking your stones. My goal in life is to get a rise out of Haley and I did."

Jax offers me his hand, I accept, and he pulls us both off the ground. He swoops up my backpack and some of the applications that had fallen out of the files, then kicks the cabinet closed. He waves the apple in the air. "Garbage can?"

With her head propped to the side as if she's watching a fascinating reality TV show, she points to the small can next to her feet. "Tell your grandfather I'm still working on that volunteer."

"No problem." Jax trashes the apple and drags me along as he brushes past her. "Later."

Like I'm a seven-year-old, I wave and smile at her before I trip out into the main hallway. Jax and I become engulfed in the mob of people heading toward first period. Jax thrusts my backpack and the loose applications at me. Great, now I'm going to have to get these back.

"What was that?" I demand. "Do you want to get a social worker involved? Like we don't have enough problems already?"

Jax steps in front of me, causing me to whiplash forward as I halt.

"Get out of the way!" some guy shouts as he walks past us.

"Go fuck yourself, asshole!" yells Jax. When he's done staring the guy down, Jax towers over me. "Tell me what happened on Friday."

"Nothing happened. I fell. The medication rolled out. End of story."

"Who the hell are you anymore? I mean, there are times I see you. You. Like a few minutes ago in the office. The girl I grew up with. The girl who talked trash. The girl who fought with and for her family. Then you got wrapped up with Matt..."

Reining in his temper, Jax inhales deeply and looks away. "I thought when you broke up with him... Why are you guarding his back? I miss you, Haley. And if you ever see the girl I liked, tell her that for me. Tell her that her family misses her."

He leaves me there....standing alone in a busy hallway. The scholarship applications crackle in my hand. How do I tell him I've been protecting him from Matt and Conner? How do I tell him I've been fighting for him this entire time?

West

FROM ACROSS THE COUNTER, the secretary slides my schedule to me. "You'll love it here."

I nod, then meet her eyes. What would she do if I told her that for the past two nights I've parked my car in a remote spot at a local park and slept there, then showered at a truck stop?

Pride kept me from asking anyone for a place to crash. Not my brothers, not my friends, not anyone. They'd give me a place, but I can't stomach the look of disappointment.

After word spread I was officially expelled from school, I was avalanched in texts and the idea of adding to the sympathy induced dry heaves. I'm West Young, and regardless of the fact that I've been disowned from the family and the fortune associated with it, I don't accept charity...or pity.

The secretary tilts her head. "Are you okay?"

No. I'm not. It's been cold for the past two nights and I've had to run the car every hour to ease the chill. The exhaustion sucks, but it's the silence that kills me. "I'm good."

Without waiting to see if she buys my response, I exit the

office. I don't care if I'm going the right way to first period. School...class...normalcy feels unnecessary, a bit insane.

I came to my new school hoping my parents would be here. Saturday I went home, packed some shit, then left, and I've stayed gone. Somewhere around three last night, I had the delusion Mom would be worried and Dad would be sorry. That the reason my cell wasn't burning with texts and calls was because it died Saturday night and I forgot my charger at home. The image looped over and over in my mind that I'd strut into school and they'd be waiting for me—begging me to return home.

If my brothers did call or text, maybe I would have reached out to them by now, but they didn't. Dad not contacting me is no shock, but for Mom to be AWOL? My gut cramps and I rub the back of my neck as I stalk down the hallway. Guess Dad was right—when it comes to my family, I don't belong.

The sight of long sandy-brown hair causes me to pause. I don't believe in ghosts, but I'm seeing one. With wide eyes and a facial expression that mirrors the one she wore when I almost hit her with the Escalade, Haley stands in the middle of the hallway. A backpack slung over her shoulder; a piece of paper clutched in her hand. People give her a wide berth as they walk past, like she's an island in the middle of rapids.

I'm not shy. Never have been. People, parties, crowds: that's my thing. But being near Haley again... I found my kryptonite.

Her jeans perfectly fit her hips, a blue cotton shirt molds nicely around her ample curves and she has the darkest eyes I've ever seen. A guy could get lost in those eyes.

She blinks several times, folds the paper in her hand and turns—heading in the opposite direction of me. Shaking myself back to life, I duck and weave through the crowd in pursuit.

"Haley!"

Right as she walks into the stairwell, she glances over her shoulder with her eyebrows scrunched together. *That's right. I'm calling you.* "Haley!"

Our eyes meet and her hand automatically covers her heart. I cut through two girls in order to reach her. One of them yells at me, but I ignore her.

"West?" Haley remembers my name. That's a bonus.

"Why is it every time I see you, you're running?"

Her lips move a centimeter. "I wasn't running." She hitches her thumb over her shoulder. "I was heading to class."

I don't want halfway. I crave a full smile from this girl. "You gotta admit, it was a sweet line."

Christ, she has an amazing smile. With her eyes shining like that, she could be her own personal fireworks show. "The line sucked. I'm more fond of guys who give me flowers."

Noted and filed away for future use. "It got your attention."

"My attention?" Her head tilts as if she remembered something awful—odds are she's replaying Friday night.

An electrical current slams through me when Haley grabs my arm and drags me into the corner of the stairwell next to the fire extinguisher. Her fingers are cool against my now burning skin.

She lowers her voice. "You've had my attention for the past three days. The last time I saw you, you were bleeding on the street with a drug dealer offering to babysit. Do you know how many times I searched the newspaper to see if there was an article about you being dead?"

My shoulders roll back. "Drug dealer?"

Haley releases my wrist and steps back. "Yeah. Abby. Everyone knows she sells drugs. I mean, she's your friend, right? Please tell me I left you with a friend. Oh, my God, she's not your friend, is she? Crap. Oh, crap. Are you okay?"

Her eyes dart around, searching for signs of abuse. She'll find them—the remnants of the two fistfights from Friday. What she doesn't see is the internal bleeding from my argument with Dad. Haley stretches her hand to touch the yellowish bruise fading on my jaw, then hesitates.

I inhale and revel in Haley's scent: wildflowers in bloom. The sights and sounds of the world dissipate—well, everything except those gorgeous dark eyes.

"Seriously, are you okay?" Haley drops her hand and I turn my head to breathe in anything that's not her.

"I'm fine," I say. "Are *you* okay? Did those guys hurt you?"

"I'm fine." She sounds uncertain, so I cross my arms over my chest.

"I'm fine," she answers again. "Honestly. What are you doing here?"

I ignore her. "What happened after I blacked out? Why did they leave my car?"

"Not important. Tell me, why are you here? To see Abby? For me? This school has a zero tolerance policy on outsiders. If they find you, they'll call the police."

"I go to school here now." From my back pocket, I pull the schedule I picked up a few minutes ago from the office.

"West..." Haley's level stare has all the makings of a firing squad. "What do you mean 'now'?"

"I got expelled from my last school."

"For what?"

"Fighting." For the first time in my life, guilt heats the back of my neck. Man, she's got to have a fantastic image of who I am. The problem? She'd be right and the fact that I care is weird.

She tosses her hands in the air. "Of course. Why not? I'm a magnet for you stinking people. Why wouldn't I be surrounded by more?" Her head falls back and she focuses on the ceiling. "Hey, God? It's me, Haley. Not funny."

"What?"

"Okay. All right. This can be managed. It can. I can manage this. This is entirely under my control. I can own this situation."

"I don't need to be managed."

Haley tosses me an are-you-for-real gaze and her hair tumbles over her shoulder. It's shiny and I bet if I ran my fingers through it, the strands would feel like silk. I like hair like that. I like kissing girls who have hair like that. My eyes flash to her lips and the memory of her stepping into me on Friday night sizzles in my mind: the walking, talking inferno. Kissing Haley would be a thrill-ride experience.

"West?" Haley motions near her eyes. "Attention here, please?"

"I wasn't checking out your curves." Though now that it's mentioned...

"Go there and I swear to God you'll have to check 'other' when asked if you're male or female."

I chuckle and rest my palm against the cool cinder block wall, crowding her. Haley shifts and practically shrinks into the corner. She's shorter than me, but not by much. I'd say she was afraid, but the way she studies my biceps tells me differently.

"Haley?" She refocuses on my face. "Eyes up here please."

Gaped. Open. Mouth. "Okay, look. Me and you. We've got problems."

I agree. She wants to kiss me. I want her body underneath mine. Nothing a dark room and a bed couldn't solve. "What are you doing after school?"

"What? No. Don't tell me. I don't care. Back to problems. Those guys that jumped us on Friday?"

My hand slips off the wall and I straighten. "Yeah?"

"They go to school here and I'm not exactly their best friend."

My muscles tighten and I have to work to keep the smirk off my face. Payback is going to be sweet with those bastards. "Do you know where they're at?"

"Stay away from them. They're dangerous."

I don't give a shit if they play poker with the devil. They took me down. That doesn't happen, and I won't let that be the final say—especially since I'll be spending the next four months in this hellhole.

Haley clutches my arm as if I were about to waltz into a minefield. "No!"

I lean into her—our heads less than an inch apart. The crazy ass bastard's words echo in my head: *I know where to find Haley.* "Have they threatened you?"

Her fingernails attempt to dig canyons into my arm. "There are things in my life you can't understand, okay? I know you meant well on Friday, but to be honest, you screwed everything up, so I'm begging you to listen to me now. Stay away from them, stay away from me and, for the love of God, don't mention Friday to anyone."

The warning bell rings. Haley releases me and runs up the stairs. What the hell?

Haley

GOD HATES ME. It's the only explanation when West appears in my first-period class. My best girl friend, possibly my only girl friend, Marissa Long, lowers the book she's been absorbed in since I sat at our science table.

"Wow" is the word that slips out of her mouth.

Unfortunately, I have to agree. The boy is fantastically pretty, that's for sure. His golden-blond hair is cut short and is styled. Trendy yet not. Exactly like the rest of him. A combination of dangerous and steaming hot.

He wears jeans, the sexy kind. A bit baggy, not overly. Just enough that his black boxers peek out when he walks. And thanks to the clingy T-shirt, the world knows he's on-fire ripped in every single delicious way.

I close my eyes and suck in air. *Stop it.* West is not hot. He's a fighter. He's trouble. Been there, done that, got the T-shirt and the associated heartache.

Marissa touches my arm, and, when I open my eyes, I find her camped in my personal space. "He's staring at you."

Sure enough, while our Biology II teacher shuffles through the drawers of his desk, West flashes me this glorious smile that causes me to melt into a puddle. Crap. Just crap. I *am* attracted to him. This isn't good. Not good at all.

"Do you know him?" Marissa asks.

Yes. "No." And it's going to be hard for anyone to believe that answer when he continues to stare at me like he's seen me with my clothes off. I run a finger around the collar of my shirt, releasing some trapped hot air. If West doesn't rein it in, he's going to get us both killed.

"Are you *sure?*"

I told him to stay out of my way because that's how West will avoid trouble with Conner and Matt. It'll be amazing if I can remain unscathed through lunch.

Our teacher motions with his hand for West to take a seat. "Any seat."

West's eyes roam to the spot next to me and I grab Marissa's hand. "Do not leave your seat. Not to sharpen your pencil. Not to use the bathroom. Not to pick up your backpack."

"Ooookay," mumbles Marissa and sticks her head back into a book.

West strides down the small space between the tables. I keep my eyes forward, ignoring he exists, ignoring that on Friday he almost pancaked me with his car, that he went kamikaze on Conner and that I had to fight to bail him out of trouble.

I ignore all of that, but more importantly, I ignore how my senses heighten as West pauses next to my table, plants a hand flat on the surface and leans into me. I swear the heat of his body wraps around mine. An extremely tempting musky scent enters my lungs when I inhale. Oh, God, he's mouthwatering.

Everyone turns and watches because the most beautiful

boy to ever step into this school is next to the girl no one but Matt has ever wanted to date.

"Hello, Haley," he says in this deep voice that curls my toes in that *Notebook* movie kind of way.

I can't look at him. I can't. One, because he's not supposed to be talking to me. Two, because he's gorgeous and I'd prefer for West to remain in the dark that I think that. "We have an agreement."

West chuckles. "You said something. I disagreed. Later, we'll come to an agreement."

Mr. Rice asks everyone to settle in, and West continues toward the back, but not before skimming one finger down my shoulder. I let out a rush of air between my lips as goose bumps tingle on my arm from his touch. West does not fight fair.

I return my gaze to the front and my heart slams out of my chest when I meet stone-cold eyes. Matt walks into class at the sound of the bell and there's no doubt he saw part of the show.

He stalks down the aisle and I wish I could blend into my chair. Without breaking stride, he mumbles as he passes, "We're talking today."

My hand presses against my neck as if that will help open my clogged air passage. Whether he wants to talk about West touching me or the fact that Conner may have told him what happened between us or if he just wants to rehash previous fights in our defunct relationship, I don't know, but as far as I'm concerned, there's no way I'm talking with Matt—not if I can help it.

West

I DROP INTO A SEAT at an empty table in the back and a dishwater-blonde slithers into the chair beside me. "You're West Young," she says.

"I am." I edge away from her. The last thing I want is my reputation with girls or my rep with fights following me. Something good should come out of this. "How'd you know?"

"I've attended some parties at Brian Miller's house with my cousin. She goes to Worthington Private."

Shit. I assess her, praying we haven't hooked up. I don't fuck girls. It's not my thing. I've witnessed guys spiral and burn because of an unplanned pregnancy, getting too emotional after the fact or a good ol' STD. Thanks, but no thanks. I might not be hitting it in that way, but I hit it in other ways and girls appreciate my creativity.

The blonde twists her hair around her finger, makes full-fledged eye contact and sends me an I'll-go-down-on-you smile—all signs indicating we have had previous carnal knowledge of each other.

"I'm Jessica," she announces. "I've wanted to introduce

myself since I saw you at a party a year ago, but by the time I get there, you're usually a little far gone."

Thank you, Jesus, for saving me from the why-didn't-you-call guilt trip.

Our teacher calls the class to order and I open my lone notebook. With twenty bucks in cash to my name, I bought this and a pen, then spent the remainder on gas. Food wasn't on the priority list this morning, and as my stomach growls, I'm beginning to regret the decision. I haven't had a decent meal since Thursday night.

I'm terrified to use my credit card and learn it's been denied. There's a limit to what my mental stability can handle.

A few tables up, Haley sits curtain-rod straight. *Come on, give me something. Anything.* I got the hell beaten out of me over her, plus I saw the attraction stirring in her eyes in the stairwell. Hell, the girl flushed the moment I stepped into the room. *Look at me. Just look at me.*

My pen knocks against the table as it bounces in my hand, then freezes the moment Haley glances over her shoulder. In rabbit-fast movements, she switches her gaze back to the front, but it won't erase the fact she looked.

Why it's important to me, I don't know. Maybe it's because everything in my life is screwed up and I need to know at least one person cares. Maybe...but who knows? Right now today almost feels doable.

"You know Haley?" The lines cluttering Jessica's forehead spell jealousy.

What were Haley's words to me? To stay away? Not happening. "Yeah, do you?"

"She's a friend of mine."

Our teacher passes out an outline for an upcoming project and mumbles something about having to leave for a moment to help a class across the hall but being able to see us from there, and that he expects us to watch the documentary he cues up on the SMART Board. With the lights off and the door behind him clicking shut, the class loosens up with low buzzing conversations.

Jessica faces me, props her elbow on the table and rests her head on her hand. “How do you know Haley? From the fights?”

The fights? “Yeah.”

A relieved grin eases onto her face. If I play this right, maybe I can figure Haley out.

“That’s what I thought,” she says. “After she and Matt broke up last summer, she swore she was done with that tough man stuff, but I knew she wouldn’t be able to hold out. Haley’s been a tomboy since kindergarten.”

A tomboy? Are we admiring the same person? Haley’s all curves. She may be in high school, but she’s miles from that in-between stage.

Jessica’s seat scrapes against the floor, creating an ear-splitting squeak as she slides closer to me. A chorus of *damns* fills the room. Most everyone looks back, including Haley. Fuck me. Another girl up in my business is not what I want Haley to see.

“So tell me,” Jessica says in a way that indicates we share secrets. “Is she fighting again? I won’t tell anyone, I swear.” Meaning she won’t tell anyone until she leaves class.

With her head lying on an outstretched arm on the table, Haley’s pen moves in circles. She’s a doodler, like my brother Ethan. When he’s trying to clear his head, to think things through, he scratches away on any paper he can find.

Haley's shorter than me. Tall for a girl, yet not. And very, very feminine. Jessica has to be joking. There's no way Haley's a fighter. "I haven't seen her fight."

"Oh. Well. Then you must have seen her cousin and brother fight, I guess."

"Yeah." Haley and her family are fighters. I roll the words around in my head as if taste-testing them. It feels off, but then I think of how she challenged me the other night when I almost hit her with my car.

Haley's a fighter. Interesting. Like the info on the flowers, it's duly noted and filed away for future use. *What other secrets are you hiding, Haley?* "Who's this Matt guy you mentioned earlier?"

"That is Matt." Jessica points to the large son of a bitch at the table behind Haley. His dark hair is shaved close to his scalp and his ears are a bit deformed. I've seen the full-blown deformity before on pay-per-view, though it was a much more intense version. Cauliflower ears. It's what happens after a fighter gets hit too much and the cartilage doesn't heal correctly.

What's important is how the guy watches Haley, his eyes memorizing her every move. Has Haley informed him of their breakup or is he pining? "What's up with the two of them?"

"They got together our sophomore year and split a week after Haley moved into the homeless shelter this past summer. I have no doubt Matt will win her back, though. He's crazy obsessed with her."

"What?" My head snaps in Jessica's direction and my heart pounds as I wonder if I heard her correctly. She said

Haley, right? Not me. But then the wonder turns to dread. Haley can't be living at a place like that.

"That Matt's crazy obsessed? It's not in a weird way, well, it is, but it's like romantic, you know—"

"Not that," I cut her off. "The homeless part."

She presses a hand over her mouth. "Oops. I shouldn't have said that. Don't tell Haley I told you. She'd be mortified."

"I won't." But what she should be mortified about is that she spilled. Minus the fake hand over her mouth, Jessica wears smug well. At my old school, girls conducted war and annihilated opponents using words. That "slipup" was meant as an execution shot to Haley's head.

"Good." She surveys Haley as if she grew a conscience, but then abandons it as she lowers her voice. "Haley's dad was laid off over a year ago and they lost everything. It's been rough for her, but we've all tried to rally around her. You know, be good friends."

I'd rather drink arsenic than enjoy a friendship like Jessica's. "Does she still live at the shelter?"

She shakes her head. "They moved in with her cousin's family. Seriously, don't tell her I told you. She's sort of private." Finally Jessica's cheeks flare. Maybe she's slightly redeemable.

"Tell you what, if you keep it a secret I'm a Young, I'll keep my mouth shut about Haley." I've got no problem with blackmail. The last name Young is common enough. Hopefully no one will associate me with the richest family in town.

"Why wouldn't you want anyone to know you're a Young? Oh, my God, I'd spray-paint it in the sky."

"I don't, all right?"

"Okay," she says.

The door to the room opens and conversation ceases. I relax in my chair, stretch my legs under the table and cross my arms over my chest. When I glance over at Haley again, she's still resting her head on her arm, but this time I'm met by those gorgeous dark eyes.

Unexpectedly, she holds the gaze. One second. Two. Turning into three. Did she overhear my conversation with Jessica?

Haley breaks our connection and focuses on the movie playing up front. My mind bounces with the new information and it only piques my curiosity.

Haley

I'VE SUCCESSFULLY AVOIDED MATT since this morning and I'm betting that the refuge of the cafeteria will save me from him for at least twenty more minutes. There's no way he'll corner me in front of Jax, Kaden and the other fighters from my grandfather's gym, right? I mean, no one's that bold.

I bite my lip, starting to rethink my plan. While I don't think Matt will, Conner might. His judgment has been off since he started using drugs.

Annoyingly enough, the buzz at my lunch table is the new boy at school, West. I stab at the pizza on my plate. The boy could be the death of me. Literally. West...the gorgeous, full of himself, infuriating, not-listening knight in shining armor is in three of my classes and there are two more periods to go before the final bell rings. I'm willing to bet money I don't have he's going to be in those, too.

West.

West, West, West. Last name Young. And right now, as he struts into the cafeteria, he releases that blazing, agitating grin.

"Check out the new boy." Jessica drools from across the lunch table. "He's definitely a walking piece of art."

"With arms like that," says another girl, "it makes you wonder what he looks like with his shirt off."

Yes, it does.

Several other girls verbalize their agreement and I focus on my uneaten tray of food. My freshman year, I used to sit with Kaden and the other guys from the gym at lunch. I stupidly fell for Matt my sophomore year and ended up sitting with him and the guys from Black Fire. I was forced to find a new lunch table when things between Matt and me exploded like a hydrogen bomb.

Up until that point, I had never done girl before. It's not bad if you don't mind strolling in a field of unmarked land mines.

"I heard you and Jax were hanging out in the office this morning." Marissa eyes the other girls still ogling West and slides a French fry off my tray when she thinks no one is watching. Marissa's always on a diet. Not because she's fat but because Marissa believes she's fat and the other girls pamper her fears. "Jessica saw you guys and told me."

Marissa has been hot and bothered by Jax since he helped her when she tripped in elementary school. Fortunately and unfortunately, Jax has no idea that the mostly mute honor student exists. Bad for Marissa, yet great for her. Jax would devour her as an appetizer.

"He kept me company while I searched for scholarships."

Marissa nervously tucks her hair behind her ear three times. "Did he mention me? We were in a group last week in gym. There were four of us, but he was next to me so...you know...he might have remembered me...or something."

Conversations like these are why I am welcome at this lunch table. As Jessica lovingly had put it: *She's the girl who knows the hot guys*. Yep. That's me. The living, breathing Wikipedia of Eastwick's hot guys. I keep it to myself that they all currently hate my face.

"You know Jax." Though she doesn't. "He doesn't discuss girls with me." He used to, but then Jax and I lost the ability to talk with ease. He and Kaden have a hard time forgiving me for leaving the gym.

She nods. "You're right."

Movement to my right catches my attention and I become one of those oil-slicked birds smothered and weighed down. Conner, Matt's little brother, enters the cafeteria with his wrist in a brace. Yellowish fading bruises cover his face and the remnants of a black eye mark his skin.

I scoot my chair back, preparing to bolt. Conner's a year younger than me, so I've been able to avoid him…until now.

A few tables away, Kaden and Jax slide to their feet. Jax leans one shoulder against the wall with his arms held tight to his body and fists clenched. He's burning a hole through me. Kaden, on the other hand, paces like a pissed-off tiger behind Jax, his sights set on Conner.

"Oh, my God," whispers Marissa. "He's coming."

He who? My head whips so fast in preparation of finding Conner at our table that my hair stings my face. Nope, not Conner, but someone just as bad. "Really?"

"Ladies," says West. "Mind if I join you?" He's asking the table, but he's surveying me.

Does the boy ever listen? I shoot up and my chair rattles against the floor. "You can have my seat."

His smile grows. "I don't have personal space issues so you can sit on my lap."

My mouth pops open. Did he just say… "You…" No words. "You are…"

West gestures with his fingers for me to continue. Oh, my freaking God, this is a game to him. "Handsome? Irresistible?"

I slam my chair into the table and head for the food line, hoping to blend in with the stragglers. The only way out is past Conner. I'll buy another lunch if it means he won't spot me. I peek over at the entrance and blow a relieved rush of air out of my mouth. Conner's deep in conversation with Reggie, his dealer. I have a reprieve in being hunted by him—at least for today.

"Me and you, Haley." Matt's familiar gravel voice sends a shock wave of shivers through my soul. "We need to talk."

"My family is watching." I have to force my eyes up and, even as I curse myself, I begin to shake. I don't want to show fear, but he scares me. Matt is the stuff nightmares are made of.

"You're the one who chooses whether or not Jax and Kaden get involved. Make this hard and they will. Make it easy and they won't."

There's a faint resemblance to the cute guy I fell for my sophomore year: tall, dark hair, hazel eyes. He shaves his head now, his ears are a bit deformed from fighting and there's a roughness to him, an edginess that wasn't present when I first met him. Who knows, maybe the edginess always existed and I was too naive to notice.

Matt turns and heads to the front right corner of the cafeteria. Toward where the other Black Fire fighters sit and in the exact opposite direction of Kaden and Jax. Matt doesn't look back to see if I follow because he knows I will. He controlled me then—even when there was blood on his hands and blood on mine. Any self-respect, any self-confidence I thought I had built disintegrates. He controls me now.

I can't glance at my brother or cousin. My cheeks are on fire and I stare at my moving shoes. Six months ago, Jax and Kaden found me as a lump, alone in a garage at a party. My body shook, my teeth chattered and all I could think was that Matt was stronger than Jax and Kaden.

With my body still pounding with the proof, I lied. I protected what I loved—I protected Jax and Kaden, and then walked away from fighting. A decision I still bleed over.

With a few hushed words, the guys seated at Matt's table disperse, leaving me and him somewhat alone in the crowded cafeteria. None of them make eye contact with me because each of them is fully aware that they had a hand in what happened. They're the ones that pointed out Conner's drug use to me. They're the ones that begged me to talk to Matt because Matt wouldn't see what was in front of him.

"He'll listen to you, Haley. You're the only one he listens to."

Nope, he didn't listen to me and I figured out quickly why no one else had the courage to speak badly about Conner to Matt. A right hook to the head is a great deterrent.

Matt crosses his arms over his chest. "I don't take to people hurting what's mine."

No, that job belongs solely to him.

Matt used to hold me in his arms. He'd caress my face, my body. I realized too late we were an inferno and that I had been chained to the stake. He touched me. He kissed me. He said words to me no one else ever had. He made me feel special.

After being with Matt, I don't care if I ever feel special again.

"Because of what we were to each other," he says, "I'm giving you a chance to explain."

My toe nudges a spot of dried ketchup on the orange tiled floor. Telling him the truth enraged him last summer. Nothing since then has changed. He steps closer and cold sweat breaks out along my neck.

"I hated it when you wouldn't talk to me," he whispers. Once upon a time, he whispered the words "I love you" into my ear and I kissed him in return. Hurt and regret can slowly kill a person from the inside out.

"You have never wanted to hear what I've had to say," I respond.

"Not true," he says. "That's not true."

It is and somewhere deep inside he knows it.

"What did Conner tell you?" If it doesn't damn me too bad, I'll go with Conner's version of the truth, because real truth doesn't exist. There are only other people's perceptions of reality.

He drops his arms and his shoulders sag. This is what snagged me initially to Matt: his ability to appear vulnerable when he's physically anything but. "He came home all beat to hell and he said you were there and I know that can't be true. You'd never cross me like that."

The little liar actually told the truth for once. Where was the fib when I needed it? "Conner told you I did it?"

"He started to tell me what happened. Said you were there. Then he realized the guys were in the other room."

"The guys" being the other fighters from Black Fire. He'd never admit to them what transpired between us. Matt continues, "When Conner wouldn't talk, we drew the natural conclusion—Jax and/or Kaden jumped Conner. Out of respect for you, I kept everyone from going after your family that night."

"Respect for me?" I echo.

A muscle under his eye jumps. "You covered for me once. Consider the debt paid."

Tremors run down my spine. He's never mentioned that night before. Just hearing him acknowledge it...

"Tell me who did it," Matt says. "And we'll take care of this in the cage."

I wrap my hair into my fist. I don't want Jax and Kaden paying for my sins, but they constantly go against guys from Black Fire at matches. Better the cage with a ref than on the street, with weapons, which has been my greatest fear. "What event?"

"No event or referee. Conner's wrist is sprained. There's no mercy rule on this."

No mercy rule meaning no tournament. No public event with rules or referees. No ability to tap out if the fight becomes sick or demented or too much. A fight like this—it's a street brawl and it could mean severe damage... It could mean death and it's what I've been working desperately for months to avoid.

"No. Not happening." I bite my tongue to keep from informing Matt that if Conner hadn't tried to use my hair to drag me to the ground I wouldn't have had to try to snap his wrist. What's unreal is that if Matt looked at me, like really looked at me, he could see the bruises behind the makeup, he'd see my red knuckles, he'd see the truth, but Matt, like always... like most people, only sees what he wants.

"Then we go after both of them," he threatens. "Hit them whenever and wherever we want."

He moves to walk past me and I grab his arm. "Did you ever think that Conner was the one doing the jumping?"

"Why would he do that? We fight Kaden and Jax in the ring. We don't need to street brawl to prove a point."

"Because Conner has a drug problem."

"Shit, Haley." Matt rips his arm out of my grasp. "We're back to this. Your lies killed us last time. Do you think it's wise to go there now?"

"Listen to me!" I'm desperate enough to permit the truth to flow. "I did it. I hurt Conner. I had medication for my dad and Conner jumped me."

"There's no way you could have done that damage." A vein bulges in his neck. "You're covering for someone. Tell me who it was and tell me now."

I close my eyes the moment I hear the voice that should be nowhere near me. I hear West. "It was me. I did it."

West

I ASSESS THE GUY in front of me: my height, my build, my problem. Actually, it's the kid skulking behind them that's my issue, but overhearing the argument between Haley and this bastard, it appears all related.

"Who the hell are you?" the guy towering over Haley asks.

"West. Same question back." Since, in theory, I shouldn't have a clue who he is.

"Matt Spencer," Haley answers for him, then gestures to the guy that knocked the hell out of me on Friday night. "That's Conner, his younger brother. West is new here, Matt, and I'm guessing he's highly medicated or high and therefore has no idea what he's saying."

I chuckle. Highly medicated. Good one.

Haley mouths, "Leave."

I subtly shake my head. Conner and I have unfinished business and I'm not impressed with the direction of the conversation between her and big brother. "Granted, on most weekends that may be true, but I remember this past Friday night clearly enough."

The skulker joins the party. "I remember my fist blacking you out."

"I have a hard time believing you remember your name." All the signs of a hard-core user are there: paled-out face, shadows under his blank eyes and jittery as hell. I've seen it before at my old school. Drugs are one of those things that cross party and money lines.

Conner flashes forward and in simultaneous movements Haley slides in front of me and Matt tackles his younger brother, demanding that he "Back off" and reminding him that he "Can't afford another suspension."

"Are you suicidal?" Haley stretches on her toes and tries to match my height. She fails. "Is that the issue? There are 1-800 numbers that can help."

The walking, talking inferno is back and I like it. "You looked like you needed backup. You helped me on Friday, so I'm helping you now."

She collapses onto her heels. "I don't *need* your help. I *need* you to listen and stay the hell away from me. Are you deaf? Maybe have a little hearing loss you're ashamed to admit to? Because I know I specifically told you to stay away."

"Did you do it?" Matt demands. Skulker boy stands next to big brother with his hands shoved in his pockets, but his grimace suggests he's just as eager as me for round two. "Did you jump Conner?"

Other guys slip into the picture. They hang back, taking seats at the table or leaning against the windows. Why are my odds always bad?

Haley turns her head so they can't see her whisper to me, "Say no and let me handle it."

My eyes widen when I look at Conner. I mean, really look

at him. The yellowish fading bruise on his jaw—I did that. But the black eye...the wrist. It can't be possible. I was the only one there and when I woke up there was Haley. "Nice brace."

"Fuck you," Conner snaps.

"Go, West," Haley murmurs. "You're making this worse."

"Who's the new kid?" A guy with a Mohawk walks up.

Haley throws her head back. "Really?" She mows down the Mohawk boy with a brutal glare. "I mean, really, Jax?"

Jax winks at her as another guy sidles up alongside of him. "It's a little hard to eavesdrop while being on the opposite side of the room and I have a feeling we're all interested in the same conversation. I'll give a cookie to whoever tells me who hurt Haley and then we'll make the decision, like the proper gentlemen we are, of what match we'll be pounding this out in."

A hushed argument breaks out between Jax and Matt. My stomach plummets into free fall. Jesus Christ, how could I not notice her bruised knuckles or how the makeup poorly hides the slight discoloration near her eye? Conner is a dead man walking.

I raise my hand and it hovers close to her eye, my palm almost connecting with her skin. Heat builds in the gap as I ache to remove her bruises. Haley tilts her head away and I drop my hand, feeling cold, rejected.

"Tell me you didn't get into a fight over me," I whisper.

She lowers her head. "Conner wouldn't have stopped. Even when you blacked out, he wouldn't have stopped."

"Haley..." There are no words. None. It's not okay for her to wear bruises over me. It's despicable that a guy would strike a girl. Regardless of whether she hit him first. Regardless of whether she was defending someone else. Regardless.

"Just go," she says. "This isn't your fight and I've got to make sure it doesn't become my family's battle, either."

These two guys must be the cousin and brother that Jessica referred to earlier. Two feet divide Haley's family from Matt's brood. Everyone's posture is open, daring, yet they remain in their neutral corners. For a few seconds, I respect them. They're smart enough to keep the fights outside of school.

"I did it," I announce.

Mohawk boy loses his outer playful demeanor and his inner demons possess him as he advances on me. "You hurt Haley?"

"No. I defended her."

"I fell." Haley grabs my wrist and her slender fingers squeeze my skin. "I fell."

I don't know how to help you. It's what I want to scream. Instead, I lay my hand over hers and brush my thumb over her battered knuckles. Her hand is frozen, lifeless. She attempts to jerk away, but I hold tight. I don't make promises lightly and I'm swearing right now to take care of her and her problems.

Releasing Haley, I face the two groups of guys. "She fell. I walked out of the store, saw Haley on the ground and Conner standing over her. I made the wrong assumption. My bad."

The sneer on Conner's face is almost enough to compensate for the blackout. "Bullshit."

"Fine. Then you explain how it went down. We fought. I won. Unless you want to admit you were beat up by a girl." I grin for effect and the asshole twitches. Several guys in his group laugh at the "joke."

"Is that the way it happened?" Matt asks Conner.

His internal struggle plays havoc with his face. I'm not sure which one is worse. Could I admit a girl pounded me? Damn, it's bad enough to know a girl kicked a guy's ass in my defense. The asshole nods.

Matt scratches his temple and swings his gaze between me and Haley and Conner until settling on me. "Who are you and why are you up in Haley's business?"

"He's a stranger," responds Haley right as I answer, "We're dating."

Haley whirls in my direction, a tornado in a cornfield. "We're what?"

"Dating," I state clearly. Because neither Matt nor her family is buying any of the bullshit I'm spewing and they won't...unless we offer incentive. "In private. But it's okay, *Haley.*" I overemphasize her name in the hopes of gaining her attention. "Now that I've transferred here, we can tell people our secret."

She transforms into night of the living dead and blinks repeatedly. I position my hand under her elbow in preparation for if she faints. Note to self: she shocks out easily.

Mouths gape. Some guys harden into stone. Then it smacks me, is one of these guys her boyfriend? Jessica mentioned a failed relationship with Matt, but Haley could be seeing someone else. Shit. Fucking shit. Fucking shit in a Crock-Pot.

"You're dating Haley?" The pure menace in Matt's tone indicates I hammered the nail into the two-by-four. "My girl? You're dating Haley?"

Haley snaps back to life. “I’m your *ex*-girlfriend.”

Thank God for small favors and the damn Easter bunny because that was one gift I needed. There’s no one else in Haley’s life and Jessica had it right: he is crazy obsessed.

Matt’s obviously the alpha in this mangy bunch of wolves, so I address him, “Is it a sin around here to protect your girl?”

He hasn’t peeled his eyes away from Haley since I announced our sudden relationship. Finally, he answers, “No.”

“Is it true?” Jax pinches his nose as if he’s smelling shit. “You’ve been dating this guy in secret?”

“I...” Nothing else falls from Haley’s lips.

“All the lies you’ve told since Friday... What I put up with at home because I covered for you... Over a guy again? Jesus, Haley.” He pauses, then sucks in a breath. “I’m done with you.”

“Jax!” Haley calls out, but he struts away. The other guy from her family wears the same expression my mom does when she talks about the daughter that died right after my birth. In silence, he follows after Jax.

Her posture droops. The look on her face...it’s like someone cut out her beating heart. I’ve got to get her out of here.

“Check it out, man.” I direct myself to Conner. “It was a misunderstanding. I saw you standing over Haley, I got protective and things went down. No harm, no foul.”

I wrap an arm around her shoulders and Haley tenses beneath me. I extend my other hand to Conner, knowing full well there is plenty of harm done and *foul* is a mild adjective to use to describe the animosity between us.

“Fuck you,” says Conner. I withdraw my hand and shrug. Hey, I tried.

"Then I'll leave you to lunch." I attempt to guide Haley away but it's difficult to do when she's grown roots and planted her feet into the ground.

"Sounds like it was an unfair fight," says Matt. "My brother being chivalrous and helping out Haley after she fell and then you jumping him from behind. It's easy to take down a guy when he doesn't know you're coming. An apology isn't enough."

"It's enough," Haley pleads. "Please, Matt, let it go."

Matt mimics the crazy grin his insane brother had right before he knocked me out. "Do you know the lies your *girlfriend* tried telling me before you showed? Listening to Haley beg for you makes me wonder if you can actually take a hit."

I rub my chin, release Haley and step into Matt. Chairs crack and squeak against the floor as his boys bolt to their feet. Matt stops them with one raised finger. "Got something to say?"

"Yeah. Thought you should know I got expelled from my last school for fighting. I got no problems taking hits."

"Then prove it."

"Take the swing, asshole." I'm not going to be accused of jumping a man from behind.

The air hums with pissed-off energy. Matt shoves his chest out, arms poised to come up, then a guy says, "Principal."

Matt backs off and I follow his lead. Some old man in a gray suit watches us as he heads for the food line.

"New boy," says Matt. "We don't fight in school, but the moment the bell rings, your ass is mine."

Haley angles to become a human shield in front of me. "No."

"Haley." My blood boils that she's begging this bastard for anything. Does she honestly think I'm that weak? "I got this."

"Listen to her, Matt," Conner butts in.

"What?" Matt asks.

"One of us should fight him in the cage. You know, make it public humiliation. Best man wins and all that shit."

Haley tunnels her fingers into her hair and clutches it as if to yank it out. "He's not a fighter. It won't be fair."

"I can fight," I snap, but not one of them acknowledges me.

"If he can't take the hits, then he shouldn't have messed with one of us," says Matt.

"Matthew." The pure desperation in her tone causes everyone to freeze. "I swear to you he didn't know."

The looks, the stares. All of them doubting me because Haley's basically signed in blood that I'm incapable of holding my own. I've got four months in this school and I'll be damned if she'll be protecting me the entire time. "Name the day and time."

Conner motions to Matt with his sprained hand as if deciding whether to have cheese on a burger. "The tournament in two months. I get the hand healed and then the two of us go at it."

Matt nods. "All right. Are you in, New Boy, or are you chickenshit?"

I smile. An adrenaline rush floods my veins. This is possibly the craziest and the most alive I've felt in years. "Looking forward to it."

The bell rings, ending lunch. Matt and his pack of wolves leave the table.

Haley closes her eyes and lowers her head into her hands. Not the reaction I hoped for.

Haley

I'M SECOND BUS RUN. When we lived in our old house, my home, I was first. That was back when things were simpler. Back before I started dating Matt and when Jax, Kaden and I weren't at each other's throats. Back when they could at least look at me...unlike now. Today, when they left to hop the city bus to train at the gym, they didn't even mumble goodbye.

I sit away from everyone else. After my breakup with Matt, I can honestly say I don't mind being alone. His version of attention left scars. I suck in a deep breath, missing the relationship I had with Jax and Kaden. Even worse? I miss who I used to be.

Both my knees bounce as I wait on the bench outside the loading dock. Blowing warm air onto my hands no longer helps. They're frozen for good. We go so many days without seeing the sun during the winter it's easy to believe it no longer exists.

"Haley."

My heart stalls at the sound of West's voice. Dear God, is he always so gorgeous? Especially now with his hat on backward and those ocean-blue eyes twinkling at me. Teeny-tiny wings flutter in my chest when he drops onto the bench beside me. He's close. Superclose. Like his jeans touching mine close. Heat rolls off his body and I sort of crave to snuggle up to him and steal his warmth.

"West," I respond. Good girl. Act casual.

I should move. At least an inch. Prove to us both that I have an inkling of self-respect. But I don't. He's warm and…well… dammit, he's cute. I rub my hands together, half wondering if I should thank him for what happened at lunch or if I should punch him for getting involved or if I should press my fingers to his face and save myself from frostbite amputation. I seriously want to do all three.

"Would you like a lift?" he asks.

"You really don't listen, do you?" I try to bend my fingers, but they're so cold they're swollen. "I told you Friday I don't ride with strangers."

"Well, you are my girlfriend."

I choke on the laugh that bubbles up my throat. West smiles and I have to admit it's a sweet sight on his face.

"You realize," I say, "that after what happened at lunch we're both undeniably screwed."

"It was an interesting first day." He stands and extends his hand. "Come on—let me drive you home."

I accept the offer and I hate the way my insides palpitate when his fingers wrap around mine.

"Jesus, your hands are ice cubes." West's hand flinches away from mine, and, with red cheeks, I pull my hand back, but West denies my retreat and reclaims my fingers.

"Don't. It's okay." I yank to free myself, but I'm unsuccessful. "I'm just cold."

"No shit. Gloves could help."

I don't have gloves. If I did, I'd wear them, but I lost them when we lost the storage unit. Ticked off by the reminder, I start to inform West the exact route to hell he can take when he draws my hand toward his lips.

The world stills when he opens his mouth and blows hot air onto my skin. My eyes widen, my toes curl and my blood explodes with heat. Holy freaking crap.

Staring straight into my eyes, he blows onto my hand again. My fingers tingle with the warmth, with his touch. His thumb sweeps over my skin and my heart skips too many beats.

"You've got smooth skin," he murmurs.

"Yeah," I whisper. Yeah.

Um…what? I blink. We are overly close, like if either of us moved, clothes would be against clothes, and I like the thought of his body brushing against mine way more than I should. I extract my hand from his. "I don't mind cold hands."

He smirks. "You don't?"

"No, I don't." I beeline it for his car and moronically stumble over a parking curb. Then, for giggles, I trip over my own feet. At least I stay upright—barely. "They're always cold, even in the summer."

West says nothing as he walks beside me, but he does watch me with an amused grin. Twice his hand flies out to grab me if I should fall. I hate him. I like him. I wish I wasn't so pathetic.

"I'm used to it." I glance around, wishing Marissa would pop out of thin air because friends shouldn't let friends ramble and stumble. I massage the hand he blew on. It's like the skin there is now hypersensitive. "It's not a big deal since it's normal."

Because I can't stupidly zip my lips, I go on to say, "My hands are always cold. It's genetics. My mom has cold hands and her mom had cold hands. Bad circulation or something like that." *Shut the eff up, Haley!*

West pushes a button on his key chain and the lights on his Escalade flash. Like a gentleman, he opens the passenger-side door. "Good to know." There's a sparkle in his eye that matches the smug smile.

"What?"

The grin widens. "The cold hands. The genetics. All good things to know."

I smile widely because I don't know what else to do. Kill me now. West shuts my door and I knock the back of my head three times against the seat. He climbs in and I smile falsely again. He chuckles and I die of mortification.

When he starts the car, rap pounds from the speakers, causing the frame to vibrate. He turns the radio off, turns up the heat and points the vents at me.

The rich smell of leather wafts in the air and every electronic and computerized gadget embedded in his dashboard intimidates me. "This car is quiet. It's like the motor isn't even on."

"My sister, Rachel..." He pauses and switches the hand he drives with. In the short amount of time I've known West, this is the first time he appears unsure. "She's great with cars. Anything good about this thing is because of her."

"That's cool." And unusual. I've never heard of a female mechanic, but who has ever heard of a female fighter?

West grows grim and we sit in awkward silence. His sister must be a sore subject and, because of Kaden and Jax, I can highly appreciate that.

Murphy's Law dictates we hit every red light. After one particularly long light, I tap my fingers against the door and replay the events of the cafeteria. Should I be mad or grateful to West? To be honest, I'm both, but still, there's this nagging inside me that if he had gone along with the original plan...

"Why didn't you listen? Friday night or in the cafeteria? If you had just listened to me once you wouldn't be in this mess and I wouldn't have to bail you out."

His head jerks. "Did you say bail me out?"

"Yep. Bail. Like a bucket and a boat with a leak."

"Nah. You've got it wrong." West readjusts the hat on his head and his jaw solidifies into steel. "You don't like accepting my help."

"I don't *need* your help. What I *need* is for you to listen to me."

The incredulous glance from the corner of his eye causes my skin to crawl. Cocky bastard.

"If you had acted like we were talking," I say, "I would have made it and we wouldn't be here."

"You don't know that." He floors the gas when the light turns green.

I stop tapping and bang my hand against the door. "I got hurt anyway. I got hurt and I lost my father's medication and I had to hit someone. Something I swore I'd never do again. Now my father is a wreck, my cousin and brother hate me more than normal and I have to worry about you dying in two months."

"I am not weak!" He slams on the brakes at the next red light.

My body lurches against the seat belt then smacks into the seat. "I never said you were."

"Yes." His blue eyes burst into twin flames. "You did. The

moment you begged Matt to back off, you announced to the world I'm weak."

A grunt of disgust leaves my throat. Boys. Stupid boys with their stupid egos. "You're mad because *I* saved you."

Because a *girl* saved him. Revolted, I cross my arms over my chest. God, the countless times I've seen that same look on the faces of guys at school. I'm the fighter—the girl who can throw a punch. Sure, they'll say it's cool, but their egos require that they be the protector.

The light switches to green and West floors it again, causing his engine to roar in anger. "Even if I had pretended to chat it up with you, they still would have followed."

"It would have worked."

"And you know everything?" he snaps. "If I didn't follow, then I would have thought about how they beat the shit out of you and how I was to blame—that I failed. Again!"

I'm mad. Shaking mad. So mad, I shouldn't open my mouth, but I do, and I scream at the top of my lungs. "I obviously can take care of myself."

"How the fuck was I to know that?"

The car behind us blares his horn when West cuts him off.

"I hate you," I mutter.

"Right back at you."

He pulls into the neighborhood and before me is the spot where our worlds collided. One second earlier or later and maybe I could have avoided Conner and his friend. One step in the other direction and West would have never almost plowed me over.

Nausea disorients me and I lay a hand over my stomach. Is this all we are? Continual actions and reactions? No control over our futures? One pink slip and we lose our house and

I lose my father? One decision to date the wrong guy and I lose Jax and Kaden? One step off the wrong curb and my life is entangled with a stranger's?

If that's true, then life is one pathetic and sick game.

West eases into the lot and shifts the SUV in Park. "We can't leave it like this."

"I know." A pause on my part. "I don't hate you." I fidget with one lone long fingernail. I've never been able to grow them long or figured out how to paint them properly. I totally stink at all things girl. "That was mean to say."

"I don't hate you, either, and, trust me, I've been told worse." He releases a breath. "I'm in this, Haley, whether you want me or not."

The gray day makes the dismal shopping plaza more depressing. A woman too thin and barely dressed hauls a crying toddler by her arm, practically breaking it. The child trips over a curb and the woman drags her against the blacktop. I hate this place. Not West. Just my life.

"I keep searching for a way to fix this so you can be free and I can't think of one." Not when he insists on continually butting in. "I'm not looking to argue again, but can you please tell me why? I'm a stranger. I could be a serial killer or I could collect road kill and turn it into stuffed animals or own two million porcelain dolls and hang their decapitated heads from my ceiling—"

"The dolls would creep me out."

I raise an eyebrow. "Just the dolls?"

West smiles again, like he did outside school, and that sweet, sweet sight causes me to smile in return. "I have a high threshold for creepy."

I laugh and the high feeling plummets when I search for

the last time I laughed before today. Last month? Six months ago? Years? "My point is, you don't know me, yet you volunteered to become a modern-day gladiator without an ounce of training."

"Cool. Does that mean I'll get a sword?"

"I'm being serious! This whole situation is utterly and completely serious!"

"You need to learn how to chill." West exhales, then slides his hand over the steering wheel. "I don't know why I'm doing this."

"Please?"

He's silent, but it's the type of silence that tells me he's sorting his thoughts. My dad, before he was laid off, had that same expression whenever we had a discussion. Dad always answered me and I have no doubt West will, too…if I grant him time.

"I'm involved now because that Conner kid hit you."

My stomach sinks. "West…" God, I hate admitting it out loud. "I hit him first." Because he wouldn't relent against West.

He holds up his hand. "He hit you. I don't care if you backed over him with my Escalade two hundred times. It's not okay to hit a girl. Besides, you had my back. I don't forget that type of thing." His lips slant. "Granted, I'm usually saying this to a guy."

There's more. I can see a pain etched on his face…in his eyes.

"You said earlier you couldn't live with the idea that you failed. What did you mean?"

"We all have demons." He stares at the bar situated at the end of the strip mall. "How about we leave it at that."

"Do you have any idea what you've walked yourself into?"

"In two months I'm going to be in some tournament. For all I know, I'll be throwing knives at this kid and he could be tossing them back at me."

"No knives. Though that could be faster and less painful."

"Good to know."

The school bus rumbles on the road behind us. "I need to get home. Can I explain everything tomorrow at lunch? Then we can devise a plan to keep you alive."

"Sounds like a date." West puts the SUV in gear and I give him directions to my uncle's. He leans against his door as he drives and watches the road intently. Something tells me he's not focused on the road as much as he's trying to digest the world he's thrown himself into.

West stops in front of the box house. "What are you trained in?"

The instinct is to divulge nothing because my fighting days are long over.

"I saw the damage you did to Conner. You're trained in something."

If West is going to survive, I've got to wade through the charred and ruined bridges I've burned and find a way to rebuild them. Might as well start with the truth. "Muay Thai."

"And that is?"

"Kickboxing."

West releases a paralyzing grin. "Holy shit, my girlfriend's a kickboxer."

I sort of giggle, but it's so halfhearted it falls flat. Never in my wildest dreams would I have imagined I'd be sitting in such an expensive car with such a gorgeous guy. Taking a page from Marissa's book, I tuck my hair behind my ear and suddenly care what I look like.

I wish I was wearing something nicer. Something more than ripped jeans and a long-sleeved cotton shirt. Something that would make me "girlfriend" material for a guy like West. "Look, the whole relationship thing—"

"Yeah," he cuts me off. "Sorry. No one was buying what we were saying so I ad-libbed. Can we keep up appearances for a while? We can 'break up' in a couple of weeks after they believe the reason I went after Conner was because I was into you."

The glare I throw him causes him to toss his hands in the air. "I swear to God, I'll keep my hands to myself. I highly respect that my girlfriend can throw a punch."

Which is the reason why the only guy I've ever dated or kissed has been Matt. Boys are repelled by strong girls. "Have you considered transferring to another school? This was your first day. You could start fresh someplace else. I can play dumb and say I have no idea where you lived because it's true. If you leave now, this could blow over."

"You mean it could blow over for me."

I nod.

"And leave you hanging? Not happening." The crazy expression I often see on Jax and Kaden spikes across his face, and suddenly I don't care what I look like anymore. I'm not interested in becoming involved with another fighter.

"It's not my style to run from a fight," he says. "Besides, I'm not sure if you heard, but my new girlfriend is going to teach me some of her kick-ass moves."

"Assume much?"

"I'm not telling you anything you haven't already thought yourself."

True. I reach for the handle and ask one last question. "Curious. Is my new boyfriend a drug dealer?"

West laughs. It's deep and smooth and gives me beautiful shivers. "No." He pauses. "I'm not much of anything anymore."

The ache from earlier returns to his eyes and it reflects the hurt tucked deep inside me.

"Whatever it is that's going on with you," I say, "I'm sorry."

"I'm good." His eyebrows furrow and he stares out the front windshield.

He's obviously not good, and I bite my bottom lip. For strangers, West and I have become uncomfortably familiar in a rapid amount of time. Our worlds didn't just collide; they merged as paint spilled on a sidewalk and it's like neither one of us will be the right color again.

"You can tell me—that is, if you want to talk. If you're worried, I'm not a gossip because I'm not exactly—" my fingers flutter in the air "—popular."

West opens and closes his mouth a few times and I hold my breath. Whatever he has to say, it's big, and somehow, it feels right for him to tell me. "My family threw me out Saturday."

The air rushes out of my lungs as if I got steamrolled by a front kick to the chest. "Do you have somewhere to stay?"

"Yeah."

But I'm not sure I believe him. For months, I've been the queen of chaos. I'm a mist, a vapor. Belonging nowhere yet stretched everywhere.

This boy drops into my life with his clothes and car and attitude that suggests he's rich and affluent and the king of the world. With one small yet enormous statement, the gap that existed between us disappears. I slide across the divide, placing my fingers as tightly as I can around his. “I get it, West,” I whisper my secret to him. “I understand not having a home.”

West

I'M USED TO PEOPLE TALKING, saying words aloud to prove they know more than me, that they're better than me. But they're just words. Syllables strung together between breaths to fill uncomfortable silences.

Meaningless words.

Haley, on the other hand, speaks volumes with a touch. The way her hand clutches mine, it rips out my heart and tosses it onto a platter.

This moment, it's too raw. It's too real. And the instinct is to snatch my hand back and slam the door shut on the sharing, but the other part of me—the part that feels as if my remaining sanity is a gift on the verge of being returned—it clings to her.

I knot my fingers with Haley's and turn my head so I'm focusing out the driver's-side window—away from her. If I look at Haley, I'm terrified of what I might say, what I might feel. And fuck me, I've already said too much.

If she understands this, being without a home, will she understand the rejection? Will she understand the devastation that everything you have ever loved doesn't love you in return? And because I can't face those fears, I'm unable to face Haley.

She squeezes once and it's like her voice caresses my mind: *I'm here. I get it.*

I squeeze back.

Seconds pass into moments. Moments into minutes. No words. No meaningless conversation. No eye contact. Just our hands combined.

My throat swells. Haley's the only string holding me together.

"West," she says as if we're lighting a candle for a loved one in a church.

"Yeah." My voice is cracked, gritty. *Don't say it, Haley. Don't say you have to go.*

"I have a curfew I need to meet." Yet her fingers wrap tighter around mine.

"Okay." I should release my grip, but it's hard. I never realized I could lose everything. Now I don't want to lose anything, especially her. Not even for a short period of time.

Haley loosens her hold and I withdraw my hand, placing it in my lap. I thought I felt alone and isolated when I tried to sleep in the darkness of my car, but the cold exhaustion left behind when Haley removed her hand indicates I had no idea what lonely was.

The door cracks open and cold air rushes into the SUV.

"Tell me if you run out of places to stay," she says and then the door shuts behind her.

With her pack slung over her shoulder, Haley shoves her hands in her pockets and slowly idles to the front door. I want to stay and see if she looks my way before she goes into the house, but I don't because what if she doesn't?

Haley

WEST IS HOMELESS. I sort of crave to crawl onto his lap, bury my head in his shoulder and weep for him because when you're the one going through something so horrible, it's too difficult to cry for yourself. Sometimes I wonder if the agony inside would disappear if someone would shed the tears for me. I'm not sure I could survive expressing all the pain.

My heart one million percent aches for West and that creates problems. I'm attracted to him, I hurt for him and, overall, I like him and I need additional complications like I need a hole in my head.

Staring at the television, my uncle sits on his La-Z-Boy throne in the living room. He's below a man, who's below a man, which makes him the lowest man at an exterminator company. From six in the morning until three in the afternoon, he kills things for a living. The things everyone else cringes to touch.

I slip off my sneakers and line them neatly near the front door and hang my backpack on one of the many hooks. Feeling like a wallflower geisha, I lower my head and position myself next to my uncle's chair. I learned once in Sunday school that wishing someone dead, wishing for the murder of someone, is as sinful as committing the act. Standing here, I have the same thought every day: when I die I'm heading straight to hell.

While staying focused on the television, he talks at me. "Where's Jax and Kaden?"

In the cramped living room, my younger sister lies belly-flat against the floor and colors a picture of a house: two stories, blue shutters, rosebushes near the front door. The sun is shining and a family of stick figures smile. It's our old house. It's what we used to be. "At the gym."

He knows this, but he enjoys asking. He enjoys knowing I'll answer.

"Why aren't you at work?"

"It's Monday. I'm off." He knows this, too. I'm a waitress, like my mom. Except I work at the pizza place for bad tips and she works double shifts at the Roadhouse for slightly better bad tips. She works so much that I never see her anymore. Ever.

My uncle avoids looking at me. It's a reminder I'm not worth being looked at. He drinks from the frosted can of Coke. Alcohol, he says, is the devil.

If I didn't believe he was Satan incarnate, he could be considered a handsome man even in his blue work uniform and with the stench of pesticide-death rolling off him. He's my father's half brother and a thirty-eight-year-old carbon copy of Jax: whitish-blond hair, blue eyes and sturdy build.

It's the half part that has made the difference between my father and him. The difference between me living in this prison for a few months and Jax living here his entire life.

My uncle finishes the Coke and extends the can to me. "Cut up the vegetables and start the meat and get me another."

Dad steps out of the bedroom and I catch his tired eyes. *Tell him to say please. Tell him I'm not his slave.* Instead, Dad glances down. When we moved in I promised him and my mother I'd keep my mouth shut and do what I was told.

I made a promise.

A promise my pride prefers not to keep. I'm not a slave. I'm not. Being poor, being homeless, being a girl doesn't make me less.

"I think I told you to do something, girl," says my uncle.

"Haley," Dad barely mutters. I flinch like I did when Conner rammed his fist into my gut. With too much anger, I snatch the can out of The Dictator's hand and stomp into the kitchen. I breeze past Dad, not once meeting his eyes.

The burner on the stove pings when I slam the pot against it and a few magnets bounce to the ground when I throw the refrigerator door open.

"Don't let him get to you." Dad picks up the magnets and snaps them back on the door. He speaks in a hushed tone because we're not allowed to have opinions in this house. No one is allowed to think in this house. "It's how Paul handles things."

I want to scream at Dad to find a job. To save us. But I don't. That wouldn't be fair of me and life hasn't been fair to him. A black forest of bitterness festers inside me and other words flow out instead. "You're okay with how he talks to me?"

Because guys shouldn't talk to girls like that. Because my own father doesn't speak to me that way. I deserve to be treated better. At least I think so. My eyes burn and I quickly blink. My life is so twisted I'm not sure what's correct anymore.

I've been hanging upside down for too long and a terrifying doubt wedges itself in my brain, asking the question... is this normal? Is this right? And the horrifying part is the small voice answering, "Yes."

Dad grabs my shoulders and I gasp. He turns me, forcing me to stare at him. Fire blazes from his eyes. "No one should talk to you that way. Do you hear me, Haley?"

"But he does." My throat thickens with every word. "And you let him."

Dad releases me as if my skin were layered with acid. "I'm sorry," he mumbles. "I'm your father... I should..."

He pivots slightly, angled half toward the living room, half toward me. The gray of his skin is what worries me and causes me to snag his wrist, to keep him from deciding between fighting for his daughter and giving the rest of his family a place to live. "It's okay."

It's not. I've never desired anything more than for my father to tell me I'm worth saving, that I'm worth being stood up for. I press my fingers into his skin until he meets my gaze. "It's okay."

The sane part of my brain knows it's selfish for me to even want it, because my uncle would throw us out and we'd have nowhere to live. But if I'm going to be honest, if I thoroughly analyze the black monsters inhabiting my soul, I'd discover I'm stopping him because if given the opportunity, even without repercussions, I doubt he'd believe I'm worth more than what my uncle thinks of me and I'm not sure I can handle the truth.

My father nods and moves his arm so we no longer touch. A hand through his hair, then he clears his throat. "I'm going to the library."

"At least take Maggie with you." At least save her. In movements so deliberate that I mimic a marionette on a string, I turn from him, take vegetables out of the fridge and close it. He's gone when I turn back.

I slice a knife through the potato and listen as he mumbles his destination to my uncle, tells Maggie to grab her coat and closes the front door.

A numbness shrouds my body. One slice of the potato, then another. The same motion again and again. There's an awareness you have when you reside with evil. A presence. Tiny whispers snapping at your energy. The only thing preserving your sanity, the only thing that helps you sleep at night is the idea that others surround you. That somehow together you can be protected. My spine straightens and a shiver runs through me.

I'm alone.

West

A FEW BLOCKS UP FROM HALEY, I lean on the glass of the pawn-shop display counter and count the wad of cash the street-hustler-owner of the joint just gave me. The owner reminds me of a fattened hog prepared especially for Christmas as the legs of the stool he sits on creak under his weight.

"You don't trust me," he says.

"No." I got played on the cost of my watch, even with negotiating him much higher than his initial price. Now I have money for food, gas and a few items for school. The temptation to rent a hotel room hovers around me, but I've got to think further than that.

"Good," he says. "It means you're smart."

The glass cases on the wall contain guns and electronics. In the display below me, a couple of old baseball players stare at me from their cards. When I count out three hundred for the second time, I shove the wad into my front pocket. An asshole pickpocket is going to have a rough time digging in the front of my jeans to get their gold.

"Anyone around here hiring?" At this point, I'll shovel shit if it means I can have a roof over my head.

A smoker's hack shakes his fat rolls. "Everyone's looking for a job, boy."

Yeah, I'm sure they are. Here's the problem with landing a job: I need a phone and unless I plan on returning home with my tail tucked between my legs to retrieve my charger or to beg Dad to take me back, I'm SOL.

I scratch my head as I leave the shop and pause against the wall. Two skaters fly past. My stomach growls and a pang shoots through it, almost doubling me over. Hunger. It's surreal that a few days ago I was here stalking my mother.

My temples throb, and as I spot a guy head out of the grocery store with a loaf of bread dangling from his hand, I bury the urge to snatch it from him. I've got money now and can buy my own loaf of bread. Maybe some meat.

Every time I came here peddling for pot, I'd mumble to some lowlife pleading for change to get a job. The pounding in my head intensifies. I'd get a job if I could. In a world that seemed black-and-white days before, now all I can see is gray.

Down the covered sidewalk, two guys stumble out of the bar, completely ripped. I used to come here to protect my mother. Each time I think of her, I feel like a frayed string is winding tightly around a nerve, cutting it off. I should find a pay phone and call her.

Gravity or just plain magnetic curiosity pulls me in the direction of the bar. There are three signs on its door and one grabs my attention. It's not the one that indicates no one under twenty-one can be admitted nor is it the one stating motorcycle gang colors aren't allowed. I'm interested in the help wanted sign: bartender and handyman. If I work here, I can score some cash and possibly some information on Mom.

Inside, the strong odor of spilled beer permeates from the drywall. To my right, a guy in a wifebeater breaks the balls on the pool table. The loud crack thunders in the boxed-in room and Hank Williams croons over the speakers. Neon signs advertising different beers hang on the wall and illuminate the dark dive.

My shoes stick to the concrete floor and, as I walk to the bar, I try to find one redeeming reason why my mother frequents this dump, even if it is for a fuck. Mom's in her fifties, but she still turns the heads of guys at those charity balls. No need to lower or demean herself.

"Hey," I call to the Vin Diesel bartender hovering over a small laptop. He's a huge son of a bitch with a completely shaved head. "I hear you're looking for help."

"You a bartender?" he asks without glancing up.

I've mixed a few drinks at parties and nobody died. "No."

"Then I don't want you."

"You should check him out, Denny," says that same damn feminine voice that keeps popping up at the wrong times. Like the beginning of a bad dirty joke, Abby waltzes into the bar. She brushes past me and reminds me of a lazy cat as she slips onto a bar stool. "S'up, West."

"You stalking me?"

She snorts. "You wish. I finished some business next door and saw you wander into this fine establishment." Abby leans over the bar. "Where are the cherries?"

Denny slams his laptop shut. "I'm not a food pantry, Abby."

"Hello, I get two of my four food groups here." Abby lifts the bowl of peanuts and swivels it. "Protein food group and the cherries are the dessert group. You'll feel bad if I die of malnourishment."

My mouth waters at the sight of the peanuts and my stomach growls loud enough that Abby lifts a brow.

The Vin Diesel wannabe actually cracks a smile. He picks up a foam container and the smile fades as his eyes land on me. "What the fuck are you doing here?" His words are angry, but his tone isn't. I have no idea what to make of him.

Abby grabs a fistful of peanuts and feeds them into her mouth, one at a time. I watch each one disappear behind her lips, almost tasting the salt on my tongue. Her eyes flicker between me and the bartender and I try to refocus on this moment, not on food. A single thought weaves through: Abby knows Mom's secret. Is this the guy my mom is screwing?

"I'm here for the job," I say.

Denny tosses the container at Abby and she catches it midair and immediately flips the lid to revel a half-eaten deli sandwich and chips. My knees go weak at the sight. He then crouches, fishes out a jarful of cherries, joins us at the end of the bar and slides it to Abby. She digs in and shoves a cherry in her mouth like she really is on the verge of starvation.

In slight, deliberate movements I'm not sure anyone but me notices, she edges the bowl of peanuts in my direction. I try to act casual as I approach the bar, but I'm so damn hungry it was probably a full-on run. After snatching a handful, I shove them into my mouth. My eyes close as I chew, part relieved, part devastated. How have I been reduced to such desperation?

When I open my eyes, I discover Denny staring at me. "You're underage."

"So's she." I tilt my head at Abby.

"I just feed her."

"It's true." She tears a hunk out of the sandwich. "See, if you had listened to my story on Saturday morning instead of cutting me off, you'd know that. By the way—" she glances at Denny "—this is West Young. We go to school together." Her forehead wrinkles as she chews. "I think. I didn't go today."

Denny crosses his arms over his chest. "Abby..."

She waves him off. "Yeah, whatever. I get it. I'm going to end up dead and pregnant then dead again by the age of eighteen. Then I'll have thirty venereal diseases and end up pregnant again before I'll die in a fiery car crash. Do you have those tiny pretzels? No? Damn."

Giving up on her, he cocks a hip against the bar and assesses me. "I've not seen you around. Are you new to the area?"

I don't know why, but part of me is disappointed. I hoped his initial reaction meant he knew who I was and therefore he would be the reason why my mother frequented this place, but no go. He could still be the fuck, he just might not be familiar with her children. "Yeah."

"I meant what I said earlier. I'm looking for a bartender—a legal one."

"What about the handyman job?" I snag another handful of peanuts. "I'm eighteen." I'm not, but I will be soon. "And as long as I don't serve drinks, I can work here."

"I'm searching for someone to fix things and clean. Are you going to do that?" There's a clear challenge in his voice.

Last week, hell no. Today? "I'm handy." It's true. Rachel's the car freak, but I'm the one who fixes odd things in the house: loose doorknobs, leaky faucets, dripping toilets. I learned early because Dad was never around and the people Mom hired to do the shit never did it right. "What's the pay?"

"Ten dollars an hour."

Abby chokes and pounds a fist into her chest. "My bad. Go on."

Denny scratches his jaw. "I don't know."

"I'll vouch for him," Abby says. "He's a stupid teenager who knows nothing looking for a job. He's obviously hungry and he's as naive as the day he was born. I think that screams employment."

My head snaps to Abby, but before I can tell her where to shove her vouching, she winks at me. "Denny has a soft spot for lost puppies. Trust me—no one else could give you a better recommendation."

Denny looks me over again, then does the same to Abby. The doubt is etched on his face and I consider begging. My mind begins to section off between sanity and crazy and crazy is pulling ahead for the win.

How can I exist without food? Food means money and money means a job and a job application means a phone and an address. It's an endless loop where if I don't have one, then I can't have the other.

"I could hire him." Abby tosses a chip into her mouth. "I've been considering expanding the business."

What? Haley said she was a drug dealer. No longer able to stand, I drop to a stool. Buying it is one thing. Selling it...

"You can't feed yourself," Denny reminds her.

The glare Abby sends him prickles the skin on the back of my neck. "My assets are continually tied up, but I know people who can pay him."

Silence before he addresses me. “I’ve got one stall down in the men’s bathroom. If you can fix it, the job is yours.”

“Give me tools and show me the way.” My older brother Jack constantly clogged his toilet.

“Tomorrow,” he responds.

“Now that this is all Brady Bunchesque, I’m thinking finder’s fee.” That damn evil grin crosses Abby’s face.

“Haven’t you ever heard of not biting the hand that feeds you?”

“No, that would have required me to go to school regularly. The way I see it, you were looking for something and I helped you find it. I deserve some appreciation.”

They stare at each other like both of them are contemplating hitting the button that results in nuclear war. Frightening how neither one of them flinches.

“You didn’t find anything,” I say. “I came in here myself.”

Denny pulls his wallet from his back pocket and slams several bills that include zeros in front of Abby. She tucks the cash down her shirt and begins eating again like the whole exchange never happened.

“Tomorrow after school,” says Denny.

When he walks into the back, I steal the rest of the peanuts. “Want to tell me what that was about?”

“No,” she says between bites.

“Is he the reason my mom comes in here?”

She demolishes her sandwich and dusts off her hands. It’s like a curtain shade descends over an open pane and the fallen fabric produces an intricate, sad design. For a few seconds, Abby isn’t the girl I hate. She’s a girl whose outside mirrors my inside. “Has there ever been anything in your life you’ve learned that you wish you could take back knowing?”

A sickeningly sharp pain slices through my stomach, the ache worse than hunger. The serious set of Dad's face while he told me to get the hell out and the bitter cold and loneliness of three in the morning in the car—I could do without those memories. "Yeah."

"This is one of those things, okay? Work here, but kill your curiosity. If you can't, then I suggest the Laundromat. I hear they need an attendant."

It's a numbing confession. Could the truth be that bad? "My mom's having an affair with someone here. Maybe that guy. I can handle it."

"If it were that easy, I would have dragged you in here last Saturday and introduced you to the issue myself. Leave it alone."

Abby hops off the stool and steps into me. There's nothing seductive about it unless you're the kind of guy that likes to have your dick ripped off and handed back to you. "Tell anyone that Denny gives me food and I swear to God I'll have you screaming like a little girl."

I smile because I can tell she means it. "And here I thought we were becoming friends."

"I'm lethal. Never forget it."

Abby leaves with as much flair as when she'd traipsed in. Who knows if anything out of her mouth today was the truth, but her last statement... Abby probably has never uttered truer words.

Haley

DINNER'S DONE. The dishes have been washed and put away and, on one of her rare nights off, my mother has become an anarchist. There's a spring in my step as I walk down the dark street with Mom and Maggie. All of us are bundled in multiple layers of clothes to fight off the cold. Behind us, Jax and Kaden push each other, laugh, then one of Jax's brothers yells out, "Go."

In a flash, all my cousins and my brother race past us with their arms pumping hard to see who will reach the neighborhood park first.

Thanks to my mother's crafty thinking, we're all being rebels by breaking tonight's curfew. Sometimes a little rebellion is good for the soul.

Maggie slips her hand in mine and does the same with my mother. She draws back as we walk forward then uses our arms to swing herself into the air. She's getting too big to do this, but I can't fault her for finding a bit of happiness.

"I don't have a school project," Maggie says, but thankfully she was smart enough to keep her mouth shut when Mom told Uncle Paul that's why we all needed to leave the house.

"Yes, you do," answers Mom. "Your weekly agenda says that you'll be starting physical fitness testing next week. You need to practice, and who better to train you than your family."

I try to suppress a grin, but I fail. Uncle Paul didn't like my mother informing him that she was taking all of us to the park to help Maggie study, but because Mom asked him nicely and said please, he let us go. Personally, I think it's because she offered to take the younger kids out. He gets irritated when they're too loud.

Curfew is a loose term with my uncle. It can change from day to day, from moment to moment. It's created to suit his whims and his whim tonight was to agree to let my mother empty out his house.

Mom releases Maggie's hand and gently nudges her forward. "Go on now. Catch up with the boys. This is your first task in preparing for the test—running."

Maggie starts to bolt after the boys, but I hold on firmly to her fingers. The park is in sight and the dark February night is chased away by multiple streetlights, but there are dark houses along the way.

I was jumped a few days ago and suddenly nothing in this neighborhood feels safe. "She should walk with us."

Lines crinkle between Mom's eyes as she studies me. "She'll be fine. I see her, and Jax and Kaden are watching us from the park."

Sure enough, the two of them have climbed the jungle gym and behave like soldiers as they scan the area surrounding us.

"Go on, Maggie. I want to talk to Haley."

My stomach sinks as it hits me what's going on. Just crap. Maggie yanks out of my grasp and races for the park. It warms my heart to hear Jax and Kaden encouraging her to run faster.

"So," says Mom.

"So," I repeat, feeling the need to hide the bruises on my face that I thought I had covered so well with makeup.

"I heard you talked to your dad this morning."

"Yup."

"I also heard that you talked to John about a scholarship."

Figures John would snitch on me, but I ignore the twitch of anger because of the hope that spreads within me. Maybe this isn't about the bruises. Maybe the makeup has worked. "Yes."

"Alice Johnson's son heard from Notre Dame."

I stop, because the ache that I was rejected is still too fresh. Mom pauses beside me and places a comforting hand on my arm. "Did you get in?"

I shake my head because I'll cry if I speak.

Mom stretches an arm around my shoulder and rests her temple against mine. "Why didn't you tell us, Haley? Your father and I want to be here for you on this. And not just with the college search, with everything. It's like you're keeping everything bottled up all the time."

I readjust, forcing Mom to drop her arm. "I was going to tell you," I lie. "Things just got busy."

"Haley," Mom starts, but I don't give her an opportunity.

"I told Maggie I'd race her on the monkey bars."

Mom's forehead furrows, but she nods, accepting that I'm ending the conversation. "No matter what, I'm here if you need me."

If I need her.

I need her and Dad desperately, but since we lost our home everything has become distorted. "All right."

"Believe me," she pushes.

"I believe you." I don't and as we walk down the street, neither of us holds ourselves as if we believe the other.

West

AN INSANITY LEAKS into my brain that makes deciphering reality from fantasy impossible. The cold creeps past my skin, past my muscles, and burrows deep within my bones. My limbs feel numb. Mainly my toes and my fingers. I blow on them and I no longer sense heat.

I'm low on funds and low on fuel, but I can't take the chill anymore.

With a flick of my keys, I start the engine and turn the heater on full force. This is my third night sleeping in the car. I think it's my third. My stomach growls. Two in the morning, I'm freezing my balls off and hungry as hell. I don't know what the fuck I'm doing anymore.

At home I'd be warm. I'd be in a pair of boxers under a pile of blankets. Stomach full.

I could go back. Pull in and walk through the door, but I stop the thought. Dad threw me out and if I walk in, he'll throw me out again.

I roll to my side in the reclined driver's seat, searching for comfort. Each night, I fall asleep, then wake up from the cold. And if the plummeting temperatures don't jerk me awake, the demons haunting me do.

Exhaustion causes my eyesight to blur, but I force myself to stay coherent. I can't fall asleep with the car running. I'll be out of gas by morning. It's in these moments when reality mixes with dreams that sleeping in the car becomes dangerous.

Wake up!

My eyes snap open and my entire body shivers. I dreamed it. I slam my frozen hand against the steering wheel. I dreamed again that I had powered on the car. My breath billows out in a cloud and my fingers hurt as I bend them. I pinch myself after I turn over the engine. I'm awake this time.

Awake.

The air first blowing out of the vents is cold, but within a few minutes hot air defrosts my frozen digits. I push a button and the radio plays. Not loud enough to draw attention, just soft enough to keep me awake.

This song played the last time I talked to Rachel—the night of the accident. She was pacing in a conference room in her golden ball gown. She was a replica of one of those fucked-up fairy tales she was addicted to when we were kids. Only Cinderella wasn't a seventeen-year-old high school junior with severe anxiety issues.

"I'm sorry, Rachel," I say as if she can hear me now—as if her memory could have heard me then.

"You stole from me, West." The gown crinkled as she completed the endless pacing loop in the small room. "You expect me to speak to you after that?"

"I was helping Gavin." Our oldest brother. My breath is a white puff of smoke in the cold air. "I stole the money out of your room because he gambled too much. I didn't know you needed it. You should have told me you needed help."

In an extremely bold and uncharacteristic movement, my sister lifted her skirt so she wouldn't trip and invaded my personal space. "Isaiah and I needed it. If anything happens to him..." She paused, then pressed on her stomach as if she was in pain.

Fuck it. I rub my eyes. She *is* in pain. The night of that last conversation we had was the night she went after Isaiah. She went after him to save him and she ended up in an accident. She ended up in pain.

And Rachel told me if anything happened it would be my fault.

A bell rings and I jump in my seat. My heart pounds hard once as my breath comes out in a rush. The cheap-ass alarm clock I bought continues to blare in the passenger side and the first light of day breaks in the east.

My neck is stiff from falling asleep against the driver's-side door. My fingernails are blue. I stretch my legs and my knees automatically lock.

I slam the clock off and I stare down at the keys that had dug grooves in my hand. Fuck it all, I never turned on the car last night. The entire torture was just a dream.

Unable to take the car anymore, I stumble out and let the sharp cold air hit my lungs. Leaning against the front of the Escalade, I try to rub the cobwebs out of my head.

Dad was right to throw me out. I'm a worthless piece of shit that let my sister down. I failed her. I failed her so badly that she saw the writing on the wall. She knew her entire world was falling apart and she knew exactly where to rightfully place the blame—on me.

Haley

WITH MY HANDS SHOVED in my jeans pockets and my nose buried in the collar of my father's old army sweatshirt, I run to keep up with Jax and Kaden. They were pissed to find me at the neighborhood bus stop this morning at four and their mood hasn't lightened as the three of us walk-run the two blocks from our bus stop to the gym. The bus ran late and John hates tardiness.

The moment we step inside, Jax and Kaden bolt for the locker room and I survey the space, searching for John. Only the completely dedicated and insane show this early and they are currently in the middle of a three-minute rope jumping set. The bell on the timer rings and all of them drop to the ground and begin push-ups. Five more of those bad boy combos to go until they start the sit-ups.

"I'm not giving you a letter." John sits behind a small metal desk in his cramped and disorganized office, banging on a laptop.

I rest a hip against the doorframe, seeking courage. I've got to be tough on this. Make him think I'm in control. "That's not why I'm here. I want you to train someone."

John's eyes snap to mine and his fingers freeze. "What do I get out of it?"

"An awesome fighter." West did take down Conner's little friend and bruised the hell out of Conner's face. It's definitely arguable that West has raw talent.

"Can he pay?"

My face tightens as I try to smile. "Probably not, but I heard you're looking for a volunteer to clean the gym and I'm sure he'll do it."

"Not enough. What else do you got?"

"I'll return to the gym and train." Swallowing prevents dry heaves, but the tingling in my head indicates I probably went green. Just the thought of fighting makes me ill.

John pulls on his bottom ear as if that will help him correctly hear what I uttered. When he accepts that hell hasn't invested in snow-removal trucks and that pigs haven't taken to air, he speaks. "Sit down."

With my foot, I push a boxful of paperwork to the side and drop into the seat across from my grandfather. He resumes his angry typing and ignores me. On the filing cabinet behind him is a picture of me and him after my last fight. He has his arm around me and both of us hold up an end of the belt I won. I barely remember what that type of smile feels like on my face.

Since there was a lack of female kickboxers in the area, I trained with the guys in the gym and we had to travel to find tournaments for me, which meant a ton of one-on-one time with my grandfather. The two of us were close, very close. Now we're as far apart as strangers.

John clicks the mouse. "What's this about?"

I weigh whose truth I should tell. "I've got a friend who's

going to be in a fight in two months and he needs someone to train him."

John's seat squeaks as he relaxes back and links his fingers together across his stomach. The smirk informs me I'm in trouble, but it's the chuckle that grates against my nerves. "Are we talking about your new boyfriend that jumped Conner?"

I officially hate Jax and Kaden. "Yes."

He chuckles again and the smile fades. "Fight for me, Haley."

I'm shaking my head before the final word leaves his mouth. "No."

"I want more than you gracing us with your presence in my gym. You remain the best talent I've seen in years—"

I interrupt, "You have Kaden and Jax."

"In years," he repeats. "And you threw it away. You want that college scholarship? You'll get more than a recommendation from me. You'll have current titles. What more do you need?"

"No."

"Haley..." John runs his hands through his gray-and-white-peppered hair.

"No!"

"At least tell me why! Tell me the truth. Tell me why you walked away."

I lean forward with the urge to bolt from the cramped office. My breathing picks up and I rub the sweat off my palms onto my jeans. "Because."

"Dammit." Both of his hands land on his desk and I jump with the impact. "What the hell happened to you?"

My pulse pounds in my ears. Did Jax and Kaden snitch about the night they found me in the garage? I wipe my palms against my jeans again, except this time I'm not attempting to expel sweat but the memory of the blood that caked my hands. "I'll train here again, but no sparring. I can't spar, okay? It's my offer. Take it or leave it."

It's silent as he stares at me. I try to count my heartbeats, but it's next to impossible.

"Then we've got nothing to discuss." John pretends he's in his office alone and writes on a piece of paper.

"He needs help." I need help, but I can't admit it. There's always been a part of me that has craved to rest my head on my father's or grandfather's shoulders and tell them the truth, but then they'd see me for who I am and how can that help? They already hate who they believe me to be. No reason to make them despise me more.

"You know my asking price."

I prop my elbow on the arm of the chair and cover my eyes with my hand. "Then I'll train him. At least let me use the gym to do it."

The scratching of pen against paper ceases. I can't look at him. I just can't.

"If you train at my gym again, then you can use the facility, but he only spars or trains with me or the others if I get you as a fighter."

I part two fingers and peek at the evil old man across from me. "I won't spar."

"I wouldn't throw you immediately back into your old training regimen even if you asked. I'll ease you in, but if you agree to spar when I say, then I'll *help* you train him."

I straighten. "I'm not sparring, old man. Get it through your thick skull."

Totally unaffected by my outburst, he continues, "How are

you going to train him without sparring? In fact, how are you going to work your job, train in my gym, then find extra time to train someone else? Agree to one fight for me and I'll take him off your hands."

My heart beats manically and a cold clamminess blankets my skin. I can't spar. I can't fight. Not even for West. "I'll train him when I get off work."

He throws his hands in the air. "You'll be here until midnight."

Now I'm the one to pound the desk. "That's my choice!"

"You're right. It always has been."

We stare at each other and I suck in air to calm the adrenaline shooting through my veins. "I want to start training him tonight."

"You can start Friday. I want to see you in my gym every morning by five. Saturdays included. I also own Sunday afternoons."

"Friday! That's—"

John stop signs me with his palm. "Consider it an act of good faith. I had to cancel fights because you walked away. I want to see commitment on your part."

I'm up against the ropes and John knows it. I nod and start to wonder when I'll ever complete my homework, but like John agreed—this *is* my choice. "What about my uncle and his obsessive curfew?"

John resumes writing. "I'll take care of it." There's only one person my uncle fears and that's my grandfather. None of us know why and nobody asks. Jax and his brothers have trained with John since they were small and my uncle allows it.

"And the extra time I need to train West?" I ask.

He assesses me with cold eyes. "What type of name is West?"

"The extra time? What happens when Jax and Kaden walk in his door and I don't?"

"I said I'd take care of it."

All righty. I stand to leave and John nails a final blow. "Our deal starts this morning. I want your ass in the changing room now and on my floor in two minutes. Your stuff is still in your old locker."

Nerves create a dizziness as I walk out of his office and head to the locker room. Every single fighter watches me. What have I done?

West

DAMN, THIS SCHOOL is crowded and if I didn't have a pretend girlfriend, I could definitely work this place. Like the blonde, Jessica, who's been twisting her hair around her finger and staring at me from across the hallway. The girl is contemplating something and I'd bet it's not calculus.

If it'd been two weeks ago, she and I would have already found a secluded corner in this dump and gone to town. I got suspended twice at my old school for being caught with a girl and it was worth the time served.

I rub at the crick in my neck. It's Friday and I've been living in my car for almost a week. I've tried sleeping with the seat reclined and by lying across the backseat. Regardless, sleeping in a car is uncomfortable and cold...and lonely.

Hours drag by. Every decision I've made, good and bad, haunts me. For the first time in my life, I look forward to school and now, because I fixed a toilet, I look forward to my job.

Jessica slithers across the hallway and, feeling twitchy, I once again survey the mass of students for Haley. I like Haley, and truth be told if my hands are going to roam any girl's curves, I'd prefer they be hers, but I won't do Haley wrong. I won't ruin her rep by cheating and I won't ruin *her* by luring her down that hallway for a quick, cheap thrill.

"You held out on me Monday." Jessica runs a finger along my biceps. "Rumor has it you're dating Haley."

"Who's spreading that rumor?"

"Matt Spencer. Actually, he was asking me if it was true. He said that Haley said the two of you were an item, but I told him I thought it was a lie."

I pop my head to the right. Damn. Not what Haley and I need.

Since Tuesday, Haley and I walk to class together and I sit with her at lunch, but the other girls at the table talk to me more than she does. We're not a couple, so we're not acting like a couple. No touching. No hugging. In fact, we've hardly talked. Every time I press her for more info on training and this upcoming fight with Conner, she says she's working on it.

To make matters worse, Matt watches her like a hawk and I don't like it. "Why would I lie?"

"Why do you want to keep it secret that you're a Young?"

Jessica waits to see if I accept the bait, and, when she figures out I'm not biting, she continues, "Everyone knows you got into a fight with Conner last Friday. Matt thinks Haley is protecting Jax and Kaden and that you two are faking this relationship to throw him off course."

Matt's smarter than he looks. "Why would I get involved in Haley's world if we weren't an item?" Because Haley defended me, because Conner hit Haley, because I won't go through the rest of my senior year with anyone believing I'm weak...because I can't fail again.

Her lips compress into a flat line. "That I don't know."

"Haley and I are the real deal. If you talk to Matt again, tell him he can kiss my ass."

"I still think you're lying." Jessica trails a finger along my arm again and surprising myself, I inch away and wipe my biceps as if to get the dirt off. Wildfires don't work as fast as this girl.

"Haley and I are dating and you're supposed to be her friend."

"Haley doesn't do attachments. She floats. By the way, I saw your Escalade in the parking lot. It looks like a sweet ride."

"It is." Come on, Haley, where the hell are you?

She leans against me, pushing her breasts against my arm. "I like sweet rides."

Meaning she gives sweet rides. "I'm taken."

"Please." She rolls her eyes and pulls the hem of her shirt down so that she exposes more of her cleavage and part of her bra. Damn. She's selling hard. "You're not taken. If you were, you would have confessed your undying love for her Monday or Tuesday or any day this week during science, but you never did."

True. "I was curious what people said about Haley." Truer.

"You kept quiet because you liked what you saw in me."

"Let me guess, your favorite position in basketball is forward?"

Shit, the way she just smiled says she eats anything she fucks for breakfast. "I heard you liked forward."

Normally, I do. Guess a lot has changed in a few days. "As I said, I'm taken."

"Besides," she continues as if I hadn't spoken. "Haley doesn't do guys."

That grabs my attention. "What?"

Her smile widens and she juts out a hip. "Haley's a fighter."

"So?"

Her voice indicates the "duh" is implied. "Fighting is a guy thing."

And cars are also considered a guy thing, but my sister is in love with the inside of a popped open hood. I can't stomach people like the chick in front of me. "I've gotta go."

She slides to block my exit. "Okay fine, she's interested in guys, but she's Matt's property."

My muscles tense. "A girl is no one's property." And Haley sure as hell doesn't belong to that asshole.

"You're all girl-power. That's awesome in a weird way. Look, I agree with you, but here's the thing—Matt doesn't give a crap about equal rights or that we earned the right to vote a couple hundred years ago. Haley and Matt may have broken up, but he makes it clear that no one sniffs around her. He'll hit you the moment you touch her."

"Let him." I've agreed to this showcase in two months for Haley's sake, but if Matt and his crew want to go at it now, then I'm game. Maybe it would be better if we did. I wouldn't have rumors floating around that I'm weak and it would take the burden off Haley.

"Matt's bad news," she says.

"So am I," I snap, pissed everyone thinks this guy is stronger than me. "Why are you even interested?"

Her eyes light up. "Because you're West Young."

Because she thinks I have money. This is the first time

I've itched to tell anyone I've been disowned. Is she still going to be pushing up on me then?

With her fingers typing intently into a cell, Abby, the queen of not giving a shit whether or not I want her around, sidles up beside me. "You should listen to her about Matt." She glances up at me. "I was eavesdropping."

"Rude much?" says Jessica.

"Jessica," responds Abby.

She widens her eyes as a "what do you want?"

"I bite."

And the blonde scurries down the hallway like a squirrel darting through traffic. If I didn't hate Abby, I'd be impressed. "You do go to school here." Haven't seen her once.

"Yep." She slips her phone into her back pocket. "Do you watch soap operas?"

What the hell type of question is that? "No."

"Curious." Her eyebrows furrow. "Because I would have thought you reenacted the crap with what you've accomplished in a week."

Not caring for anything else Abby has to say, I head to my first period class. Maybe I missed Haley and she's already there.

"You're a soap opera writer's wet dream." Abby keeps step beside me. "The funny part is, I've never seen one, but, holy shit, has this been fascinating. In a span of seven days you've managed to piss off Isaiah, Jax and Kaden Williams, and Matt and Conner Spencer.

"You're dating Haley Williams, plus you've got slut of the month Jessica...well...slutting up on you. Throw in a switched at birth storyline and bam, I'm thinking daytime Emmy for sure."

Abby pivots, walks backward and snags the shirt of some kid with bloodshot eyes. She drags him with her, forcing him to her level. "Unlike the rest of corporate America, I'm not into competition. Last time I'm telling you, keep it off my block."

She releases him with a shove, then resumes walking forward. "Sorry, business negotiations. As I was saying, it's amazing no one's plugged a bullet into your head."

Abby's probably right. I pause outside the doorway to my class and she, not surprisingly, joins me. "Why are you telling me this? We hate each other."

Her phone vibrates and she pulls it out, texting back instantaneously. "True. But I kinda like this fairy godmother, guardian angel bullshit, plus oddly enough I believe in karma. One last tidbit for the day before I return to mild-mannered drug dealer."

I hold out my arms. "Lay it on me."

Pushing Send, she refocuses on me. "Watch Matt. He'll be gunning for you, but he'll wait to see what your weaknesses are before he does. Jax and Kaden have always been protective of Haley and I don't see that ending anytime soon, even if they are mad at her. Stay out of Isaiah's way. He's giving you a reprieve because your family kicked you out, but don't test his patience. With Rachel in pain, he's looking for an excuse to snap."

Abby turns to leave, but I stop her. "How did you know Dad kicked me out?"

"When it comes to my neighborhood there isn't much I don't know. I heard that an Escalade has been at the park every night, all night. Then I saw you in the bar." Abby shrugs. "I know kicked out and hungry when I see it."

"Does Rachel know?" I stop myself from asking if my parents appear upset.

"Your parents are holding their cards close to their chest. Isaiah's monitoring the situation because he doesn't want anyone to tell Rachel. It'll upset her."

The asshole has gained some of my respect. "Thanks. Can you keep it to yourself that I'm a Young?"

Abby rolls her neck. "Does Jessica know?"

"Yeah."

"Then it doesn't matter if I keep my mouth shut. Jessica doesn't shut hers and, yes, I mean that in every way possible."

"I'll take care of Jessica. Will you keep it to yourself?"

"What, you're so much better than this school that you can't tell the truth?"

This from the self-proclaimed liar. "Being a Young here will create problems. Don't Haley and I have enough of those?"

"And the boy has a point. I'll keep your dirty secret...for Haley." Abby releases a smile that causes the hair on the back of my neck to stand on end. "But now you'll owe me a debt. Toodles."

I just made a deal with the devil.

Haley

MY LEGS ARE JELL-O. Actually, Jell-O is sturdier than I am. This is my fourth morning training at the gym and tonight I have to start training West.

This morning, I ran and ran and ran. Then I began on the sit-ups and push-ups. I crave a nap, a hot bath, then another nap. I fold my arms on my desk and rest my head on the makeshift pillow. A tension stretches across my shoulder blades. I worked out on the bags this morning. Tomorrow, the muscles in my back are going to be begging for death.

"Haley." It's a low whisper that has to be one of those strange illusions during that semiawake, semidreaming state.

"Haley!"

My seat jerks beneath me when my head pops up. It's not that the voice was loud this time, but it's a shock when Marissa says anything louder than a whisper. Next to the two-seater science desk we share for Biology II, Marissa holds her books tight to her chest. "We need to talk."

"Okay." I rub my eyes and wait for her to sit, but she doesn't. She remains standing, edging her books closer to her chin as if she's contemplating hiding her face.

"What's up?" I ask.

She glances to the left, to the right, then to the left again, like she's preparing to cross the street, then leans toward me. "Jessica came on to West in the hall this morning. She touched him...and everything and well...he didn't leave."

The unsaid "everything" would include breasts pushed out against any available male body part. Jessica likes to play with the male species. Sort of like how black widow spiders snack on their mates.

"Well, crap!" Half of the room turns and stares at me. The surge of anger is a shock and I'm not sure why I'm mad. It's not like West is my boyfriend, but he's supposed to be acting like my boyfriend and she's supposed to be my friend and...and...

West enters the room. The moment our eyes meet, I look away. Jessica hit on him, which means he probably hit on her back. She's pretty and forward and guys fall all over themselves so they can be near her and I'm...me.

I slouch in my seat, a hurricane combination of ticked off and hurt and confused.

If he's smart, he'll stay away.

If he's smart, he'll come over here and apologize for fake cheating on me.

Either way, I want to punch him *and* Jessica in the jaw.

Maybe I should rethink my stance on sparring.

"I've been looking for you." I shut my eyes at the sound of West's deep voice. Butterflies have a field day in my stomach. He's not my boyfriend. He's a friend—a complication—and he's probably kissed Jessica. Butterflies are not allowed.

"Marissa, do you mind if I sit here today?" he asks.

"No!" I open my eyes and Marissa is MIA. For real? Are all

my friends abandoning me? First Jessica makes a move on West; then Marissa flees at one request.

The chair beside me scrapes against the floor and the heat of his body caresses my left side as he takes a seat. If I inched my arm over a tad, I bet we'd be touching.

Jessica walks into the room and frowns. Warm, heavy fingers lace with mine on top of the desk and the heart that had picked up speed moments before is now supersonic.

I study our joined hands on the table and I have to admit I like the image. My fingers are dwarfed compared to his. At school, I've always been the fighter—the girl who's not really feminine—but against West's masculine hands, my fingers appear slim, graceful even.

And if I'm going to daydream for a sec, I might as well concede that I like the tingle in my blood. The skin of his fingers is rough but not sandpaper. Strong but not weighted. And warm. Very, very warm. If our entwined hands create such bliss, I wonder if his lips against mine would cause fireworks.

"Your friend Jessica is a piece of work," he mutters and I pull out of my daydream.

Cautiously, I peek at him from the corner of my eye. I've seen Jessica work guys over before. Did West fall for it? "Rumor has it she's been extremely friendly with you and not a friend to me."

"Damn, word here spreads fast. Do you guys have a text gossip notification system? If so, I need to warn the other guys she's willing to molest anything with two legs and a dick. There's something wrong with her. She doesn't understand no."

I giggle and let my fingers relax in his though I don't

understand why he's touching me. We've been pulling off "together" without PDA.

"Maybe she's testing you. You know, to see if you're really into me." Maybe, but probably not. The way Jessica stares death daggers over her shoulder tells me she's not happy. Over what, I'm not sure. I'm assuming it's because I've pretend scored a guy she wants.

He surveys the room. "Anyone else I should be aware of?"

"Probably everyone." I'm not much competition when it comes to keeping a guy as gorgeous as West. Even though we would never work. Even though I shouldn't want us to work.

The warning bell rings and Marissa chooses a seat in the back next to a hot guy. My lips curve up. Go, Marissa. Though the guy would probably notice her more if her face wasn't glued to the inside of a book.

I rock our knotted hands on the table. "What's with the hand-holding?"

A smile erupts on West's face that transforms me into gooey brownies fresh out of the oven. "Besides the fact if I don't your fingers will fall off from frostbite?"

"Ha, ha, ha." My cheeks warm. "Besides that."

His glorious smile fades, leaving me empty. "We're in science. Consider it an experiment."

"On what?"

He turns his attention to the front of the room. Matt walks in and the pure menace radiating from his glare causes me to yank away from our joined grip, except West doesn't give. In fact, he holds on tighter. "On that."

West

"WHY ARE WE SITTING HERE?" Haley slams her lunch tray on the table and sinks into the chair across from me. Still pissed at our show of hand-holding during science, she stabs her fork into the chicken patty. I chuckle. I don't need much of an imagination to guess what part of my anatomy she'd like to stick that fork into.

"Consider it a continuation of my science experiment." I chose a solo table in the back for the two of us under the half-broken florescent light. It could be romantic, if I did romantic and we were an actual couple.

"By baiting the tiger? Really, West? Why don't you pull out fresh meat, smack Matt on the nose a few times, then open the door to his cage? It's like you want to cause problems."

"Are we having our first fight as a couple?"

Her mouth twitches. "Yes."

"Do you still have feelings for him?" I hold my breath while she answers, but try to act like I don't care. Which I shouldn't. We're only faking a relationship.

"No," she answers immediately. "Matt and I have history.

I was young and stupid and now we have history. History that will never, ever be repeated."

Satisfied, I settle into my seat. "Then why do you care if I bait him?"

"Because I like you enough that it would suck if you died."

"I can take Matt."

No response from Haley and I push down the urge to rattle her. What do I have to do to prove I'm capable?

I shove a forkful of corn into my mouth. Haley plays with hers and I can tell her mind is a million miles away. This morning, Jessica easily dismissed her and what has also been a shock is the way guys walk by her without noticing her existence. Haley's gorgeous with all that sandy-brown hair and dark eyes that promise long nights full of kisses and laughter.

Maybe that's what happens if you go to school with someone since birth and you only recognize them by their label. How many girls have I wrongfully overlooked at my old school?

Haley's eyes meet mine. She slowly glances over her shoulder, then back at me. "What?"

"What what?"

She kicks my shin underneath the table and I laugh as I shake off the sting. "You're hot and I like looking."

Haley turns an adorable shade of red and she traces a make-believe line in her corn. Thinking of how Rachel hates to be embarrassed, I offer Haley an out. "What type of tournament am I facing? Knife throwing? Quilt making? Dueling pistols at sunrise?"

"Mixed martial arts."

I scratch my chin. Now I understand why Haley didn't

want to discuss this in front of anyone else. If I had been thinking straight, I would have forced her to eat lunch at a separate table days ago, but my head's been jacked up as I contemplated my own problem: the forecasted temperature plummet tonight.

I had hoped for boxing, but I had doubts it would be that easy. Not that boxing is easy, but MMA is a whole other animal. It's the best of the best. The ultimate badass contest. It's not just discovering who is the better man in boxing, but who's the better man in boxing, jujitsu, Muay Thai, grappling and whatever the hell else combat fighting thrown in for good measure.

"Cage and all?" I ask.

"Cage and all," she echoes. After a second, she peers at me from under those long dark eyelashes. Does she curl them or do they naturally have that sexy wave? "You don't have to do this. You could transfer to another school."

"How?" I snap. "My dad threw me out. I doubt he'd sign the transfer papers."

Haley's face falls and she drops her fork onto her plate. "That was awful of me to say—"

"Stop. I didn't mean it that way." I didn't mean to upset her.

"If being stuck at this school is the reason why you're taking this on, then I'll figure out another way to fix this. Give me the weekend, I'll think of something—"

"Haley, I'm in this and it's not because I'm stuck at Eastwick."

She opens her mouth to protest, but I cut her off. "I'm in this."

"You never listen to reason, do you?"

"I listen to any reasoning that makes sense and yours doesn't."

"Impossible," she mutters. After several beats she continues, "My grandfather owns a small gym in the industrial park. He's given me permission to train you there. I get off at eight tonight, so I thought we could meet up at nine."

Wow. Lots of things going on in that statement. I fork my own patty, then cut it up into pieces. "Where do you work?"

"I'm a waitress at Romeo's Pizza. Sorry. I should have asked about your work schedule."

"It's all right. I didn't have one until Tuesday." Benefit of being a trust fund baby—work was optional. Funny, I thought of college, but I had never thought of supporting myself.

"Oh." She lowers her gaze. Regret heats my neck. I bet every guy she knows has had a job since they were sixteen. In her eyes, that makes me the unemployed loser who lives in his mom's basement and bums rides off friends. Worse, she's aware I don't have a basement to live in. And here I thought Dad was the only one I unimpressed.

"My hours are after school and flexible." At least that's what Denny said. "How do you get around?" That's called changing the subject.

"City bus." Haley's voice becomes muffled as she talks into her cup before she drinks.

City bus. Something clicks and I edge my tray away. I've got half a tank left in my car and the remaining cash I have, I need for food. I get paid next week, but I won't be breaking bank. Now Haley's supposed to be training me and I don't have money for the gym or the equipment. My fist clenches and this overwhelming urge to hit something—someone, anything—rages through my veins.

A hand folds over mine and my eyes jerk to Haley's.

"You okay?" she asks.

"Yeah." I suck in a breath. "No. I'm fucked."

"Are you running out of places to stay?"

I nod, unable to admit I lied to her earlier in the week about where I've been sleeping.

"There are shelters." Her voice cracks. "But they're downtown. The bus routes to there are a little...dangerous. If you drove, your car would be jacked in minutes."

I figured. "How are they? The shelters?" Hell. She's never told me she's stayed in them. I'm tipping information from Jessica.

We stare at each other for seconds, longer. Her face is blank, but her eyes are moving. She's thinking. Haley is always thinking and, like I did before, I offer the out. "If you let me pick you up, then we could reach the gym by eight-thirty."

It'd be worth the last bit of gas I have to end a conversation I never should have started.

She memorizes her plate as she eats and contemplates my last statement. Who knows—maybe she's still pondering the shelters. I've noticed this about Haley over the past couple of days—someone asks her a question and instead of immediately answering, she mulls it over. Possibly two minutes pass and I have a hunch she's an overanalyzer.

"It's a car ride, Haley. Not an invitation to stay over after we have sex."

She chokes on her chicken patty and downs her water. "We are not having sex."

"We could," I say, then grin at her.

She coughs into her hand and I laugh. I laugh harder when her foot connects with my leg.

"What do you say?" I lean back and rest my arm on the back of the chair next to me. "Eight-thirty or nine?"

She sighs as if this is a huge concession. "Eight-thirty."

"You don't like it, do you?"

"What?"

"Accepting help."

The fork impales the chicken again. "You honestly make it impossible to like you."

The bell rings and I catch Haley's tray before she has a chance to lift it. "But you do."

A tiny smile forms and she quickly hides it.

"And after today's conversation you'll also be thinking about the two of us in bed."

She straightens. "That is not going to happen."

"The daydreaming?"

"Yes!"

"Then you're good on the actual sex?"

A fire ignites in her eyes. "I could drop-kick you now."

I bite back any response because the truth is, even with me being heavier in muscle and several inches taller than her, the aftermath of Conner says she could. On occasion, even I know when to stop, but damn, teasing her is fun.

Haley pauses beside me as I dump the trash and deposit the tray. In classic pissed-off girl stance, she folds her arms over her chest and pouts that beautiful bottom lip.

I should tell her I'm sorry and that I'm a jerk. That's what boyfriends do, but I've never been boyfriend material and Haley and I aren't actually dating. I give into the temptation and rub her silky hair between my thumb and forefinger.

She stares up at me with those hypnotic eyes. There's an attraction she can try to deny, but it won't make the tension crackling between us any less true. I would easily renounce my trust fund to fist my hand in her hair and kiss those perfect lips. God, this girl turns me on.

Knowing there are teachers and principals and students waiting for me to screw it up and kiss her in public, I flick her hair over her shoulder and run my hand down her arm. "That's all right. You don't have to think about it, but I'll dream about it for the both of us."

Haley

MY GRANDFATHER THINKS he's being crafty, but the old man is obvious. Paperwork at nine at night on a Friday? He barely tolerates paperwork during the day. John stays somewhat busy as he clicks buttons on a laptop, but every thirty seconds his eyes flash to me and West.

We walked in a few minutes ago and by the way West has spun his hat backward, I can tell he needs time to soak in his evening home for the next two months. Maybe now West will see how serious this is and he'll learn how to back down from a fight.

I sidle closer to John's office and when he does his next scan, I catch his eye. "Do you need something?"

His jaw clenches. "He's cocky."

I agree, but I'm not sure girlfriends are supposed to admit such things to their grandfathers because I should be so puppy and rainbows in love I wouldn't notice. "I'm glad you can judge sound moral character in less than a minute."

"The way he walks—he's cocky."

"Name one guy who trains here who isn't."

John looks past me to West. With a gym bag slung over his

shoulder, West curls his fingers through the caged-in Octagon and grips the metal.

The ring engages his entire attention and it should. This isn't a game or a television show where the good guy always wins. This is reality and the moment he steps into that cage with someone waiting for him on the other side, he can die. I hope I'll never see his blood on the caged-in floor.

"Welterweight?" John asks.

West still hasn't moved and there's tons I need to explain to him. "That's my guess. I'll find out when I weigh him."

"He doesn't look big enough for a middleweight, even if he gained muscle."

I know and I rest my temple against the doorframe. Both Conner and Matt are welterweights, meaning they weigh 170 pounds or less. Part of me is pinning my hopes that West greatly exceeds weight and can't fight them, but even if he did they'd get a middleweight fighter from Black Fire to take their place. I'm not sure I can train West in enough time to defend himself in the welterweight division, much less middleweight.

"He'll have to cut before he fights," John says.

"Yeah," I answer absently. Cutting weight before a fight is rough, necessary at times, but rough. John relaxes back in his seat and appraises me. For once every muscle isn't tight, preparing to strangle me for my past decisions. Somehow, despite the fact he hates me, the two of us have fallen into an easy conversation.

I miss easy. I miss John. "Matt and I didn't end well."

John's gray eyes shoot to mine and I immediately regret the slip. I've never said anything like that to anyone. I've never even hinted at it, but somehow being at the only place that has felt like home in months has broken through a wall that shouldn't be breached.

"Kaden and Jax...they came to me..." His pauses are so awkward that the contents of my stomach swirl like a whirlpool. "They were concerned...but you wouldn't talk—"

"Can you register West for the fight? The one in two months?" I made a mistake by speaking the words aloud and now John's too near a subject that causes absolute panic.

"Haley—"

"I just need you to register him." My chest constricts and my throat swells. "Please."

He sighs, then flicks a pen across the desk. "Jax said your new boyfriend has a problem with Matt. Is that the reason for this? Are you training him so they can take out their differences in the cage?"

That sounded pathetic out loud, but it's better than the previous conversation. "West and Conner have issues." John's been around Black Fire fighters long enough to understand that means West has a problem with that entire gym, Matt included.

He gestures with his chin toward West. "Should I be worried about you and him?"

"He's harmless."

"You said the other one was harmless, too."

It would have been less painful if John had taken a railroad spike and driven it into my skull. I do only what I can do: change the subject. "Take West on. You can train him a million times better than I can."

"You know the old saying about teaching a man how to fish?"

That he can feed himself. "Yeah."

He motions with his hand that I have my answer, but I don't. Instead I have a raised brow. Maybe Grandpa's drinking again. "Does that mean you're training him?"

"It means if you agree to spar, like we negotiated earlier, then I'll help you train him."

Whaaaat? "But if you train him, he can fight all the fish he wants." Or something like that.

John scratches the back of his head. "Hays, I need you to learn how to fight."

"I know how to fight." Each word comes out slowly, as if I don't believe it myself.

"No, you don't."

I want to ask him what he means—what he's hoping for—but there are things so dark and dirty and hopeless inside me that I'd prefer everyone, like me, continue to ignore they exist.

"The fight," I say. "Will you register him?"

"Is he eighteen?" John asks. "If not, no. Even better, if he's a minor, I want his parents' permission to be standing in my gym and if he's eighteen, then he's got a shitload of forms to fill out. I'm not looking for anyone to sue my ass when he dies."

I roll my eyes at his last statement if only because he's putting my worst fear for West into words. "West! Are you eighteen?"

Say no. Say no. Say no. Legal age to fight MMA in Kentucky is eighteen.

"You don't know your boyfriend's age?" asks John. I ignore him because...well...really? If West and I were a for real couple, his birthday would be hearted in red on my calendar. Okay, maybe not my style, but still...

From across the room, West nods and I mumble, "Damn."

So much for an easy way out. West struts in my direction and I push off the wall. If John isn't training him, then I'd like to permanently avoid introductions.

"Will you do it?" I ask John as I back away. "Will you register him?"

"If he's got the money for the fees, then I'll get him in." He holds his fingers up in the air and rubs them together. "And for that you stay in my gym until the end of summer."

My hands slam onto my hips. "Summer?"

"Take it or leave it." John focuses on the computer again.

"Fine." I've become an indentured servant teaching myself how to fish in the desert without a net or a pole.

The word *fees* eventually sinks in, and, as I stroll up next to West, I say, "I hope you make good money."

West

HALEY RAKES A HAND through her hair, then grips it at the base of her neck like she's going to tear it out. "Shirt off."

"Yes, ma'am." I've already lost the shoes and socks. "I'll take the shorts off, too, if you'd like."

I thumb the edge of my waistband and Haley shakes her head too quickly. "That won't be necessary."

"You know you want me to," I say and enjoy every second of watching her skin blotch red and the slight tilt of her lips. In typical Haley fashion, she chooses to ignore me. One day, I'll climb into that head she constantly withdraws into.

Her grandfather left for the night and Haley is sexy as hell in her sports bra and shorts. Her flat stomach looks so soft, so smooth. My fingers twitch with the need to caress it.

A rush of air escapes her lips. "Crap."

"Want to fill me in?"

She blinks as if she's noticing me for the first time, which does nothing for my ego. Girls usually pay attention to me when I have my shirt off.

"You weigh 177 pounds."

"Yeah." Not news.

"I need you to weigh 170." Her eyes roam my body. "And there is not an ounce of fat on you." Haley bites her lower lip as she stares at my abs and I grin. Now I've got the girl's attention.

I step off the scale and the lever clanks against the metal. "You keep telling me this is going to be hard-core. I'll lose the weight."

"Yeah, but you'll also gain muscle. I'll figure it out later. Come on." Haley pulls at her hair again, then lets it cascade through her fingertips.

I've filled more than one night this week driving out the darkness and loneliness by fantasizing about rumpling Haley's silky hair and placing my mouth over those gorgeous lips. It's taking every ounce of willpower I possess not to push her against the wall and kiss her. The image in my head almost causes me to groan. My shirt's off, her stomach is exposed, hot flesh would be touching...

Damn, I'm killing myself. I snatch my shirt off the floor and trail Haley to the open spot near the mirrors. I'm doing the friend thing with Haley. Just friends. No benefits. She's proven time and again she deserves the respect. "You say that a lot."

"What?"

"That you'll figure things out."

She raises one shoulder as she snags a yellow ball off the floor. "That's because I will."

"The weight of the world isn't on you, you know? There're a couple other billion people who can help you figure out the solution to global warming."

I earn a half smirk from Haley as she rolls out the two-inch wide material. "I'm not worried about global warming."

"You know what I mean."

She pretends I didn't speak. "Have you ever wrapped your hands before?"

"None of the fights I've been in have included advance notification so I bare-knuckled it."

"And that," she says with her best under-eyelash schoolteacher glare, "has to stop. Outside of this gym, there are no fights."

"Hey, I don't go looking for trouble. It finds me."

Haley inclines her head at a stool and I sit. "Put your hand up, like this." She sticks her hand in the air, palm down, with spread fingers.

I follow directions and Haley hooks a circle of material at the end of the wrap on my thumb. "Do you see the tag?"

I nod.

"It goes faceup. The trick to wrapping is to think in threes." She winds the material around my wrist in layers. "Three up the wrist and then three back down. Tight enough that you create tension, loose enough that you don't cut off circulation and cause your fingers to fall off."

Haley's thigh applies pressure to my own and I drop my knee open so she can slide between my legs. Every cell within my body hums and, when I breathe in, all I smell is the sweet scent of wildflowers. Her fingers work diligently, brushing against my skin as she weaves the material around and around again.

The seriousness of her face tells me she has no idea how close she is. How with each caress of her fingertips, I go up in flames.

"Is that why your hands are cold?" I ask in a poor attempt

to keep from grabbing Haley and permitting my fingers to roam that tempting flesh. "You cut off circulation?"

Another under-eyelash glare. "Ha, ha, ha. The boy's a comedian."

"I forgot," I needle. "Genetics."

"I can take you now," she says in a singsong way.

She could and the thought causes me to smile. "I'm game, except I forgot protection."

Haley smacks my shoulder. "Fighting, not sex. My God, you have a one-track mind."

"When I'm around you I do."

"Create an X around your palm and then wrap it around your knuckles. Do this three times and don't forget to keep your fingers spread apart. How's this feel?" Haley moves her leg, creating this heart-stopping friction. Lightning zaps up the vein of my inner thigh and straight to very private areas.

"Is it too tight?" she asks.

Space is becoming an issue in my shorts. "Nope. It's just right."

"I hope you're paying attention because you're wrapping your other hand."

"Do you ever think about kissing me?" Because I think about kissing her. Often. And a deep urge that sinks down past my bones wants her to feel the same.

Haley's head snaps up and those gorgeous dark eyes stare into mine. Red creeps across her cheeks and neck. I have my answer and it only stirs the flames.

"It doesn't matter," she whispers.

"Why?"

"I don't date fighters anymore."

I keep it to myself that we don't have to date to kiss or that

I've kissed lots of girls and have never once had a girlfriend. Haley's a nice girl and I don't want to scare her with my experiences. "Because of Matt?"

Haley goes quiet and pensive, focusing on the yellow strip like it has all the solutions. "Because of Matt."

"You know, I'm not actually a fighter."

"You are. It's not about the gym, it's about who you are. You may not have trained until now, but you're a fighter."

She continues her wrapping, creating a cross, padding the knuckles, then brings it back to my wrist. "You can use the excess material however you want. I choose to use it to wrap my wrists again."

At the end of the strip is Velcro. She pats it into place and a shadow of lust darkens her eyes. Haley quickly withdraws her hands and puts space between us.

I stretch my fingers and admire her handiwork, but what I'm really doing is buying time. There's more to Matt and Haley than a steady relationship that ran its course. There's more to all of it—her, Jax and Kaden. "I meant what I said earlier—this isn't all on you."

"It is. No one else is going to watch Kaden and Jax's back but me."

"I don't get it," I admit. "From what I understand your family and Matt and Conner go at it all the time at sanctioned fights. Why the cloak-and-dagger? You and I know what really happened that night. What harm would it have done to let Kaden and Jax take the fall? They're going to fight anyhow."

"Because." Haley's chest moves as she inhales. My gut twists at seeing her so sad. "Because Matt would have taken it outside the cage. He would have fought them on the street with no ref and there is so much bad blood between them because of me that Jax and Kaden would have accepted the fights."

"And the problem is?" A member of their family got jumped; retribution and justice were theirs to take.

"West..." Her gaze moves beyond my shoulder to the caged-in Octagon behind me. "Every time you walk into that cage, you're saying you're okay with dying, but at least you have some rules, a referee and a coach who can stop the fight if you don't tap out. Can you imagine the bloodshed without rules, without a referee? And who says if Jax or Kaden try to tap out that Conner or Matt would let them walk away?"

I feel sucker punched. "The reason they want me in the sanctioned fight is because everyone thinks I'll be crushed and it'll be fun as hell to do it in public."

Haley won't meet my eyes and she shifts.

"Do you think they'll crush me?" A heaviness bears down on my stomach. Haley returned for me that night and this fight is the only way I can repay that gift.

"I don't know," she says quietly. "This isn't a movie or a TV show where the guy practices a few times, then takes on the world champ and wins. Matt and Conner and Jax and Kaden...they've trained for years and they still aren't good enough to go pro. I'm hoping I have enough time to teach you how to defend yourself."

An edginess claws its way into my muscles. "If you have no faith in me, then why the fuck are we here?"

Her head jerks up. "I feel awful you're standing here in Jax and Kaden's place. Every second of my day, I think about how to shove you out."

"If you did figure out a way to *shove* me out, you'd be on

your own to deal with Matt and Conner. When you're busy taking care of and protecting everyone else, who's protecting you?"

"I can take care of myself."

I laugh and Haley straightens: a pissed-off, sexy warrior. *Give me all you've got, Haley, because right now, I'm handing it back.* "Every time you think you have everything under control you don't."

"Says Mr. Disaster. You never think anything through and end up in messes like this and the guilt is on me if anything happens to you. Tap out of this right now, West. Walk away."

"Do you always roll over and die? Since I've met you, you're either running or scheming. The one thing you never do is fight."

"I fought for you!" she shouts. "I fought for you and it cost me. It cost my whole family!"

"You're not fighting for me now! You admitted you're trying to shove me away!"

"Sometimes walking away is fighting!"

"Walking away is abandonment and I don't abandon!"

I'm breathing hard and Haley's eyes become glassy. "I...I... don't abandon. I don't."

Her lower lip trembles and I'm so pissed at myself that I ram my wrapped fist into the bag. The bag swings and, when it returns, I smack it again. The strike feels clean and it feels powerful and I crave to do it again and again.

Haley blows out a shaky stream of air and I catch the bag. Our backs are turned toward each other, but I can see her in the mirror. It would be easier on me if she cried. Tears, for some reason, cause me to tune people out, but Haley doesn't cry. Doesn't even blink or wipe at her eyes. She wears the look of a person who continues to breathe though their soul is dead. It's the same expression my mother wears when she sits in the room of her deceased daughter.

My insides ache as if salt is being poured into a million internal paper cuts. Haley never asked for any of this. "I'm sorry."

It took me years to say that statement to Dad, yet only days to say it to Haley. I wish she understood how difficult those words are for me.

"What are we fighting about?" she whispers.

"I don't know." But I don't think I'm fighting her. My eyes roam over the cage and suddenly I wish it were two months from now. I wish I could enter that cage and see an opponent across from me, because then I'd know where all this anger, all this rage should be pointed.

"I don't want you to get hurt," she says to the floor. "I like you and because of that I'm struggling. There is no way I can prepare you to fight in two months."

"So I don't win." I turn to face her, but she keeps her back to me.

"It's not winning that concerns me. I'm terrified you won't walk out of that cage."

I flinch as if someone nailed me in the gut. It might have been less painful if she had. Pride screams at me to lash out at her again, but, in the mirror, her shoulders curve inward. Harsh memories surface of all those times Rachel was sick from anxiety and I never paid attention. I fucked up with Rachel. I've fucked up with my whole family.

It doesn't matter. It changes right here. Right now. I've let everyone else I love down. Haley needs me and helping her protect her family is my one shot at redemption and I'll be damned if she steals it from me.

I advance on Haley and, before she can retreat, I round on her and gently rest my hand on her face. My fingers weave into her hair and her jaw fits perfectly into my palm.

"Listen to me because I'm tired of saying it. I'm in this for good. You can't get rid of me even if you wanted. If you shoved me out that door and locked it, if you never spoke to me at school, it doesn't matter—I'm taking the fight in two months."

Because I need this fight. For once, I need to know who I'm fighting against. I need to know I can do it. I need to know when I've been thrown away that I'm worth more.

"I'm doing this with or without your help, but I have a better chance of walking out of that cage with you on my side."

Her eyes search my face, looking for something…a sign I'm lying, a sign I'll take back the words. Haley licks her lips. "I can't convince you to tap out on me?"

"No tapping out."

Haley strains, wanting freedom, and as much as I'd like to keep her close, I drop my hand and let her go.

She circles the room, slowly…thinking. I can't get the girl to stop overanalyzing. Finally she halts. "Okay. If this is how it's going to be, then you need to wrap that other hand, then start jumping some rope."

Haley

MY BREATH CATCHES when I step out of the locker room. Waiting for me, West leans against the wall next to my grandfather's office. His blond hair is darkened from his shower and his shirt clings to him, like he's still a bit wet. God, he's beautiful.

We've been training together for a week and each night we keep playing out this same scenario. I'll admit it—seeing him there every time... I go weak in the knees.

"Ready?" West glances in my direction and his lips tilt up into this endearing smile. It's sexy and wicked and adorable all at the same time. I tuck my damp hair behind my ear. There's one locker room and, within it, two showers. I loitered in the gym when we finished cooling down—washed down the mats and bags, cleaned the mirror, untangled jump ropes—anything to keep from being in the same area as him when he was naked.

I'm attracted to West. There's no denying it. Whenever he's around, my heart does this insane fluttering like millions of hummingbirds have taken up residence in my chest. So space…it's definitely what we need. "I told you I'd take the bus home."

"I know, but it's late." Eleven at night, our latest training session yet.

"Afraid I'm going to kick the bus driver's butt?"

He chuckles and the flutter changes as the hummingbirds soar into the sky. "Yes, that's exactly what I'm worried about. Come on—let's go."

We walk out and I shiver from head to toe. The cold bites at my face, my fingers, my neck and burns my lungs. "The white flag will be out tonight."

"What?" His breath crystallizes into a fog.

"It'll be below freezing," I say quickly, mentally kicking myself for the slip. "The homeless shelters ignore capacity and take in extra people when it's this cold. Hold on for a sec. I've got to take care of something. You can head on to the car."

I cut to the right of the warehouse and pick up the pace, half-grateful for the chore. Discussing homeless shelters is not on the top of the list…or the bottom. Last week, I told West I understood what it's like to be homeless. He later asked me about the condition of the shelters. Does he know that's where my family and I lived for a short time or did he make the assumption? Living in the shelter is my dirty secret. Just as dirty as my breakup with Matt and almost as dirty as my current living conditions.

Because West can be the most annoying guy on the face of the planet, he follows. "What are you doing?"

"I'm pretty sure I told you to stay put."

West must have a hearing deficiency. "I'll come along."

"You never freaking listen, do you?"

"No."

West continues to tread on areas of my life where I've never allowed anyone. I stop and so does he. "Will you go wait for me in the car?"

"Are you cold, Haley? Because I'm cold. I'm going with or we can stay here and freeze to death. Either way, we're together."

It's cold enough that my wet hair is forming into icicles. "You are *so* high-maintenance."

The parking-lot lamp behind him creates a shadow along his face, but that smile is hard to miss. I'm irritated with him and I want to stay irritated with him, but those types of smiles make it hard to stay mad at him for long.

"Have you looked in a mirror lately?" he asks.

My mouth gapes. "I am not high-maintenance."

He rocks his eyebrows. "I'm messing with you. For real, it's cold, so let's move."

"Will you stay here? Just one second. I swear I'll never be out of your sight."

In a sweeping motion, he waves his hand for me to continue.

The blacktop beneath my feet crackles as it gives way to gravel and, with West a safe distance away, I approach the tiny camper and knock on the door. The muted and distorted sound of a crowd roaring fades away. John's always watching a fight—for entertainment, for training, for scouting, for tips on how to beat an upcoming opponent.

The entire vehicle shakes as John opens the door. He's in the same clothes as usual, a T-shirt and nylon athletic pants. He rubs his eyes as if waking from a deep sleep. "You're done?"

"We're done," I say. "I forgot to get the keys from you so you'll need to lock up."

John grabs his coat. "I'll drive you home."

"Thanks, but West will do it."

He peers over my shoulder. "I'll lock up after I finish watching this tape."

Nerves cause a flash freeze in my bloodstream. "What about my uncle?" I've never come in this late before. Jax and Kaden have, sometimes they roll in later, but never me.

"I talked to him and he knows you're training. I'll warn you, he's not happy, but he'll let you in. You've got to be there by eleven on a school night and midnight on the weekend."

I shift, suddenly consumed with the urge to run and meet curfew. "It's eleven now. When were you going to tell me?" Anytime this week could have helped.

"I would have come and gotten you by eleven-thirty and taken you home."

I assess sleepy "Grandpa." "Uh-huh."

The old man cracks a rare grin. "Go on before you do miss curfew."

I hesitate. "Jax and Kaden weren't here tonight."

"They weren't."

"But they train at the gym every night." I know because I've been stuck at the hellhole house without them. John cocks a hip against the doorframe, waiting for me to catch up, and it doesn't take long for the synapses in my brain to fire. "They say they're training and then they go out."

"Good night, Haley." He shuts the door. Jax and Kaden had a way out and they didn't include me. My insides drop to my frozen toes. Oh, my God, they must seriously hate me.

I say nothing as I pass West.

"Is that his other office?"

"No." It's where he lives.

West unlocks the passenger-side door and holds it open for me. "You okay?"

He searches my face and the sympathy screams he knows the answer. I slide into the seat and a few seconds later, he joins me. West revs the engine, blasts the heater and angles the vents at me. It's a sweet gesture. One that makes me sort of regret not dating fighters.

Thinking of Kaden and Jax and all their secrets, I kick my shoes off and curl into a tight ball in the seat. How did everything become so screwed up?

"It'll get warmer in a second." West pulls out of the parking lot and heads to my uncle's.

He assumes I'm cold. I'm always cold, but I'm trying to hold myself together. Sure, Jax and Kaden weren't happy with me, but to not tell me John would cover for us...

I'm like an injured antelope abandoned by the herd, but I guess I asked for it. Somewhere between dating Matt and leaving fighting, I became the stray left for my uncle to devour.

My uncle never touches me. He doesn't have to. His words, his voice, his glares... They have a way of clawing past my skin, becoming a toxic layer along my bones and creeping into my bloodstream. *You're worthless,* he once told me. *You're weak and you're worthless.*

I'm not. My throat tightens and I rest my temple on the window. *At least, I don't think I am.*

Too fast, West eases in front of my uncle's. Sometimes I expect a black mist to surround the house, an indication of the evil inside. Even if there was, where else would I go?

I turn to say goodbye to West when the light of the streetlamp flickers on and something shiny draws my attention from the backseat. Two gym bags rest on the floorboards. Both are open and clothes poke out of the openings. His schoolbooks and notebooks litter the backseat.

"Why didn't you tell me you've been living out of your car?"

No response, and the weight of my words crushes us both. Wind hits the SUV. A storm front is blowing in tonight, bringing ice, snow and plummeting temperatures. "You can't stay out here tonight. You're staying with me."

West

THE THOUGHT HITS ME as I'm halfway up the trellis that this is the first time I've snuck into a girl's room and oddly enough, it isn't to hook up.

I'm too heavy for the rotting wood, so I work quickly and quietly up the tangle of decaying vines. Haley left the window open and I climb in, shut it behind me, then slide off my coat. I straighten and swallow the curse when pain shoots through the top of my head. I'm too damn tall for the ceiling.

Haley was drill-sergeant strict on her orders of no noise. She threw out a lot of instructions and the wide-eyed fear on her face kept me from asking questions. The girl was serious. Very serious. With temperatures threatening to drop below zero and wind chills in the negative double digits, I wasn't in the position to play.

A lamp on the floor highlights a portion of the cramped attic. Most of the space is filled with varying sizes of cardboard boxes heaped one on top of the other. A fake Christmas tree with tinsel still hanging from the branches is shoved between the wall and a collapsed pile of mounted deer heads.

On the floor next to my feet is a blow-up mattress with

a blue daisy-printed comforter. Haley's backpack leans against the mattress and an old green chair appears to serve as her dresser as piles of her clothes are stacked neatly upon it. I catch sight of black underwear and a bra. Both have a layer of lace along the seam and damn if I don't go hard.

The door on the other side of the attic creeps open. I duck into the shadows, then reappear when Haley enters with a plate and cup in hand. She uses a foot to close the door with a snap and her hips sway as she crosses the space to reach me.

Without meeting my eyes, she rests the plateful of food and the cup on the floor next to a clock radio. "It's not much, but I've got a heater and walls."

"It's great." It's great she's obviously breaking rules to give me a place to crash.

Haley realigns the comforter and fluffs the lone pillow. "This isn't my house. It's my uncle's. We're staying here for a bit. I used to have a room, like a real room with stuff, but, you know, this is temporary..."

She continues in the same forced cheery tone as she refolds a couple of shirts and her cheeks turn red when she spots the same underwear set. Haley rattles on about temporary and how they'll have a real home again soon and after she strategically plants a pair of jeans over her private garments, I snag a finger through one of her belt loops and drag her closer.

Haley stops midsentence and her dark eyes widen. Her fingers grasp another pair of jeans she was in the process of refolding. If it weren't for the damn things, her body would be touching mine. "I don't care. I live in a car. You live in an attic. There's no judgment here."

She sags and, for a few seconds, Haley is the most pliant

she's been since I met her. I take advantage of it by letting my hands form to her hips and nudge her in my direction. She allows it, releases the jeans and drops her forehead to my shoulder. "We live with my uncle—Jax's dad. We lost our home six months ago."

My hands move up her back and I engulf her into my body. Haley answers by wrapping her arms around my waist. Through my shirt, I can sense her cold fingers, but the rest of her is warm. Extremely warm. She relaxes into me and lays her cheek against my chest.

There's a peace in this moment—a settling in my soul. Like I've been searching for home and finally found it. Tired of fighting the urge, I run my fingers through the ends of her silky hair. "It's okay." We're okay.

"It's not," she whispers. "Living here isn't okay."

We stay like that, holding each other. I think of Isaiah at the hospital the night Rachel was hurt. His two friends held him up and I wonder if that's how Haley and I would look. Am I holding her together as much as she's keeping me from falling apart?

With a sigh, Haley untangles herself from my body and sends me a shy smile. "Sorry. I don't tell people that or bring them here. It's just hard."

"I get it." And if she's sharing secrets, I can spill mine. "You're the only person who knows I've been kicked out and that I've been living in my car."

Haley's forehead wrinkles as she lifts the plate. "Really?"

Well... "Abby knows."

She sits on the floor and motions for me to join her. The moment I'm beside her, she picks up a strip of thinly cut meat, then hands the plate to me. "Here. FYI, it's deer meat."

My stomach growls. I haven't seen a decent meal that didn't include a fast-food wrapper in a week. Along with the strips of meat is a helping of mash potatoes and green beans. Who knew I'd miss vegetables? As much as my mouth waters, I can't. "This is your dinner."

"And yours," she answers. "I've been hungry before. I wouldn't wish that on people I hated, much less those I like. I would have brought more up, but my uncle is a serving size Nazi."

I consider arguing, but the hollowness of hunger wins. I'll take some, but the majority of it will be hers. The taste of deer is different than what I expected, a little like beef, but not.

Haley watches me intently and places the plate on our joined legs. "You've never had deer before, have you?"

When she reaches for another piece, I do, too. "How can you tell?"

"Your expression. It's like when I used to watch my younger sister try baby food for the first time. Your face squishes up because it's new and then it goes blank as you try to decide if you liked it or not. What do you think?"

"I'm eating it."

She giggles and the sound warms my blood. "I've eaten crap that looked like someone puked. Eating it and liking it are two different things."

I savor my second piece a little longer. "It's good. Though I'd probably enjoy it more if Bambi wasn't watching. Has that cannibalistic feel. Is your uncle gun crazy?"

"Crazy, yes, but he's not a militant gun guy or anything. He likes to hunt, and so do my dad and brother. I tried it once, but I suck at it and it's boring. Dad likes deer season and goes turkey hunting occasionally. My uncle hunts everything and he expects everyone to eat it. What's up with you and Abby?"

Nice abrupt change in subject. Haley eats half of the green beans, then passes the fork to me. Something tugs inside me, at my heart. It's strange and I like it.

"She's my sister's best friend," I say between bites. "Abby and I tolerate each other."

"You're kidding? I thought maybe she was making that up."

"I wish. Rachel's not like Abby. She's sweet and kind and..." In the hospital. Using a pay phone, I call the hospital every day and, because I'm family, they give me an update, but there's only so much I can gather between "still in the ICU" and "condition appears to be improving." My throat swells and I return the plate to Haley. "I miss her."

Haley scoops up some potatoes and grants me a reprieve. Silence with her is never uncomfortable. She picks up the cup and I watch her delicate throat move as she swallows. Haley hands it to me and her eyes hold mine as I drink. The water is cold against my mouth, but every other part of me heats.

The wind blasts the house and the window rattles. Hail begins to pelt the siding.

"Where did you park your car?" she asks.

"At the strip mall." That was one of Haley's instructions—the car couldn't be left anywhere near the house.

"Sorry." She's referring to the thousands of tiny dents I'll find on my car in the morning.

"It's fine. At least I'm not in it." The space heater clicks on and the metal wires glow red. We both stare at it, like it's a fireplace. I can almost imagine it: Haley and I at a lodge in the Smoky Mountains, relaxing after a day of skiing and snuggling near a warm fire. I could have offered her that a couple of weeks ago. Now I've got nothing more than my word.

"Why were you kicked out?" she asks.

It seemed clear when it happened. I was mad. Dad was mad. I hated him and he was wrong. Dad obviously felt the same way. But night after night, alone and cold, the replay of the fight between us distorts and the blame shifts. "Someone made fun of my sister and I hit them."

"So your family threw you out?"

"Yeah... No." I inhale, then let the air out. "My dad and I don't get along. We haven't for years. My sister was in a bad accident and she's in the hospital and he blames me."

Haley puts the plate on the floor and kneels beside me. "Were you driving?"

"No. Dad was, but I was the reason why Rachel was where she was at. She was in trouble and needed money and if it wasn't for me..." How do I explain my messed-up family? "I let Rach down. I let my whole family down."

She weaves her fingers through mine, but my hand remains limp on the floor. "Have you ever thought they let you down?"

There's a pain inside me that's worse than an ache. It's continual and I've fought it night after night. "I failed."

"I may not understand everything going on with you, but I can't imagine failing at anything that's worth being thrown out over. Whatever it is, it's not your fault."

"It is." My fingers tighten around hers, hating the truth,

hating that Haley persistently sees my weaknesses. "I promise I won't fail you."

"I know you won't." She tilts her head and the dull lamplight creates a halo around her hair. Haley is gorgeous and strong and kind and she's more than I deserve. "It's late and I've got to be up early. We should sleep."

I nod and join Haley as she stands. She flitters her hand at a pair of pajama bottoms and I turn to give her the privacy she needs. The sound of cotton shifting off her body makes me close my eyes. If I turn, would she be naked? I imagine her beautiful curves.

"Okay." She wears pink flannel bottoms and a matching tank top. Her hair falls over her nearly bare shoulders. Talk about breathtaking.

Haley crawls onto the bed and lifts the comforter up as if inviting me in.

"I can take the floor."

"Well, you are my boyfriend." The tease in her voice causes me to chuckle. The window rattles again and the gust penetrates the frame. "I don't have another blanket or pillow and the temperature will drop up here. Besides...I trust you, West."

I flip off the lamp and the space heater follows with a click, leaving us in the dark. The air mattress dips with my weight and I take my time unlacing my shoes and slipping them off.

Thank God it's not a twin mattress or we'd be on top of each other—literally. Haley lies beside me, curtain-rod straight, and I knot my hands over my stomach. At home, I slept in my boxers. Because of the past two weeks, I'm getting used to sleeping with everything on.

"Where are you going to stay tomorrow?" she asks into the darkness.

"I don't know."

Under the covers, her fingers find mine and I clutch hers with both hands. There's something intimate about lying here with Haley. Maybe it's because I've been alone, but honestly, it's her. Sleeping in my car, I've had a lot of time to think and even though the silence is new, the loneliness isn't. How is it possible to have been surrounded by people and never feel complete?

"This is a huge risk for me," she says. "If we get caught, my uncle would throw my entire family out onto the street. I wish I could offer you more than tonight."

Lacing our fingers together, I tug on her hand until she allows mc to move it up and out of the warmth of the blanket. Not knowing or understanding why, I kiss her hand. The skin is smooth and tastes sweet, just like her constant smell of flowers. My lips linger much longer than needed, and then I guide her palm back to my chest, right next to my beating heart.

Haley

MY MOUTH GOES DRY. No one has kissed me since Matt. No one kissed me before Matt. I avoid thoughts of kisses and of dating and of boyfriends and relationships, because the last time didn't work out so well. But Matt never kissed me like that, not even when I gave him my virginity.

Never did he kiss me in such a way that my insides bloomed, or in a way that I saw color in darkness, or in a way that made me want to kiss anyone back like how West kissed me. It wasn't even on the lips; it was on my hand. I inhale deeply to calm my breathing. Just wow.

"Will you tell me what happened?" West rolls, and, even in the darkness, I sense him staring at me.

I stiffen and my head pops up. "What?"

"With your family. Will you tell me how you ended up here?"

"Oh, yeah." I sink back into the mattress. For a second, I thought he was asking about me and Matt. "My dad was an engineer and my mom stayed at home. He was laid off a year ago last Christmas. There was some unemployment and some savings, but we got behind on everything and my younger sister had an emergency appendectomy and then we found out the insurance had lapsed and everything turned into a huge mess. Dad couldn't find a job. Then he got depressed and whatever dollar store job he did take, he couldn't keep. We lost everything."

My hand slams against the air mattress, the anger still as fresh as it was when I found out. I pull on my hand and West lets me go. "It's... I hate them, you know? My dad worked at that company for twenty years and, poof, they decide it's cheaper to move to Mexico."

There's silence from West. I'm probably freaking him out. I cover my face with my hands. Oh, God, that was too much information. He scratches the top of his head and asks, "Who did your dad work for?"

"It was a small factory, bought and sold many times. I think the last name they had was Sillgo."

"I'm sorry," he says, and by the tone in his voice I can tell he takes it personally.

"It's not like it's your fault. It's what people do, they buy and they sell companies not caring that souls are involved. They only see profit margins and they never think about the families. I often wonder how much my family and the other families were worth. I mean, are we different from animals on an auction block?"

The heater clicks on again and part of me wishes West never brought up my family. I'm tired of being angry. I wish he was still holding my hand, but then again, that would mean me falling for a fighter and that can't happen.

Flipping to my side, I turn away from West and try to create space between us. I told him I trusted him. I do, but I obviously shouldn't trust myself.

"Haley..." He hesitates.

Silences seem longer in darkness. I think it's because it's harder to lie when the lights are off. There's a rawness that only belongs to the night and the truth can't help but be set free.

"Yes?"

"I hate to ask, but I need to know. What are the shelters like?"

I fold into myself, absolutely crushed. My dirty secret isn't such a secret after all. "Did Jessica tell you?"

She knew because her mother had volunteered her to work the shelter's kitchen one day as a punishment for stealing money out of her purse. I can't begin to express the utter embarrassment and horror I felt the moment our eyes met over a tray of scalloped potatoes.

"Yes," he admits.

"And you were going to tell me you knew when?"

"I'm telling you now."

I bring my knees to my chest and tug the blanket to my face.

"What was it like?" he insists. "Staying there?"

"They separated us. Me, Mom and Maggie from Kaden and Dad. The three of us at the family shelter and Dad and Kaden had to go to the men's."

We had heard of family shelters and when we arrived, desperate for a place to stay, my mom broke down when they informed us men above the age of thirteen weren't allowed to stay at the family shelter.

"But we're a family," my mom begged. Tears spilled down her face and Maggie sobbed with her arms wrapped tightly around my father's leg.

"I wanted to puke, West. I wanted to find a bathroom and

puke. I mean, we had just lost our house and we had nowhere to live and now we were being separated. I was terrified. It took everything I had not to grab on to my father and beg him to make it go away."

The world became this tunnel-vision blur as my mom asked if an exception could be made and the person behind the counter kept telling her no.

Right as the tingling sensation in my head grew into a roaring, Dad grabbed me by my shoulders and looked me straight in the eye. "You've got to be strong on this one, Hays. Do you hear me? I need you. Your mother and Maggie need you. I need you to do tonight and any other night what I can't."

"You stayed strong, didn't you?" West says into the darkness and I jump, feeling a bit crazy as I wonder if I said the last part aloud. "Because you could protect your mom and sister."

"Yes." Tears well up in my eyes. I didn't cry then and I won't cry now.

I inch closer to the wall, not wanting his pity, but he parallels my movements. West doesn't touch me. Instead, his body heats my back. His hand hovers near my shoulder and, after a second, his fingers comb through my hair. The gentle pull, the tenderness of the motion almost causes the tears to cascade down my face.

"What happened?" he asks.

I swallow to clear my throat. "We were fine, but things were rough for Dad and Kaden. The population at the men's shelter was more...unstable. I found it impossible to sleep at night without knowing if Dad and Kaden were safe. My mom cried all the time and Maggie was starting to have night terrors.

"The shelter wouldn't let Kaden in a few times because he had bruises on his face from training. They thought he was violent, so Dad and Kaden slept in the car or at the gym. One night, at the shelter, some guy tried to steal their stuff and Kaden hit the guy. All of them got thrown out. Then outside the shelter, Dad and Kaden were held up by a man with a gun. The next morning my mother went to my uncle and begged for him to take us in and here we are."

My uncle demanded our car and she gave it to him. The bastard took the last thing my parents owned. If that hadn't worked, then we would have lived on the mats in the gym: waking between three and four in the morning to be gone before classes began and not returning until well after eleven at night. It would have been the same as living out of the car.

"You saw where my grandfather lives," I say. "There's barely enough room for him and until my mother begged, my uncle wouldn't take us in..."

The memories burn brightly in my brain and I wish they would fade. "I know what it's like to be scared. To wonder if anything will feel normal again. There's this hopelessness, a sadness that permeates through your pores, when you have no idea what home is or what the word means. I may be under somebody's roof, but it's not a home. I just want a home."

West edges closer and his musky scent envelops me like a welcome blanket. His lips press against my shoulder and I allow myself to melt into him.

Goose bumps rise on the back of my neck and I shouldn't, but I angle my head so more of my neck is exposed. He kissed me. I should tell West to stop, that he's crossed lines, but his lips against my skin created a feeling of togetherness, a closeness I've been longing for.

In quiet acceptance of my invitation, West skims his nose

along the sensitive skin near my hairline. "What did home feel like?" he whispers into my ear.

"Warm," I whisper back. West's fingers roam along the end of my tank and when he discovers bare skin, he splays his palm across my stomach. His heat radiates into my bloodstream.

"What else?"

"Safe, protected."

He pulls me into him, creating a shelter—one like I haven't experienced in months. I feel small against him, fragile. Like he's realized the secret I've hidden: that I'm breakable, if not already broken.

I've noticed his muscles before—his biceps, his abs—but there's a difference between seeing them and being held in them. I release a breath, one I've been holding for six months, for a year, possibly forever.

"When I had a home, I never felt alone," I whisper. His lips press against the hollow of my neck and my fingers find his. We lace our hands together and his leg rubs against mine. Every part of him connects with a part of me.

"I'm here, Haley," he says. "You're not alone."

"Do you know what my favorite part of the day is?"

West settles his head into the pillow. His mouth continues to drift against the curve of my neck; then he lazily kisses the sweet spot near my hairline. "When?"

"Those brief few seconds when I wake up and I forget and I think I'm at home."

"Until now, that's also been my favorite part of the day. Sleep, Haley. Sleep knowing tonight, I'm not letting go."

I listen to his breath, enjoy the rise and fall of his chest and focus on the gentleness of his fingers against mine. My mind wavers and I no longer exist in an attic and the darkness no longer taunts me with my fears. Sheltered in warmth and in strong arms, I sleep.

West

THE SUN DOESN'T RISE for another hour and Haley's alarm went off twenty minutes ago. She headed downstairs to get ready and I wait like a man on trial with the jury out for deliberation.

Outside, a new layer of icicles hangs from the eaves of the house. Last night was possibly one of the best nights of my life and as I slump onto the corner of the air mattress, I feel like shit.

Sillgo. I rake my hands through my hair, pulling at the roots. I swear that's one of the companies Dad bought. I don't pretend to know everything about Dad's business, but he had a crap ton of documents on his desk with that name on the letterhead last year when I got called into his office for cutting class. My father—he did this to Haley and her family....

And I'm falling for her hard.

Haley already knows that my family does well financially, but she doesn't know I'm a Young and I have to admit I like it. I like that Haley doesn't see me as a meal ticket or act weird around me because my family is the equivalent to royalty in this town.

Even if she knew I was a Young, she probably wouldn't know that the Youngs are the ones who bought Sillgo and shipped the jobs to Mexico. But keeping all this to myself? I'm lying to her. Before I drop that bomb, I need to be sure that my dad is the one that owns the company.

The door creaks open and Haley sends me a shy smile and I automatically smile back. Last night, the two of us said too much, felt too much, and I had somehow convinced myself that the moment we shared would remain that—a moment. But it didn't; the emotions between us linger and I don't know what that means.

Haley closes the door behind her and crosses the room to me. "I've got to go in a few minutes to catch the bus. John wants me there early to train."

I stand, understanding she's handing me an eviction notice. "Can I drive you?"

"No. Jax and Kaden are working out this morning, too, and I don't want them to know that you stayed here, so do you mind..." Her eyes flicker to the window.

"Got it. I'll head out."

Haley smooths the hair trailing from her ponytail. "Last night...we...uh... I don't think..."

Shit, she really is handing me an eviction notice and not just from her room.

"If we get involved," Haley continues, "and then things don't work out...it'll make what's going on between us complicated."

"Right." Complicated. "And it has nothing to do with the fact you don't date fighters?"

She shrugs. "Maybe."

I nod, getting it, yet not. Because the truth is, she's too good for me; plus she's right. We have an agreement and I need this shot at redemption. Reality—the truth of who I am would ruin us anyway, but I'm a selfish asshole.

I step into Haley's personal space and her breathing hitches when my body slides against hers. "How about we don't overthink it and just see how this plays out."

Haley licks her lips as if they're dry and stares up at me from under dark eyelashes. Damn, she's gorgeous.

Footsteps pound against the stairs and Haley pushes me into the shadows. She races across the attic and my heart beats hard at the thought of causing her trouble.

Haley grabs the door right as it opens and blocks the view of the room with her body. "Everything okay, Jax?"

"We're heading out in five," mumbles Jax.

A few more worthless words between them, then his footsteps retreat back down. I edge out of the shadows and Haley turns to me. "I'll see you later. For training."

"Don't overthink this," I tell her.

"I'll think about it."

I chuckle and Haley smiles while lowering her head, obviously figuring out the irony of her statement.

"Thanks for the place to crash, Haley."

"You're welcome." Then she disappears down the stairs.

A few hours later, I loiter down the aisle of the grocery store, buying time until Denny opens the bar and I can earn money. It's noon and I won't train with Haley until the evening. I used to love Saturdays; now I hate free time.

Abby passes my aisle, then jerks back and heads in my direction. "Come with me."

"Drug deal gone bad and you need protection?" Why else would she need me?

Her hazel eyes bore into mine. "It's Rachel. She's dying."

I don't wait on the elevator; instead I fly up the stairs. Two at a time. Three at a time. Whipping around the corners. Driving faster. Harder. The door bangs against the wall when I wrench it open. A heaviness in my chest causes my breath to come out in gasps. And it's not from the running. It's from the breaking.

My sister... She's dying.

I round the corner, swing into my sister's room and my heart tears out of my chest. "Fuck!" My hand covers my mouth as nausea climbs up my throat. I bend over to fight the dry heave. I don't win. I never win. My body convulses. "Fuck!"

It's not happening. It's not. My fingers form a fist and slam into the wall. Pain slices through my fingers, floods into my wrist. It's nothing like the pain ripping the skin from my bones. "Fuck!"

"What are you doing?" It's a nurse. Smaller than me. Blue scrubs. I glance up and the entire hallway watches.

I point at the empty room. "Rachel..."

"Is down the hall." She continues to talk, but I don't give a fuck. I run. Past her. Past others. Past the stares. Past the ICU. Past the waiting rooms. Everything on the periphery blurs. Looking, searching, and then I catch blond hair in a bed and I pause.

Blue eyes. A smile. "West!"

My heart is so out of control I've forgotten how to breathe.

I stumble into the room, gulping in ragged breaths. "Rachel?"

My sister is up. She's propped by a million pillows, but she's up. And pale. Rachel was a small thing to begin with, but she's lost weight. Scratches fragment her face like a web of broken glass. Her legs are bulky under the blanket.

"Oh, my God, you're here!" Her smile grows and that smile has always been infectious, but instead of grinning back like I normally do, I scrub a hand over my face and sag against the wall. She's alive. Air rushes out of my mouth and I inhale again. She's alive.

A huge bouquet of balloons enters the room first. Three of them bump against my head and block my view of Rachel. I bop them out of the way and throw a dagger glare at Abby as she emerges on the other side of the helium nightmare.

"You said she was dying," I whisper from behind the wall of bobbing plastic.

Abby rolls her eyes. "Of boredom. It's not like there's anything interesting to do around here. Someone tries to bring in a puppy and they get all pissed. It's not my fault it pooped."

I grab the string of balloons to keep her from going any farther. "You lied to me."

That evil smile spreads on her face. "Shocking. What are you going to do, spank me?"

I release the balloons and she blows me a mock kiss. That girl is fucking psychotic.

"What's with the balloons?" Rachel asks.

Abby places them on the nightstand next to Rachel's bed and collapses into a chair. "We're being festive."

"Festive?"

"Like a party, fiesta, you're-in-a-normal-room celebration. I need to get you out more."

My family isn't here. Not a single one. Isaiah, Rachel's asshole boyfriend, sits in a chair parked tight to her bed radiating badass: tattoos, earrings, hair shaved close to his head. Through the tangles of tubes and wires hooked to Rachel's body, they hold hands.

A muscle in my jaw twitches. Ethan and I found out over a month ago that she was seeing this guy behind my family's back. She ditched school to see him. She ended up in debt to a street hustler because of him. She fought with me and Ethan over this guy when she's never fought with us before. He's why her best friend is a drug dealer. It was through him that Abby and Rachel were introduced.

Isaiah's bad news and he's the reason why she's here. He took her to the dragway. She thinks she loves him, but she doesn't. "Want to get the fuck off my sister?"

"West!" Rachel chastises.

With his hand still entwined with hers, the son of a bitch barely looks at me. "It's going to take a lot more than you to pull me away from her."

Rachel's head whips in his direction. "Isaiah!"

The balloons thump together. Abby flicks her finger against them until we stare at her. "Festive, people. Urinating on the floor like a pair of dogs does not make for a good party. Well...at least one Rachel should be attending."

Isaiah mumbles something that makes Rachel giggle and Abby starts into some nonsense story. Their voices shift into background noise as I focus on my sister. There's less than a year between us. She has a twin, but I secretly feel like their triplet. My earliest memories are of Rachel, of her laughing and sometimes of her being sick.

She suffers from panic attacks. Bad ones. It makes her shy and it's also made her a target, which is where I come in. From elementary school 'til now, I've never had a problem connecting my fist to the jaw of any guy that's tortured my sister and most girls know better than to talk shit about her when I'm around. They'd find themselves having to hang with a new group of people.

My parents don't understand Rachel or any of their children, me included. They don't know all I've done to protect her since we were small, but they do know about the one time I failed.

Rachel shifts, but her legs don't move. There's a buzzing between my muscles and my skin. Like a trapped fly that needs to be surgically removed. Isaiah stands, his mouth moving, but I hear no words. He helps Rachel readjust and once again her legs remain motionless.

As he reclaims his seat, her face pales out and Isaiah and Abby lapse into silence.

"Talk to me." Isaiah possesses a calm that causes me to hate him more.

Rachel sucks in air as if she were in labor. She white-knuckles the railing on her bed and my fingers twitch with the need to tear something apart...to make someone pay for her pain.

My sister's heart-monitor beeps increase. Isaiah pries her fingers off the railing and takes her hands in his. "Abby, go get a nurse. Breathe, Rachel. Give me the pain. I can take it."

Abby stands and I step back.

"West?" Rachel asks through a breath. "Are you okay?"

The hurt in her voice knifes through me. I meet her eyes and shake my head as my sight flickers to her legs again. I've got to get out of here before I implode.

A hand lands on my shoulder and I snap my head to the side to take in Dad. I expect him to yell, asking what the hell I'm doing here. Instead he keeps his hand on my shoulder while he mumbles words like "daughter, pain and medication" to a passing nurse.

He urges me into the hallway and I follow. The breath is knocked out of me when my mother collides into my body. Her hands capture my face, then slide down to my shoulders while her glassy eyes survey me. "Are you okay?"

"I'm fine." From over her shoulder, I try to judge my father's reaction, but his poker face gives nothing away.

"Why did you leave?" Mom shakes me. "What on earth would make you leave?"

"Miriam," Dad says softly. "Let's take this into the family waiting room."

Mom observes me like I'm a ghost. "You left. You know I don't handle leaving well."

Fuck, I hurt my mom. "I'm sorry."

"Miriam," urges my father.

As if I'm five, Mom slips her hand into mine and grasps it as if her life or mine depends on the contact. Together, we head down the hallway.

"I didn't know that you were gone until yesterday." She speaks in a quiet voice reserved for conversation during a church service.

"Dad knew," I respond while attempting not to flinch. She didn't notice for two weeks.

"I know." There's a rare bite in her tone. "And I'm dealing with that."

Mom hesitates and I shove my hands in my pockets as I pause with her. Two weeks. Mom didn't notice I was gone for two weeks.

"I've been all but living here at the hospital and when I was at home briefly and didn't see you, I just assumed that you were out with friends. Making new ones at your new school and keeping up with old ones. We all knew you weren't coping well with Rachel being here, so I thought... you were...dealing with this in your own way. I..." Mom drops off. "You've always been so independent that I never stopped to think..."

That's the point: when it comes to me and my brothers, Mom never stops to think.

"Your brothers knew," she says, but before she can continue Dad calls for us to join him.

In the empty waiting room, Dad pours three cups of coffee and hands one to Mom, then me, and gestures for us to sit. The rich aroma drifts in the air. It's surreal being here with them and crazier that the atmosphere fits a business negotiation more than a family reunion.

"How's Rachel?" After all, that's the reason I'm here. "She didn't move her legs."

In his pressed white shirt, starched black pants and black tie, Dad pulls a seat around, creating a triangle as he faces me and Mom. "I'm flying a new specialist in this week. We should know more soon."

I hold the hot drink between both of my hands and think of Haley's cold fingers. Rachel would like Haley. That's the type of friend she should have instead of drug dealer Abby and punk Isaiah. "Isaiah's bad news."

Dad nods.

"So's the girl," I say with a twinge of guilt. Abby's been helpful, but she's a drug dealer and regardless of what she's done for me, Rachel's safety is the priority. "They're both trouble."

He nods again.

Even now, our father is worthless. "Then why the hell are they in there?"

Dad sips the coffee and leans forward. "How do I tell her no when she's in pain?"

"I guess the same way you told me to get the fuck out of your house."

Dad and Mom glance at each other. Mom angles her body toward me and Dad inspects his coffee. "I was angry and said things I shouldn't have. I didn't think you would listen."

Anger crashes through my bloodstream like a tidal wave. "You didn't think I would listen when I was informed I was trash and you didn't want to see me again?"

The man honestly has the nerve to meet my glare. "It's not like you've listened to anything I've had to say for years. Why would I have thought you'd start now?"

I start to rise and my mother slams a hand on my knee. "You're not leaving." She directs herself at Dad and yells, "He's not leaving. I have buried one child and I have come close to burying another. I will not have stupid pride costing me a third."

"Mrs. Young?" A nurse pops her head into the waiting room. "The dietary nurse would like to speak with you."

Mom is charity-ball smiles as she tells the nurse she'll be

right there, but the moment she's gone, Mom releases an expression that could rival Abby's any day of the week as her cold eyes work over Dad. "He's coming home. Fix this. Now."

She stands and smooths out her gray pants and checks the cuffs of her sweater before resting a hand on my cheek. "I love you and I want you home. There is no other option."

Her tone tells me everything else: I disappointed her. She's hurt, angry, sad. That once again I failed. But mostly, she loves me.

I nod, unable to say or do anything else. Her heels click against the faux wooden floor and fade the farther she goes down the hallway. I place the coffee on the end table. "What now?"

"I don't understand you, West."

No shit. He doesn't understand anyone in our family.

Dad eyes the floor. "Why were you in the Timberland neighborhood?"

"How did you know?"

"The GPS in your car. I had one installed in all your cars when you got your licenses. I've been trailing you the entire time. You didn't actually think I would just let you walk away? Jesus, West, give me some credit. You are my son."

My eyes jump to his at the word *son* and a dangerous glimmer of hope flickers inside me. Is it possible he regrets throwing me out? But if that's the case, how come he never showed? How come he didn't ask me to return home?

"Your mom tried to call you," he says.

"My cell died."

"I figured." He scratches his jaw. "You haven't answered me. Why were you in the Timberland neighborhood? Why not with one of your friends or my parents?"

"Dump's in that side of town. Just going where you told me I belonged." I'm pushing him. We've been tearing at each other for so long we have no idea how to stop. At least I don't.

"Why, West?" he presses. "I need to know, why there?"

"Why does it matter?" Does Dad know Mom's been going to that bar?

"Answer the question. Why do you make everything difficult?"

"If I do, it's because I learned from the best."

"Just answer the question." His voice rises with his anger.

I stay there because it's close to Haley, but I don't want her anywhere near a conversation with Dad. "It doesn't matter why."

His fist clenches. "My father once told me you can love your children, but you don't have to like them. I never understood him. I thought his words were cold and callous, but then I realized I don't always like you."

Fuck it. I stand, memorizing what I'll tell Mom because I refuse to live under his thumb. Not after holding Haley last night. Not after figuring out my life's jacked up. I'll take the damn shelter. Living in the damned car wasn't as bad as listening to this.

"I was in the Timberland neighborhood because I got a job," I say. "That pays. Tell Mom I'll call her once a week."

The surprise registering in his eyes causes me to smirk. He honestly thought I'd return home with my balls cut off and he sure as hell didn't think I'd be willing to walk again.

"A job?" he asks.

"Yeah. I don't need you anymore."

The moment I step for the door he says, "Your mother's been through hell. Are you willing to put her through more?"

Fuck him for using guilt. “No, I’m not.”

“Then come home for her.”

A knife straight to my gut. Come home for Mom, not for him because he could give two shits about me. Regardless of how much I tell myself I don’t care what he thinks of me, I do. I’ll never hear him say he wants me or that he’s proud of me, yet whenever he opens his mouth, I hope for the words.

“What are your terms?” I won’t fool myself that this is anything more than a business negotiation. Haley’s words echo in my mind: Are we different from animals on an auction block?

“I’ll give you until graduation to clean up your act, your grades, your life, your attitude, and if you do, I’ll let you stay in my house. Otherwise, I want you out this summer. Who knows, maybe you can find a way to make me proud.”

“Yeah,” I mutter as I leave. “You never know.”

Haley

IT'S EIGHT AT NIGHT and West is late.

I untangle the last jump rope and loop it neatly with the others on the hook on the wall. Two million explanations as to why he hasn't shown yet have deluged my mind, but it's the reasons that cause my heart to ache that stick around to torture me. Nibbling on my bottom lip, I scan the gym to find something else to fiddle with to pass the time.

"Prince Charming chip a nail and decide the sport wasn't for him?" My grandfather turns off the light to his office. "Tells you a lot about a man's integrity for him to show late."

"I'm sure he has a good reason."

"Humph."

"He'll show." He will. Though doubt tiptoes in my mind like a linebacker through tulips. After the intense night we shared together, I sort of freaked and blew him off this morning. My eyes drift over to the clock again. As much as each tick of the second hand causes a painful sinking of my heart, in theory, isn't this what I wanted? West to walk away?

The door opens, cold air rushes into the gym and the groan of a tractor trailer rumbling down into a lower gear from the freeway enters alongside West. My muscles actually relax at the sight of him, like I stepped into a hot bath. Until this moment, I hadn't realized how much I had come to depend on him keeping his word.

With his baseball cap on backward, heavy jacket and gym bag thrown over his shoulder, West smiles when he spots me. My answering grin actually makes me feel like I'm floating, but then I notice his blue eyes. There's no light shining from them. Just a bland dimness and the high within me plummets.

John mumbles something to West as he leaves. West nods his head and says, "Will do."

I sit on the mat and roll out my yellow wraps, pretending I'm not dying to know why he's not on time. "What did John say?"

"He told me to make sure you got home safely."

"Hmm." I have nothing intelligible to say to that.

West plops down beside me, unzips his bag and pulls out his set of wraps. "Sorry I'm late."

"Why were you?" Hey, he brought it up.

He smirks with a muffled snort. "You don't let anything slide, do you?"

"Answer the question." Because while I hate to admit it, John's right. Being late is an integrity issue and it's one I plan on nipping in the bud now.

West pulls his cap off and scratches the top of his head. His blond hair sticks out in a hot crazy mess. He shoves his hat into the bag, then stares at the ground. "I saw my parents."

My eyes flash to him, but he doesn't meet my gaze. "Where? How? What happened?"

"At the hospital. I visited my sister and they were there."

He pauses and I have no idea if I should fill the silent gap. Time passes. Enough I'm uncomfortable. "Is she okay?"

"Yes. No. I don't know." He shakes his head and the shadow of pain darkening his face physically hurts me. "She's out of the ICU and in a normal room, but she looks like hell and her legs..."

Because both of his hands are untangling his wraps with the fury of a sailor untying knots on lines during a storm, I place my hand on his thigh, on the spot above his knee. "I'm sorry."

West drops his wraps and places his hand over mine. He doesn't respond. He doesn't squeeze my hand. He just holds on.

The wall-length mirror reflects us—me and West. My mother read a story to me once where a girl walked through a looking glass and discovered that the world on the other side was the opposite of our reality. I can't help but wonder if the opposite Haley and West are happy or if they're drowning in worse circumstances.

With a sigh, West pats my hand and stands, taking his wraps with him. He leans his back against the mirror and weaves the fabric over his wrists and knuckles. Following his lead, I do the same, but because I've been doing this years longer than West, I finish before him.

I stand and try to ask as casually as I can, "What happened with your parents?"

West pulls hard on the material over his knuckles, then wraps the leftover material around and around the length of his wrist. "They told me to come home."

Home. The word ricochets within me like a bullet. "That's... that's...great."

But it doesn't feel great and it feels worse knowing I should be happy for him. West won't have to sleep in his car anymore, he won't have to face the shelter and he'll be fed. More than fed. For a guy who drives an Escalade and wears brand-name clothes on his body, I'm sure he'll be full of all sorts of fancy food. He'll have a warm bed with high-thread-count sheets and he'll probably have every creature comfort that I could only dream about.

Somehow, this loss of a home was the bond between us and it made me feel less alone. Now, with him returning, I feel more isolated than I did to begin with.

I pull on my ponytail. Brat. He's going home and I'm throwing a pity party. What's important is that West will be safe. Even though I don't understand what's going on between us, I want West to be safe.

"That's a good thing," I repeat.

"Yeah," he says and the heaviness in his tone indicates that returning home isn't his dream come true.

I replay the conversation. West only said that they asked him to go home; he never said he agreed. "Are you going home?"

West slams the Velcro into place and rests his hands on his hips. "Yeah."

"Is there a problem? I mean, is there something else going on there? Is it not safe?"

"No, it's safe." His face contorts. "But the problems... They're still there."

He's going home and I'm not. He'll be safe and I'll still live in the presence of evil.

I think about my home. The place that Maggie drew with the stick figures. Nothing was perfect there. My mom and dad would have the occasional fight. Kaden and I would get on each other's nerves. The hot water heater suffered from manic depression and would either be really hot or really cold. But for all the problems that surrounded me at that brick-and-mortar address, they were nothing like what I face now.

"I'd give anything to go home," I whisper.

West's head jerks up and the apology on his face is apparent, but I wave him away as I grab two jump ropes off the hook. "Three minutes jumping rope. Twenty-five push-ups. Then twenty-five squats. We'll repeat the cycle five times."

"Haley," he says and I only offer him the rope.

He reaches over, but instead of taking the rope from me, he glides his fingers onto my wrist and swipes his thumb over my pulse point. His caress sends fire straight to my toes, but there's a part of me, no matter how pathetic, that resents him. I yank my hand away. He's going home and I'm not.

"As I said this morning." I shove the rope into his hands. "We need to keep this simple. No complications. Now let's get moving. You've got a fight in less than two months."

Without allowing a response from him, I turn up the volume on the stereo and let Eminem drown out West's voice and my emotions.

West

I'VE NEVER SLAPPED A WOMAN, but the pain that slashed across Haley's face earlier this evening when I told her I was going home... I felt like I had. My entire body flinches. I hurt Haley tonight. Like I always do, I acted and didn't think.

I'm on autopilot as I race down the rolling hills of our sprawling gated community. Mansions dot the land every quarter to half mile. Some properties, like my parents', are practically their own zip code.

Turning, I spot our house and my foot falls off the gas. The house is larger. Somehow even bigger than I remember and I remembered it huge. The towering white columns and white marble stairs are illuminated against the night sky.

It's massive and for the first time in my life a pit forms in my stomach as I ease into the driveway. It's not just massive. It's excessive.

I bypass the attached garage used only by my parents and whip around the back to the structure built for me and my siblings to park our cars. On instinct, I reach for the garage opener attached to my sun visor and a sickening nausea spreads through me as the door opens. Where three cars should be sitting, there's only one. Ethan's car looks lonely in the spot to the left. I park the Escalade near the right wall and close my eyes, unable to glance at the empty middle.

That's where Rachel's Mustang should be. In fact, that's where she would be if she'd never been in that accident. The entire garage rings loudly with memories.

At midnight on a Saturday, Mom would be asleep and Rachel would have escaped out the kitchen door to slip in here to work on the cars. She'd be knee-deep in grease and would have sent me a smile the moment I rolled in next to her.

Rougher than I mean to, I push the door open and slam it behind me, doing my best to ignore what's not there...what I want to be there.

The house is quiet. Dark. With the flick of a switch the lights of the kitchen spring to life. The air from the heater rolls out of the overhead vent and the sound only presses against the silence.

A loaf of bread sits on the counter. A bowlful of apples on the island. The pantry door's cracked open and a dozen or more boxes of assorted foods pack the shelves. My stomach growls and my hand lowers to stop it. I've eaten two meals a day for two weeks. Sometimes one. The meal always small. And here...we throw food out.

"Welcome home." Ethan leans against the doorframe leading to the foyer.

"Miss me?" I ask casually. I didn't hear shit from him or any of my brothers.

"I texted and called," he says. Sometimes it's hard to look Ethan in the eye. He's too much the spitting image of Dad. "You didn't answer."

It's a convenient excuse that's probably true. "My phone died."

Ethan nods like that explains everything away. "I was worried about you."

I pause, knowing that means I left Ethan here alone...by himself...worrying not only over our sister, over our mother's sanity, but also over me. "I'm sorry."

"You're a goddamned asshole for leaving. You know that, right?"

"Just an asshole." I drop my bag, readjust the hat turned backward on my head and open the fridge. "Let's leave God out of this one."

Ethan chuckles and the thick tension between us eases.

Ham. Cheese. Milk. Eggs. Leftover spaghetti. My stomach cramps at the thought of eating it all. I grab a chicken leg out of a bowl and start devouring it while swiping a Tupperware container of potato salad. With the chicken in my mouth, I flip off the top of the potato salad, fish a fork out of the drawer, then spike it into the container.

"Hungry?" Ethan asks.

Famished, and my response is scooping a forkful of the salad into my mouth. I sit at the island and Ethan joins me. "Where the hell have you been?"

I shrug and mumble between bites, "Living in my car."

"Sounds cozy."

"Fucking Four Seasons."

I continue to eat and Ethan fills me in on the status of our household, which is the equivalent of saying nothing changed while I was away. Rachel's still in the hospital. Mom's still a basket case. Dad's back at work.

Speaking of work. "Can I ask you something?"

"Shoot," says Ethan.

"Did Dad's company buy Sillgo?"

"Sleep in your car for two weeks and now you're coming home a corporate tycoon?"

"Not even close. I remember the paperwork around but don't remember if the sale went through. Was it Dad's company that bought it?"

Ethan shrugs. "Dad mentioned something over dinner last year that there were problems with the deal and that someone else might buy it, but I never cared enough to ask what happened. Why?"

"Curious." Maybe I don't have anything to be worried about. Maybe Dad isn't responsible for the destruction of Haley's family. Even though it's a shred of hope, it falls short within me.

"Why?" asks Ethan.

"I told you, curious."

"No, why did you decide to live in your car?"

My gut tightens—too much food too fast. I slow up. "Dad threw me out."

"Not that why," he says. "Why didn't you crash with Jack? Hell, Gavin's already living there. One more of us there wasn't going to hurt."

I move a potato chunk in the container, searching for an answer. Why the fuck didn't I go to Jack's with my tail between my legs, begging for a place to stay? I slam the top back on the container, toss it in the fridge and throw the chicken bone into the garbage. "I didn't need someone else in my face reminding me how I failed."

"You didn't fail," says Ethan.

"If that's true, then tell me why I'm here and Rachel's not."

"Because this is your home!"

Home. According to Haley, home meant a safe, warm place to fall. I scan the room as if I've never been here before. It's cold. It's unwelcoming. Dad was right the night he threw me out. I've never felt like I belonged. "It doesn't seem right. I shouldn't be here without Rachel."

I never should have come home. All this luxury, all the excess— I don't deserve it, especially since Rachel isn't enjoying a damn thing lying in that hospital.

Ethan lowers his head, and, when he doesn't say anything, I head into the foyer, then up the winding staircase. My footsteps echo as I climb the steps two at a time.

Rachel's in the hospital with no comfort on the horizon. Haley offered her soul to me when she thought I had nothing and I hurt her by callously dropping that I get to go home when Haley has no escape from her nightmare. I've hurt the two most important girls in my life.

At the top of the stairs, my foot angles to the right, toward my bedroom, but my head turns in the direction of the gravitational pull of Rachel's room. How many nights have I ended up in there?

All the nights that I felt the guilt creeping up for the sins I had committed. All the nights of being in the middle of a crowded party and suddenly struck by the sensation that I was out of place. All those nights I knocked on Rachel's door, walked in and found relief in my sister's easy acceptance.

And there's the punch in the throat...Rachel always accepted me for who I was...the bad and the downright ugly... and, in my mind, I repaid the debt by protecting her. I stood up for her. I took on fights for her. I made sure she knew she was never alone.

Standing in her doorway, I can't find the courage to turn on her light. I strain to listen...to hear her soft voice tell me to come in...to tell me that she loves me...to tell me that it's all going to be okay.

I hear a voice...a whisper in my mind. The voice doesn't belong to Rachel, but to Haley, and it only reflects the loneliness inside me: *"I'd give anything to go home."*

My fingers grip the edges of the doorframe. "Me, too, Haley. Me, too."

Haley

TALK ABOUT A NIGHTMARE come true. I fidget in the seat of our school's social worker's office, feeling a little like I've been chained to the stake. Government officials give me the creeps. They have the power to destroy the pathetic remnants of my family by forcing separation.

With her blond hair slicked back into a bun, Mrs. Collins sweeps in and closes the door behind her. "Sorry for the delay. I had...well...a thing." She smiles widely on the word *thing.* Do they get excited when they ruin families? Is it their occupational benefit?

"That's okay." I nibble on a fingernail as my mind searches for the reason for this meeting. It can't be illegal for us to reside with my uncle, or is there a limit to the number of people that can live under one roof?

Her cluttered office reminds me of my grandfather's except hers has a woman's touch with pink polka-dotted curtains and cutesy frames with cutesy sayings on the wall. No wonder the two of them got along.

"Did your grandfather find a volunteer for the gym?" she asks.

"Sort of." John was searching for a volunteer so he didn't have to pay anyone to wash the mats and bags, but because West can't pay gym fees, the two of us have been cleaning after we train on Friday and Saturday nights.

West and I have been training together for three weeks and I've been impressed. He does possess raw talent and he's a quick study, but when I start to contemplate how much he needs to learn to go against Conner, I grow nauseous. There's no way it can be done.

As if I'm a prisoner searching for an escape, I survey the room again. West, West, West, West. I can't stop thinking about him. His family asked him to return home and he did, but I can tell by the hurt in his eyes that things aren't fixed.

Thinking of West causes me to sigh and Mrs. Collins squishes her mouth to the side. She lets it slide as she clicks her mouse and her computer springs to life. "If you don't mind, I need to send a quick email."

"Okay." West and I have never discussed the night he stayed with me. It's like it never happened and sometimes I wonder if I dreamed it. But the memory of his lips hot against my skin, of his hand on my stomach– My breathing hitches. It definitely happened.

Actually, West did mention that night the first day we trained together after he moved home. He only said, "It'll be simple. For now. Until I know you're ready for more."

For now... Ready for more. My heart flutters. No. No fluttering is allowed. West and I work better together as simple. Not complicated, but the thought of his mouth near mine....

Stop it! Focus on something. Anything.

With her fingers still moving, Mrs. Collins glances at me

from the corner of her eye. "Is there something you'd like to talk about?"

"No." Not at all.

She finishes. "You seem a bit nervous. I promise—I'm completely harmless. Though I have one ex-student who claims I can't drive, but no need to worry. We won't be leaving the office." She winks and grins like we're friends.

Guess I've been as twitchy as a rat in a meth lab.

"I pulled you out of class because one of your teachers told me you're trying to apply for the Longworth scholarship?"

I nod. Is it a crime to ask for teacher recommendations?

"It only pays for books," she says.

"I know."

Mrs. Collins opens a file, slips out a piece of paper and hands it to me. "This is the Evans scholarship. It'll pay for four years of tuition for a person majoring in kinesiology."

I sit straighter and handle the paper as if it's gold. "A full ride?"

"Yes." She brightens and I wait for rainbows to appear behind her and blue birds to land on her shoulder. Mrs. Collins definitely is too happy of a person or maybe I've been down for so long that I've forgotten what happiness is.

She loses a bit of the rainbow as she folds her hands on her desk and settles into her serious face. "But it's an extremely competitive scholarship and this isn't a simple essay and transcript situation. Students from across the nation will be sending in videos showing why they would be the best candidate."

I scan the three pages while dread and hope battle for dominion. Oh, my God, I actually have a shot at winning this, but I'll have to find some footage of my old fights and videotape me training West. I can show his training from beginning to end. And this is where the dread eats the hope. He's going to need to spar, which means I will, too.

"Haley?" Mrs. Collins says. "Are you okay? You look a little pale."

"I'm fine." I run a hand through my hair. "Thank you for this. I can't tell you how much this means to me."

The smile on her face is so sincere that I relax in my chair. Maybe she's not out to destroy me.

"Your grandfather speaks highly of you. He's very proud of your accomplishments in his gym and at school."

The relaxing turns to sagging. Great—guilt. One parent-teacher conference and they're best friends for life. I pretend to read the application while she taps a pen against the desk. "When I first began social work, I was hired as a case worker in a homeless shelter."

My eyes shoot to hers and she steadily holds my gaze. She knows. Dear God, she knows.

"It's not easy to be without a home. It's confusing and scary and if it's that way for an adult, it has to be twice as terrifying for a teenager. I know you're no longer there, but I also know things are still floating. Unfortunately, the state isn't allowing me to take you on as a client, but because I work in this school you can talk to me anytime and my door will always be open."

"How do you know?"

"Your parents didn't sign up for the parent-teacher conference and then I couldn't reach them by phone and the letter was returned, so I found your grandfather. Haley, he really does care about you."

Care about me? I crave to crush his throat. He told *her* our family's private business. Why didn't he lie? Why didn't he say it was a mistake? Why didn't he tell her that we have a home?

I stand, wanting to leave, but not sure if I'm allowed. The scholarship application crackles in my hand. "Are you taking me away from my family?" The words slip out and I immediately wish I could take them back.

She shakes her head. "Regardless of what you believe, the state isn't interested in destroying you or your family, and, from what I understand, you're living in a safe environment. We're here to help, Haley. I'm here to help."

At the word *safe,* a bubble of hysterical laughter wells up inside me and bursts out of my mouth. The sound is definitely out of place and instead of making me feel better the laughter twists an already too-tight spring. Dizzy with the crazy emotions, I stumble for the door. Right as I touch the knob, I sober up and freeze.

Not that I'm complaining. "What do you mean you aren't allowed to take me on?"

She leans back in her seat and the quirky set of her lips and eyes reminds me of how Jax stares at his opponent before entering the ring—as if she's trying to figure out my next move. "My job at this school is to help those who the state believes need a little extra push in the right direction. Regardless of how I tried to convince the powers that be, you don't fit the requirements for my program."

I slump against the wall in relief. Oh, thank God, I can stop worrying about CPS arriving at the door and dragging me and Maggie away. "That's good."

"I guess," she says. "But my gut says you need to talk to someone, and I have a sinking feeling once you walk out, I'll never see you again."

A twinge of guilt rocks me because every word out of her mouth is absolutely true: I do need to talk to somebody. I want to open my mouth and vomit out all that has happened, to take the darkness and give it to somebody else. I want the nastiness and decay out of my body, out of my soul, and maybe if I expelled it in words, then maybe, just maybe, the rot would be gone.

But it's like my windpipe has collapsed and my voice box was taken hostage. To tell her about my life—losing my home, what happened with Matt—that would mean exposing myself.

I trusted Matt and that didn't work out, and I was stupid enough to talk to West and he hasn't acknowledged a word I said since it happened.

"Thanks," I say to her while turning the knob. "But I'm fine."

West

IN THE CAFETERIA, Haley drops into the seat across from me and immediately pops a French fry into her mouth. "I'm considering tying your hands to your head. Maybe that way you'll keep your guard up."

I chuckle. Haley isn't a "Hi" and useless conversation type of girl. She's direct, to the point, not capable of bullshit, and I'm falling harder for her every day. I'm completely fucked because she's damned insistent that we keep things "simple." "I'm keeping my guard up."

"What. Ever."

I've been waiting for some sort of confirmation that she might see us as more than friends. More than coach and student. I slather a French fry in the ketchup, then push my tray away, wondering how much Haley's had to eat all week. "Want to go to dinner tonight? Before we work out? My treat."

She shakes her head without looking at me. "I've got to work before we go to the gym. You know, bills and all." Weak smile on her part.

"What time do you get off? I'll pick you up and get you to the gym."

Haley scowls at her plate. She hates accepting help, but she mumbles, "Seven."

For the first time since Rachel's accident, I spot Isaiah at school. He walks in the side door pure night of the living dead—pale, dark circles under his eyes, the whole dead-on-his-feet montage. I stare at him and he assesses me like I'm scum.

I glance away first. He's been standing by my sister, holding her hand, making her happy when I can't. That deserves some respect.

Haley's gaze flickers between the two of us. "You know him?"

"He's Rachel's boyfriend."

Both of Haley's eyebrows rise. "No kidding."

"Wish I was."

"How'd that happen?"

I shrug because I only know what others have told me. "They met drag racing."

"Wow. Adrenaline rushes must be a family thing."

I chuckle, never having thought of it that way. "Do you know him?"

"He lives in the same neighborhood as me, but I don't know anything more than rumors and we both know that rumors typically aren't true."

We drop the subject of Isaiah and move on to fight strategy. When a scuffle in the corner draws her attention, I toss my remaining French fries onto her plate. I hold my breath when she turns back and breathe again when she doesn't appear to notice. If I got caught doing that shit, she'd kick my ass.

"So I have this thing," she says.

Interesting. "A thing?"

"Yeah, a thing." Haley rummages through her backpack and withdraws a stapled-together pack of papers. "It's a scholarship. A full ride and I really need it."

She pauses and I feel like shit.

"Anyway," she continues. "I have to submit a video and I'd like to tape me training you and some of your workouts to show why I'm a good candidate for the scholarship."

I wiggle my fingers and she places the paperwork in my hands. Haley sucks in her bottom lip as she watches me from across the lunch table. "I'll understand if you say no."

Like I could say no to that face. "You didn't have to create a big deal to get a video of me with my shirt off. I'd take it off if you simply asked."

"Bwha..." It's a short, sexy sound that accompanies an open mouth and red cheeks. I love it when she blushes. Since our night together, I've cut back on the sexual innuendos, but if she's going to draw attention to her lips, then all bets are off.

I flip through the scholarship paperwork and the guilt that's been killing me for the past three weeks mushrooms. With Haley's current family situation, she needs this money and my father may be to blame. I'm home. She's not. My life continues on as normal. She's still living the nightmare. "Whatever you need, I'm your guy."

Those gorgeous dark eyes brighten and her fork clangs against the tray when she drops it. "For real?"

"Yeah." The least I can do is let her videotape our sessions.

Becoming the exact opposite of the hard-core drill instructor busting my ass at the gym, Haley claps her hands. Last night she continually screamed at me to keep up my guard as I ducked and weaved while pounding out a three-one kick combination on a bag.

She pushes her chair back and springs to my side of the table, wrapping both arms around my neck. "Thank you!"

Her hair falls forward, caressing my face, and her intoxicating scent envelops me. The memories of holding her all night flash in my mind. Never in my life have I felt such belonging and peace as when I lay awake watching her sleep.

My arms slide along her spine and, as I go to stand, she shifts back and kisses my cheek. Soft lips caress my skin and my fist clutches a strand of her hair. My heart beats hard and I turn my head, hoping to catch her mouth with mine. Our gazes meet and lust darkens her eyes.

Haley stiffens, like her mind caught up to her actions. She practically leaps away from me and presses a hand against her lips. "I didn't mean that."

I couldn't stop the grin if someone paid me a million dollars because, yeah, she did mean it. Haley, whether she's willing to admit it or not, wants more.

"Thank you," she says as she continues to step back. "For helping me with the scholarship, I mean. Um... As in I'll see you tonight."

In a blur, she pivots and is out of the lunchroom with Marissa by her side. Damn, no girl has ever left me speechless or with this type of smile on my face. Then again, no girl has ever caused me to collapse on the floor in a pool of sweat.

I pick up her tray, then mine, dumping the garbage and placing the trays on the rack. Watch out, Haley. Simple just went out the window.

Haley

I'M LATE WALKING OUT the door of the pizzeria and West will be more than happy to throw it in my face after I gave him a hard time a few weeks back. The cold wind slaps my cheeks and there's a sense of comfort when West backs his SUV out of his spot and eases his car next to me.

I open the door, slide in and smile. The heater is on full force and every single vent is pointed in my direction. Sitting in the driver's side like he's done nothing amazing, West sure does make it difficult to not fall.

"How was work?" he asks.

"Slow." Which means that I didn't make the tips I was hoping for.

West reaches to the backseat and I quickly lift my freezing hands to the heater. Yeah, they're cold again and, yes, I'm trying to hide it from West.

"Hey, Haley," he says.

I drop my hands. "Yeah?"

A handful of pink roses appear in front of me. Air catches in my throat and I lose the ability to speak.

The roses shake in front of me and I snap out of my shock long enough to take them. “Thank you.”

West presses on the gas and turns onto the main road. “This is what I was thinking. We work out, you process this and then later we’ll discuss how we’ll handle moving things from simple to complicated.”

“A little full of yourself, aren’t you?” Yet I say it as I inhale the sweet scent of the largest rose.

“You like guys that show with flowers, remember?”

I laugh and West smiles at the sound. How on earth did he remember?

“Okay,” I say. “We’ll work out first and then maybe we’ll discuss complicated.”

“Not maybe.”

“Maybe. And, West?”

He glances over at me.

“There’s no way I’m going easy on you because of this.”

West

"KEEP YOUR GUARD UP!" Haley shouts. We've been at it for two hours and my arms move as if they've got hundred-pound weights attached to them. "You've got to step into me when you go for the punch and stop stepping back. This isn't self-defense class, which means there are no points for running."

We're in the ring and Haley raises the pads she wears on her arms to her face as we continue the combination. I inhale deeply and throw a double jab, a cross, and my shin meets the pads down by her thigh as she instantly lowers them. With each punch, a breath exhales out of my mouth and Haley marks each hit with a grunt in order to keep me in tempo.

On beat with the music pounding out from the speakers, Haley's feet switch—a crazy crisscross she's yet to teach me. She rounds on me and she expects me to match her pace. "Come on—you've got to move. Keep it parallel otherwise I'll crack you in your head or slam you onto the floor."

She makes those types of remarks often, but since we've

been training, Haley's never taken a swing. I believe she could toss me to the floor, and I wonder why she hasn't.

I wipe the sweat from my forehead, but another wave floods from my scalp onto my face. My hands are hot in my gloves and my biceps beg for a rest.

"One more time all the way through," she demands. I shoot her a glare and swear the sadist smiles. "You've got it in you. Dig deep and find it. Same combo."

Same combo meaning she wants me to put it all together. Jesus Christ, I can barely catch my breath never mind remember the entire combination.

Her legs switch again, but this time I move with her and I like the exotic slant of her mouth. "Good boy, now, if you'd keep those guards up, you might still be standing in the ring."

Fuck. My gloves slam to my temples and Haley holds the pads up. I throw a jab and Haley ducks out of the way. "Who are you fighting, your grandma? Come on! Throw it like you mean it. Throw it like you're actually trying to hit. What the hell, West. I'm not playing here."

As if she injected anger into my veins through a sharp needle, energy rushes to my muscles and the double jab strikes, followed by a cross, a left hook to the head, another cross, a reload and then a low kick to the legs.

Haley drops the pads. "You need to step toward me and punch at the same time. Stepping first is going to tip your hand. He'll back out of the way or worse, read the punch and take advantage of your dropped guard and plug you upside the head."

I rest an arm against the cage for support. I lost the shirt an hour ago and my shorts stick tight, becoming an additional layer of skin. "Why so many damn jabs? My cross is more powerful."

"Your jab is your most important hit. It's your closest punch and it's not going to throw you off balance."

Maybe because I'm too damn tired to think, I shake my head to let her know I'm not getting it. She gestures with her head for me to straighten and when I do, she wiggles her fingers at my cross. I rub my arm against my forehead. "What about the pads?"

I've never thrown a punch straight at Haley before and the thought twists my stomach.

"You're not going to hit me," she says. "If you want, mock throw it and you'll still get the point."

My pretend girlfriend is cocky. "All right." I widen my stance and "throw" a cross. Haley's arm snaps out and deflects the hit and in a second her cross is frozen at my chin.

"You're leaning," she says.

I am. My body tilted with her deflection. Damn.

"If my cross struck you, you would have been off balance and I'd have the upper hand. All hits are good, West, especially if they connect, but a jab is your bread and butter."

Haley picks up my wrists and shifts them near my temples. "You need to keep your guard up at all times. Drop it for a second and you'll get the hell pounded out of you."

"I know." I start to lower it, but she keeps a firm grip on my wrist.

"No." Haley becomes the only thing I see in the small gap between my gloves. "I need it to be ingrained, not a useless tidbit of information to be discarded as trash."

With her delicate fingers holding on to me, we stay that

way, silent, as the music continues to play. After a second, she says, "What are you scared of?"

Failing her like I've failed Rachel. Getting my ass handed to me in the cage. Being kicked out for good after graduation. I go to drop my wrists, but Haley keeps them in place.

"Tell me," she says.

"Nothing."

"No, you keep messing with your guard. If you do hold it up, you're not keeping it tight near your temples. You move it out— Why?"

I stare at Haley through the small crack. "I can't see anything else."

"Can you see me?"

"Yes." The top of her cleavage is exposed by her tank top and small pieces of her hair fall from her ponytail. She's an erotic mess that my hands itch to roam.

"Then what's the problem?"

"I feel blinded like this." With my guards by my temples, it obstructs my peripheral vision. "I can't see what's going on."

"You're seeing everything you need to see. You're not getting jumped by a gang—you're fighting one person. For three rounds of three minutes each, you get to ignore everything else in the world and focus on the one thing in front of you. Think of it as a gift. How many other times in your life will you be allowed that type of focus?"

Haley—that's the gift in front of me. A girl who's trusted me with her secrets and has protected me from the elements. Possibly one of the few people who likes me for me and not because of my last name.

She steps closer and her fingers glide against my skin. Haley turns my wrist toward my face and my gloves block her out. "If you're overpowered, a tightly held guard can be your best defense."

She repositions my wrist back out and consumes my line of sight again. "And when you're ready to attack, you simply open up and take the swing."

When our eyes meet, her breathing hitches. If I kissed Haley, would she kiss me back? Desire slams into me as hard as it did when I wrapped my arms around her three weeks ago and allowed my lips to brush against her skin. In the darkness, she became an angel bent on saving my soul. She angled her neck and I knew I could kiss her without an ounce of hesitation on her part, but I didn't because Haley doesn't know who I am—she doesn't know I'm a Young.

"See." Haley mock swings and nudges her fist against my glove. "You're protected. I can't hurt you."

Yes, she can. Haley can learn who I am, who my family is, and hate me. I can let her down and, once again, be a failure. Haley has no idea how much I need this last shot at redemption and how much I need her.

She drops her hands and I lower my arms to my sides.

"But here's the important part." She waggles her eyebrows. "You're never going to win a fight unless you take a chance and actually engage."

"What about you?" I ask.

Haley's eyes jump to mine. "What about me?"

"When are you going to engage?"

Her forehead wrinkles and her dark eyes harden. She's sexy as hell pissed. "What is that supposed to mean?"

It must mean that I don't mind angering her enough that she'll cut off my balls. It means that when I give her roses, she tells me maybe we'll talk. "You keep telling me what I need to do, then, instead of going for a blow, you show me shadow boxing."

Haley lifts her chin, almost daring me to challenge her again. "Do you have a problem with how I'm training you?"

"No, but it doesn't take a head shrink to figure out that you're holding back."

She leans into me just like the night we first met. "I am not holding back."

"Yeah, you are. We've been together day in and day out for over a month, and holding back is what you do. With people at school, your family, in training, with denying what you feel when you're with me."

"Feel with you? Me and you—we are friends."

"We crossed beyond friends the night we spent in your room and you know that. Fuck, Haley, there isn't a moment that we haven't been into each other and I'm not the only one in the room aware of it."

Haley shakes her head and waves a hand in the air. "Keep your mind where it needs to be, West. In the gym."

"Hey, you're the one who kissed me in the cafeteria today."

"Bwha." A large puff of air leaves her mouth and blood leaves her face. "I was thanking you. For helping me. Not coming on to you."

I ease closer to her. "You want me. Admit it, Haley. You. Want. Me. You wanted me the first night we met, you wanted me the night in your room and you want me right now, but you've buried it deep. It popped out today when you least expected it and now you're mad because I'm calling you out."

Haley goes blank, and, like the time we confronted Matt and Conner in the cafeteria, she goes into the frozen shock. I'm used to girls who tell me everything that crosses their minds...everything. Including the things that should be self-censored, but Haley keeps every thought locked away and maybe she doesn't do it on purpose. Maybe that's her way of keeping up her guard.

I glance down at the gloves on my hand. "I step when I punch."

Haley's dark eyes jump to mine and the hope, the gratitude swimming in them for changing the subject almost brings me to my knees. "No, you don't."

"And I throw more jabs than crosses."

A smile starts to play on her lips. "That definitely never happens."

"And I am the king of switching up between going on the defensive and offensive."

Like I knew she would, Haley laughs loudly. The spark that has returned to her eyes is nearly impossible to resist.

"If I throw a jab..." I lift my left arm and mock throw the punch.

Haley giggles as she absently blocks. Instantaneously, I step and "toss" a cross at her and she takes a mirroring step back as she blocks it again.

"The boy can be taught," she says through another laugh.

"Been known to happen with me and monkeys on occasion." With each halfhearted throw, I step in, and in smooth, rhythmic movements, Haley continues to counter, keeping a safe distance between us. She stays close enough to block me, close enough to go on the offensive if she chooses, but far enough away I can't touch and that's what I want... I crave to touch Haley.

Without warning, I slide into her and back her into the cage. Haley's breath leaves her body in a rush and those dark eyes focus on me. Her hands rest on my chest and her fingers flutter, as if not sure whether to push or to explore. With my gloves against the fence on either side of her head, I lean into her and draw my nose up her jawline to her ear. Her body is warm and firm and she smells so damn good.

"What do I do if I get pushed against the cage?" I whisper into her ear and close my eyes when a tremor runs through her body.

Her fingernails tease my chest as her hands drift to my sides. "You hit here." She squeezes my right side and electricity blazes out of her touch and into my system. "And here." Then squeezes the other.

I nip at her ear and Haley's hands tighten against my skin. Images of her underneath me appear in my mind and I want the fantasy to become reality. "What do I do if he takes me to the floor?"

I watch her throat as she swallows. She has beautiful skin—soft, smooth. The gloves on my hands turn into a nuisance as the urge to touch her evolves into an obsession.

"Grappling," she says a little breathlessly.

Now those are lessons I look forward to. "When will we start that?"

"Soon."

I part my mouth and kiss her neck. Haley dips her head to the side, allowing me more access, and through these damn shorts, she has to feel how much I want her.

"We shouldn't do this," she whispers, yet her hands wander to my back and trace my spine. "I won't date another fighter."

"Then walk away." I trail a line of kisses along her collarbone, up her throat, then pause, staring straight into her eyes, giving her the chance to end this now. "I won't lie. I want this, Haley. I want you."

Hot, shallow breaths leave her mouth and brush against my lips. The vein at her neck pulses as her fingers perform this light dance on the small of my back that drives me insane. I'm a bastard if I do this. She doesn't know I'm a Young or that my father may have destroyed her life.

"West." She says my name as a question, as an answer. Damn me, it was an invitation.

My name. That was my name on her lips. Fuck everything else. Haley knows the real me and for once in my life I'm going to know what it's like to kiss a girl who means something.

"This doesn't mean anything," Haley whispers as she reaches up and pulls at the Velcro of my glove.

"Yes, it does." I bring my arms to my sides and the instant the gloves fall to the floor, my hands latch on to that beautiful body. "Tell me, Haley. Please tell me it does because this means something to me."

Her forehead wrinkles and her eyes are moist as if it's physically painful for her to nod and breathe out the words. "It does... It means something."

Need begs for the physical fast, but Haley isn't one of the girls I duck into hallways with. She's more, and a shiver runs through me. I lower my lips to hers and, with the first taste, I moan. Her lips are sweet, soft...perfect. She exhales, a contented sigh, and my body melts into hers. The metal fencing behind her crackles with our weight.

As if flawlessly synchronized, our mouths move in the same rhythm. Lips drawing in, hands learning curves and muscles, our breaths coming out at faster rates. And when Haley knots her hands in my hair, self-control ruptures.

My arms become steel bands around her waist and I lift her so she fits perfectly to me. Haley latches her arms around my neck and joins me as the kiss races past innocent and into heated—bordering on out of control.

Her neck beckons to me again and the most beautiful sound escapes from her when I give in to the temptation. The spinning in my head spirals toward delirium as Haley shifts her legs. One thigh moves and the other one follows to wrap around my hips. I relish her warm weight pressing into my body. Heat surges through my bloodstream and my fingers dig into her skin.

Then the entire gym starts to shake. Haley drops her legs and I shove her onto the floor, my heart racing and my body covering hers. Metal screeches against metal and I glance over my shoulder.

Haley pushes at me, her nonverbal cue to let her go, but intent on keeping her safe, I ignore her request. The overhead heating unit releases an earsplitting shriek as the fan fights for one more rotation. Another bang vibrates the metal frame that holds the punching bags, and the entire unit shudders, then completely stops.

From beneath me, Haley whispers a curse. "John's going to be pissed."

Haley

WE LEFT JOHN WHILE HE WAS in the middle of a particularly eloquent cursing rant. The moment I knocked on his camper door and told him the heater blew, he forgot my existence. Sneaking out seemed like the best course of action.

West and I haven't said anything to each other since the kiss, which means this car ride is officially awkward. Resting my head against the back of the leather seat, I watch the night as we roll by. What the hell was I thinking?

When he backed me against the cage and nipped my ear… I close my eyes. I can still feel the heat of his lips on my neck and what drives me stick-a-knife-in-my-eye insane is as much as I hate myself for kissing West, my body is screaming for a repeat performance.

Stupid body. Stupid, stupid traitorous body.

West eases his car in front of my uncle's and the pathetic part of me wants to dart into the house without acknowledging him. I rub my forehead, covering my eyes. Oh, crap, I'm embarrassed. How can I look at him again? We're not even dating and I freaking all but molested him. And that brings up a ton of issues because I don't want to date him... He's a fighter.

"Haley," West says. "About tonight—"

"I don't hook up." I peek at him and whatever he had to say seems to have escaped him as he stares at me with a slack mouth. It's like someone pushed fast-forward on the remote and my thoughts are skipping and racing. "I don't know who that was, but it wasn't me. I mean, have you done this before?"

West runs a hand over his face. "Yeah. It's what I do. Fuck that. It's what I've done, but that's not what was happening between us."

Oh, crap, I've digressed into an Octagon Bunny, bouncing from one fighter to the next. Soon I'll be in a bikini, announcing the next round. Just when I think I can't go lower...

"Haley, I swear to God that wasn't a hookup. I told you that this means something to me. That you mean something to me."

He's saying the right words and a small voice in the back of my mind tells me to listen, but the crazy portion is winning. "Because that's what you tell girls when you drop them off. You don't look at them and say 'I used you.' You lie and say it meant something! I watch MTV!"

"You watch...what?" He shakes his head. "Don't care. What happened between us—"

"Stop it." There's an ache near my heart and my hand claws at my chest. I can't think and I can't draw in a deep breath and I kissed West and I loved kissing him and he makes me laugh and he's a fighter and I like him.

I like him. I more than like him and it terrifies me that I have feelings for West Young. "I can't do this."

"Do what?" West tosses his arms out as if he's mad or frustrated or I don't know what, because I don't trust my reactions on anything anymore.

"Hook up or date a fighter or like or love or anything. I don't want anyone close again." Sheer terror widens my eyes with the rawness of the words. "Have you ever seen the paint sets that have multiple colors?" I've boarded the bus for crazy and somehow I can't get off.

West

"HAVE YOU EVER SEEN THE PAINT sets that have multiple colors?" Haley rushes out the words as if they'll erase what she said before them.

"Yes," I say slowly, trying to buy us both time. How the hell did this get all screwed up? One moment we were kissing; then it blew up in my face. This is karma biting me in the ass for every girl I said pretty things to in order to satisfy myself.

The leather seat squeaks when she faces me. At least she's not running for the safety of the house. "When you open up the set, it's beautiful, right? Each color is perfect and if you're careful, you can paint and paint and paint as long as you take the time to rinse off the color you just used into the water, maybe use a towel and dry the brush before moving on."

She shyly glances away. The tension building between us causes me to shift. I may not understand it, but Haley's attempting to explain something. I nod, willing her to continue. "Paint, brushes, water. I'm keeping up."

Haley inhales. "Sometimes you get too excited and dip

the brush into the paint and the colors get mixed up. All of a sudden I'm no longer yellow and you're no longer blue."

"We become green," I finish for her.

Haley lifts her head and she's raw, completely open. Too open, almost bleeding. "I dated Matt and I sort of became gray and I'm over being gray and I'm not ready to be green. I'd like to try yellow again for a while."

Haley needs time, and I can give her that. Maybe I'll find a way to get my own shit together and figure out how to tell her about my family by then.

She sucks in air as if she swallowed too much water and I throw out a life preserver. "When will you teach me grappling? You said it would be soon."

Haley blinks and what was meant to help her causes her to drop her head back and then forward into her hands. "Damn."

"What?"

"Grappling's out of my league. I'm a kickboxer, not a wrestler," she mumbles through her fingers. "I'm going to fail you."

Yeah, Haley needs time, but I'm not ready to give her space. I pull on her hands and, when she refuses to look at me, I place my fingers under her chin and force her eyes to mine. They're glassy and in pain and I don't want any of that over me. "There's no possible way you can fail me. The fact that you believe in me enough to train me...to let me help you with your scholarship... You are not capable of failing." That's my arena.

She tilts her head and I brush my thumb against her cheek. Haley closes her eyes as if she enjoys my touch and when she reopens them, she struggles to smile. "This sort of feels like green."

"This is me being blue. Don't worry—you're still yellow."

Her eyes laugh for a brief second and I burn the sight into my memory. I withdraw my hand and Haley opens the passenger-side door, steps out and closes it behind her.

I roll down the passenger-side window. "Haley."

She raises her eyebrows.

I lean my shoulder against my door and grip the steering wheel. "You need time, that's fine, but we're no longer pretend dating. Not sure what it is, but we're more than that. Thought it'd be simpler if I made that clear."

With lines bunched around her eyes, she nods once but won't look at me. She turns for the house, takes two steps, then rushes back to the car. Haley swings the door open, grabs the roses, then blushes when our eyes meet. "You're right. I like guys that bring me flowers, but just so you know I am so still yellow. Okay?"

"Okay."

Haley slams the door shut and bolts for the house. I pull away feeling like a man who's flying.

Haley

THE DOOR TO THE BATHROOM RATTLES, followed by three knocks. “Occupied!”

I undo the strings of my red half apron and wash my hands in the sink. The scent of pizza and pasta smothers me and my hair is horrifically frizzed from waltzing in and out of the steamy kitchen. This is not how I want to look or smell when I hop into West’s SUV. I comb my fingers through my hair and it does nothing to tame the wild monstrosity.

The door rattles again. There’s one bathroom each for men and women and someone obviously has to pee. The outfit isn’t so bad: my best jeans and a dark blue button-down shirt, but the hair…the lack of makeup…the fact I’m pathetic enough to care…

It’s not like West and I won’t be sweating, sweltering messes in an hour. But still, the past couple of weeks with West have been…well…nice. Last Friday night, West backed me up against the cage, he kissed me, made my body come alive, and now…he’s letting me be yellow.

I barely recognize the silly grin sliding across my lips.

Somehow West is reducing me to giggles and grins and butterflies. There's hope for me being a girly-girl yet.

With a deep breath, I leave the bathroom and ignore the long line of angry-faced women doing the I-gotta-pee dance. It's not my fault they sucked down gallons of Diet Coke. It's Friday and the restaurant is packed.

I walk out into the cool late March night and glance around the parking lot for West's SUV. My sigh materializes into a white mist and quickly evaporates. He's not here. I'm a few minutes early, but my tables paid and were out the door. If I stayed inside, my boss would have stuck me with more tables and then I would have been trapped for a minimum of thirty minutes, maybe longer.

To my right, a girl's shrill laughter echoes from the back of the building. A crowd lingers there and my stomach sinks. It's been months since they've hung out here—honestly since our breakup—but I have no doubt the back-alley loiterers are Matt and his crew.

I pivot on my heels, willing to take my chances on another table, when Matt emerges from the shadows.

West

I FINISHED THE LAST ITEM on my thin to-do list for Denny a half hour ago, but for the fourth time today, I sweep the stockroom. Guess with moving home, I could have quit, but I've stayed on as Denny's monkey for multiple reasons.

One, I need the money in case Dad changes his mind and throws me out again. Two, oddly enough, I like what I do here. I fix things. I'm useful. For once in my life I actually do something right. But the last reason, the most important reason, deals with Mom.

It's the fourth Friday of the month and six-fifty in the evening. Rachel had surgery last Friday and Mom was chained to her side. If life goes on as normal, I'm betting Mom pushed back the visit by a week, and all I want for my birthday is to discover why she visits.

My cell buzzes and I ignore it. My mother whispered a happy birthday to me this morning from the door of my bedroom when she left at five to see Rachel. Dad mumbled something as he left for work that sounded like an acknowledgment of my existence while I ate breakfast in the kitchen. My brothers and friends have texted their birthday wishes and the continuing texts have been from my closer friends—friends from my old life.

Most of the messages say the same things. *Where have you been? There's a party tomorrow night. You've gotta come. It's been too long.* Weeks ago, I would have, but with the fight looming a month away, my nights belong to Haley.

The door to the bar opens and Denny sticks in his head. Johnny Cash sings about a ring of fire and a woman's drunk laughter drifts with him into the room. "Have you become learning impaired or crippled since I last saw you?"

I continue to sweep the nonexistent dirt. "Got a point?"

"Yeah, you should have been done a half hour ago."

Our eyes meet and my heart beats once. Denny has never pushed me out. He has to be in on the secret. "I get paid by the hour."

The Vin Diesel stunt double shakes his head and widens the door. "He's not coming out so I guess you're going in."

My hands freeze on the broom handle and for a short second I expect my mother. Instead, Abby walks in with a Hostess CupCake on a plate and a single lit candle.

"Don't get delusional and think this means I like you," says Abby. "Because I don't. I'm being blackmailed and I don't appreciate it. I do the blackmailing, not the other way around."

Denny leans against the open door with his arms crossed over his chest and a smirk planted on his face. "You have the rest of the night off with full pay. Get the hell out of my bar."

"How did you know?" I ask.

Denny gestures toward Abby and Abby holds up a cell. "Rachel."

Rachel. The two of them might as well have used razor

blades against my soul. I take the phone and a moment before saying, "Hey."

"Happy birthday!" I can hear Rachel's smile. "Did Abby give you a piece of cake?"

I survey the prepackaged glob of sugar. "And a candle."

"Good. Make a wish and blow it out."

With an owner of a run-down bar and a drug dealer watching me, I stare at the burning candle and wish for Rachel's health, for her happiness and for her forgiveness. I release a breath and watch as smoke rises into the air. "It's done, Rach."

"I love you," she says.

Me, too. "Thanks." I'm not sure how to react when my eyes burn.

"Abby says you have a girlfriend."

Abby rocks her eyebrows when I glare at her. I sigh, not wanting to lie to Rachel, but the truth is, I like Haley. A lot. As much as I'm dying to see her naked, I'm just as content hanging out with her fully clothed. There's a strange tugging inside me and I try not to focus on it because that chaos scares the shit out of me. "Yeah."

"I want to meet her."

"Maybe." I consider adding on "freakasaurus." I used to call Rachel that, but I lost the right to tease her months ago.

"I've got to go. A nurse walked in. Happy birthday again." She ends the call and I hand the cell to Abby.

In a whirl, Abby turns on Denny. "If you give me twenty dollars, I'll make sure he goes out the back."

With a look used by marine interrogators, Denny assesses Abby. "You better." He yanks a twenty out of his pocket, gives it to her, then leaves, slamming the door shut behind him.

"I'm not leaving," I say.

"Didn't expect you to think you would, but you will. And FYI—when you freak later because you rush out of here like your penis is on fire and like your eyes have been sprayed with Mace, know I stayed to watch your mom's back. Then you will, once again, owe me. Since you're in good graces with Daddy, I'm thinking cash this time. In increments of lots of zeros."

"Don't hold your breath because I'm staying."

Abby cocks her head. "Aren't you supposed to be meeting with Haley soon?"

"You do stalk me, don't you?"

"Don't flatter yourself. Everyone at school knows you and Matt will be going at it in April and that Haley's all Mr. Miyagi Karate Kid to your Daniel-*san*. Has she taught you wax on and wax off yet? If so, can you teach me? I'm totally ready to kick some ass."

"Conner and I will be going at it, not me and Matt," I correct her, then ignore everything else.

There's a gleam in her eye I don't like. "Whatever you say. Check it out—I'm feeling generous today, so are you ready for your present?"

I hold out a hand, waiting for her worst.

"Okay, this isn't your present, but it's important. Matt figured out your weakness."

This ought to be funny since the only weakness I have at the moment is Rachel and no one at school besides Jessica and Abby knows I'm a trust fund Young. "What does he think it is?"

"Haley," she says in a "duh." "A blind man could see you falling for the girl with your long ass stares and tongue hanging out of your mouth. Matt and his crew are chilling at Haley's place of employment tonight and his birthday gift to you is to rattle her."

The broom snaps against the floor as I drop it. "How do you know this?"

"I told you already—there isn't much that happens in my territory that I don't know."

I step for the back door and Abby grabs me. "I haven't given you your birthday present."

"I don't give a fuck about a present." I need to get to Haley.

Abby clings to me and stares straight into my eyes, not caring I'll haul her ass with me in order to protect my girl. "It's your mom," she says in a rush. "She's not having an affair. She comes here to see her brother."

Haley

MATT HAS A GIRL draped on his arm. She's a genuine bikini-wearing, sign-strutting Octagon Bunny from the fights. Blond hair, big breasts and very much a girly-girl. Her laughter fades the moment she spots me.

The three of us eye each other and I hate the seasickness of seeing him with someone else. Once upon a time, regardless of what happened between us at the end, I cared for Matt. I briefly close my eyes and suck in a deep breath. I lost my virginity to him and now he's *doing* that. I'm consumed with the need to take a hot shower and scrub my skin off.

Because I don't live under a rock, I've heard the rumors of how he's done it with every girl backward, sideways and forward since we broke up. Matt terrifies me and I hate him, but as she winds her arm tighter around his, nausea causes me to turn away and head to the front of the building. When I'm far enough away, I drop to the curb.

"You broke up with me." With his hands shoved in his pockets, Matt's a good six feet away and the Octagon Bunny is nowhere in sight.

"Stay where you are." Because the thought of him any closer causes my hands to tremble.

I consider standing, but my knees have that weak feeling. I'm in public. If Matt comes near me, I can scream and he'll walk away. I wrap my arms around my body, to keep myself warm, to keep myself intact. With each rock, I repeat the mantra: I'm safe.

Matt sinks to his portion of the curb, maintaining the make-believe restraining order. "I saw the pain on your face when you looked at her. I don't like hurting you."

My mind warps and separates, then crashes together. I bend over as I laugh. It's manic and maddening and I try to shove the hysterical giggles back in as I slap a hand over my mouth, but they won't stop. I shed blood because of him. I lost my family over him. He has done more than hurt me; he's destroyed me.

The laughter runs dry and I'm suddenly overwhelmed with the need to cry. "She doesn't bother me."

It's the truth. The nausea—it's not from seeing him with her. It's from hating myself. How could I ever have loved somebody like him? How could I have given him something as sacred as my virginity?

"She bothered you," he insists. "I fucked up with us. I know it and I'm sorry. If you give us another chance, I swear, I'll be different."

I shake my head before he finishes. "I'm with West." Even if it is pretend or not pretend or this strange middle ground purgatory, I'm with him and I've never spoken sweeter words.

There's silence between us and two cars drive by.

"Your story isn't panning out, Haley. If it was true, then someone would have seen West leave the store and go after

Conner that night, or would have known that you and West were a couple. I've asked around. No one knows him except for a small-time weed dealer. Dating a pothead isn't your style. You need to end this lie and stop protecting Jax and Kaden."

The muscles in the back of my neck tighten. Fabulous—West smokes pot, but to be honest, what do I know about him? We've told each other things, in the middle of the night, in a raw moment where lying felt impossible. We admitted truths you don't say aloud or to other people, but we've never actually learned anything about the other.

Maybe that's why I'm attracted to West. Maybe that's why I like the game we play. He's anonymous and so am I. "If I'm lying, then so is your brother. Are you ready to admit Conner is capable of not telling the truth?"

Matt's head snaps in my direction and I have to fight to keep from scrambling away from him. We're in public. I'm safe. Please let me be safe.

"Aren't you tired of arguing over the same old shit?" Matt rubs his anger off his face with the balls of his hands and tries again. "Break up with West and I'll call this whole thing off. No fight and no going after Jax and Kaden. Consider this a blank slate."

"I never told them," I whisper. "About what happened between me and you."

"I know." His shoulders roll forward. "Figured you didn't when they didn't show at my front door."

"They would have come after you and you would have retaliated." And it never would have stopped. They'd go after him and he'd jump them in return. It would have been a bloody, endless cycle. I glance at him, begging him to give me this. To know that all the sacrifices I've made haven't been in vain.

Matt pops his neck to the side. "I am who I am, Haley. I can't change that."

A brief moment of justification and I hold on to it tight. I did have a right to be afraid for Kaden and Jax.

I process Matt's offer and I'm terrified to inhale. This is what I've been hoping for. "That's it? Break up with West and no repercussions? No one jumps West or Jax or Kaden or anyone over what happened with Conner? Bygones are bygones?"

"You've got my word."

I'm almost dizzy. Is it possible one thing is going right in my life? But then a horrid pain slashes through my chest—this means giving up West, walking away from West. Everything within me plummets. Oh, God, I don't just have feelings for West. I've fallen for him.

Matt watches me intently. Too intently. There's more to this deal—a deal I should accept, but don't think that I can. "For real, that's it?"

Matt rests his arms on his knees and joins his hands together. "Come back to me. I liked who I was when I was with you. I liked how you made me feel—like I was somebody worth caring about. If you try and it doesn't work, then it doesn't work, but at least try. It'll be different—I'll be different—I swear."

West

I SLAM THE SUV'S DOOR and stalk to where Haley sits on the curb, but I keep my eyes glued on Matt. There's a pulsating in my blood that begs for a fight. He's done something to her. She's shocked out, pale as a ghost and her fucking hands are trembling.

"Is there a problem here?"

Matt surveys me with boredom from his spot on the curb. "Only if you make something of it. Are you man enough or are you going to continue to hide behind Haley?"

"I'm game." A smile stretches across my face. "I've got the balls, what about you?"

I've been dying for this moment since my first day of school. To hell with the fight next month, I'm ready to finish this. I stride past Haley and a tug on my wrist pulls me to a stop. I glance down and she grabs on to me with both hands. "Not here. Not now."

"Haley," I say, utterly exasperated and pissed. I've never had anyone doubt my strength as much as she has. I'm over her assumption that I'm weak and done with her thinking

I don't care enough to lay down my life for her. "I can take him."

"This is where I work." Her fingers shake against my skin and her eyes are hazy, as if waking from a dream. The urge is to kick his ass and it's hard as hell to listen to what she's telling me...that I could cost Haley her job.

"Fuck." I crouch beside her and place my hand on her frozen cheek. Being a selfish bastard, the connection isn't for her. It's to keep me from losing control and smashing my fist into that asshole's face. Jesus, why is she always so damn cold? "Are you okay?"

Haley nods and her eyes automatically dart back to Matt. The bastard stays seated on the other end of the curb and watches us; specifically, he focuses on my hand on her face.

"What's it like to be pussy whipped?" he asks.

The muscles in my body jerk, but instead of removing his balls with my foot, I slide my thumb against Haley's skin and kiss her forehead. She sags into me and I kiss her one more time before glaring at Matt. *That's right, she's not your property. Haley chooses me.* "Sorry I'm late. You ready to go?"

"Yes."

I enfold her into the shelter of my body the moment she stands.

"Consider it, Haley," Matt says as if I'm not here. "I'm not expecting an answer tonight. You and I could save a lot of people from a lot of heartache. It's your choice."

"Yes," she says slowly. "It always seems to be my choice."

I hate the tilt of her head, the faraway glaze in her eyes, all of it screaming that whatever he said to her has her thinking, analyzing, and I don't want one word from that bastard circling in Haley's mind. "Let's go."

I guide her to the SUV, tuck Haley safely inside, then join her when I climb into the driver's side. With the car on, I blast the heater and tear out of the parking lot, craving to put as much distance between Haley and Matt as possible.

With her head lolling against the headrest, Haley stares out the window, looking as lost as I felt after Abby's "present" to me. Abby's got to be lying again because Mom's parents are dead and she has no siblings. Abby's confession from weeks ago echoes in my brain: Have you ever found out something you wished you hadn't?

I peek at Haley out of the corner of my eye. I asked her once if she still had feelings for Matt, but I've never asked for details on their relationship. In fact, I've never asked her about anything and the kick in the nuts is the realization that Haley hasn't asked anything about me, either.

All this time I thought I had coasted at school and with Haley in regard to my past, but it's easy to coast when no one gives a shit.

Lights and cars become blurs as I speed down the road and head for the highway. Haley doesn't seem to notice when we pass the turn for the gym and I fucking hate the sensation that only her body is present because her soul is still at that damn curb.

"What the hell is going on with you?" I ask. "With Matt?"

As usual, she's silent, choosing to be locked away inside her brain—thinking, analyzing, not sharing, not talking. Haley plots and she plans, but she hardly ever discusses. "Say something!"

"Take a right."

"What?"

Haley peers toward the oncoming street and her fingers

hover near the window like she's a child frightened to touch a broken piece of glass. "Take a right."

Muttering a curse under my breath, I hang the right and we enter a neighborhood. My headlights hit one of those signs with a kid chasing a ball informing me to slow my ass down. I do and idle along at twenty-five as I wait for her further instructions.

Most of the homes are two-story brick houses that flaunt amateur landscaping. It's better than her uncle's but lower scale than where I live. Overall it's nice, pleasant and very suburban.

"Stop." There's a longing in her voice that pricks at my chest. Haley presses her hand against the window; condensation forms an outline along her fingers. "That's my house."

I shift the car into Park. It's a lot like the others: two stories, a chimney, but this one has a front porch, blue shutters, rosebushes and a for sale sign with the word *sold*.

"Mom would force Kaden and me home from the gym because she wanted us to eat dinner together. On Sundays, we'd order pizza and watch a movie in the living room. And that's my bedroom. The corner one with two windows. There was always a lot of light in my room. I miss that—having a lot of light."

Having no idea how to steal her pain, I gently stroke her hair one lock at a time. Rachel asked if I had a girlfriend—if I was Haley's boyfriend. If I was, I would know how to make her better. I would have the words or the actions, but I only own silence.

I've never felt so much over a girl before. The emotions are unknown and confusing.

"I had a yellow lab," she says. "She slept in my room and

died a little over a year ago. Did you know..." And Haley stops and her breathing hitches. It's like being slashed open with a knife. "Did you know she's buried in the backyard?"

"No." Because I wouldn't know, but somehow it feels like I should. I think of me and Ethan at ten and nine dressed in our best suits to help Rachel bury her hamster in a shoebox in the backyard. It was my idea to hold the service when Mom was locked in her room, crying over a long-lost daughter, and Dad, once again, was busy with business.

Rachel sobbed and sobbed as Ethan held her. I dug the hole and I repacked the dirt. There is nothing I wouldn't do for my brother and sister.

"Do you know what I miss the most?" Haley whispers.

"What?" I ask, terrified of her answer.

"The feeling that no matter what happened or what I did, there was someplace safe to fall." Haley looks at me and my insides wither at the moisture in her eyes. "What's it like to go home? I fantasized about it and I'm sure you did, too. What was it like?"

I'm in love with you. I'm in love with you and I don't know how to make you better. I'm in love with you and I shouldn't be. I'm in love with you and once you figure out who I am, you're not going to love me. I'm in love with you and I seem to fuck up the ones who love me back.

"Do you want to go there?" Each uttered word is cut against my heart. Once she sees where I live, once she knows I'm a Young, whatever it is going on between us will be done.

Haley nods and as I U-turn it out of her old neighborhood, I lace my fingers with hers. I hold on to her and what kills me and warms me at the exact same time is how desperately she clutches me. Like the two of us are drowning and the only way to stay afloat is to never let go. I've got minutes left with Haley and I want the memory of her skin touching mine burned into my brain for eternity.

Haley

MY FINGERS TRACE THE SPLIT of my lips as I stare at the sprawling house from the passenger side of West's SUV. I'm not sure if my fingers are there to keep the words in or to help them out. I think of those sci-fi movies where a character sets his gun to stun. I'm stunned. This—speechless, frozen, numb—this is what being "stunned" feels like.

"There's a five-car garage around back." West's keys clank together as he circles them on his finger. "I can show you that if you'd like or we can head inside."

My chest moves as I inhale, then exhale. Never would have I imagined that this is where he lives. "It's a mansion."

"It is."

"They threw you out?" Aren't people with money supposed to be better than...well...everyone? The way his hands clutch his keys tells me how terribly wrong I am.

"Yeah." A pause. "I'm not like you—I'm not a good person. My dad had valid reasons for throwing me out. In fact, it's amazing he didn't throw my ass out sooner."

West focuses on his lap and I have to force myself out of my stupor. Words. Words would be good right about now. But I don't know what to say. He lives in a mansion.

But mansion or not, I hate the pain on his face. I bite my bottom lip and reach out to West, just like he reached out to me in the parking lot with Matt a few feet away. I rest my fingers on his shoulder and brush my thumb against the material of his shirt.

When he doesn't respond, my heart flutters at the thought of becoming bold. My mouth dries out and I swallow. I'm not a bold person, not when it comes to intimacy—to touching. I inch closer, and, like I've dreamed of a thousand times, I caress the hair on his head, sliding my fingers into the golden-blond strands, then retucking it behind his ear.

West finally allows his deep blue eyes to meet mine.

"Will you take me inside?" I ask. "Will you show me your home?"

We're out of the car in a heartbeat, and, with our fingers knotted tightly together, West leads me up the white stone stairs as if he's terrified I'll change my mind or he'll change his. He shoves the floor-to-ceiling door open and the air rushes out of my lungs.

And I thought it looked huge on the outside. "My God."

West shuts the door and my eyes dart about, trying to comprehend the splendor. I stand on a marble floor and in front of me is a sprawling staircase that winds with immeasurable grace. The ceiling appears to soar to the heavens and at the very pinnacle above us is a domed skylight. Because this house is perfect, the moon itself is centered in the middle.

I glance at West and I expect to see quiet expectation or a glimmer of pride. Instead, his expression contains an ache. I squeeze his hand. "It's beautiful."

"It's excessive."

I appraise my clothes: my best blue button-down shirt, my best pair of jeans and black shoes. There is no way my best could ever measure up. My grip on him loosens and West clings tighter. A constant seesaw between us of holding on and letting go.

High heels click against the floor and I raise my head to notice a slender woman gliding into the foyer from a back hallway. She has mail in her hands and she flips through it with an air of absentness. I bet she doesn't receive collection notices.

"Hi, Mom," West says and I flinch, startled by his voice breaking the silence.

She stops abruptly. It's obvious where West inherited his good looks, golden hair and blue eyes. A tender smile brightens her face as she surveys him. "You're home. I thought you'd be out celebrating with your friends."

Celebrating? My forehead scrunches. Is he purposely avoiding my gaze?

"This is Haley Williams. Haley, this is…." West pauses and the pleading glance he sends me causes me to shift. Meeting parents can be awkward, but West is acting like he's about to slash open my heart or his. "My mom, Miriam Young."

Young. I suck in a breath as my heart pounds faster. He's Young.

West Young. I've heard his name—have said his name—a hundred times and it never clicked. Not once…until now.

He's not just any Young. He's *the* Young. This is the family that half of the buildings in the city have been dedicated to. They're the reason why the zoo can throw a Halloween party.

Because of a plaque at the check-in desk, I knew they were the ones who paid for the mattress I slept on at the shelter.

I let out a slow, steady stream of air because breathing is helpful. Breathing can keep me upright and deter the black dots encrypting my vision. Breathing may possibly make this moment less real.

"It's nice to meet you, Haley." His mother's eyes dance as she spots our joined hands. "And I'm assuming Haley is your..."

"Girlfriend," answers West.

A sound leaves me that's akin to a squeak. West Young claimed me as his girlfriend.

Mrs. Young's smile overtakes her face, and, as she moves forward, I let go of West and extend my hand because that's what you do with royalty, right? Crap, maybe I should curtsy. Mrs. Young accepts my hand with both of hers, then draws me in for a hug. "West has never brought home a girl before."

"He hasn't?" I hug her back, sort of, because I'm wondering if I'm allowed to touch.

Mrs. Young pulls back and stretches out my arms in that weird assessing way. "She's beautiful. Really, West, she is. Simply gorgeous."

And *she's* touchy. "Thank you?" Am I a contestant in a dog show?

I shoot a please-help-me glance to West, and, thankfully, he swoops in for the rescue. He lobs an arm around my shoulder and his mother finally drops my hands.

"I thought I'd show her around," he says.

She claps. "That is a wonderful idea. You do that. I'll change into something less formal, and then we can meet in the kitchen. It'll give me a chance to properly celebrate your birthday."

We both stand as still as pillars of salt and watch as Mrs. Young sweeps up the stairs and out of sight. "That's my mom," he says with a hint of apology but mostly the pride I'd been expecting earlier.

"She's—" enthusiastic "—welcoming."

He chuckles. "She's a nutcase, but she's my mom."

"You're a Young," I say and there's a sad hollowing out in my stomach. He didn't tell me, but at the same time, he didn't not tell me, and I never cared to ask for details.

"Yeah." West lowers his head, then raises it. "I am."

West points in several different directions. "Kitchen, formal living room, formal dining room, Dad's office, bathrooms, sunroom, a couple more other rooms and the basement is for lounging."

West claims my hand and starts up the stairs.

"Where we are going?" I ask.

"My bedroom. We need to talk."

West

WE DIDN'T REACH MY BEDROOM. Mom was changed and out her door in less than thirty seconds.

The moment I introduced Haley to my mother, Haley's face drained as she connected the dots—I was a Young. Instead of allowing Haley time to decompress, my mother, the blinding social snowplow that she is, grabbed on to Haley and has yet to let go.

With a hip cocked against the doorframe and arms crossed over my chest, I watch as Haley graciously laughs and chats with my mother at the massive island in the overly large kitchen of stainless-steel everything.

I don't understand a lot of what's happening, but I know one thing: Abby told the truth. I did tear out of the bar like my skin was on fire and the guilt rides me hard that I left Mom to fend for herself. I assume Abby stayed to protect my mother's back. For that, I do owe Abby.

Mom opens another photo album, flips through the pages and slips it over to Haley. "This was taken on the day we brought West home."

I'm eighteen today and I have never brought a girl home.

Damn, Mom must have been dying to do this for a long time. Except for the fact that she spends her days and nights at the hospital instead of at a charity function, life has returned to normal...at least for everyone else. It's like, to them, I never left.

Haley examines the photo and glances at me with laughter in her eyes. "Your onesie says *angel.* I'm *so* going to remember that."

"That's because he was." Mom slides her fingers against the photo as if she could make the newborn me pop out and be real. "I had West to save Colleen."

Mom told Haley about Colleen a few minutes ago. Colleen was Mom's firstborn and she died of cancer when she was a teenager. Mom and Dad had Colleen, Gavin and Jack in a group and they considered their family done. When Colleen became sick, all bets were off.

"Colleen needed bone marrow, so I had West in hopes he'd be a match."

"Was he?" Haley's eyes flash to mine. She's aware Colleen passed but doesn't know the when, the how or the why. But in the end, do any of us know the why?

"No," I answer for Mom. "I wasn't a match." A failure since birth.

"It didn't matter." Mom touches the picture again. "Colleen was too sick by then and died shortly after West was born."

My legacy in this house was formed a few days after my first breath: I failed at my sole purpose of life and my birth will forever be associated with Colleen's death. Mom went on to become pregnant with Ethan and Rachel shortly after because I wasn't enough to make her happy. All Mom desired was a girl, a replacement for the child she lost.

"Well then." Mom shuts the album and forces a fake smile. "What are your plans?"

"Quiet night," I answer. "I thought I'd show Haley my room. Maybe watch some movies." Have her break my heart into pieces because I've lied about who I am.

Mom narrows her eyes as she stands. "I want the door unlocked and I expect you to behave like a gentleman."

I laugh. If she knew what I've been doing behind locked doors at other people's houses, she would have given me this modified sex talk years ago. Mom pokes me in the stomach as she passes. "I mean it." Then leans in and kisses me on my cheek. "Happy birthday, West."

"Thanks."

Mom softly pads out into the foyer and up the stairs. She won't sleep in her bedroom tonight. Instead, she'll go into the mausoleum that once was Colleen's room.

The patter of different feet draws me back to the kitchen and cool fingers against my wrist connects me with Haley. "Why didn't you tell me it's your birthday?"

"I'm not a birthday fan. Sucks to be reminded once a year you weren't wanted."

Haley tilts her head. "She wanted you."

"To save Colleen." I was brought into this world to save somebody else. "I've done this for eighteen years now. I know what she sees when she looks at me."

Haley nudges the floor with her foot. "Are you going to show me your room?"

I scratch my jaw, trying not to put too much hope into her statement. "You sure?"

She nods. Not giving her a chance to change her mind, I link our fingers together and, for the second time tonight, walk her up the stairs. At the landing, I pause and notice light shining from the cracks of Colleen's door. Across the hall, Rachel's door remains shut. Thank God Rachel didn't die. Mom wouldn't have survived an additional loss.

I lead Haley away from Mom and in the direction of my bedroom. Once inside, I flip the light on and, out of respect for my mother, keep the closed door unlocked.

With her thumbs hitched in her pocket, Haley surveys the room: king-size bed, flat-screen television, gaming systems, a stereo, and, with another flick of a switch, Haley finds the full bathroom.

"Wow." Her voice echoes from within. "You've got a Jacuzzi tub." Her head pokes around the door. "Do you actually use it?"

"No. When Ethan, Rachel and I were little we used to pour bubble bath into it, then turn it on so the bubbles would overflow onto the floor." I smile at the memory of Rachel laughing.

She exits the bathroom. "Your mother must have hated you as children."

"At least we were clean."

The joke earns me a giggle, but the happiness fades as she straightens a picture of me, Ethan and Rachel on my mirror—Rachel's in the middle and Ethan and I have our arms locked around her. "You lied to me about your age."

She means I lied to her about me. "I was close to eighteen. I figured it didn't matter."

Haley raises her eyebrows, either in agreement or disagreement, I don't know. Regardless, she keeps her comments to herself. While it often drives me crazy that she lives in her own head, there are times I appreciate her silence.

"Why were you kicked out?" Haley's slow to face me, and when she does there's a hardness to her. She's playing judge and jury and she has a right to.

"My oldest brother, Gavin, has a gambling problem. He became indebted to some bad people, so I stole money from Rachel to help pay the debt. Turns out Rachel had her own problems and needed the money. To make up for it, she and her boyfriend drag raced to raise the funds I took. Long story short, Rachel's now in the hospital and my father, rightfully, blames me."

"He kicked you out because you tried to help your older brother?"

"He kicked me out because I don't trust him and he doesn't trust me..." Say it. "And because I'm a disgrace. Look, I smoke pot. I drink. I party every weekend. I've been suspended more times than I've had first days of school and I fight more often than I laugh. And as for girls..." I'd rather rip off my own skin than admit to her the reality of those sins.

She massages her temples and I wish I could crawl into her mind.

"Who are you? None of this—" and she motions around the room "—fits what I know."

"Maybe because what you've seen isn't the real me."

"I've seen you. I know I have but...all of this..." Haley sags against my dresser and brings her hands to her face. "You're a Young."

Every bad decision I've made catches up to me and it

will push away the one person I've learned to love. How can someone like her want to be with someone like me?

"I'm not just any Young. I'm West Young. I'm the unnamed delinquent son you read about in the papers."

Haley

I FOUGHT IN A COMPETITION where I was overmatched. The girl had more experience than me, more wins than me, was just more than me. After the first round, my mind was a mixture of confusion, chaos and despair. She knocked me from one end of the ring to another, all but picking me up and using me as a mop for the floor. Right now, I don't feel much different.

My hand slips to my stomach as it churns. What makes this sickening isn't that I'm training West; it's because I've fallen for West. Blindly. Deeply. Hard. All the ways I'd sworn I'd never fall again. And I fell for the fighter. When will I ever learn?

"I can't train you if you drink or smoke pot." We'll continue the training if he intends to proceed with the fight. "It's not acceptable for an athlete. Plus I don't like it."

"I haven't touched either one since Rachel's accident." He holds out his hands. "I'm plain-day sober and plan on staying that way."

"We should have stuck with simple," I whisper. I glance around the room. Flat-screen television. Stereo that costs more than two months' deposit at the cheapest apartment complex in our school district. Everything that life could offer him right here at his fingertips.

"This isn't news—that my family has money," he mumbles.

"Yeah, well, being a Young is!" I snap. "You never thought that was important to tell?"

"I never hid the last name, either."

"You lied! Even if you didn't say the words, you lied!"

"You're right, okay?" he shouts, then calms downs. "I lied. I liked that you didn't see me as a Young. For the first time, someone judged me for me, for who I was alone and not who my parents were and what their money could do for them. Being with you…it was like being offered a second chance and I'm sorry if I fucked it up."

For the first time since West broke down and showed me the truth behind the iron curtain, I look at him. Really look at him. West casts his gaze away, tucks his chin near his throat, then crosses his arms over his chest. Leaning against the door of his room, he's closed off, shut down…his guard is up. West is expecting a beating.

It's his birthday. I sweep my bangs out of my sight and straighten. It's his birthday and not a soul here tried to celebrate it with him. Even his mother spent more time talking to me than she did him. West hovered, watching us, but never engaged.

My heart trips over itself—West never engaged.

A few weeks ago, his father kicked him out while his sister fought for her life in ICU. What does that say about his family? Even better, what does it say about West and his relationship with his father that West didn't want to come back to live here? I scrub my fingers over my face. I'm doing what West says everybody does to him: I'm judging him. I'm judging him based on a last name, based on an assumption of money. I'm just judging.

Think, Haley. West Young. My West Young. The guy who fought for me when Conner and his friend tried to jump me. The guy who took on a fight to help save my family. The guy who held me while I mourned my own losses. That's West Young. The man I'm falling for.

I don't know who his family sees, but I see who West really is.

"They don't know you, do they?" I move toward him as the confusion and chaos fades.

West glances up, startled. "Who?"

"Everyone."

A grim smile pulls on his mouth. "They know me. They know me very well."

"I don't think they do." I touch his biceps. I've trained with West for over a month. He was fit before but he's leaner now, sculpted and shaped. West has made me laugh, he's held me at my lowest and he's stood by me when no one else has. Matt had words—plenty of useless words. West is all action.

The same fight from before barrels into the forefront of my brain. At the end of three rounds and the winner declared, I sat defeated on a stool. My grandfather squatted in front of me, gave me that rare smile and patted my knee. "You did good, kid."

It almost killed me to meet John's eyes. "I failed."

He shook his head. "In my book, you won. You've got fight in you, girl. Three rounds of pounding to be exact. More importantly, you've got heart. I couldn't be prouder."

Who West was before he slammed the brakes of his car

inches from me isn't my concern because the man in front of me...he has heart.

"Matt offered to end all of this," I say. "He'll put an end to the fight in a few weeks. He'll prevent any retaliation on my family that I've feared from him or the Black Fire boys... He'll make everything go away if I broke up with you and returned to him."

He grinds his teeth. "Over my dead body. If you even think of returning to him—"

"I'm not accepting," I cut him off. "I've chosen you. I'm ready, West. I'm ready to be with you."

His eyes widen. "Why?"

"Because..." I inhale deeply. "Because you have heart."

West

DID SHE JUST SAY...? No, I heard it wrong. It's not possible.

The scent of wildflowers fills the air as Haley skims her fingers along my biceps. It's a tickling touch, pleasurable enough to heat my blood and awaken parts that should remain silent.

"I like you," she says. "When it comes to you, everyone else has it wrong."

Haley wraps her hand around my wrist and as much as I want to ignore the truth, I can't. "I've made mistakes," I say. "Big ones."

"So have I. You're not the only one who's messed up. You told me once to let you know when I was ready for us to be a couple..." She trails off and my brows rise.

"Are you sure about this? About me? Us?"

"I'm scared." She sucks in a breath and her hand trembles. "Matt and I didn't work out."

The need to protect her sweeps through me. I cup her face and slide my fingers over her cheeks. "I'm not Matt."

She moves her head in my hands as if she agrees, but the fear consuming her eyes tells the story engraved on her soul.

Someday, she'll trust me enough to tell me the truth. For now, I'll be that home she lost—I'll be that soft, secure place where she can land.

I lean so that our foreheads almost touch. "I mean it. I'm a lot of things, but I'm not him."

"I know," she whispers. "But it doesn't make falling any less frightening."

My nose drifts along hers and the pull I've been fighting strengthens. "Don't think of it as falling. Think of it as jumping—with me."

I feel the curve of her smile beneath my lips. "How is jumping better?"

"Falling happens. Jumping you choose." And you chose to do it with me.

"I still don't see—"

"Haley," I cut her off while tunneling my fingers into her hair. The girl way overanalyzes. "Stop thinking and jump."

My muscles react like I'm stepping into a hot shower as my lips melt against hers. Our bodies transform into liquid, shaping and forming into the other. Her hands roam my back and mine fist her hair. The kiss builds in intensity. Her lips are soft and pliant, and as we angle closer, Haley opens her mouth and I accept the invitation.

Our tongues meet and every cell in my body explodes to life. My hands seek lower—the curve of her waist, the hollow of her back, craving hot skin. Haley caresses my face and the intimacy of her touch weakens my knees and causes me to lose track of reality and time.

I wrap my arms around Haley's waist and lift her so that her head is above mine and her feet dangle off the floor. Her silky hair brushes against my cheeks and I moan with the sensation. She's tiny in my arms—a weightless feather tickling my skin.

We never break the kiss as I carry Haley to my bed. Both of her hands explore my jaw, my hair, tease the strands near the base of my neck. All of it sends a ripple of excitement through my bloodstream and the resulting shockwaves cause me to silently beg for more.

I brace her head and back for the soft tumble onto the bed. My leg lands over hers and I keep it there as I taste her neck, caress her midriff. Half of me covers her and it feeds the images of what I long to do—to completely blanket her body with mine. I yearn to touch her skin, to unbutton her shirt, to...

Haley turns her head and gasps. "West." It's a desperate sound full of lust and want and a whole lot of slow down.

I inhale deeply as I rest my arm across her stomach and nuzzle my nose into the sensitive part behind her ear. Haley's delicious. She smells delicious. She tastes delicious. I could spend the rest of my life devouring her. "Yes?"

Her fingers move in my hair and her body inches closer to mine, but it's not a sign to continue; it's a sign that she desires more than something physical. I've never done more. Whenever a girl breaks away, I'm usually out of bed and out the door. For Haley, there's more because she is more. She's slowly becoming my everything.

With a slow kiss to her neck, I kick off my shoes and she squirms as she does the same. I draw Haley with me to the top of the bed, ignoring how her thighs shifting across my legs encourage my fantasies.

Haley's hair cascades into a light brown halo as she settles her head into the pillow. She looks up at me with those large dark eyes and a shy smile. “This is a soft pillow.”

“I like it. It’s my favorite.”

“Is it?”

“It is now.” I warm at the sight of her in my bed lying next to me. I tuck a stray hair away from her face and the pieces of myself that felt missing suddenly return and fit.

For weeks Haley and I have talked about what home is and what it means: a building, a structure, a memory. It’s none of those things. For me, home is the contentment currently bubbling up inside me. Home is the rush of emotions buzzing in my veins.

“You asked me earlier what it was like to come home,” I say.

Haley nods. I lace our fingers together and raise them into the air. “I couldn’t answer you because I didn’t know, but now I do. This—” I rock our hands “—I finally found home.”

Haley

WEST AND I HAVE BEEN OFFICIALLY together for a week. I swapped shifts so that I now work on Mondays and have Fridays off. This way, I can train with John in the morning, train West in the afternoon, then spend quality time with my boyfriend.

On the flat screen in West's room, the movie ends and, to be honest, I have no idea what it was about. West watched his fingers tease and explore my body until my skin vibrated and my blood buzzed. I, for the most part, watched West.

I love the serious set of his jaw and the way he'd occasionally run his hand over his golden hair. The biceps in his arm would flex as he moved and, every now and then, his shirt would ride up, exposing his gloriously defined abs.

I'm flat on his bed and West is propped up on his side next to me. His fingers sweep across the plane of my stomach and his deep blue eyes follow an imaginary line like an artist would a paintbrush along a canvas. "You're the sexiest damn thing. Jesus, your skin is soft."

West shuts his eyes and I suck in a breath. This is dangerous. Very dangerous. My lips are still swollen from earlier.

Kissing West is addictive. It propels me to want to kiss and touch more and travel with him to unknown and hidden places. And I secretly begin to imagine the type of kissing that involves darkness and covers and whispers.

His fingers slip under the already tucked up fabric of my shirt and he gently skims the trim of my bra. Heat explodes throughout my body and my breathing hitches. It's frightening how I react to one simple caress.

Not good. Not good at all. Actually, it's very good and I all but purr with his hands on my bare skin, but I need to think. I need air.

Without warning, I go to roll off the bed, but in lightning-fast movements, West captures my waist and draws me back to him. "Where are you going?"

"You're going to kiss me again," I say a little breathlessly.

"Yes, I am. Not sure if you knew, but last week was my birthday so that means I get a two-week grace period of presents. Kisses come with the territory. It's a state law."

I giggle. "*Now* you're playing the birthday card."

"Play it. Use it. Own it." His voice hums over my skin as his fingers begin to roam. Oh Lord in heaven, I've never experienced this type of mesmerizing intimacy in my life.

"Anything to kiss you again," he whispers into my ear and I shiver.

An overpowering urge screams to melt into him, to hold him, to wrap my body around him, but it's the small voice begging me to listen to reason I cling to. "I need this to go slow."

"Slow." He nibbles on my ear and pleasurable goose bumps form on my neck. "I can make this as slow as you need."

This is killing me because I crave his kisses, but… "*Er.* At least slow*er.*"

West sighs, then falls back onto the bed, rubbing his face with both his hands. "I can do slower. It's possible." With a moan, West shoves off the bed, puts on his shoes and offers me his hand. "Let's go for a drive. That should be safe."

We end up in West's SUV, driving around for hours talking about Rachel and hospitals, Isaiah and Abby, his relationship or nonrelationship with his father, how he's been following his mother for over a year and Abby's confession that his mother visits her brother at the bar.

"What are you going to do?" I ask as West stops at the last red light before we turn into my uncle's neighborhood. "About your mom?"

He switches the hand he drives with and stares off into space. "I don't know. I'll try to talk to Abby again, but the more I talk to her, the further down the rabbit hole I fall."

It's like how I feel when I have a conversation with Matt. For a few seconds last week, I considered his deal. I could return to Matt for twenty-four hours, for a day, and then he'd be forced to keep his word and wipe the slate clean. But due to what's happened with West, for better or worse, the option is no longer on the table.

Unable to look at him, I pick at lint on my shirt. "What number girlfriend am I?"

The light changes and West takes the right. "I've never had a girlfriend before."

I laugh, then sober up when his mouth bunches to the right.

"You're kidding," I say.

He shakes his head and my imagination clicks at full speed. "You don't kiss like you've never had a girlfriend."

West scratches the shadow forming on his chin and is unusually silent for him. My stomach sinks. Crap. Just crap. "How bad?" I ask. He said he hooked up before, but how many hookups is he talking?

Silence. A long silence. Silence should be forbidden.

"Bad," he finally answers.

The interior of the SUV darkens as we enter the lightless viaduct of the neighborhood. My skin pricks as the ghosts of West's beautiful, bold and uninhibited lipstick- and thigh-high-wearing hookups hover near me. I bet they knew every secret move, every intimate whisper, and never blushed or fidgeted when touching went too fast and clothes were shed too quickly.

"Matt's the only boyfriend I've ever had," I admit. "The only guy I've ever kissed."

The washed-out sympathetic glance he throws me makes me want to shoot myself. He already knew. Sitting here in a pair of faded jeans, I have never felt as homely as I do now. I'm going to freaking strangle Jessica. I'm sure she gave him an entire history lesson on me.

West eases in front of my uncle's and his expression hardens as he gazes past me to the house. "What the hell?"

I whip my head and panic shocks my nervous system. My hands fumble for the door handle, and after three tries I fling myself out of the SUV as West yells out behind me to stop, but I can't stop. It's Jax and if I don't intervene, my uncle will throw him out.

West

HALEY BOLTS AND I MUTTER a curse as I shove the car into Park and chase after her. On the front lawn of her uncle's house, Jax and an older version of Jax stand nose to nose. Both of their shoulders stiff and tight, hands and arms ready to strike.

"Do it!" yells the older guy. "Become a man and take the damned swing!"

"No!" shouts Haley and she rushes them. The front door bangs against the worn siding and Kaden's out of the house. He jumps off the stoop and collides with his cousin.

"Let him go!" The older guy, the asshole, moves within eyeshot of Jax. The moment their gazes meet again, Jax attempts to surge toward him, but Kaden interlocks their arms, chest against chest, so that Jax goes no more than a step.

Using his shoulder, Kaden pushes him back, in my direction, and Haley's following them. In a movement so smooth it appears coordinated, Kaden slides to the left, keeping Jax in his grip, and Haley slips in front of Jax and cups his face near his eyes, distorting his peripheral vision. "You don't want to do this," she says.

"I do." Jax jacks his head to get a view of the dick still dropping insults. "I want to fucking kill him."

"A year," Haley says rapidly. "A year and you're out. Think of your mom. Think of your brothers. You can't protect them if you're not here. If you give your dad what he wants, he'll throw you out. He'll call the police. It's what he wants. He wants to prove John is wrong."

With her last sentence, Jax darts his eyes to hers. "John's not wrong about me."

"He is!" The asshole spits at the ground. "Never seen such a waste of skin in my life."

"Don't listen to him." Haley keeps her hands on Jax's face. "I know you, and John's not wrong. He's right. He's very, very right. You're going to succeed."

I stay near the car, but I have a foot angled toward the asshole, ready to protect Haley. I don't know Jax. He doesn't know me. I've encroached on his family and he hates that an outsider is involved with someone he loves. I understand that. I get it. And the rage in his eyes, the hurt radiating from his posture—I understand that, too. We both have fathers who should be roasting in hell.

"John's wrong," taunts the asshole. "Just like he's wrong about the girl. Want to tell her what you said, Jax, or should I?"

Jax grimaces and Kaden readjusts his grip. "Get out of here, Haley."

"What?" Haley lowers her hands as the pain contorting Jax's face is mirrored on hers. I inch closer, not liking the change between them.

"Go, Haley!" There's a force in Kaden's voice that could terrify a pissed-off rattlesnake. "You!" And he glares at me. "Get her out!"

Don't have to tell me twice. I move in Haley's direction as the screen door creaks and a guy resembling Kaden joins the party. "What's happening?"

"Get her out, West!" Kaden yells. "Dad, go back inside."

Haley's eyes flicker between her cousin and brother. "I'm not going anywhere."

Jax's dad laughs and he's the only one who thinks this midnight scenario is funny. "Jesus, Jax. You don't want her to hear what you had to say about her dating one of the Black Fire boys? I'd imagine Saint John thinks the same thing."

Haley steps back and the pain darkening her eyes also rips my heart. Jax sags and Kaden releases him. "It's not what you think."

I slice in between them, facing her, not letting her cousin access. "Let's go."

But she's not even on my planet as she peers around me. "Jax?"

"I was mad," he explains. "I was talking to Kaden after I found out about you and West. I didn't know anyone was around to overhear and it's not what you think."

The regret weighs his tone and I ache for him and for Haley. I understand regret. I understand being hurt, but Haley is my lone concern. I lace my fingers with hers, holding on even though her hand lies cold and dead in mine. "It doesn't matter what he said. Let's walk."

"It matters," she whispers. "Did you say it, Jax? Did you say it again?"

“That you’re a slut?” the asshole announces into the night. “Yeah, he did.”

The bear hibernating in me roars to life as I round on Jax’s father. “What did you say?”

“Slut.” His grin twitches. “I don’t know who you are, so get off my property.”

I’m on fire. Haley’s voice becomes distant as I cross the yard. He called her a slut. He called the girl I love a slut. Inches from him, I throw my fist back to pound the hell out of him when arms are everywhere. Behind me, in front of me, beside me and dragging me away.

“Want to say that again?” I shift my arm and I’m out of the grasp.

“Stop it!” Haley screams as she appears in front of me.

But I can’t stop. I love her. I love her and this asshole guy has made her life hell. He’s hurt what I love and he won’t do it again. With a hard yank, I’m free.

I rush forward again and a foot hooks against my calf and a hand grazes up my arm. In a flash, I’m in a free fall with my arm twisted behind my back. I grunt as my body crashes to the ground and Haley crouches beside me.

“I’m sorry,” she whispers in my ear. “I’m sorry. If you do this, he’ll kick us out. He might already and we have nowhere to go. Nowhere. I’m sorry. So sorry.”

Searching for freedom, I jerk and she releases me as the apology continues. Rising to my knees, the world shifts into slow motion as I glance at her brother, her cousin, then to her father.

Not one of them came to her defense. Haley’s uncle hovers over me. “Get off my property. If you come back here again,

I'm calling the police." He glares at Haley. "If you continue to see him, you and your entire worthless family are out."

The front door slams shut as he goes into the house. Everyone else—her father, her cousin, her brother—solidify into frozen dumb-ass lawn ornaments in his screwed-up world. I drop my head into my hands as the anger begins to fade and the reality of what I've done sinks into my bone marrow. Just fuck.

"We're not over," I say so only she can hear. Haley massages circles over her temples.

The April night isn't cold enough for my breath to show, but it's cold enough for the air to burn my lungs. I hate the agony in her eyes, on her face, but what I hate more is the silent acceptance by her so-called family.

"You shouldn't have done that," she says.

"He called you a slut." I stare each one of them down. "She is not a slut."

"Shit!" Jax turns his back to me and walks away into the night, slamming his fist into the mailbox. The metal door tips open and the entire box vibrates on the pole.

"It isn't what you think," says Kaden. With one final look at Haley, he follows his cousin.

"What's your poor excuse?" I ask her father.

Haley touches me now: a grip on my biceps, fingernails digging into my arm. "Don't. Not him. Yell at me, not at my dad."

"I'm sorry, Haley." Her father shoves his hands deep into his pockets. "I'm sorry."

Her hold on me tightens and she gulps for air. "It's okay, Dad. Don't worry. It's okay."

The forced cheer in her voice causes me to fall back onto

my ass. “Fuck this.” Taking a page from Abby’s book, I’m going to pretend I didn’t hear Haley excuse her father for permitting anyone to call her a slut.

We remain silent as he stands on the front porch stoop, frowning at the brown winter grass. Her fingernails keep their teeth locked on my arm and the skin underneath begins to throb. I watch Haley, willing her to acknowledge me. Instead she focuses on nothing, on everything, once again locked inside her head.

“You have ten minutes before you need to be inside for curfew,” her father says. The screen door squeaks shut behind him.

Against the cold dirt and sparse grass, the two of us sit alone. “I’m waiting.” For an explanation, for a mere word, for a glance.

“For what?” she snaps.

Is she for real? “For you to explain what the hell is going on and why the fuck your family stood by and let some asshole treat you like shit.”

Flames blaze out of her eyes. “Because they have self-restraint. Because they aren’t like you. Do you want to know why I freak out over you being in the cage? It’s not because you aren’t capable or strong—it’s because you don’t think. Ever. You are impulsive and let your emotions rule your decisions.”

“He called you a slut!” She’s not getting it.

“Yeah, he did and you took off swinging. In order to survive, you’ve got to be smart. You’ve got to think. With a temper, you forget your training and start swinging wildly. That type of attitude will get you killed.”

“And you think so much that you never act. Rolling over

and dying or letting people treat you like shit isn't the answer, either."

Haley closes her eyes. "I'm not a slut."

"Never thought you were. In fact, I'm the only one willing to defend that."

Besides the rumble of traffic on the nearby interstate, we stew in silence. She's mad at me, I'm mad at her and, if I don't do something drastic, I'll lose the only good thing in my fucked-up life. "I'm in love with you."

Finally, the girl looks at me. "What?"

"I don't know." I gesture to the house, the yard, the dirt surrounding us. "I'm not sure what suggested romance. Maybe it was the screaming match or the way my girlfriend kicked my ass to the ground, but I love you."

Her mouth gapes. "I...I..."

"I don't want you to say it back now. One of us should have some class." Or maybe she doesn't feel the same or maybe she'll listen to her uncle and dump my ass. Either way, I don't want to find out, at least not yet. "Can I say one more thing?"

She barely nods once.

"I don't like how every time I've tried to defend you that you step in my way."

"My uncle would have thrown us out!"

"And with Matt?"

"I would have lost my job."

She's probably right on both counts, but there's something dark in her eyes. It's the same shadow I see whenever she stops me. "You're worth fighting for."

"I'm not." The way she answers too fast with too much conviction twists my insides. When the three men who should be taking bullets for her stand by and let insults be thrown at her, how can I convince her otherwise?

"You are. You deserve better than this."

The air thickens with her quiet resolve. I slide over and wrap an arm around her shoulder. She stays frozen, unmoving. *Come on, Haley...* "I mean it. I'm in love with you."

She releases a long stream of air and I briefly close my eyes when she settles her head on my shoulder. "Tell me we're still together, Haley."

"I slept with Matt," she says.

My head drops back, but I keep her body tight to mine, even when she tries to pull away. She slept with Matt. Slept with him. Had sex with him. They were together for a year. What the hell did I think they would be doing?

I long to reach inside my brain and tear out the images those four words produced. Thinking of her with another guy—kills me. Thinking of her with the bastard I hate the most—slays me. I say I love her; she announces she slept with the guy. Unfortunately, her admission seems to fit into this mess.

"Okay?" I'm not a good enough person to keep the edge out of my voice.

"While Matt and I were together, Matt told Jax about our... um..." Haley covers her eyes with her hand and her shyness, her embarrassment, chips away at some of my anger.

"Extracurricular activities?" I need a shotgun to blow the scenarios out of my head.

"Yeah, that. Matt told him before a match to piss him off and it worked. Jax lost his temper, which means he lost his game plan, which means he lost the fight. Sound familiar?"

"Temper. Fights. Moving on."

"I'm serious. You need to work on impulsive decision making."

I mess a hand through my hair. "I've got images of Matt too near you for comfort. Keep talking before I perform my own lobotomy."

"Anyhow...I was mad at Matt. So mad I wouldn't talk to him for days."

She hesitates and I want this conversation over as quickly as possible. "So?"

Haley folds into herself. "After the fight, Jax called me a slut."

Jesus. And there is finally a contender against my family for the most screwed-up award.

"Jax later apologized," she says in a quiet voice. "He came to my home and got down on his knees and apologized. I had never seen him so upset over anything in my life..." Haley sighs. "Until when he thought I had lied to him about dating you...and then there would be tonight."

"He should have never said it."

"No, he shouldn't, but you don't understand me and Matt. My grandfather, Kaden and Jax hated him and I thought it was because he fought for Black Fire. They were mad at me for not listening. I was mad at them for not giving him a chance, so I switched gyms and began training with Matt and if the story ended there, then it wouldn't be so bad, but it doesn't."

I ache for Haley because I understand downward trajectories. Regret, in my experience, can be sharper than a knife. I lift Haley, gather her onto my lap and kiss her temple. My arms create the shelter her family should be providing. I like the light weight of her against my legs, the warmth between our bodies and her beautiful fragrance filling the air.

For comfort, for strength, I rub her back like I used to do with Rachel. Haley's a private person and sharing with me has to be like yanking a camel through the eye of a needle.

"I was mad at them, and then Jax called me a slut." She exhales sharply. "I taught Matt how to defeat Kaden and Jax by showing him their weaknesses. I taught him how to defeat my family. I wish I could take it back. I wish I could take it *all* back."

I rest my cheek against the top of her head, hold her closer to me and rock her in my arms. Her fingers grasp my shirt as if a hole is threatening to appear below her feet and consume her. I think of Rachel and all the rotten decisions I made that led her to the hospital...that possibly cost her the ability to walk.

"I understand," I tell her. "I get it. So say it. Tell me we're still together."

Haley

NOTHING IS EVER EASY. My relationship with Kaden and Jax is as messed up as ever, Matt wants me back, my father wouldn't even talk to me last night after the fight with my uncle, West Young told me he loved me and I told him I needed time.

There's a darkness inside me, this shadow that keeps me from delving into my emotions too deeply and saying it back. The last boy I loved hurt me and I'm, once again, dating a fighter.

As I walk into the gym, the uneasiness spreads. Actually, it battles against the overwhelming sense of home. When I'm here, when I'm training, it's the only time the darkness fades away. I pause outside the locker room and watch as Kaden and Jax spar in the ring.

I try to deny it, but West also drains the darkness from my soul. I don't want to love him, but I do. Something within me is broken; a contagion that obliterates my relationships. Like with Kaden, Jax and my father. If I continue this with West, will I also destroy him?

"You're late!" Jax dips between the ropes and yanks off his

headgear as he trots over to me. "I came early hoping we'd talk."

I stayed locked in the attic last night and arrived late hoping we wouldn't. "Had stuff."

"Yeah." He scratches the back of his head. "I didn't call you a slut again. I was talking about what happened last year and Dad heard."

Whatever. I roll my eyes and Jax plants a hand on my arm. "Come on, Hays—give me this. I don't apologize to just anyone."

And I'd really prefer the avoidance route. "I'm late and need to change."

Jax tilts his head and sort of grins. "Are you gonna make me do this?"

"I'm not making you do anything."

I attempt to step past him and Jax falls to his knees. He stretches out his arms to create his massive wingspan. The pounding on the bags stop and guys yell and taunt Jax from around the gym. My eyes widen. He's humiliating himself for me.

"Hear me out," he says. "Otherwise, I'll be following you around like this for the rest of the day."

A few guys slip out of the locker room and I slide to the side to let them pass and motion with my chin for Jax to join me. He stands and the gym returns to routine.

"Of all the stories you could share with your dad, why share that?" I whisper.

His eyes narrow at the mention of his father. "I wasn't sharing with him. I was outside, talking to Kaden, and I didn't know he was around to hear."

"You regularly bring up I'm a slut?"

"You're not a slut. Look, you're dating West and it's bringing back bad memories. Kaden and I were talking because we're both worried. You blocked us out when you dated Matt and you're blocking us out again. Matt hurt you, Hays, and we don't want to see you hurt again."

I search his eyes, wishing I could ask what he knows. "Matt didn't hurt me."

"Every time you walk into this gym you go ghost white. That never happened before Matt. I don't know what he did to you, but he did something. He killed a part of who you were and Kaden and I will be damned if West finishes you off."

"West isn't Matt." He's not. A shimmer of panic weaves through me. What if I'm making the same mistake twice?

The metal cage vibrates when Kaden beats his hand against it. "Let's go, Jax."

Jax shoves his headgear back on. "Just saying that history seems to be repeating itself. Think about it."

Just crap.

The door to my grandfather's office opens and out steps my father. Pure, utter joy skips into my bloodstream and my face aches with the smile. My dad came. This means he's back and he'll be okay and he'll sleep again and he'll smile again and he'll be my dad. I don't care about the job. I don't care about the money. I care about my dad.

Dad gestures for me to join him and I'm hesitant as I head over. Any time with my father is like Christmas morning, but a vibration of nerves strings me out like a drug.

John offers a halfhearted smile and any type of smile from him scares the pee out of me. "Shut the door behind you."

I do and sink into the chair across from John. Dad leans against the filing cabinet and stares at a large envelope on

John's desk. John picks it up, opens his mouth to say something, then shuts it while handing the envelope to me.

Nausea kicks in as I think of the million horrible things it could be, but none of them make sense until I see the return address: the University of Kentucky.

My hands shake and I inhale deeply. Large envelope. I got in. I was accepted.

"Congratulations." There's a heaviness in my Dad's voice that catches my attention. The smile I hadn't even known formed on my face fades.

"I picked up the mail today," he continues. "I hope you don't mind, I already opened it."

I flip it over and slide my hand along the already unsealed flap. Mind? Yeah, I do, but I could never say anything to upset my father, so instead I empty out the contents.

While my father and John scrutinize my every movement, I scan through the mountains of papers and brochures, finding everything but one crucial item. "The financial aid?"

John fingers a paper on his desk. "Some grants, a small student loan, work-study, but no scholarship. I'm sorry."

My ACT scores weren't high enough. I suck at tests but rock it out in class. While my brain knew this would be the outcome, my heart didn't. I nod and bite the inside of my mouth.

"I was accepted." I try to lift my lips, but they tremble. Dammit, this should be a good moment.

"Haley," starts John. "Your dad and I talked and I'm going to try to take out a loan—"

"You can't," I cut in. "You put everything into this gym and the heater just died."

I'm not stupid. John doesn't live in a camper because he

thinks it's cool. He, like everyone else, has made hard decisions to stay afloat. There's no way he can handle more bills.

"It's the only option," says my dad.

"I'll work two jobs or I'll go to community college." Though that also costs money I don't possess. "I'll find a way to save money, work for a year—"

"No!" Dad bangs his hand against the cabinet and I jump. My father has never been one to lose his patience, to lose his calm. "Not acceptable. You'll take what we give you."

"Dad—" I argue.

"I said no!" he shouts, then tears out of the office. The blinds on the window of the door sway when the door slams shut.

I look at John and my mouth grows slack. "What did I do?"

"It's a hard position for a man to be in when he can't care for his family, especially his daughter."

"I don't want him to worry about me. I can figure this out on my own."

"That's just it. He wants to provide for you and he sees how hard you're working to take care of him." He pauses. "He told me what happened last night. Your boyfriend almost cost you the roof over your head."

I wilt and wish the earth would engulf me. "I know and I tried to apologize to Dad."

"There it is. Right there. You shouldn't be apologizing to him. It's killing him. You're his daughter. He's your father. The roles at this point shouldn't be reversed."

"I promised to make it work with my uncle and I failed. This is my fault."

"Your fault? Did you cost him the job? Did you force Maggie to get sick? Did you create the recession that caused half of those fighters out there to not be able to pay gym fees?

There is no fault. There's how life works. Your father's having a hard time accepting the hand he's been given. And you've chosen to roll over and play dead. I'm not sure which one of you is worse."

We're silent and the packet becomes a pregnant elephant on my lap. "I lost his meds."

"That was a battle. Not the war. You used to have better perspective."

For months I worried about being accepted into college and now I wish I would have never received the acceptance. I toss the paperwork to the floor. "How do I help him?"

"This is something he has to work out. In the meantime, you keep going forward."

Forward. But I want to go back...back home, back when Dad had a job, back when there was hope. "I'm worried about him."

John's silent for a few seconds. "I am, too. I'm worried about all of you, your mom included. It's a heavy burden on me that I can't provide a proper home for *my* daughter."

"Mom's aunt Vi contacted her again. She wants us to move to California to live with her," I say this to gauge his reaction. My great-aunt Vi is his sister-in-law, my grandmother's sister. She and John hated each other, but she loved her sister and my mother.

"Your mom told me." He glances away. "I told her she should consider it."

"Mom wants to wait until Kaden and I graduate." If I don't win a scholarship by then, I could be moving with them. "Maybe Dad will do better in California."

The grim set of his lips creates a crawling sensation along my skin. "What?"

"Your father's in a bad place. He used to be a fighter, but I'm not sure he has fight left in him anymore."

"He's a fighter." Even the best fighters have a rough time running uphill with weights on their backs. I just have to take a couple of those weights off. The first place to start is to win that scholarship. "I'll spar. Today. Tomorrow. Whenever. In exchange, I need a letter from you for a scholarship and I also need you to train West."

"I'll train West if you agree to fight for me. Not spar."

I can't fight. "Then I'll spar if you give me the letter and Jax and Kaden. Tell them they have to help me with West."

John cracks a rare real grin. "Now we're talking."

West

ON THE FLOOR, I TIGHTEN the screw, then test the half door attached to the wall that, in theory, keeps people from behind the bar. Last night, somebody tore it off the hinges during a fight. Today: good as new. Satisfied, I sit back and observe the few people milling about. The same thought circles my mind: Is one of these guys my mom's brother?

It's Saturday and for the millionth time, I wish Haley had a cell. This whole only talking to her when I see her is too old-school for me. Last night I asked her if we were still a couple and she asked for time. Waiting until Monday at school to discover the answer is driving me insane.

"It's killing you, isn't it?" Abby plops onto a stool and I stand. How the hell does she know about me and Haley? She swivels to survey the tables. "Wondering which one it is."

Ah, the brother. "Is he here?"

She pops peanuts into her mouth. "Nope."

"Would you tell me if he was?"

"Uh-uh."

I lean my back against the bar and rest my elbows on it.

"You could be lying to me about my mom coming here to meet her brother."

"I could. But I'm not." She glances around. "Where's Denny?"

Abby's completely deadpan. There are two sides to the chick: full of shit and lethal. Either way, she's hard-core. "He's in the back with a delivery truck."

"Did he leave me food?"

I reach behind the bar and hand her a foam container. Her eyes light up. "Spaghetti!" Abby twirls the noodles onto a plastic fork, then motions toward the swinging door. "You actually are handy. Impressive."

I push the door again, awed by the sense of pride. "My dad will be disappointed I didn't fuck something up."

She humph-chuckles at my statement. "Your father is rather bitchy. By the way, Rachel might come home soon."

Abby gains my full attention and my hands sweat. I want Rachel home. She needs to be home, but... "Her legs?"

"She'll move around again, but with or without assistance, they don't know."

I rub at the muscles of my neck, somewhat relieved, somewhat devastated. Rachel should be maneuvering around the hood of her car, not constrained. When she's home I'll have no choice but to face her and I've got to find a way to make this up to her.

I watch as a new guy walks in. He has blond hair, like my mom. Blue eyes, too, but he's rough as hell. "That one?" I ask.

"Not telling," she mumbles through the food in her mouth.

"You didn't even look."

"Because I wouldn't even answer." She drops her voice to try to mimic me.

"Why would Mom lie? She told us she was an only child and that her parents died."

"You can't get it out of your mind, can you?"

I shake my head.

"Trust me, you don't want to know more. It's the stuff of nightmares. It even gives me cold chills if I think about it at three a.m."

A sickening darkness curls in my gut. "It's my mom, Abby."

"And if she wanted you to know, she would have dropped the bomb during one of your swanky dinners." Abby tears off a piece of a roll and shoves it in her mouth. Is Rachel aware how often Abby goes without food?

"Don't do it," she says to the noodles. "You're in my world because Rachel loves you and I love her. Just 'cause Daddy took you back, it doesn't give you the right."

"The right to what?"

She peeks at me from the corner of her eye. "Feel sorry for me."

The guilt that I pitied her slices through me. "Then I'll go back to hating you."

"Good. Did you do it?" she asks. "Did you give Matt what he wanted?"

"Is it a medical condition that causes you to talk in riddles?"

Abby actually smiles. "Fine. Matt wants the fight next month to be between you and him, not you and Conner, but he doesn't want to be the one to cause it because he's trying to stay on Haley's good side."

"You're making shit up now." Because there is no way she can know all this.

"I have super hearing." She pokes me in the head with one

finger. "I even have the ability to hear your thoughts. You're thinking about Haley and sex."

I wasn't, but now I am. Jesus, Haley can kiss and her skin is so damn smooth... I sigh. And Haley may no longer be mine. "You're full of shit."

"Maybe, but I do sleep with one of the guys from Black Fire and he's a talker."

Damn. That was blunt. "Then aren't you betraying your guy by spilling to me?"

She snorts. "I said I sleep with him, not married to him. What I do for a living—it's better to be a free agent. If he wants to get all sentimental afterwards and talk, that's his problem."

I assess Abby. "You don't give a fuck what anyone thinks of you."

"Nope." She sucks up a noodle and it smacks her on the lips. "I take that back. I care what Rachel thinks. She's the only person besides Isaiah to ever like *me.*"

The way she emphasizes the *me* causes me to look beyond the dark hair, hoodie and lethal. "You're doing it again," she says.

I hold up my hands. "I'm back on the page—you're a heartless bitch."

"That's better. Here's the info dump. Matt wants to fight you because he hates you. He figures if he can kick your ass, Haley will dump you because you're weak or you'll bail on her because you'll hate that she thinks you're weak."

A slurp of spaghetti. "But he wants you to provoke him into taking the fight, so Haley will be all like, 'No, West, no! Stop being mean to Matt. He's harmless in that psychopath way.' If he provokes you, then he's the mean guy and he's campaigning as Mr. Nice Guy. Fallen for it?"

"No." But my intestines twist at how close I was to taking a swing at Matt. I hate being played. "So what if Matt and I go at it instead of me and Conner? I'd rather go against that bastard."

"Good, because you probably will. I'm ready for the spoiler— If it does come down to you and Matt in the cage, if he hands your ass to you, will Matt be right? Can you stand to look the girl you care for in the eye knowing that in public her ex proved he's stronger than you?"

Haley

MY MOUTH DRIES OUT and a weird pressure compresses my throat, almost as if a ghost cups my neck and squeezes. Sitting on the mats next to the ring, I slowly wrap my hands. Each layer a confirmation of a death sentence. It's strange how I used to love this ritual and how I loved being in the ring. Stepping under the rope, I'd leave behind who I was in my everyday life, and I'd emerge on the other side with a clear mind—every thought and movement calm and precise.

With one hit, Matt stole my joy and made me terrified of the few things in life I enjoyed.

There's a shift in the gym—a jovial mood among everyone else. The guys I've known a good portion of my life are eager to see my return to the ring and the new guys that have heard of me from rumors or have possibly seen one of my fights in person or on YouTube seem to be excited, too. Not too long ago, I held a national title. Now I'm a fraud.

Jax crouches in front of me, swiping my boxing gloves off the floor. "Me or Kaden?"

I lift my eyebrows, confused as to what he's asking.

"Who do you want to spar with? Me or Kaden?"

He undoes the Velcro and holds out the hole for me to sink my hand into. I remain silent, too stunned by the offer. I love him and my brother. There's nothing I wouldn't do for them.

I shove my hand in and Jax secures the glove. "You've avoided sparring, so I'm guessing you've got a mental block. We'll go easy. A few hit series, a couple of low kicks for shits and giggles. Nothing fancy."

I slip on my headgear, then let Jax help me with the other glove. "That's not what John had in mind. He wants me to spar."

"You're wrong. He wants you back."

Jax stands and I place a glove on his arm. "I'm sorry."

"For what?"

"For Matt." For betraying my family. "For everything."

Jax glances over his shoulder and I'm startled to see Kaden on the other side of the ropes. He nods and Jax playfully mocks a two-one combo in his direction. "Water under the bridge, but this doesn't mean we're good with West. If he's with you, he's got to earn our respect."

I go to rip off the gloves. If they aren't going to help me train West, then I'm not sparring. Jax plants his hand over the Velcro. "You go into the ring—we help you. The kid is bad news, but at least now we'll be there to have your back."

"You've always had my back," I say with a grin to lighten the mood.

He shakes his head. "It's hard to help someone when they're damned insistent on doing all their own fighting."

Jax offers a hand off the floor and I accept. "West's a good guy and I care about him." Possibly more than care.

"He's an unknown and he's got a temper. Remember, I saw him lose it last night."

My heart plunges because Jax is right. West permits his emotions to rule him and that will be a problem in the cage.

John slams the door to his office. "If I wanted an audience, I would have sold tickets. Back to work!"

The smack of punches on the bags and the tap of fighters knocking out combinations against each other fill the gym, but it doesn't take much to notice it's halfhearted.

John grabs a pair of punch mitts, bends under the ropes and enters the ring.

"I thought I was sparring." I motion toward the mitts on his hands.

"You will, but I told you we're starting slow."

I follow him into the ring. Since returning to the gym, I've only done bag work with John. I've used the mitts with West, but I've yet to really throw a punch at anyone. John holds the mitts near his head. I inhale deeply and my guard goes up. One second. Another.

I hit Matt in anger, but he struck me first and it hurt. If I didn't fight back, would it have gone as far as it did? If I weren't trained, would he have even hit me? Where do Matt's choices end and mine begin? I drop my guard. "What if I can't do it?"

John widens his arms so that the targets are at arm's length. "Then we'll ease you in slower. Jab, cross." He shakes his right hand. "Then jab, cross." And shakes his left. "Let's warm you up."

"Okay." Some of the tightness unfurls. No punches toward the head. I can do this. "Okay."

My gloves slide back to my temples and my feet rock into position. Okay.

West

WITH ABBY'S WORDS FRESH on my mind and Haley's decision to be made, I head straight to the gym. If she's going to butcher my heart, she can do it now, not at school.

The bags near the front door are empty, but a crowd gathers around the boxing ring. A roar of approval ripples from the guys watching the show. In the corner of the ring, Kaden slips on his headgear and gloves, then says something to Jax, who stands on the other side of the ropes. The two of them confer like a coach instructing a student.

I work through the BO-laden crowd, bobbing my head to find Haley. The guys decked out in workout clothes yell again and I discover her in the last spot I'd thought to look—the ring.

John and Haley dance around each other, a demented tango. With mitts on his hands, John aims for her head. Haley ducks and fires back with machine-gun punches to the mitts near his face: double jab, right hook to the head. John grunts with each punch, just like Haley does with me—keeping up the tempo, rewarding her for the hit.

Haley is lean and gorgeous with a sheen of sweat over her

body. Her long hair is gathered together at the nape of her neck and her face is barely visible from the headgear and with her held guard. There's a lethalness about Haley. It's more than the way her shoulders roll forward and how fast she strikes. It's the serious gleam in her eye. Haley in that ring means business.

"Never forget she can kick your ass." Jax saddles up beside me. "And if she doesn't, I will."

I ignore him as John combines both mitts and lifts them in the air. Haley nails a double high kick with a power that could kill a man. My eyes widen as the crowd shouts for more. John slams his mitts together and continues to dance around Haley. "That's right, Hays. That's right!"

John turns and shouts for Kaden. The guys clap as John whispers instructions into Kaden's ear.

"What's the big deal?" I ask.

Jax surveys me, head to toe, then back up. "You really don't know, do you?"

I scratch my jaw, pride preventing me from giving an answer.

He grins at my nonresponse. "Haley's a national titleholder."

Shit. I never asked and she never told. I shift and Jax chuckles.

"Beyond that? This is the first time Haley's honest to God trained here in over a year and in a few seconds this will be the first time she's sparred in over six months."

My head snaps to Jax, the shock registering an earthquake in my system. "She trains here all the time."

"When she left Black Fire, she left fighting. She agreed

to come back to the gym, but she refuses to engage. What you're witnessing is her resurrection."

"Last time I checked, you and I aren't friends. So why the feel-good moment?"

"She's more than you and better than you and I'm fine with you seeing it. Haley's already been through hell and neither Kaden nor I will permit a return visit. Got it, amigo?"

I turn my attention to the ring, trying to sort through Jax's words. Haley left fighting when she left Matt. I run a hand through my hair to shake out the mental cobwebs. She didn't stop just dating fighters; she stopped fighting. The image of her nursing her hand the night we met, the fight we had in my car and how angry she was that she hit someone and was hit in return—it all flashes in my mind.

In the middle of the ring, Kaden nods his chin and lifts his arm, glove out. Haley's hesitant on her side of the ring as she leans against the post. The crowd yells at Haley to accept and I step forward. Jax throws out his arm like a railway gate. "She made a deal with John over this. Don't embarrass her."

"What deal?"

"Like you don't know, and if you don't, figure it out."

I roll on the balls of my feet, gravity begging to rush the ring. "He's bigger than her."

"And Haley can drop his ass. This isn't a real fight and she knows it. A few hit series. That's it. If she's going to be worth a damn again, inside or outside of that ring, Haley's got to engage."

I straighten and go toe-to-toe with Jax. "She doesn't have to."

His green eyes harden as he invades my space. "She does

if she wants to save your ass like she says she does. Haven't you wondered why you aren't training with the rest of us?"

Fuck this. I round away from Jax and fight through the crowd right as Haley pushes off the post. Before I can reach the ropes, Haley taps her glove against Kaden's and the two immediately slam their guards against their heads and begin to circle.

She's smaller than him, possibly a hundred pounds lighter, and every instinct screams to slide in front of her. If he wasn't her brother, I'd be in between them in a heartbeat. Kaden turns his guard, hiding his face and exposing his wrists. Haley answers with a jab, cross into his gloves. With their guards still in check, they move again and Haley turns her wrists to Kaden and he throws the same jab, cross.

Haley slips back and lowers her guard. Color drains from her face. "I can't."

"Come on, Hays. Don't give in. Just a few hits." Kaden turns his wrists out to Haley again.

She sucks in a breath and my pulse pounds in my ears. There's fear in her eyes. With the release of air, she rejoins the dance. They continue to hit each other's wrists, the punches increase in frequency, adding low kicks to the thighs, all of it methodical.

My grip on the rope tightens as the round continues and each strike grows in intensity. Kaden throws a jab and Haley fumbles with her guard right as Kaden goes for the hook. His glove connects against her headgear behind her ear. Her head snaps to the left with the blow.

Kaden's hands drop and he reaches for Haley. "I'm sorry—"

The answering cross comes hard and fast, too fast for Kaden to raise his guard, and she lands the punch on his jaw. He reacts by tossing out an arm to block the jab, but Haley throws another cross, following up with a cut kick behind the knees. Kaden's body pounds to the floor and the gym vibrates.

A flash of blond breezes past me and, following Jax's lead, I'm under the ropes. Haley is already turned away, tearing her gloves off with her teeth, her breath coming out hard and fast. John's in front of her, mumbling shit, and she screams at him, "Get away!"

Haley

JOHN'S FINGERS WRAP around my biceps and I freak. Completely. I jerk out of his grasp and throw back my arm, prepared to punch if he touches me again.

He tosses his hands in the air. "Easy, Haley."

"I said get away!" The words tear through my throat with such force that the chords of my voice box strain. "I can't do this! I told you I can't do this!"

The world blurs from colors to shades of gray, then back to colors again.

John nods but doesn't do what I ask. He's too near. Everyone is too near. It's like the gym is shrinking. I rip at the Velcro of the hand wrap and I need the material off now, but it won't come off. It's attached to me. Just like Matt's blood is still attached to me.

I'm stained and ruined. I hit my brother in anger and sent him to the floor. An ache develops in my chest, near my heart, and breathing becomes difficult. Why can't I get these wraps off? "Get them off!"

But when John nears me, I step back and shake my head to the point he trembles in my vision. I need the material off,

I need to get away and not fight ever again. I'm evil when I fight and if John touches me, I'll hurt him, too.

"Let me do it."

I suck in a breath when West dips under the ropes. Oh, my God, he's seeing this. He's seeing me. The real me. The poseur. The fraud. The patheticness. "I don't want to hurt you."

West moves toward me with the slow, confident swagger that only he possesses. "Only way you could do that is to tell me to stay away. You know kick-ass girls turn me on."

As if there was a breeze, the haze clears just enough to create a small focused thought. "I want my wraps off." I lift my palm to reveal how I've murdered the set on my left hand.

Like a thief, West slips into my personal space. "I can see that. Do you mind if I give it a crack? I'm quite talented when it comes to taking clothes off of pretty girls."

I'd normally laugh because that statement is so West, but I don't. Instead, I extend my arm. West cradles my hand in both of his and slides his thumb against the exposed skin. "I'll do this slow and then we'll get out of here. Just you and me. What do you think?"

Something wet threatens the corner of my eye. Sweat maybe? I'm not sure. "Okay."

"Good." He begins to untangle the material that's knotted like necklaces shaken together in a jewelry box. "There's too many people here for my liking. I prefer to kiss you in private."

As if from a distance, someone shouts something about clearing out and I sort of recognize the voice as John's.

"Kaden hit me behind the ear," I say as if that will help him understand.

"I saw." He meets my eyes and his hands pause. "Are you hurt?"

I'm broken. "No."

Guilt rushes through me. My eyes dart until I spot Kaden, but I don't have to look far. He's beside me and Jax is next to him. How could I not have noticed? "Are you okay?"

He beats his chest twice. "Made of stone, remember? Plus it's not the first time you've taken me down. How about you, Hays? You okay?"

No. "I'm sorry." And I stop because my throat closes. I hold my breath when my eyes burn. I hit my brother. When Kaden's glove connected to my head, my mind flashed to Matt and I hit my brother. I caused him pain—on purpose. I can't fight. I shouldn't fight. "I'm sorry."

"She's shaking," says Jax.

Cold air caresses my fingers as West frees the wraps. "I'm getting her out of here."

"Not to her uncle's." John walks up next to West. "Her blood sugar's dropping. Get her something to eat and that'll help with the shock. Kaden, Jax—meet Haley at the front door of the house at midnight. She doesn't need her uncle's crap tonight."

West slides his jacket off and tosses it around my shoulders. He shouldn't be nice to me. "I hit my brother." In anger.

West brushes his fingers against my cheek and cups my face in his palms. "It's okay."

"John," says Jax. "Maybe she should stay with us."

"I want you," I whisper to West.

"Then you'll have me. Can you walk?"

I nod, but my legs don't move. West bends over; then my

feet are dangling and my body is cradled tightly to his. I rest my head on his shoulder because it's too heavy to hold and plus…I like his warmth.

"It's okay, Haley," West says as he carries me past the bags for the door. "It's okay."

West

FRESH OUT OF THE SHOWER and in a borrowed purple sweater and jeans from Rachel's room, Haley twirls the fettuccine Alfredo I heated for her onto the fork and slides it into her mouth. Dad's away on business, Mom's staying the night at the hospital and my brothers are God knows where. Long story short—we're completely alone.

Haley and I sit next to each other on the floor of my room and lean against the end of my bed. Some girl-movie Rachel's watched a million times plays on the flat screen. I put it on for Haley, hoping it would make her smile and distract her. She watches it, and, while color has returned to her cheeks, her eyes are flat and dull.

"This is a lot better than deer meat," she says.

It seems like years ago when the two of us shared a simple meal on the floor of the attic. "We have a guy who cooks a couple of times a week. Our fridge is always stocked."

She creates an *H* in her nearly demolished bowl of noodles. "That must be nice."

Until I was thrown out, I took it for granted. Along with

a million other things. "Are we going to discuss what happened earlier?"

In midbite, Haley coughs, then forces down the swallow. "Do we have to?"

"Yeah."

"I got hit and freaked out. I guess I'm rusty."

"What did Matt do to you?"

She slams the bowl to the floor and the fork clanks. "Nothing."

Bullshit. "You turn white every time you see him, and Jax told me you stopped fighting six months ago—the same time you broke up with Matt. Jax also told me you held a national title. National titleholders don't walk. Matt did something and I want to know what he did."

A fire ignites in Haley—the same inferno as the night we met. "Jax needs to keep his mouth shut."

"Maybe you need to learn how to talk." And I hit the nail on the head and I'm much closer than I'd prefer. The pieces fall into place: Haley freaking about fighting, about dating a fighter, then how hard she's fighting me now. A dangerous undercurrent of anger floods my veins. "Did Matt hit you?"

"You don't get to ask me that." Haley's on her feet and across my room in seconds. I'm up after her fast and I grab her arm before she can reach the doorknob. When I turn her toward me, she jerks away, then slams her palms into my chest. "Don't touch me!"

She gasps and stares at her hands as if they're covered in blood. "Oh, God, I did it again."

I worked too hard getting her back to reality and I'm not going to let her slip away. I take her hands and plant them on my chest. "Do it again. If you need to shove me. Do it. You know I can take it."

Haley snatches her hands back and stumbles until she smacks the door. "This is why I gave up fighting. I did something horrible and I don't want to do it again."

This is it. This is as close as I've come to being inside Haley's head and if I say something wrong, if I move the wrong way, she'll shut down and I could lose the only good thing in my life. "Do what? What don't you want to do again?"

Her fingers splay open and she holds them up in a stopping motion, but I'm not what she's battling. There's something in her brain, someone there torturing her.

"Do what?" I urge.

It's like a shadow descends and she shrinks from it. "I don't want to hurt anyone."

I've never been a praying guy, but the goose bumps forming along my neck tell me something evil is attacking her soul. "You're only hurting yourself by not talking to me."

Haley breathes. One breath in. Another released. A steady movement of her chest rising and falling. Hours could have passed as I watch her wage a war in her own mind.

"There is no answer you could give that will make me change how I feel about you."

"And if he did—" a strangled sound escapes her throat "—do it...it still doesn't make what I did right or what I did to Kaden...or how I hurt Jax and my family and my grandfather. What I did was wrong and I'm useless and I'm pathetic and..."

"You are none of those things." Anger swells up in me, directed at Matt. If I'm not careful, I'll take it out on Haley. Not wanting to hear her berate herself any longer, I bridge the distance and pull her in to me. "There is nothing you can say to change us. Nothing."

Haley's hands fist the material of my shirt. For once in our damned relationship she's relying on me. I rain kisses into her silky hair and rub her back.

"Nothing," I repeat.

I hold on to Haley, wishing I was twisting that son of a bitch's neck. He hit her and not in the sparring type of way. "What happened with Kaden?"

Haley rests her head on my shoulder and gestures to where Kaden's glove had made contact. "The hit to the head. It triggered some stuff. Do you think I'm crazy because I freaked?"

"No. I think Matt's an asshole." I think Matt's a fucking dead man. "How often did it happen with Matt?"

My heart beats several times.

"Once," she whispers. "That's when I walked away."

"Jesus."

"I hit him back," she mumbles into my chest. "I made him bleed. If I showed restraint, then maybe it wouldn't have been so bad."

Every muscle in my body convulses. He's dead. He's fucking dead. The damned bastard won't walk another day. "I'm glad you hit him back."

She becomes limp in my arms. "It's funny. I spent my entire life learning how to fight and I never thought of it as hurting someone. It was a sport—the ultimate chess match—and I was good at it. When I stepped into the ring, my intentions were never to hurt. My intentions were to use my skills against another person with skills. But with Matt, I meant to hurt him and I did. Doesn't that make me as bad as him?"

I set my hands on her shoulders and move so I'm eye level to Haley. "He *hit* you."

She flinches with the word *hit*. "He hurt me."

"Hit." I flip back through our conversation and realize she's never fully admitted what he did. "He attacked you and you defended yourself. This wasn't a sparring match or a tournament. Someone you trusted failed you. That makes him an asshole and you justified."

Haley cracks her neck to the side and steps from me. I allow her the space, because she's heading away from the door. Her fingers brush along the top of my dresser, touching two of my watches, a class ring and a bottle of cologne.

She assesses the room. The judgment I'd been waiting for since the first night I brought her here settles on her face. "Why are you with me? You could have anyone, yet you're with me."

"What you mean to say is that I'm rich."

"And I'm poor. I lived in a homeless shelter."

I shrug. "And I lived in my car."

"You can't understand me." She dangles the Rolex from her fingers. "It's not the same."

"No, it's not. There are things about us that are different, but don't try to make me out to be something other than what I am when I'm with you. Being with you is the only time I'm okay living in my own skin."

"Why me?" There's a taunt in her voice and she's looking to pick an argument. "Did you get tired of girls who would give you whatever you wanted and decided to go for the chase?"

"Why are you pushing me so hard?"

"I'm not," she says. But she is. She doesn't like what I said to her about Matt.

"Last night you weren't sure you wanted us. Now that I know something intimate about you are you going to do what you do best? Are you going to hole up in your head and run away?"

"You're a jerk," she spits out.

I throw out my arms. "I sure am, but at least I'm not playing dead. Are you fighting or are you running? Because this is on you. You can say whatever you want and you can push me as hard and as long as you want, but I'm not tapping out."

Haley stands by my bed, unblinking and unmoving, and because I've already tossed it all on the table, I decide to give up the last of my pride. "And so you know, I'm a virgin, Haley. I've never had sex with any of those girls. You were *never* about the chase."

Like I've announced I have eight nipples, she clumsily sits back onto my bed. "Why are you telling me this?"

"Because you're the girl I've been waiting for. If you want to break up, then you're going to have to do it because I won't. You're *it* for me, and I'm not walking away."

Haley stares at the carpet. A sad song begins to play on the television. It's the part in the movie where the couple breaks up. Eventually, they get back together. It's what happens in movies, but as Haley has reminded me time and time again, this is real life. People lose their jobs, their homes... They lose each other and in real life, the pain actually hurts.

"I'm falling for you." It was a whisper, barely audible. I heard it more with my heart than I did with my ears and it was the most beautiful sound. "I'm falling for you, but I don't want to."

She bends forward and her hair hides her face. I crouch in front of her and tuck her hair behind her ear. “I’m not Matt. Me and you, we aren’t a repeat of the past.”

“I know.”

“No, you don’t.”

She nods like she understands, but the truth doesn’t reflect in her eyes.

“I’m not Matt.”

“I know,” she whispers again.

“Then you say it.”

Haley twists her fingers into her hair and barely whispers, “You’re not Matt.”

“Then why do you keep comparing me to him?”

Haley

WEST'S STATEMENT IS LIKE a front kick to the gut. "I don't."

"You have been the only person to see who I am. You've never looked at me as a Young. You've never looked at me as a free ride. You have always seen me—the good and the bad."

West slides his fingers into my hair and rubs the strands between his thumb and forefinger before letting it fall back to my shoulder. "But whenever we're close, I see Matt's ghost in your eyes. When we fight, sometimes I don't think it's me you're fighting against. I love you, Haley, but I'm not willing to share you, even with a memory."

My eyes flash to his and I see the honest ache telling me how much speaking the truth costs him. West isn't Matt. I know this. West and Matt could never be sorted into the same category. West: refined in his own bad boy way and smoldering blue eyes that whisper his secret thoughts, both the heart-warming emotional and the blush-inducing erotic.

But it's more than that. The emotions growing inside me... It's more than the warmth, the constant flutters, the excitement of meeting his gaze from across the room. It's more than a crush. The longer I'm with West, the more I realize that's exactly what it was between me and Matt. I crushed on Matt...hard...because if it was love, he wouldn't have treated me like he did.

"Maybe we're doing this backwards," says West with a crazy gleam in his eye.

"How's that?" Because this all feels rather hopeless.

"The only way to get rid of a ghost is to exorcize it."

"Exorcize it?"

"Yeah." West brushes his thumb against my knee and I watch the muscles in his arms ripple as he moves. "Fill you up with memories of me so there's no room left for him."

I wrap my arms around my waist, trying desperately to disappear. "What if it's not the memories that frighten me?"

"Then what scares you?"

"What if I'm not terrified of you or him?" I swallow, unsure if I have the courage to say the words. "What if I'm terrified of me?"

His nonresponse confirms there's no hope—none at all. Then my skin prickles with the light caress of fingers against my cheek. West urges me to lift my chin and it's hard when the weight of his silence crashes on my shoulders.

"Then I'll teach you how to fight the fear."

"Teach me?"

"Teach you. First you've got to trust me."

West's fingers linger on my skin and I tilt my head toward the pleasing tickle. "I trust you."

"Some," he says. "But not all the way. When things get rough, you lock yourself in your head...resort to where you feel safest. Let me in, Haley. Let me bear some of your load."

I know what he's talking about...that smothering feeling when things grow too complicated. Those moments when I would have turned to my father or my brother, but then everything became lost and I had to learn how to depend on me. "How?"

"Start by talking to me." West edges onto the bed near the pillows and offers me his hand. Tension thickens the air and I have to work harder to breathe. This is it; I either trust West or I don't. I either tap out or fight.

My hand inches for his, a battle between falling and leaping. I'm choosing this—I'm choosing West. It's like stepping out of a two-dimensional universe and walking into another when my fingers meet his and he draws me up along beside him. Colors seem richer, smells stronger. West snakes his thumb underneath my shirt and heat builds between our skin.

"Talk to me," he says again. "Uncensored."

I suck in air and I'm immersed in West's heady scent. "What do I talk about?"

"You can admit I go too fast, but at the same time you don't want to stop." West slides his hand along the curve of my waist, then slips one fingertip past the fabric of my jeans near my hip. Electricity jolts my body and I move with the thrilling shock. While I love the sensation, it also terrifies me.

"Nope. Gotta say it, not think it."

"I like kissing you." More than like. I love it. I crave it. I dream of it at night and wake up frustrated when I find myself alone in a cold bed.

West sinks lower and skims his hand along my thigh. "Just the kissing? You're not a fan of this?" And he mimics the delicious movement.

I melt into him. "I'm a fan."

West leans down, his breath hot on my ear. "And this?"

Superb, divine goose bumps. "Superfan."

"And the kisses along your neck?" he murmurs.

I wiggle against him, wishing he would. "Love those."

His hands snake around me and his strong palms glide along my spine while he blows warm air along my neck. I turn my head, exposing more of the skin there, silently begging.

"What do you want? No more staying locked inside your head. You have to tell me."

"Kiss me."

West's lips connect with my skin behind my ear and I go weak with the teasing pleasure.

"More?" he whispers.

I nod with the frequency of my rapid heartbeats, then remember he'll wait until I say the words. "More." He immediately rewards me by parting his lips and kissing the same spot again.

My breathing hitches when West flips us and lays me down on the bedspread. Air rushes out of the fluffy blanket and my hair spills all around. West hovers over me, our bodies not quite touching. His knee rests between my legs.

My hand shakes as I stroke the smooth skin of his face. West is beautiful with his blue eyes and golden-blond hair. My fingers explore down his shoulder, along his arm. He's always been strong, but with the training his muscles have become powerful, refined. Greedy, I yearn to admire the results.

Bolder than I have ever been, I ignore the redness forming on my face and tug at the hem of his shirt—a nonverbal West happily agrees to. With his shirt up and over his head, I trail a path along the plane of his chest and stomach; tracing the well-defined lines.

West closes his eyes as if my touch affects and seduces him.

My pulse thuds to the point my frame quakes. I know what I want and the courage to say it evades me until West brings my hand to his mouth. His lips press against my palm and I rush out the words, "I dream of you at night. Of this."

"Me, too." He releases my hand and I draw forward, holding my arms in the air. West grasps the hem of my shirt and he slowly edges the material up while leaving hot, lingering kisses along my stomach, between my breasts and onto my neck. West's body is blazing and what I love is the thump of his heart against my skin.

"I love you," he says.

Nervous adrenaline creeps into my bloodstream. I love him. I do. I love his strength, his tenacity, his loyalty and even his impulsiveness. But I'm frightened how those three words said aloud will change everything.

With his body blanketing mine, our hearts in tune with each other, the emotion I've been fighting overpowers me and I've never liked the feeling of losing control. My lip trembles as a hot tear escapes and streams down my cheek.

West catches it with a kiss. "We're strong together, Haley. Stronger than we are apart."

"I don't feel strong," I whisper.

"Then I'll be strong enough for both of us."

My fingers dig into his shoulders and I cling to him. "I love you."

West captures my lips and the intensity of the embrace unravels all train of thought. Our hands are everywhere: touching, exploring. His on my body. Mine on his. A strap of my bra down, then another.

We roll and his hands are tight in my hair, our tongues

slide urgently against the other, and, as I hook a leg around his, we roll again and my body arches with the way we fit.

Hands wander lower and with warmth spreading everywhere I whisper his name—one time, then another—and with a few more touches he whispers mine. West's fingers pause on the button of my jeans and we both snap open our eyes.

Our breaths come out in gasps. "I want you to be my first. This means something—making love means something. It's why I haven't done it before. I've been waiting for you."

I lick my lips and nod, wanting to know what it's like to be with someone who loves me and I love in return. My lips brush against his and West slips the button through the hole and the unzipping of my jeans becomes the only noise in the room.

Silence as we stare at one another. My jeans are unzipped. We can go forward or we can go back, and even though I'm scared as hell, I don't want to go back.

My fingers find his jeans and West's grace eludes me. A metal button through an open space of material. It should be easy, simple, uncomplicated, but my fingers fumble. One time. A second time. With the third, I feel an indention of the button forming on the tip of my finger.

West lays his hands over mine and I close my eyes, wishing I'd die. He doesn't push me away. Instead he guides my fingers in a fluid and effortless flick and his zipper crackles.

I swear to God my heart can't beat any faster.

With my bra and jeans half off, I flounder with the blanket beneath me.

"Are you cold?" he asks.

Nope. Not at all. In fact, I'm burning up, but being naked

is intimidating. I guess I'm more experienced, but really...I'm not. "Do you mind?"

He shakes his head and under the covers we shed the last of our clothes. We lie on our sides, facing each other, and West runs his hand along the curve of my body. He unashamedly looks through the gap, seeing more of me than anyone else has. "You're beautiful."

My mouth slants up and West gathers me to him. We lie there for a while, enjoying the warmth and the new feeling of being *next* to each other. I steal a few glances at *West* and I know he knows that I'm satisfying curiosity by peeking, but still...it's weird and exhilarating.

"Can we... Can you turn the lights off?" Because while West is stunning, there's an intimacy I'd prefer in the dark.

The kindness in his eyes almost removes the sting of the blush on my cheeks. He turns off the television, shifts off the bed, and I bite my lip as I watch his bare butt and the way the muscles in his shoulders move as he crosses the room.

With a flip of a switch, blackness envelops the room and it takes a second for my eyes to readjust. Little lights glimmer from his assorted electronics, and from the glow of the cracked-open bathroom, I can see just enough. West's feet pad against the carpet back to me. The bed dips and his heat reaches me before his body.

We're slow in returning to the edginess—the rawness that causes me to forget I'm naked and West is naked and that we're sharing something so intimate, so intense...

West breaks away and mutters a curse. Cold air slaps my body and panic tenses my muscles. I replay the past few seconds, searching for what I did wrong. "What is it?"

He falls back to his pillow and I tuck the sheet over my breasts. "West?"

"I don't have a condom."

I blink. He doesn't have a... "But I thought all guys..." Guess they don't.

He rubs his eyes. "I told you. I don't have sex."

"Oh." Giddiness invades my voice. "So you still want me?"

West peers at me out of the corner of his eye and motions downward. "Obviously."

I nervously giggle, then stop, feeling relieved and somewhat...frustrated. Like waking up from a dream of kissing West and not finding him in my bed. "I won't do it without one."

"Neither will I." He rolls to a sitting position and grabs his jeans. "Then we'll get one."

I don't know why, but that freaks me out. I reach out and snatch his hand. "Stay."

"But—"

I squeeze his fingers. "Stay. We can do...other...*things*... Just stay. I don't want to go to a store and pick it out because then it's not...the moment...this moment..."

West is silent for a bit, then nods. "Okay."

I breathe out a sigh. "Okay."

He slides back beside me and kisses my lips. "But I'm buying some."

"All right." I lose my breath again as his hands resume their exploration.

"I mean it," he says.

"I one hundred percent believe you." And with a few more touches we become lost.

There's a building of sensation and all the emotion drives

it to an inferno. Our bodies weave into an intricate web and, if given the option, I don't want to escape. I grab hold tighter and so does West. We gasp and then the entire world fades away, leaving only us.

We collapse into each other; muscles weak and minds drifting. Our arms and legs are tangled and West tucks me into his body. One arm draped protectively over me. My cheek rests against his chest and his heart beats steadily in my ear. I love him. I do.

West kisses the top of my head as his hands trace meaningless patterns on my back. "I love you, Haley," he whispers. "I love you."

West

I STARE AT THE REPORT CARD I received in first period. No matter how many times I unfold it, the letters never alter: solid Bs. The smile, once again, spreads across my face regardless of the anger that's been simmering inside me since Saturday night.

The bell rings for lunch and Haley stands. She tosses her light brown hair over her shoulder and, for a few seconds, I'm back in bed with her and I swear I feel that silky hair sliding against my bare chest.

"You're going to rub the ink off. Then no one's going to believe you," she says.

I refold the paper and slip it into my notebook. Haley's met my demons, grades included, and loves me anyhow. Her arm swings next to mine as we maneuver through the crowded hallway to lunch. I enjoy the satisfied tilt of her lips when my hand connects with hers. It's Monday. Saturday night changed everything for us—it made us better, made us stronger.

"It's amazing what happens when you study," she teases again.

"Or attend class." This afternoon I'm nailing my report card to the door of Dad's office.

"I was thinking we should skip lunch today." Haley flutters her eyelashes and her sexy expression almost blows me off course. Almost.

"I'm hungry."

She squishes her lips together. "I've got some pretzels in my backpack."

"I'm really hungry."

Haley stops dead at the entrance of the cafeteria and her grasp tightens. Hoping she'd continue, I walk forward until my arm completely stretches behind me. When I turn, Haley's lost the cuteness. "Don't do it, West."

"Do what?" We both know that in the cafeteria I'm going after Matt hard and fast.

The second I dropped Haley off at the corner near her uncle's house on Saturday, because we can't be seen together since his ultimatum, I've thought about this moment. The anger has built and stewed and I'm damn ready for it to boil over. Haley won't give me details, but Matt hit her and I'm done with everyone acting like she's roadkill, her family included.

"Remember what I said about you leading with your emotions," she says.

"Yes."

"Well, this is you doing it."

"Haley, this is premeditation at its best."

"It's not how long you think about it—it's the emotion. Anger is going to get you nowhere. I take that back. Anger is going to get you killed." Haley glances around the cafeteria. Sensing the anger pulsating from me, people watch us like bottleneckers with a car wreck.

"I can stop you," she says simply.

I look deep into her dark eyes and shake my head. "You wouldn't humiliate me like that."

"This is insane," she hisses. "You'll be lucky to get one punch in before the security guards take you down and the two of you get kicked out of school. Zero tolerance policy, remember? Doesn't matter who hits first—you both get suspended."

A wildness inside me creates a grin on my face. "I have a plan."

"Ah, hell, really?" Haley tosses her backpack to the ground like she's throwing in the towel. Matt's gym rules: he can't train for a week if he gets suspended for fighting at school. "When will you get it through your thick skull that I'm not worth fighting over?"

"Yes, you are. And you know this won't go to blows. The real fight will be in a few weeks in that cage."

Haley shifts into shock mode with her paled-out face. "No, West. Don't you dare challenge him. You have a better chance against Conner."

"I don't want to fight Conner. I want Matt and I want him suspended from his gym."

"You have a decent shot of standing after three rounds with Conner, but you're going to make it emotional by going after Matt. How are you going to keep your head on the game plan in the cage when Matt rattles you? When he calls me names? When he calls me a slut?"

The bastard will be dead if he goes there. "I'll be fine."

"When are you going to learn? This isn't a tough man

contest where guys beat their chest, then sees who hits harder. This is the ultimate chess match. Yeah, you've got to be strong and have skills, but a lot of times the smarter guy wins."

"Then it shouldn't be a problem. Matt's a moron."

"He's trained—a machine—and that's what I need you to be. No emotion. When I yell at you to watch for something or to do a certain combo, I need you to do it. You have to be focused and search for those open moments. Not pissed off and looking for vengeance because if you lead with your emotions, you won't find vengeance. You'll find your ass handed to you."

"All noted," I say. "Are we done, because I've got a fight to start."

"When are you going to stop acting on every impulse? It's going to get you killed."

"I'll stop." I clutch her hand and she tries to yank it back, too pissed at me to let me touch. I flash her a grin and she rolls her eyes, annoyed I can easily disarm her. I lift her hand to my mouth and kiss her fingers. "After I settle this with him."

"You're like loving someone sentenced to death row."

"But you love me." I drop her hand and stalk to the corner. Matt places his tray at a spot at the end of the table and laughs as he says something to his friends. His low-life little brother, Conner, sits at his left-hand side. No more game playing. It's time we call this fight what it is: a war.

Matt's head snaps up as my fingers grip his tray and I push it off the table. The tray, a plastic plate, two bowls and a carton of milk clank and bang to the floor. Food splatters everywhere.

“My bad,” I say. “I must have tripped.”

“He’s mine alone.” Matt jumps to his feet as well as the rest of his crew, but before Matt can gain traction, I grab his collar and slam him into the wall. “If you look at Haley again, talk to Haley again or touch Haley again, I’ll kill you. You want to hit someone, you’re hitting me. Got it?”

A shadow darkens his features and he knows I know. Matt’s fist flies for my face and my guard goes up and I block the blow. My jab immediately retaliates. Purple shirts are everywhere as the school’s security guards pummel us.

Matt lunges for me. “You’re fucking dead, Young!”

“Bring it!”

He points as the security guards pull him back. “It’s you and me in the cage. You and me!”

I relax so the security guards ease up on their manhandling. Mission accomplished.

Haley

THE CUTTING OF VEGETABLES turns into a rote movement. The sizzle of the meat on the stove is the saving buzz that drowns out the noise from the living room and keeps me from blowing my brains out. Out of the corner of my eye, Jax drums his fingers in a heavy metal beat against his arm and gives the floor a death glare. "I can help you cut vegetables."

Chop, chop, chop. The onions on the butcher block shape into smaller pieces. "It's better if we keep you away from sharp objects."

"True. Nice what your boy did at lunch today. I found an ounce of respect for him."

I sigh loudly. West got suspended for the rest of the day over his stupid stunt with Matt. "He'll be fighting Matt now."

Jax grunts. "Like he wasn't going to be fighting him before."

"Do you think West will be ready?" Because I sparred, Jax and Kaden have upheld their end of the agreement and have been helping me train West. Jax has been working with him on boxing and Kaden on grappling.

Jax has that thoughtful-owl look again. "I don't know.

Maybe. He's got raw talent, but he's just that—raw. Plus he's got a hell of a temper. You've gotta tell him to control it."

"I have."

"Then tell him again."

My uncle's voice rises. "...biggest screwup on the planet..." Jax's mom hums a church hymn louder from her forever sanctuary in her bedroom. She's mending something...again.

I pour more oil into the skillet, so the hissing sound of the fryer will mask listening to my uncle berate my younger cousin for walking into the house with dirt on his sneakers.

"It could catch fire if you do that," Jax says. Our eyes meet and an insane spark of hope stirs within me and the sad part is the same delirium burns in Jax's eyes.

"The Red Cross gives shelter to people whose homes burn down." I return to the vegetables. "In small disasters they often give hotel rooms. Sometimes multiple rooms depending upon the size of the family."

"Interesting. I'll keep that in mind."

The more time I spend in this house, the crazier I become. The aura of my uncle is embedded in the paint in the walls, a fine layer on the floors, hanging from the ceiling. It lurks and consumes and digests. Sometimes I find myself wishing he'd choke while he eats, fall asleep at the wheel or just drop dead.

I toss the onions into the hot oil. "I think I'm becoming evil."

"It's the house. If we survive until we graduate from high school, everything will be fine."

Mom walks into the kitchen with Maggie on her hip. Music blares from the earbuds stuck in my sister's ears. Even though my sister is eight, she clings to my mother like a toddler. Maggie isn't immature; she's afraid of evil. She should be scared, instead of being numb like me.

My mother settles Maggie into a chair. "Have you seen your father?" In her jeans and black Roadhouse shirt, she's seconds away from stepping out the door to start her second job.

After my acceptance to the University of Kentucky, he's been akin to a ghost. One more thing I've screwed up. "He's probably still at the library. Dad's really trying for a job."

Mom sucks in a breath like she's going to talk, then stops before slipping paper and crayons in front of my sister. "Please take care of Maggie while I'm gone."

Jax snatches a piece of raw potato. "With my life."

"Making sure she doesn't hear yelling, eats her dinner and goes to bed will suffice. I'm hoping none of you will be reduced to life sacrificing."

Jax chuckles. "Just saying."

"You're a good boy." She pats Jax on his arm. "And you're one of Dad's favorites."

Jax pops the potato wedge into his mouth and the grin on his face speaks volumes. Mom kisses his cheek, my cheek, then Maggie's and is out the door. Somehow the room loses warmth.

"You know I've seen your dad a couple of times up at the strip mall."

The knife in my hand pauses. "He's probably wasting time before the bus shows."

"He could be going to the bar."

I viciously slice through another potato. "Have you seen him there?"

He's silent as the blade of the knife thumps into the wooden board with each stroke.

“We don’t have the money for it,” I say. “And Dad doesn’t drink. At least not like that.”

“Beer at the bar is cheap.”

I slam the knife down and round on Jax. “My father wouldn’t give up.”

“Not the enemy.” He picks up my sister, who sits staring at us wide-eyed. “Come on, Mags. Let’s hide in the basement.”

West

THE PRINCIPAL SUSPENDED ME for the rest of the day because I slammed Matt into a wall. I chuckle. That would have gotten my ass expelled at Worthington.

At the breakfast bar in my mother's kitchen, I pile high another layer of ham and smash the bread on top. Haley's been on me about weight. She's threatening me with hours wrapped in plastic in a sauna if I don't stop eating high-calorie garbage. I've got five more pounds to drop and ham shouldn't kill me. The sandwich melts in my mouth. After the tournament, I'm eating everything in sight.

I've got thirty minutes before I have to head to the gym to train for the evening with Jax and Kaden. Haley's taking the night off to watch her younger sister.

The rumble of wheels causes me to halt midchew. Rachel came home yesterday and I've managed to avoid her. I glance at the back door, the sandwich still in my hand, but Rachel's fast in her wheelchair and I wouldn't make it out without her noticing. She rolls into the kitchen and our eyes meet. My throat constricts and I have to force down the food in my mouth.

She doesn't say anything as she coasts past me to the fridge. I shift my weight as she attempts to maneuver so she can open the door. Her movements become crisp and her eyes narrow on her wheels. I step toward her and she snaps, "I can do it."

I step back and toss my hands in the air. Everything inside me twists as she moves the chair forward, backward and forward again until she can finally open the damn door. Her eyes fall to the right and my heart sinks when she lowers her head.

The housekeeper forgot to store drinks on the lower shelves. Just fuck.

She slams the refrigerator door and rolls over to the windows. Rachel blinks rapidly as she looks out at the garage. That building was her home. Whenever she became frustrated or mad or lonely, she went out there and tinkered with her car. Besides the fact she can't drive anymore and that her beloved Mustang became toast in the wreck, Rachel can only touch a closed hood.

Rachel lost her home.

"I'm sorry," I say.

"It's bad enough I've lost the ability to walk or stand, but did I have to lose you, too?"

The floor creaks and Rachel and I both turn our heads to see Dad standing in the doorway to the kitchen. He clears his throat and motions for me to follow him out. "West."

A million words form in my mind. Rachel didn't lose me. I love her. I would cut off my own legs and give them to her if it meant she could walk again. Because I'm an idiot, I say none of them. Instead, I open the fridge, grab a diet soda and leave it on the table.

Dad's already at his mahogany desk when I enter his office and slink into the chair across from him. The table behind him is full of pictures of our family. Most of them are of Mom and their lost daughter, Colleen. It's the loose picture of me and Dad stuck to the corner of an eight-by-ten matted framed picture that's my favorite. I was eight in the photo and thought my dad kicked ass.

Dad's in a white button-down shirt with no tie. His suit coat is hung on the back of his chair—an indication he just arrived home. He finishes typing on his laptop, then focuses on me. "Your guidance counselor called and told me about the fight."

Prepared for this, I'd packed the moment I walked in the door. I've got three full bags ready to go and a wad of cash thanks to my job at the bar.

"Would you like to tell me what happened?"

"What?"

"Tell me why you got into the fight."

Dad hasn't asked why I've done anything since my second suspension in eighth grade. "The guy hurt Haley."

"Haley's your girlfriend." It's a question said as a statement.

"Yes."

He reaches into a file folder and produces the report card I hammered to his office door. "You could have handed this to me."

"Could of." But nailing a straight B report card to his door was the equivalent of flipping him off. The suspension screams I'm a failure, while the report card is my "fuck you" to him.

Dad flattens his lips and stares at his desk. I know that

look. He's seconds away from losing his patience and tossing out the "You're a disappointment" lecture. I scoot to the end of my chair, ready to leave.

"Is it possible for us to talk?" he asks.

"You know I got suspended, right? Still feel like sharing a feel-good moment?"

"I don't remember the last time we've had a conversation."

My eyes flicker back to the picture of us, and Dad follows my line of sight.

"It hasn't been that long," he says.

Yeah, it has, but I relax back in my seat. I'll admit—I'm disarmed yet cautious. He's never waved a white flag, but I wouldn't put it past him to knife me in the back. "Let's talk."

"All right. Let's talk." Dad taps his fingers together. I search for the last conversation Dad and I had without it turning into a slam fest. I look over at the photo again. Dad and I had made a birdhouse together for a school project—the same day I first used a hammer and a nail.

"I fix stuff," I say. "At a bar. It's what I was hired to do, and I'm good at it."

"I know what you've been doing. At the bar, at school and with the gym."

Anger tremors deep within me. The lone outward sign is the grim lift of my lips. "You've had me followed."

"You're my son and you left home. What did you expect me to do?"

"You *kicked* me out and I expected you to come after me. Not let me live in a car for two weeks." The words slip out and I shift, immediately wishing I could take them back.

As a child I wondered if Dad's hands were a crystal ball with all the answers because of the way he'd lose himself in them when I stood in the middle of this room waiting for whatever punishment for my crimes. I know now there's no magic—just staring.

"I wanted you to ask me to return home," he finally says.

"Wouldn't have happened." I would have lived in a car forever rather than crawl to him.

"I know," he mumbles, then clears his throat. "And I don't think you would have returned home even if I had come after you. I hated using your mother as the excuse to force you back, but I didn't think you'd come home any other way. It was obvious when you didn't return that weekend that you were set on proving something and I know how you are when you get determined."

If he had asked me... No, if he had begged, I would have come home, but begging isn't his style and crawling isn't mine. Maybe Dad's right. Maybe I was set on proving something.

"Do you know what I see when I look at you?" Dad asks.

"A failure? A loser? A disappointment?" If I say it first, it steals the sting from his words.

"Me." Dad unbuttons the top of his shirt. "Every time I look at you, I see me and it's a mirror I don't like looking into."

Jesus Christ. I lean forward and scrub my face with my hands. For years we've torn each other down. That's how we communicate—in glares and words of hate. How the fuck am I supposed to respond to this? My head spins as if I've been knocked around.

"You remind me of myself," he says. "Especially at your age. I thought your grandfather was going to kick me out before I graduated from high school."

Neither he nor his parents have mentioned this before. Dad, in my head, has always been excruciatingly perfect. “What stopped him from doing it?”

“Your grandmother.” His eyes become distant and so does the grin on his face. “Just like your mother would have stopped me if she wasn’t involved with Rachel at the time. She’s still mad at me—for kicking you out.”

I massage my neck. The muscles tighten there, creating the sensation of choking. “You messed up? When you were my age?”

“I messed up then...and I messed up now.”

Is he apologizing? I glance over my shoulder to see if Mom is there, coaching him. The door is shut and it’s only the two of us. “How bad did you fuck up?”

“Worse than you.” Dad picks up the report card. “I never made straight Bs. I never voluntarily worked a job or kept one and I never found something to focus on like you have... When was the last time you hung out with any of your old friends?”

I shrug. “A while.”

“You spend a lot of time at the gym.”

“Yeah.”

Dad slides over a brochure for top-of-the-line equipment for a home gym. “Rachel will be spending most of her time in physical therapy, so I’m converting the front living room into her own gym and I’m hiring someone to personally oversee her recovery. While I was researching, I found this. I thought you’d like to pick out a few pieces.”

I have the same heroin-induced haze as when I talk to Abby and fall down the rabbit hole. “Thanks, but I like the gym.”

"Your mother would like to see you home more since you'll most likely be going to college in the fall and...so would I."

"Did you get hit in the head recently?" I hold out my left arm. "Shooting pains down this arm accompanied by chest pain? Numbness on one side of your face? New medications or just dabbling in recreational meth?"

Dad chuckles and his dark eyes shine. He's given this look a hundred times to my brothers, but never to me. Fuck me—is that pride?

"I've talked to the administration at Worthington. You can return to school, and I've talked to the admissions office at the University of Louisville. They're willing to review your application again."

Gaped mouth. A couple of breaths in. "You know I was suspended for fighting, right?"

"Yes. But over the last few weeks, something has happened inside you. Something that didn't happen inside me until I was in my twenties. You're coming alive and I want to be a part of it."

Wait... "Twenties? I thought you and Mom met in your freshman year of college." The tale was one of those all-American love stories. The well-brought-up boy and girl fall in love over a shared love of education, money and extracurricular activities.

Dad's eyes flash to mine and I slump back in my seat. "You lied."

He rolls his neck and his silence confirms the truth. "Did you even meet at college?"

"No," he answers. "I know what I'm talking about and I don't want you to repeat my mistakes. Let me help you."

For the past two months, everything has been bleak and

dark and now there is light. I was stupid before. Made stupid choices. Had a future I willingly threw away. Then I discovered hunger and loneliness and my lone salvation was Haley.

Haley. "I'll stay at Eastwick and graduate there."

His face falls. "Worthington is one of the best schools in the state. A diploma from there will open countless doors for you in the future. Eastwick has nothing to offer you."

It has Haley. "I'm staying there."

"Are you scared you can't make the same grades at Worthington? Apply yourself like you have there. The problem has always been within you, and you're finally motivated."

My skin crawls like I'm being cornered in a dark alley. "I'm motivated at Eastwick. I like it there and I'm staying."

"Is this over the girl?"

My chin lifts. "You mean Haley?"

"I sent you into a situation where you could have made every wrong choice and instead you found a way to clean your life up. If we're mirrors of each other, take my advice. This is a honeymoon period. You'll do well at first but then sink under the bad influences. You've got the motivation now. Let's get you back to where you belong and keep you from backsliding."

"I won't backslide." Haley is the reason I'm halfway decent.

"From where I sit, the fight today at school is the beginning of the backslide."

"If we're mirrors of each other...if there's more to you and Mom's story than what you're saying, then you'll understand that I have a reason to not backslide."

"I'm telling you, from experience, a girl can be your worst

downfall. It can change your path, but not always in the way you think."

What the hell?

Dad's cell pings and he scratches his head when he scans the message. "I've got to cut this short. I want you back at Worthington. We'll work on getting you into U of L. Quit the job at the bar and I'll find you a position with me. The gym equipment will be here at the end of the week. You can start working out at home."

I harden into a statue. "I'm not giving up my life."

"Not your life. You're returning home after spending two months figuring yourself out. You're doing okay now, but the people you're around will cause major damage. You're capable of more. I know it and now you know it. Your body is here, but you haven't mentally returned home. You wanted me to ask, so I'm asking now. Come home. Take advantage of everything I can offer."

Internally I'm screaming as my insides tear in two. This moment... It's what I've craved for years. To hear my dad say he's proud of me as a son, but the crushing notion that in order to keep his approval, I have to walk away from a life I like... I stand.

"I'm sorry. I can't. I need to go to Eastwick. I need the gym. I need—"

"Haley," Dad finishes for me. "You don't. I understand you think you do, but you don't. Things between you two will end up bad. Trust me on this."

"Haley and I will be fine. Besides, she needs me. I'm helping her with a scholarship—"

"I laid off her father," he says simply. "I've had eyes on you since you didn't come home that Friday night. I know where she lives and I know who she is. I know what she's lost. I know it all, but does she know my decisions created her nightmare?"

The fear that kept me from kissing Haley the night I stayed in her room resurfaces. "No."

"I also know about the fight in two weeks," Dad continues. "I'm sorry, but I can't permit the fight to happen. I lost Colleen. On the heels of everything that's happened over the past two months with Rachel, I can't risk it. Your mother can't take anything else. I can't take anything else."

"I'm eighteen." My voice sounds far-off as I comprehend what he's telling me. "I don't need your permission to fight."

"No, you don't. But I think you'll want to wait on your decision until you consider what I'm about to offer. If you walk away from the fight, if you return home and leave Haley and this entire new life behind, I'll give her what her father can't. I'll pay for her college tuition."

Haley

I STEP OUT OF THE BACK DOOR with a full trash bag in hand and stare up at the rolling gray clouds. It's been sunny for days, but tonight thunderstorms are supposed to move in. Small drops of water sprinkle onto my arms, but I don't care. I'd rather be wet than inside.

Besides West getting kicked out of school for harassing Matt, today was a good day. I finished the paperwork for the scholarship and my teachers let me skip classes so I could work on the video at the computer lab. Now all I need is the ending: the fight between Matt and West.

West winning would be a fabulous ending, but my hope doesn't lie there because that is the stuff of fairy tales. This is reality and I've built my whole premise around taking a scrapper and training him in a few techniques in the hopes he could listen during a fight and last one round.

The ultimate irony: my advantage is I know how Matt fights and I've taught West how to use Matt's weaknesses against him. I've given West the best ammunition I have. The rest, unfortunately, is up to him.

"I've been waiting for you." Matt turns the corner of the

house and I jump out of my skin. The instinct is to throw the trash at him and run back inside, but heading in isn't much better.

I toss the garbage into the can and wipe at the drizzle gathering on my forehead. Avoiding Matt is what I should do, but I'm done running from him. I'm done being a coward. "What do you want?"

Matt rubs a spot over his eye before shoving both of his hands into his pockets. "We're two weeks away from the fight. Have you considered my offer?"

"I'm with West now. We're over, Matt."

"Did you know he's a Young?" he asks.

I curse internally. West has tried to keep people from knowing his roots, afraid his family's money would complicate matters. We both knew the truth would eventually surface. "I know my boyfriend's last name."

"No, Haley. He belongs to *the* Youngs."

Crap. "He doesn't have any money. His dad cut him off—"

"I don't give a fuck about the money. I give a fuck about you."

"He's good to me."

"*I* was good to you and I screwed up one time. I'm curious if you'll hold a grudge against him like you've held a grudge against me."

The rain picks up and beats against my uncle's car. The air is warm, but the drops are cold. I shiver against them. "Is there a point before I drown?"

"You know my dad was also laid off with your dad, right?"

I nod. My dad worked in the office. His dad on the line. Fortunately for Matt, his dad found work at another local plant.

"The Youngs are the reason why our dads lost their jobs. They're the ones that bought the company, then sent the lines to Mexico. Ask your boyfriend how long he's kept that from you."

West

A BLUISH LIGHT GLOWS from Rachel's bed and I freeze in her doorway. It's late and she should be asleep. The clothes I let Haley borrow are in my hands. Sheets shift and, with a click, the lamp on Rachel's beside table illuminates. With her head propped against a stack of pillows and the covers pulled up to her chest, Rachel squints against the light. "You okay?"

I slip into the room and close the door behind me. Mom sleeps lightly, attuned to any sound in case Rachel should need her. "I was hoping to sneak in and put back your clothes."

"Hold on. I need proof. Ethan won't believe me." Rachel raises the phone in her hand and snaps a picture. "Didn't see the whole cross-dressing thing happening. Maybe I should have. You are pretty for a guy."

I smile, forgetting how much I love her dry sense of humor. "Sorry I woke you."

"I was already up." Her cell buzzes and a silly grin plays on Rachel's lips as she reads the text. Her fingers type a response and then she shyly glances at me. "It's Isaiah. My sleeping patterns are insane so he..." Her cheeks turn red. "He keeps me company."

Isaiah—the guy who hasn't left my sister's side and walks around school like a zombie. The guy who attends every single physical therapy appointment and follows every rule my parents have created. The guy who loves her. Just like I love Haley. "You love him?"

"Yes." The answer is swift.

Before the accident, I would have flopped onto her bed and messed with some breakable item in her room to get a rise out of her, not skulked near the door. I lost that right the day I waltzed into this room and took the money she needed. "I'm sorry. What's happened to you...it's my fault."

All of Haley's warnings over the past couple of months crash in my head: I act without thinking, I'm impulsive and my impulsiveness hurts not only me, but the people I love. It hurt Rachel and now it's hurting Haley.

I recklessly wound my way into Haley's life, reacting each time, thinking I knew more, but the truth is I'm an idiot. Haley once wondered if we were nothing more than actions to reactions—helpless against our own fate. It's true. I react and others pay.

"I did this," I say to Rachel. "I'm the reason why..." And my eyes snap shut with the burn.

"West." The hurt in Rachel's tone scrapes at the already pulsating wound. "You have to come here, because I can't go to you."

The impulse is to leave—to run as far as possible—but I'm done with impulses. I'm done doing what feels good. Everyone has told me my sister needed me, but I was too selfish to listen. I was too concerned about the ache.

I sink to the floor with my back against her bedside table, not because my sister needs me, but because I'm a bastard and need her. I fucking need my sister and the past two months without her have almost driven me over the edge. Rachel rests her head on a pillow and stretches out her arm. Without looking at her, I take her hand.

"It's not your fault," she says.

The muscles in my face pull down. "It is."

"It's not."

"You can't walk," I snap and I feel her hand flinch in mine. "I stole your money and now you can't walk and there is nothing I can do to fucking fix it." I suck in a ragged breath and nausea creeps into my windpipe. "I'm sorry, Rachel. I'm so fucking sorry."

Rachel pulls on my hand and, like a house of cards, I tumble. I hurt Rachel and I'm on the verge of hurting Haley. When will I stop paying for all my past sins? How many things will I lose that I love in exchange for all the pain I've inflicted?

"I don't cry," I say. I don't. Men don't fucking cry, but as Rachel touches the top of my head, I fucking lose my shit.

"I know," she answers.

Yet we stay that way until Rachel squeezes my hand and I eventually squeeze back.

Attempting to reclaim my pride, I sit up and wipe at my face. "If I could fix this, I would. If I hadn't stolen the money..."

"If I had told you or Ethan or Mom or Dad about the trouble I was in...if Gavin never gambled...if Colleen had never had cancer...it doesn't matter anymore. None of it does. Will you please let this go, because I can't carry any more burdens."

"I want you to be happy."

"I know. I want the same for you... I'm going to walk again."

I try to pull my hand back, but she keeps it.

"I mean it. I'm going to walk again and I want you there when I do."

"Okay," I say if only to appease her. One of us deserves a happy ending.

"Promise you'll be there," she says.

"I promise."

She squeezes my hand again, and, after I return the gesture, we both let go.

We're silent and I'm grateful just to have the opportunity to sit with her again. Too many horrible conversations will be had tomorrow. I'm fine with silence tonight.

"The what-ifs," Rachel starts.

I know the what-ifs—I've asked them my entire life. "Yeah."

"If Colleen had never gotten cancer, me, you and Ethan would never be alive."

"Yeah."

"It's an awful thought to have. To know you're alive because someone else died."

"It is." And I say what I think every day and what she needs to hear. "But I'm still happy to be here."

Rachel glances down at me. "Me, too."

I nod and mischief twinkles in her blue eyes. "So, why do you have my clothes? And FYI, you'd look better in the V-neck."

God, I've missed my sister. "Haley needed something to change into this weekend."

"Abby's told me about her. So it's true? My notorious girl-using brother has been tamed? Wait, don't answer yet." Rachel slides her finger frantically over her phone and pushes an app that records. "Okay—answer."

"Yeah." Her enthusiasm's contagious, and I smile in spite of myself. "You would have liked her."

"Liked?" Rachel closes the app and her smile falters. "As in past tense liked?"

I don't want it to be liked. I want Haley and me to be forever. "Dad will give her a scholarship if I leave her."

"No, West..."

I throw her a sharp look. "Don't lecture me unless you're going to say you wouldn't do everything in your power to grant Isaiah his dreams. Dad will give Haley what I can't. What the world won't give."

Rachel settles back into bed and stares at her immobile legs. "I ran away from you guys and ended up in a car accident that's left me like this. Going to the dragway that night saved Isaiah's life. If given the choice, I would do it all over again."

"See."

"No, not see. It's not the same because Isaiah wants me and I want him. Doesn't Haley get a vote?"

"Haley's a little too self-sacrificing to think it through." I want to keep Haley, but letting her go means she'll have a future. I stand and head to the door though the pain emanating from my chest comes close to doubling me over.

"Don't do anything stupid," Rachel says.

"Nah, not stupid." Just heartbreaking.

Haley

AT SCHOOL, I STAND UNDER the overhang and watch the parking lot. My fingers flip through the pages of my book like shuffling cards in a deck. The motion and the crinkling sound of the pages soothe me. I couldn't sleep last night as I contemplated the same question over and over again. Does West know?

Adrenaline kicks into my bloodstream when West's SUV pulls into the lot. He's early, which is good but also weird. A fine mist hangs in the air and the droplets sparkle on his car as he parks under a streetlight. I can't see his face past the dark windows. I can't see inside.

I close my eyes and inhale, trying to calm the terror in my veins. What if that's all West has been? Pretty on the outside, but hiding on the inside. No. I swallow and open my eyes. West loves me. This is going to be okay.

West steps out of his SUV and my entire body rocks back. Nausea climbs up my throat and I turn my head, expecting the dry heave. Please let this be a mistake.

He's sickeningly gorgeous as he walks toward me. A black tie hangs from his neck and it stands out against the crisp white button-down shirt. His black dress pants fit him like they were tailor-made and his golden hair is gelled into style. He's poised and perfect and beautiful, but he's not my West.

I honest to God pinch myself to check if I'm dreaming. What is in front of me has to be a figment of my fears—a nightmare. The prick of pain on my arm does not compare to the slicing at my heart.

West shoves his hands in his pockets when he stops a foot away from me.

We stare at each other—me like I've never seen him before. "Why are you dressed like that?"

"I'm going back to Worthington. In fact, I'm going back to everything."

Everything? "What does that mean?"

West surveys the school building, the cars, the other students who turn their heads like owls in order to observe our showdown. "I don't belong here. I never have. It's time I stop acting like somebody I'm not and return to my world."

A fresh surge of anger rushes through me; I'm pissed off at myself for loving him. "Spit it out."

"Look, the suspension made me rethink everything. When I got home last night, I expected my dad to throw me out again and he didn't. We talked and he got me back into Worthington and he convinced me that even though I returned, I hadn't really been home. He's right. I need to be home. It's time for me to be a Young again. Haley, I loved you. I did, but we've run our course."

"We've run our course?" I snap my mouth shut. A million thoughts collide in my mind… A thousand emotions. The urge is to ask him why, to convince him to stay, to ask if he ever really did love me, but the words that slip out are the ones that cause so much ripping pain that I actually sway as I say them. "I was just another girl."

"No. Never." He steps toward me and my arm flies out as a warning. West rocks on his feet and I lift my chin.

"Are you tapping out on me?"

It's possible that pain softens his blue eyes, but I don't think it is. It has to be pity. He used me and now he's pitying me.

"Are you tapping out on me?" My muscles tighten with every word. I welcome the anger. I crave the anger because anger is a hell of a lot better than hurt. "Are you walking away from me and the fight?"

He nods and glances away. My eyes burn with tears. I'm stupid. So, so stupid. "Did you know who I was? Did you know your father is the reason why we lost everything?"

West barely looks me in the eye and the answer is so quiet I almost miss it. "Yes."

I roll with the impact of his words as if it were a physical punch, but, like I've been taught, I rebound and step into his space. Tilting my head, I give him no room to focus on anything but me. "I wouldn't have cared if you told me, but this..."

I flip his tie before I press both of my hands against his chest and push. West staggers back and it's not because of my strength, but it's because he gives. "This I can't forgive. Guess I wasn't worth fighting for."

Not allowing him a chance to reply, I pivot and disappear into a swarm of students unloading off the buses. My lower lip trembles and I fight the tears. I walk fast into the school and as the first hot tear cascades down my face I race into the nearest bathroom.

Girls chatter and talk and I ignore them as I duck into the last stall. With the door slammed shut behind me, I slide down the wall and feel as if the ground beneath me is collapsing into a black hole. I suck in air, but none goes into my lungs and then I hold my breath to halt the sob, but it comes regardless—racking my body as if I'm having convulsions.

I've lost it all… My home, my family, my hope, West. There's no place left to go. No more backup plans… There's no more fight.

West

I CHANGED INTO JEANS and a T-shirt before driving to the bar. The private-school dress code would get my ass handed to me by a mob of angry laid-off union workers. Though getting the shit kicked out of me by a mob doesn't sound like a bad idea. It could possibly hurt less than the memory of breaking not only my heart, but the heart of the only girl I've ever loved: Haley.

A few guys play poker at a table in the corner. It's sad I've grown fond of the sour stench of spilled beer. Like always, Denny hovers over a laptop near the end of the bar. "You're late."

Worthington starts an hour later than public schools. I glance around. It kills me how much pride I've got in the dump. The tables and chairs I fixed, the mounting of the speakers, the woodwork along the bar. I finally found something I'm talented at and it all goes down the drain.

I suck in air to keep my fists from closing. I'm not reacting anymore. I'm thinking and I'm giving Haley what she needs. "Thanks for the opportunity, but I'm quitting."

My boss's muscles ripple as he straightens. Denny's the

most peculiar person I've met: a big-ass man who feeds a stray drug dealer and gives a job to a throwaway. "You crawled back to Daddy after all. I thought you had grown a fucking pair of balls."

I never told him I was the rich boy. "You're talking about stuff you don't know about."

He crosses his arms over his chest. "I'm talking about shit I've known about since your momma was in damned diapers. Sit you sorry ass down and wait."

It's like I've been absorbed in a tunnel when Denny shuts his laptop and heads into the back. All the sights and sounds and smells of the bar fade away as I sink onto a stool. Thoughts race in my mind... The months of wondering why my mother comes here... Was she having an affair... Abby telling me she came to see her brother...and as Denny slips out of the back with an overstuffed scrapbook in his hand, the horror of the truth makes me dizzy.

"You can still walk away." Abby slinks up next to me. Doing something she's never done before, she touches my arm. Nudges it and tilts her head to the exit at the same time. "It's okay to not want to know some truths. Pretending is much easier. Trust me on this."

I'm slow meeting her eyes. "Did you lie to me about why she came here?"

"I lie." The confession with no apology. "It's what I do to survive and every now and then I do it to help others survive. I need all the good karma I can get."

The door to the entrance is propped open by a wedge of wood. I could leave and return to my old life like Dad suggested. So many routes to take: head to the party tonight at Mike's, fill out the new paperwork for the University of Louisville or stay. Leaving could be blissful—to remain ignorant of things that I have no doubt will change me.

Denny drops the scrapbook onto the bar and the sound awakens the drunks and me. Like it's a spell book that contains magic that can alter history, my hand hovers over the cover, fingertips barely brushing the edge.

"There's no going back after this," says Abby. "No take backs."

There was no going back the moment I met Haley. Regardless of what's in this book, I'm changed for good. I open it and close my eyes. It's me— It's a fucking picture of me. My body convulses like I've been shot multiple times.

I reopen my eyes at the sound of pouring liquid. Denny fills two shot glasses with straight Maker's. He inches one to me and toasts me with the other. "To family and whatever the fuck that means."

He swigs the shot. I stare at mine, half thinking the burn of bourbon will erase the information, but I made my bed... I chuckle... No, Mom made her bed and now I'm lying in it.

"Dad said they didn't meet in college." But even when he said that, I assumed Dad was the one who messed up, not Mom.

"Tell you that, did he?" Denny laughs like one of us told a joke. "That man's a real piece of work."

"Mom said she made mistakes." Especially when she grieves over Colleen. Mom would sit in a ball on the floor of Colleen's room and wonder if her death was the punishment for Mom's past unknown crimes. I imagined the worst thing she did was speed on the freeway.

Denny pours himself another drink. "She made a mistake by screwing a Young and accepting his marriage proposal over mine. Colleen wasn't a mistake, even if she was biologically a Young. You weren't a mistake, either. You were a glimpse of what Miriam and I should have had to begin with."

The world loses focus and I rip out the picture of me as an infant in this very fucking bar. "I was conceived to save Colleen, so this is bullshit."

"That idea only occurred to your mom after the stick turned blue. Half genes had to count, right? Your mom was born and bred in this neighborhood. She always thought fast on her feet in order to survive. Except when that Young decided to flip off his parents by slumming it on our side of town. She couldn't see straight when he showed."

"They met at a bar?"

"This bar. My dad owned it then." His eyes flicker to Abby, who's stayed unusually silent. "Dad also had a habit of taking care of those who needed it."

"How long has the affair been going on between you and Mom?"

He smirks. "The one your mom had when she cheated on me with your father and got pregnant with Colleen, or the one night your mother and I spent together when she found out Colleen's cancer progressed to stage four and your father took a business phone call after getting the news?"

Mom's from this neighborhood.

Mom's from this neighborhood and her boyfriend used to be the guy in front of me. Dad said that he went wild when he was younger. I guess this is where he ended up. In this bar, hitting on my mother and they created Colleen. Then they got married and lied to us.

They lied.

They lied because everything with the Youngs is about image.

When life became complicated, after my parents had built a marriage with three children, they buckled under the weight of a sick child and my mother came here...to Denny... She returned to what she knew and she made me.

"Sounds like he's not my father."

"He gave you what I couldn't." Denny stretches his arms wide. "You're looking at my palace. Screams day care, doesn't it?"

I shove the picture into my back pocket. "Don't fuck with me. I know she comes here on the third Friday of every month."

Abby reaches over and flips the album to the middle and there are more pictures of me. "She comes to bring him pictures. It's what he asked for when he gave up rights."

"Why not mail them?" I push. "She visits because you two are still involved."

Denny shakes his head. "If I had to give you up, your mother had to show here once a month and face the decisions she made. She has to look me in the eye, knowing what she's denying me. Me and Miriam, it didn't continue. Even after that night we spent together, she still belonged to your dad. That was never a question."

What was he forcing her to face? That I wasn't in his life or that she wasn't? But the question stays internal.

"Here's the truth." He shuts the album. "Your mom and dad made mistakes and so have I. We were young and didn't know who the fuck we were. I've seen you change over the last two months. You can go back to that huge house and play marionette for the Youngs just like your mom and dad did or you can break the chains and make your own decisions."

I jump off the stool, then kick it out of the way as I step into his space. The stool snaps and rattles against the ground. "You don't know what I'm up against."

"If it's the Youngs, it contains control and money. Just a tidbit of fatherly advice—once you start down that path, it's like entering a savage garden. It's beautiful until the vines tear you apart. Your mom used to be a different person. She used to be full of life."

I loathe the pity flowing out of Abby's eyes and I suddenly understand why she hates it. "Why the hell am I listening to you? You gave me up."

"Funny," says Denny, "how you still ended up here. The kid who walked in here two months ago thought being a man meant calling out every asshole on the block. Tell me, are you the same stupid kid or have you figured out what being a man truly means?"

Haley

THE SKIES FINALLY OPENED UP and erupted in rain. My hair sticks to my face and my shirt clings to my body as I enter my uncle's. I shiver against the combination of the warmth of the house and the cold drops of rain that slither down my arms. My toes go behind my heel to kick off my shoe, but I stop when Mom walks into the living room with a phone pressed to her ear. Her face is white and her fingers shake.

"If you hear from him, you'll let me know?" she asks. Everything is wrong. The house sits silent. My uncle doesn't rule the world from his chair. My younger cousins aren't shoving each other against a wall. Maggie isn't drawing on the floor.

"Okay, thanks." She clicks off the phone and she looks at me. "I thought you were heading to the gym after school."

I fight the automatic tears with the mention of anything associated with West. "I changed my mind. Where's Paul?"

"Your aunt persuaded him to leave with her to help me out. I need time."

The way her hands shake sets me on edge. "What's wrong?"

"It's your father. He's missing."

West

IT'S CLOSE TO MIDNIGHT and I slam the back door to the kitchen. My mother spins. Her cell phone is tight to her ear and her eyes are wide and puffy. "He's here."

Mom pushes a button and lowers the phone. I've spent hours driving, thinking about my mother: her asking me continually to use a napkin at the dinner table, the glares when I'd wear a hat backward at a charity event, teaching which fork to use at a dinner party, the countless tux ties she'd undone and done again. "You lied."

"I didn't think Denny would tell you."

"For eighteen years I've thought I was a failure. I thought *I* was the reason Colleen died, but I was never going to be a match to begin with."

Her hand flashes to her heart. "They said there might be a slim hope, so I did hope, and it gave your father hope, and he was able to see past my mistake and love you because you were going to be our answer."

I throw my arms out. "And then he hated me once I failed!"

"That's not true." Dad walks into the kitchen.

Dark hair, dark eyes and nothing like me. "Is it a relief

I'm not yours? You must have been dying to tell me since when, fifth grade?"

Dad loosens the tie stuck at his throat. "You're my son. *My* son. I never wanted you to know."

I yank the picture out of my back pocket and slam it on the island. "I'm not your son."

The moment I hit the hallway, I turn. "I gave up Haley because of you. I gave up the one person who meant a thing to me."

Mom comes up behind Dad and sets a hand on his shoulder. I don't understand the two of them. They hurt each other, betray each other, lie and cheat and yet they still act like they are in love.

Dad covers her hand with his. "You're wrong about Haley. You didn't give her up because of me. You gave her up to help you. To help her."

I chuckle. The son of a bitch has actually said something right. "True, but if it wasn't for you trying to control me, I wouldn't have been faced with a choice between living in hell without her or being a bastard for keeping her from her dreams."

"Let's sit," he says. "Let your mom and I explain."

I don't say no. Instead I walk away.

Haley

JAX SHINES THE FLASHLIGHT on me and I raise my hand up to keep from becoming blinded. "It's almost curfew, Haley. Go home."

"I'm n-n-o-t-t-t g-g-g-oing." My teeth audibly chatter. The rain hammers the pavement and pools on the street. The three of us of have been searching for hours for my father. He's been gone for two days. It turns out Dad started staying out all night over the past three months. Mom kept it a secret from us because he showed early the next morning, and she was able to smuggle him in before my uncle woke for work. This was the first time he's been missing this long.

The spring rain ushers in colder temperatures and with midnight looming, the three of us comb the neighborhood one last time. Jax takes my hand and guides me under the freeway viaduct. A tractor trailer passes overhead and the steel and concrete surrounding us rumbles.

Kaden rips off his soaked sweatshirt to expose a long-sleeve undershirt. He pulls the dry shirt off and hands it to me. I shake my head that I don't need it as I rub my hands over my arms to fight the chill. "Take it, Hays, or I'll strip you myself to put it on you."

Both of them turn as I pry the wet material off and shrug into Kaden's semidry and warm shirt. I roll the sleeves up and wish I was under a pile of dry blankets. "I'm done."

They face me again and Kaden yells over the roaring rain. "Now go home!"

I wish I could. "He's my father, too!"

Jax inches closer. "You've never slept on the streets. It's going to get damned cold soon."

"Three sets of eyes will find him faster. You're wasting time! What if he's out here? What if something happened to him?"

"Go tell Dad what we're doing," Jax says. "Maybe he'll let us in tonight if he knows we're searching for his brother. You know your mom and Maggie are upset. Be with them. They need you."

My jaw aches with the constant chattering. "You're trying to get rid of me."

Jax's whitish hair is plastered to his head. "You're becoming hypothermic and we don't need a hospital run on top of finding your dad. Go home."

"What about you guys? Where will you stay if it gets too cold?" The last bus to the gym left a half hour ago.

"When are you going to learn we're tougher than we look?" Jax flashes a sly grin. "Go on. Get going. There are minutes left until curfew."

Begrudgingly, I walk into the pounding rain. A car comes up the road and I step into the grass to avoid becoming two points against the driver's license. The lights hit me and I look away to avoid the brightness and that's when I spot movement down the freeway ditch.

My heartbeat rushes to my ears as I recognize the tan coat. "Kaden! Jax!"

I race down the gully, fumbling and sliding down the hill, and scream for my family again. They yell back my name and their footsteps pound behind me. Beams of light bounce on the dirt before me. The saturated ground gives and my feet slip out from underneath me. My hands fly back to break the fall, and Jax catches me from behind as Kaden rushes past.

Kaden bends over the form. "It's him! Jax, I need you!"

I steady my feet and Jax jumps down and helps Kaden draw my father up. Shivers run through me and it's not from the cold, but from the fear. "Is he okay?" He has to be. My heart can't take much more loss.

"Fuck!" mutters Jax as he crouches in front of him. "He's drunk."

Not caring if the entire hill has dissolved into a mudslide, I collapse back onto my butt. My father, the man who hardly ever drinks, is drunk and there's no way my uncle will allow anyone who touches alcohol in his house. "We're all screwed."

West

I LIE IN BED AND BLUR MY VISION so that the ceiling-fan blades merge into one. In my hand, I click the remote to my stereo on and off. Sound to no sound. Haley's ghost surrounds me here. Her laughter echoes in my head; the memories of her touch whisper against my skin.

The house is too still. Too silent. The impulse is for sound, noise, music, dancing and alcohol, but I can't live like that anymore. Haley said I was better. I am better. I told her she was worth fighting for and as she was on the verge of believing it—I abandoned her.

The burst of agony through the numbness causes me to roll off the bed and head out the door. Haley said impulse has to do with emotion, with not thinking. The urge is to forget. I bypass the dark stairs and slow when I reach Rachel's door.

The bottom of the door brushes against the floor as it opens and this time there is no bluish glow. She had physical therapy this evening and her breathing is light. Asleep in a chair across the room with a closed laptop on his lap is her twin, Ethan.

I ease down to the floor with my back against her bed.

The silence in here is by far more deafening than my room, but I'm searching to fill the emptiness, the shell that I've become.

There's a shift and a hand slides down and touches my shoulder.

"I gave her up, Rachel." My voice cracks and the desperation, the pain I've tried to bury, breaks through to the surface. "I gave her up and, right now, I don't know why."

Wetness fills my eyes and I slam my fist into the floor, pissed. Rachel moves to the edge of the bed. "Then you win her back."

"Dad will give her what she wants." I stop. Fuck me. Fuck him. Fuck all of this. "He's not my dad."

She's silent for a second and the sigh that escapes her lips cuts deep. "Mom told us."

There's a flop next to me and my eyes widen when a groggy Ethan rests his head against the bed. "Can we get the mental breakdown over so I can get some sleep?"

"Why are you in here?"

"The same reason you are," he says. "The same reason the three of us ever do anything and end up together. Though our problems seemed a lot less complicated when we were pouring bubble bath into the Jacuzzi. It doesn't matter who your dad is, West, because the real Youngs, they're in this room. It's always been the three of us against everyone else. For some reason, it's just taken us longer to get back together."

I lower my head into my hands and I fight the wave of grief that sweeps over me. "I don't know who I am anymore."

"Well, if we get a vote, can you stop being Dad?"

"Ethan," Rachel chastises.

Anger curls within me. "What did you say?"

"He's here, Rach, and he's asking for help. We either say this now or lose the opportunity."

She settles back onto the pillows, a silent acceptance.

"You're pissed because Dad painted you into a bad spot with Haley, right?" Ethan says.

I nod, but I'm madder at myself.

"Shouldn't Haley be mad at you for taking away her choice? To me, that sounds a lot like how Dad treats us."

"You say you don't know who you are," adds Rachel. "But the question should be—who do you want to be?"

Haley

MY UNCLE WAITS FOR US on the stoop. With the front porch light off, he's more of a shadow, but the evil pulsating from the house tells me it's him. He leans against the metal pole supporting the overhang and watches as Kaden and Jax drag my half-conscious father toward the house.

"What time is it?" asks Kaden.

"Doesn't matter," answers Jax. "The bastard isn't going to let any of us in."

Yet we continue forward. "It's his brother. He'll take him in," I say. Maybe not us, but hopefully he'll take my father. "We'll tell him Dad's sick."

"Is there a flu where you reek of beer?" Jax readjusts his hold on my father. The rain continues its onslaught and it makes holding on to anything close to impossible. "There's a reason why my dad's a psychotic control freak. Dad's dad would get drunk, then beat the hell out of him. PTSD isn't just for soldiers."

Jax and Kaden stop on the street in front of the house and share a long, hopeless look. Kaden nods to the curb and both he and Jax lower Dad to it. "Keep an eye on him, Hays."

Dad sways and I rush to his side for support. Chills run through my body as I sit in a stream of water rushing to the sewer grate. Dad mumbles something and I can't hear it over the pounding of the rain against the rooftops and the roaring of the water in the sewer tunnels below.

Above us an aging streetlamp buzzes to life. The dull light flickers, creating an eerie strobe. I close my eyes as rain flows over me like a violent waterfall. How did I end up here? How did my life get out of control? "Why?"

Dad lifts his head and John's words echo in my mind: *He's lost his fight.* Anger swells within me and becomes a tidal wave pouring onto shore. "Why!"

Behind me, Jax and Kaden begin to plead. Dad rubs his hands over his face. "You weren't supposed to find me."

When I was twelve, my father fought his last match. His opponent was half his age, stronger and agile, but my father had skill. I remember watching the bout, my hands wringing together and I kept my eyes glued to my father as if my will was enough to push him to win.

It was a bloody fight. Twice he went down. Twice he got back up. At the end of five rounds, my father stood victorious. Now, he sits in a gutter.

"You don't drink. This isn't you," I whisper.

Dad raises his head to the sky and he blinks as if he's drifting into coherency. "I don't know who I am anymore."

I think of home...my home...my bed. I should be there, lying in that upstairs corner room. When it rained, the wind chimes beneath my window on the porch would tinkle and I'd snuggle deeper into the blanket, grateful for protection.

But I'm not there. I'm here. I'm rotting in the sewer next to the father that disappointed me. This disillusion, this overwhelming sense of being let down, it has nothing to do with losing the house or homeless shelters or that we live in hell. "How could you give up?"

I shiver, not from the cold but because I feel like someone died—like my father died and he died months ago, but I'm just now discovering the truth.

I glance over my shoulder as footsteps approach. Jax grabs his father's arm as he stalks in our direction. "He's sick, Dad. Let Kaden and I get him in bed."

My uncle twists away from Jax and I lean into my father. "You've got to lie. It's past curfew and it's the only way we're getting in. John's out looking for you and the last bus to the gym is gone. We're out of options."

He reaches over and pushes the drenched hair away from my face. "Why did you come after me? You should be safe in bed."

My teeth audibly click together and the hurt overpowers me, taking me down as if I was tackled below the knees. I want to cry. I want to scream, but I can't. Those are the ways of a child and I'm no longer one. I'm the adult chasing after her father. "Because I don't abandon the people I love. I wouldn't do what you're doing to me right now."

"Help me up."

I stand and hold my hand out to him. He takes it and with more effort than it should take, he shakes to his feet. My uncle rounds on us. The rain has already soaked through his black T-shirt. "What's wrong with you?"

"He's sick," I answer. "Let us get him inside before he passes out again."

The glare he throws me causes my spine to straighten. "Unless I speak to you directly, keep your mouth shut."

I bite my lip to halt a response from spewing from my mouth. I hate him. I hate how he demeans me. I hate how he makes me feel as big as a speck of dust and what I hate more is that he's done the same thing to my father, to Jax, to everyone. There's definitely a hell and he's on the expected list.

I pray my uncle keeps the distance between them. Maybe, just maybe, through the rain, he won't notice the strong scent of alcohol.

"I felt sick this morning," Dad says. "And it got worse on the bus ride home. I sat down near the side of the road and must have passed out."

My uncle moves closer and the anxiety within me surges to new highs. He rocks forward and sniffs. I briefly close my eyes. He knows. My uncle knows. "You are a damned failure."

The world tunnels as I stare at my uncle. My father a failure? Kicked down maybe, but not out. I've seen him struggle to his feet before and he can do it again.

Dad lowers his head. "I know."

I step in front of him, clutch his shirt with both hands. "You're not!"

"I am." His voice breaks.

"Listen!" I bend my knees so I'm smaller than him in his broken state. "You are the strongest person I know. We can do this. You just have to get your fight back."

"Let me go, Hays. It's better if you let me go."

"But..."

Dad pulls my hands off his shirt and stumbles back to the ground. My fingers still curl in the air as if I'm still holding on to him and I realize blankly that's what I've been doing for months—holding on to a corpse.

I flinch as if someone shot a high-powered rifle into the

night. There was a shot except there was no sound. Only the rain against the street. For months, my uncle has been firing bullet after bullet in my father's chest and my father stood there and took it until he completely bled out.

And I'm no different. I've done the same thing. My head tilts and the world spins as I look over at my uncle. He can fire all he wants because I'm finally firing back.

Before rational thought catches up to the emotion, I explode into my uncle's face. "He's more of a man than you'll ever be! You're the one that's pathetic. Hiding behind words, behind threats, and when you're too scared you shift into a waste of a little boy and belittle those who can't protect themselves. If you're so strong and so powerful, then hit me, you son of a bitch, because I'll hit you back."

He doesn't even shrink from my proximity. Instead he becomes blank stone. "Pack your shit, get out of my house and take your pathetic family with you."

Dizziness wavers my vision and I suck in raindrops as I try to breathe. Months of telling West to contain his anger and I go and lose control of mine at the wrong critical moment. What have I done? "I'm sorry."

"Too late."

My uncle steps onto the grass and I cut in front of him. "I'm sorry. Please. I was wrong."

"Get of my way before I move you myself."

"Touch my sister and I'll fucking kill you." Kaden stalks toward us.

I stay focused on the evil in front of me. The evil that gives a roof over our heads. That puts food in our stomachs. That offers protection from the streets. He's evil and he's a bastard, but he's saving our lives.

There's a craziness that invades my brain, an insanity worming inside my soul. It distorts colors, sights and sounds. The world becomes gray and cold. Years of fighting, years of confidence, years of any self-worth disintegrate, scatter and drop along with the pouring rain.

One knee goes down and sinks into the freezing mud, then another, and in front of pure madness, I beg, "Throw me out. Just me."

Because I am nothing.

West

GIVE HER THE CHOICE. Stop being an impulsive, controlling jerk and give her the choice. The same choice Dad should have possibly given me countless times. Not a choice between ripping your heart out from the right or the left, but the choice of controlling my own future.

Outside school, I get a few raised brows from people. The rumor mill must have already spit out I broke up with Haley and returned to Worthington.

A Plymouth older than my parents backfires. The brakes screech and the car stops. The side door pops open and Abby barrels out. "Thank God you grew a fucking brain."

I glance at the Plymouth that shakes out of the way. "Who's that?"

"Nobody. You've got problems."

"Not worried about Denny right now. I've got to talk to Haley."

"That's it," she says. "Her uncle kicked her out last night and her family followed. I saw them packing up a car this morning. Her little sister said they're leaving for California."

I slam my hand into the concrete wall. Fuck.

Haley

I FOLD THE BLANKET JOHN gave me last night and leave it on the pillow in the corner of the gym. My grandfather canceled today's sessions because of what happened last night and the gym is unusually quiet.

Jax grunts when I nudge him with my toe, and instead of waking up, he rolls over.

"Come on, Jax. John's going to be back with my parents soon."

With an even louder grunt, Jax sits up and the blanket falls away. After blinking repeatedly, he shrugs on a shirt. "Where's Kaden?"

"Taking a shower." I plop on the matt beside him and think about how many years the two of us have spent in this place together. When we were six, one of us used to hang on a bag while the other pushed it as a swing.

Jax is more than a cousin, more than a brother; he's a part of me and I'm not sure how I can live life without him. "I'm going to miss you."

"Fuck!" He slams his hand onto the mat, then rubs his eyes. "Just fuck."

My uncle did what I asked. He threw me out and me alone. What I didn't expect was my brother and cousin yanking me to my feet and Jax spitting into his father's face. I left and they voluntarily left with me. When we arrived at John's half-drowned and desperate for shelter, he reopened the gym and called my mom.

Mom and John had a long talk and the result is he's giving us his car and we're leaving for California—today.

"You didn't have to leave with me." Guilt consumes my stomach because my thoughtless comment to my uncle caused Jax to leave his home.

"Yeah, I did. I should have left a lot sooner. He's toxic." Jax presses his finger against his head. "He worms his way in, past your skin, past your muscles and into your soul. Once he's in, he continues, eating you until you're dust. I'm already half-dust, Haley, and I'm tired of trying to hold together what's left."

I lay my hand over his. "I love you."

He lowers his head and grabs on to his hair, causing his knuckles to go white. "I'm gonna fucking miss you."

Jax jumps up and slams his fist into a bag as he takes off for the showers. My mouth turns down and I rap my head against the wall. Jax and Kaden are staying. I don't know who I am without them.

The door to the gym opens and my grandfather walks in. He starts for his office, but one glance at me and he changes directions. Air rushes out of my mouth with such force that my hair moves. I escaped questions last night. My luck, like always, has run out.

John's slow as he slides down to sit next to me and he does something very un-John-like: he pats my knee. "Stay."

"The camper's barely big enough for you and one of the boys. I have no idea how you're going to squeeze Jax and Kaden in it." As much as it will kill my mother, Kaden won't come. His life is here—with the gym. I don't know where I belong anymore.

"We'll figure it out. There's the bed, two bunks and the floor once I clean it up. I'm not sure Jax would be comfortable on a mattress after all this time."

I check to see if he's teasing, but he's not. "Why is my uncle scared of you?"

"I saw him grab Jax by the arm once when he was a toddler when we were at your old house." John grasps his biceps. "Left a huge mark on his arm. I said nothing to him then, but paid him a little visit later that night."

It's not surprising he and my uncle had a chat. John's an advocate of keeping fights in the gym. "What did you say? I can't imagine one word I could have said that would have changed him."

John scratches the stubble on his chin. "I beat the shit out of him."

I choke on my own spit. "You what?"

"Beat the shit out of him. I then told him if he lifted a finger to any of his kids again, I'd call the police and let them watch us as I beat the shit out of him again and then they could arrest us both."

"Damn."

"Yeah. But I could never stop him with the words."

"Jax is a good guy because of you," I say.

"Your cousin doesn't have much and it's going to kill him when you go."

"I can't stay."

"I hoped by training West you'd find your fight again."

"My fight's gone."

"You're too young for that, Haley. Take a look at your father. Is that what you want to be? We could blame what happened with Matt, but you still had some fight in you then. When you lied about what happened with Conner to save Jax and Kaden, I thought maybe you were on the right track."

I turn my head as the deep, dark secret I fought to protect rolls off his tongue. "How did you know?"

"Jax and Kaden knew the moment you came home with no meds you were jumped and they knew Conner was the one to do it. Besides, they also knew you could kick Conner's ass."

I chuckle, though I don't know why. Matt never flinched from the assumption that West was strong enough to take on Conner, but I wasn't. I trained Matt. I dated him. You'd think he would have known.

John continues, "I told Jax and Kaden to let you fight your own fights. With Matt, Conner and your uncle—with whoever. Unless you asked for help. I thought if you had to fight in some area in your life, it would prove to you how strong you really are or at least teach you how to rely on us. Even if we wanted, we couldn't help unless you let us."

I think of meeting West, arguing with him, teaching him to fight. "It almost worked."

"It doesn't have to be almost. Stay, Haley. You've always had the heart. You just need to start leading with that instead of your head."

I snort. Here I've been trying to convince West differently. The memory causes a slice of pain. God, I've lost the guy I loved. I loved him. I loved him so much and he walked away the moment his father snapped his fingers. He couldn't have loved me back.

"Mom needs me." And until last night, I've been able to pretend the truth hasn't existed. "Dad's a mess."

"You're eighteen. There comes a point in time when you need to start making your own decisions about your life. You can't control your father and you can't help your mother. They'll either make it or they won't."

"What about Maggie?"

"I raised your mother. She'll take care of Maggie and, trust me, your great-aunt will keep Maggie in line, too. The old bat is too mean to die."

John scratches his forehead and I've never seen such an unsure gesture from him.

"What?" I hope it's not bad. I'm already free-falling and I don't feel like hitting a few rocks on the way down.

"When you get to California, you should talk to someone."

"Talk?"

"Yeah." His hand waves in the air. "A professional—like that Mrs. Collins."

Uh...no. "I don't need—"

"You do," he cuts me off. "Something happened to you and as hard as I tried I couldn't fix it. If you have to go, go, but don't continue to live a half life."

Mom sticks her head in the gym. "Can you lend a hand, Dad?"

John stands and Mom smiles at me. It's not a reassuring smile. It's the type that says she wishes she could reassure me. "Get your brother and cousin. I want to say our goodbyes and get on the road."

I nod. That describes my life—nothing but goodbyes.

West

WITH ABBY RIDING SHOTGUN, I weave through the streets of the industrial park at sixty miles per hour and slam on the brakes when we reach the last warehouse. I throw the car into Park and I'm out the door with the keys still in the ignition.

John steps out of his camper. "Heard you broke my granddaughter's heart."

"Where is she?"

"Gone. She left with her mother and father for California a half hour ago."

He's talking, but my back is already turned toward him. I slam the door to my car and the tires squeal as I back out and floor the gas.

Abby grabs on to the console. "What are you doing?"

"We're going after Haley."

"That was a stop sign. What the hell? Slow down. Slow down! West, fucking stop!"

I slam my brakes and we both lunge forward at the red stoplight.

"We've got to catch up. I've got to give her the option. I shouldn't have tried to control her life."

"Did you notice Kaden standing in the entrance of the gym?"

I blink. "No. Do you think John lied? Do you think she's still there?"

Abby reaches over and shifts the car into Park. "She's gone, West. Haley's made her choice."

Haley

IT'S OUR SECOND DAY on the road and we're taking it slow to California because John's car constantly threatens to spontaneously combust. Out of the four of us, only Maggie is excited about the move with the promises of beaches and waves and all the chicken nuggets she can eat.

I wish I could be excited about chicken nuggets. I wish I could be excited over anything.

To give the car time to rest after pushing it two hundred miles, we've stopped off in the middle of nowhere Missouri to let Maggie climb on the largest bale of hay known to man. She giggles in the distance and I roam the inside/outside flea market associated with the gas station.

My father sits on the curb and absently watches Maggie and the farmland. It's a strange, numbing sensation each time I see him—as if he died two days ago and I'm at the funeral home staring at the empty shell of a body.

On the corner of the sidewalk, a dealer hangs a punching bag from the ceiling of the sidewalk overhang. My fingers whisper against the vinyl and the man notices. "Got it this morning. Do you have a brother or boyfriend who might be interested?"

I pivot on the ball of my heel and throw a back kick followed by an elbow to the "gut." The wooden ceiling trembles as the bag swings. I catch it with both of my hands and smirk at the seller. "No, I don't."

Instead of frowning, like I expect, he flashes a half-tooth grin. "You're good."

"Thanks." The pride inside breaks through the numbness.

"My grandson watches that MMA. He was telling me a few weeks ago that he saw two women fight and I couldn't believe it. Wasn't that MMA though. It was something else."

"Muay Thai?"

"That's it. Do you fight?"

"I used to."

The old man eases down into a worn lawn chair that creaks under his frail body. His skin has the consistency of leather—too many days spent in the sun. "Shame on the used to."

Right. A shame.

"Why did you stop?"

The question catches me off guard and because I don't know him and don't owe him an explanation I wander away and end up at the bumper of the car next to Mom. She shouts encouragement to Maggie as my sister struggles to the top.

"She doesn't think she can do it," says Mom.

I smile, remembering how she almost beat me a few months ago on the monkey bars. "Maggie can do it. She has a ton of upper-body strength."

Maggie's arms visibly shake, but she's almost there. Thinking how awesome it will feel within me to see that victorious smile on her face when she reaches the top, I silently will her to dig deep and find that last oomph of energy. One of us needs to accomplish a goal.

Right as Maggie almost reaches the top of the bale of hay, she lowers her head. I step toward her. No. She's almost there. "Keep going, Maggie!"

"I can't," she yells.

She can. She has to. One of us has to. I take off for the field, running over the damp ground, watching as she clutches her fingers into the hay. "You're almost there. Just keep going!"

I reach the bale. Her sneakers dangle near my head. I could place my hand near her foot and nudge her up, but this overwhelming urge inside me says that if Maggie's going to be proud, she needs to do it on her own. She needs to know she's capable.

"Catch me," Maggie calls.

"No!" I shout and hate how hard it came out, but she needs to listen. "You're almost there. Dig your feet in, push up off with your legs, then pull yourself up."

"Haley—"

"Do it, Mags."

She mutters something that I'm sure is an insult in my direction, then kicks at the hay until she discovers a foothold, then struggles up the rest of the way. The sun distorts my vision of Maggie and I step back, shielding my eyes, but the moment I make her out standing on the top with her arms in the air I laugh. Clapping. Shouting.

She did it… She did it, and then the tears form.

I bend over slightly as if I'd been punched in the gut. She did it. My sister pushed forward and she did it. I circle, searching for my mom, when I spot the punching bag. Why did I stop fighting? Why did I walk away from the one thing that brought me joy?

My uncle comes to mind as do names like Matt and Conner and Kaden and Jax, but then it all gets lost in a tangled web because in the end, what did any of them have to do with me and my ability to fight?

"I don't know," I mumble to myself.

"Don't know what?" my mother asks as she joins us by the bale. My mother is smiling. Really smiling. Enjoying Maggie's brief taste of victory.

"I stopped fighting," I whisper and my mother's smile falters as she tilts her head to understand my words.

Like it's calling me home, I stumble to the bag hanging from the roof. The old man is gone and, from behind me, I can feel my mother's and father's stares. My sister still giggles in the distance from her success.

My thumb caresses the bag like I'm greeting a long-lost friend. For three rounds of three minutes, I used to be granted the gift of focusing on one thing and it was the one thing that brought me a sense of pride and a sense of satisfaction...a sense of self.

I've spent my entire life idolizing my father. He's been this god on top of a mountain that I've always tried to climb in order to be part of his glory. But my father's not a god; he's a man and man, if anything, is fallible.

My father stopped moving forward and in my effort to drag him along, I also lost my way. Forget about everyone else and their issues and their expectations.... If I clear my mind and look deep inside me, I know who I am. I know what I'm capable of.

With a surge of power, I pull up my guard and tap out a

combination: two jabs, a cross and a low kick. The moment my shin connects with the bag, I close my eyes as a feeling of home washes over me. The bag flies high in the air and this time I let it swing as the smile pulls on my face. "I'm still a fighter."

West

TWO DAYS AND LIFE has returned to normal. I attend the best school, I have the best opportunities, the richest friends, reopened credit card accounts, a swank home and all the food I can eat. It's what my parents want as my normal, but I have never felt more like a person living in a foreign land than I do now.

It's Friday and if I'm back to normal that means family dinner night. I've avoided my parents and they've given me my space. Tonight, for some reason, feels inevitable.

I hit the last step of the stairs and the doorbell rings. I open it and discover Rachel's boyfriend, Isaiah, standing there with his hands shoved in his pockets. The guy hasn't changed: shaved head, earrings and tattoos cover his arms.

"Little early, aren't you?" I take it back; he has changed, and that burn on his arm from when he saved Rachel from the accident proves it. Rachel said she saved him. He saved her. Guess they saved each other.

"Nope." Isaiah shows every day, but he typically waits until after dinner on Friday.

"He's coming for dinner." Rachel's wheels hum against the

floor as she exits the newly created workout room. In a fresh pair of jeans and sweater, she whips around the open front door with a huge I'm-going-to-see-the-guy-I-love grin. "Hi!"

The don't-fuck-with-me guy sure as hell gives her the same grin back. "Hi."

I nod my head for Isaiah to enter and I close the door behind us. "Do Mom and Dad know about this?"

A glint strikes her eyes. "No, but you're going to help me, right?"

Isaiah folds his arms over his chest and the glare says he doesn't have Rachel's faith in me. Which he shouldn't. I've done nothing but give him shit since he's been around my sister. I extend my hand to him. "I can't promise it'll be pretty. In fact, I can guarantee it'll be the equivalent of wearing a sweater in hell."

Isaiah assesses my outstretched arm, then meets my eyes before accepting my hand. "Didn't expect anything different."

"See," Rachel says behind me as I head to the dining room. "He's changed."

I chuckle to myself. That's right. I have.

My heart stops. Have I?

I spin and Isaiah grabs Rachel's chair to stop her from running into me. In a second, I'm on my knees in front of her. "Do you think I'm different than who I used to be?"

"What?"

"Am I the same person? Do you think I'm different?"

"No. Yes. Wait. You aren't the same person. I mean, you are, but you're different. None of this sounds right."

I stand. "I've got to go."

"Whoa." Rachel snatches my hand. "I know you've been

avoiding Mom and Dad, but dinner won't be that bad. It's sort of why I invited Isaiah tonight. There's no way they'd go into the biological stuff with him there."

He grunts. "Thanks."

She waves him off. "It's a kill two birds with one stone thing. It'll be so awkward we'll inhale our food and run."

"Again. Thanks," he says.

"I've got to take the fight," I tell her.

"West..." It's like she's preparing me for impending news of death. "Haley's gone."

"Yeah, she is, but she's still worth fighting for. When I was jumped, Haley came back and fought for me. She changed me, for the better, and now it's time to fight for her."

"What about the scholarship? Dad said he'll find her in California and make sure she gets it. If you fight, she'll lose the money."

A heaviness consumes me and the urge is to fix Haley's problems and control her destiny, but it's time I start controlling mine. "I've got to do this."

Her forehead crinkles and I hate I'm causing her pain. "You're leaving again, aren't you?"

"Just this house, not you. Never you. I'll be around so damn much you'll be sick of me, but I need to do this. It's time I start acting like a man."

Rachel opens her arms for a hug. I wrap my arms around her and kiss her cheek. "We'll get you back in that garage, okay?" And after fixing the door at Denny's bar, I came up with an idea of how to do it. Mom will hate it. Rachel will love it.

I ignore her puzzled expression as I rise and suck in a

pride-eating breath. "I'm going to need a place to crash. If I'm taking this fight, I can't live here."

This time Isaiah extends his hand first. "Bed's mine, but you can have the couch. Just leave some cash occasionally on the table upstairs and my foster parents won't care."

"Deal."

Isaiah didn't have dinner with my parents. Instead he drove me to his foster parents' house as I used his cell to text my parents to inform them where I was, what I was doing and to remind them I'm eighteen. In a separate text to Dad I told him where he could shove the scholarship.

Determined to do this on my own, I packed some clothes and then left—everything: my phone, my car, my belongings. But this time I'm accepting help from some friends.

Outside the bar, Abby tosses me a prepaid cell and I hand her thirty dollars. "You've got fifty minutes. Don't use them all at once."

It's the cheapest damn phone I've ever seen. "Are you sure it works?"

Abby tilts her head to the left. "Ha." Then to the right. "Ha. To get to the gym, take the forty-two bus. It'll go straight there."

A red Honda Civic pulls up and Abby nods her chin at the driver. "Here's my ride."

"Hey, Abby."

She glances over her shoulder.

"How'd you know about my mom and Denny?"

That wicked smile crosses her lips. "That's a story from a whole other book that you aren't old enough to read yet. When you're out of diapers, maybe I'll tell it to you someday."

Why would I expect any other answer? "Thanks, Abby."

"Watch it, Young. People may think that we're friends or something. By the way, welcome home." Abby slides into the car and it takes off down the street.

I lean against the sidewalk railing and survey the strip mall. Farther down people lug piles of clothes into the Laundromat; they carry bags out of the dollar and grocery stores. Months ago, this was my foreign. Today, it's where I belong.

Damn, who would have guessed it—this is my home.

The feeling grows stronger when I walk into the bar and my feet stick to the floor. Farther down, Denny wipes down a table.

"Heard you were looking for someone to fix things," I say. "Is the job still open?"

Denny freezes, then returns to the stubborn spot in front of him. He tries to hide it, but I catch the smile on his face. "Yeah. Job's still open."

Haley

WATER BEATS AGAINST the tub as Dad starts the shower. Lying on the bed on her stomach with her feet in the air, Maggie wallows in chicken nugget and Nickelodeon heaven. I peek past the heavy motel curtains and spot Mom sitting on the curb looking at the flashing Motel 6 neon sign.

The door clicks as I open it and Mom's shoulders relax when she sees it's me. She scoots over and creates a space. Even though the very tip of the western sky bleeds pink and stars twinkle directly overhead, the concrete still radiates the day's heat.

"Kansas is flat," I announce. For months my mother's been a specter disappearing and reappearing in my life and I miss having a mom.

"Yes, it is." Mom reaches over and entwines her fingers with mine. "I'm sorry I couldn't keep everything from unraveling."

"I was going to apologize for the same thing."

The way she sighs cuts deep into my bone marrow. "Keeping this family together was never your job. It was your father's and mine."

"Are you mad at Kaden for staying?" I shuffle my feet

against the loose concrete, anxious for the answer. Decisions shouldn't be this agonizing and I envy that Kaden was able to easily make his. If I leave and return to the gym, I'm letting down my mom, my father and Maggie. If I stay, I'm letting myself down. I'm a fighter and I belong in that gym.

"No," she says and stares out into the horizon. "Sad, yes, but not mad."

Crap. Sort of the answer I desired, yet not. Then again, maybe I'm supposed to stay away from Kentucky. So many things went wrong there: Matt, Conner...West. I close my eyes with the ache.

"You okay, honey?"

I open my eyes to see Mom worrying at me like she did when I was sick as a child. "I miss West."

She nudges me with her shoulder. "Broken hearts mend. You got through Matt—you'll get through this."

West hurts, but not in the way it hurt when I left Matt. Losing West causes my heart to break; my soul feels empty—hollow. With Matt, my bones ached, my body throbbed and my self-worth was burned to a crisp. If I had more time with West, if I had given my heart faster to him, would it have made a difference? Would he have chosen me?

I'll never know. I permitted Matt's memory to haunt me and the scary part is he's still an unseen phantom stalking my every move, infesting my decisions. "Matt and I didn't end well."

I said this before...to John, but I couldn't say more than that. My throat tightens and I pull at the collar of my shirt.

Mom angles her body and for the first time in over a year, I have her full, undivided attention. "What do you mean, didn't end well?"

Say it, Haley. Say it. My mouth opens and consonants stick in my throat. The only sound that falls past my lips is a sick strangling click.

Mom pushes my hair over my shoulder. "Talk to me, Haley, but you have to breathe, too. Come on, honey."

I do what she says and welcome each clean intake. Stupid me. Stupid, stupid me. Why can't I say it? Why can't I admit it? Through another breath of air, I rush out, "It was bad."

"All right," she says as if I admitted something huge and I guess it was huge, but it wasn't the full truth. "All right. It's okay."

Mom kisses my temple, wraps both of her arms around me and pulls my head onto her shoulder. That's when I realize I'm shaking. Not just me—the entire world. Then it blurs. "He hurt me."

He hit me. I crave to say it. The words beg for freedom, but there's a whisper of guilt—a whisper that I'm stupid and that if I say more, then the entire world will see my shame…that they will judge and crucify me.

I was stupid. I fell for the wrong guy. He hurt me and I paid. He hurt me and I broke. He hurt me and the rest of the world will forever condemn.

"It's okay," Mom says again as she rocks the two of us. "We're going to be okay."

West

EVEN THOUGH I TALKED TO JOHN on the phone and told him I'm still competing next Saturday and would appreciate his help, I'm apprehensive as I walk into the gym. He agreed to see me but didn't agree to what I asked.

The moment the door shuts behind me, I drop my head. Damn. In the ring and in full gear, Kaden and Jax knock out a kick series.

John's office sits dark and, if I'm manning up, forward is my only option. I broke the heart of a person they love. If I'm lucky, I'll leave here with bones still intact.

I weave through the bags and call out to them, "Is John here?"

Their heads snap up in unison. The scratching of Velcro being undone breaks through the silence. Jax flies under the ropes and throws his headgear and gloves to the side. "Gotta death wish, Young?"

I show him the palm stop sign. "I'm here to talk to John. He knows I'm coming."

With sweat pouring down his body, Jax mock glances around the gym. "Don't see him."

"Look, I made a mistake. I broke up with Haley because my dad said he'd pay for her college if I did."

Jax advances on me like I said nothing. "I think you're full of shit. I think now that Haley's gone you want the benefit of this gym without having to respect the girl."

"Where's John?"

"Dunno. He told us to be here. Guess he wanted to give us an early Christmas present."

Fuck. I've been set up. Jax widens his stance and I mirror the position and tighten my fist. Haley's voice screams in my head to hold up my guard, but I don't want to invite the hit. I'm not searching for a fight. "I'd get on my knees in front of Haley, tell her the truth and beg her to take me back if I could."

Fire blazes out of his eyes. "Wrong choice of words."

Jax swings and my guard goes up. I duck below the hit and sidestep out of the way. "I don't want to fight you."

"Too bad."

He throws the cross and I block and meet the jab. Jax gains the low kick, but I quickly spin out of reach. "Fight!" Jax yells. "Are you a fucking man or not?"

"I'm not fighting you. I'm not here to fight *you.*"

We begin the dance. He attacks, and I counter but keep my blows to the block. Jax goes for the cross again, but in a snap he's at my knees and I'm down. Dammit. I roll to keep him from gaining position and jump to my feet, guard up, ready to go again.

I do a double take when Jax leans against the ring and drinks from a water bottle. "Haley's right. He sucks at the floor."

Kaden slips under the ropes. “I needed more time. Never said I was a miracle worker.”

“We’ve got a week. Surely you can teach him some crazy shit by then.”

“Something’s better than nothing.” He nods at me. “You’re lucky she taught you how to block so damn well. You’re going to need it against Matt. He’s got a mean hook.”

I lower my arms when John emerges from the locker room. “She hasn’t taught him how to block a hook or an undercut. She was sticking to basics.”

Jax’s shoulders shake as he laughs. “Basics against Matt. Maybe she wanted him to die.”

Son of a bitch. “What the hell is going on?”

“Checking to see if you’re salvageable,” answers John. “And good thing for you, you kept that temper in check. Otherwise, your ass would be out of my gym.”

“Did you really break up with her because your dad would pay her tuition?” Kaden asks.

All three of them stare at me in silence and I keep my fists tight in case they don’t agree with my decision. “Yeah, but by showing here I’ve negated the deal.”

“She wouldn’t have accepted the money,” says Jax. “Haley has more class than that.”

She has more class than to be with me. Jax may not have thrown a physical hit, but he landed a blow full of guilt. “I know that now.”

“Does this look like the YMCA, girls?” asks John. “We’ve got a week until the fight.”

Jax straps on his gear and I angle my body so John knows I’m talking to him alone, but I have no doubt Jax and Kaden are listening. “I don’t deserve her forgiveness, but when this is done...tell Haley I kept my word and she's worth fighting for."

John pats my shoulder as he enters the ring. "That she is. Now get changed and get your ass on my floor."

Haley

I HAVE NEVER ENVIED anyone in my life like I envy Maggie. Lying next to me, Maggie's arms are flung over her head. One socked foot hangs off the bed; the other sockless foot has broken free of the blankets. Only her middle is covered. She breathes lightly, rhythmically and I wish I could share such deep, dreamless sleep.

When I sleep, I dream of West: of his smile, his laughter, his hands on me. We kiss and we touch and when our bodies are intertwined, West whispers he loves me and every time… I wake up feeling cold and alone and with tears.

Tonight, maybe I won't sleep. Insomnia sounds like a wonderful habit.

For once, sleep isn't a problem for my father. He's turned away from me, tucked tightly in a ball on the other bed. Maybe this will mean he's on some sort of road to recovery. Unfortunately, I'm pretty numb on hope.

"I don't know, Dad…" Mom dragged the phone with her into the bathroom. She's called John every night since we left and each night she emerges with red, puffy eyes. After John's car broke down, we spent almost a week at my mother's cousin's house. Now, we're back on the road. The door to the bathroom clicks open and a ray of light floods the cramped room.

"Haley," whispers Mom. "Kaden wants to talk to you."

I slide off the bed and Mom squeezes out of the bathroom as I slip in.

"Are you sure?" I ask. Kaden avoids conversation in person. He loathes phones.

Her answer is the closed door. Limited on options, I sit on the edge of the tub and press the phone to my ear. "Hello?"

"You need to come home, Hays. It's West. He's taking the fight."

West Young broke up with me in a deal he made with his father. He was to leave the life he built behind and his dad would have paid for my college tuition. I briefly close my eyes. Stupid boy. Stupid, insanely sweet, going to get his ass kicked by me, stupid boy and I'm in love with him and West lied to me knowing I'd never agree.

He's right. I wouldn't have and I wonder how he thought I would have accepted the money, but none of that matters now.

Sitting on a bench outside the bus station, I grip the backpack hanging between my bouncing knees. It's full of my clothes and the few precious items I won't be separated with. When our house foreclosed, I had boxes and boxes of stuff I claimed as important. Funny how priorities change.

In the space in front of me, the bus's motor purrs. Mom and I left a half hour ago, leaving a note for Dad. Maggie's curled up on the bench beside mine, sound asleep and cradling her American Girl doll. The early morning air nips at my skin and I rub at the forming goose bumps.

Mom exits the office, sits on the bench next to me and lays

the ticket on my lap. “Tell your grandfather I’m now trusting him with over half of my heart. It was hard enough to leave Kaden and Jax behind. Now the scale is completely imbalanced.”

Guilt eats at me as I handle the ticket. It was cheap, but it’s still money we don’t have. But Mom agreed. Returning for me is necessary. My knees continue to bounce as a chaotic ticker crosses my mind: I’m leaving my parents… I’m leaving my mom.

“Will you promise me something?” she asks.

“Sure.” Anything.

“Don’t listen to the lie in your head keeping you from discussing what happened with you and Matt. Speaking out takes courage, but fear can make a compelling argument. I’m not saying it will be easy, but telling the truth gives you power… It sets you free.”

I nod, unable to say anything back. I can’t imagine saying the words out loud, but I can’t imagine living like this forever.

“Are you going back for West?” she asks.

“Yes… No…” The answer is both, but I say the simple truth. “I’m doing this for me.”

“Good. You’re a strong girl. Please don’t forget that.”

But I don’t feel strong. A huge part of me wants to crawl onto my mother’s lap and cling to her for dear life. All those years of holding her hand, the squeeze of her fingers stopping me when I attempted to cross the street before looking, the glances of approval, the hug after a hard day…her gentle presence in my life… I’m willingly leaving it behind.

My throat tightens. “What if I’m not ready to be on my own?”

“You’ve been on your own for a while and you’re just now

figuring it out. You'll always be my baby, Haley, just like I'll always be your mom."

She wraps her arm around me and I rest my head on her shoulder. When I was younger, my mom read to me every night. Back in our old home, back when life was simpler. She snuggled in my bed and brought peace and security. "Why did it have to change?"

"I don't know," she whispers. "But it did and all we can do is go forward."

"I'm trying." Air is harder to inhale. "But how do I walk away from you?"

"You aren't walking away, baby. You're growing up. But remember, I don't care if you're eighty and I'm a hundred and thirteen. I will always hold you, I will always love you and I will always be right here."

West

I STRADDLE A CHAIR as John wraps the yellow strip of material across my hand. An official watches us in the corner to make sure John stays within regulation. He pulls each new layer taut and concentrates like he's performing surgery. Outside the crowd roars and there's no mistaking the anger. They hate it when the match goes to the floor. Matt and I are the last amateur fight on the card and the waiting is slowly killing me.

"She trained you well." John never mentions Haley by name. It's as if saying her name creates pain. Part of me wants to tell him I understand. "Stick with the combinations she taught you, keep up your guard and keep your emotions in check."

The wrap is new and John applies it tighter than what I'm used to, but without the gloves, I'm going to need firm. I swallow, thinking how Haley tried to warn me off this. The realness and heaviness of the situation sinks in. The moment I enter the cage, I might as well be dodging traffic on a busy interstate.

The only solace I have is if the fight does go in the wrong

direction that I'm doing what needs to be done. I'm not a man because I'm walking into the cage. I'm a man because I'm standing up for Haley and myself. No more relying on my parents and their money. No more letting a past I can't control dictate my choices and future. No more being a child.

I called Mom an hour ago and told her I loved her and I told her to tell Dad the same thing. I made peace with her as she cried and, somehow, I found peace within myself. My lone regret is not being able to hold Haley again and whisper to her those three precious words.

The door to the small room at the convention hotel opens and Jax in full Mohawk mode strolls in. "After this fight, you're on deck."

John finishes with the wraps and slips his hands into the practice pads. "It's time to warm up."

The official pulls the cap off a black marker with his teeth and signs his name over my wraps. I'm regulation, not illegal, and one step closer to the cage.

After practicing with gloves, my hands feel naked and vulnerable. John holds up the pads and I widen my stance. Attempting to ignore the nerves, I blow out air. I could kid myself and say this is all for Haley, but this is also for me.

John stands in front of me and I'm flanked by Jax and Kaden. Behind the door to the hotel convention center, I sport hand wraps, a cup and a pair of wrestling shorts. I swing my arms, trying to keep them loose though tension begins to build in my neck.

Doing a bad job parroting a real MMA announcer, the master of ceremonies comes off like a sleazy carnival gamer as he advertises my weight and city.

Jax pops his head to the right and opens the door as my name is called. "Let's do this."

The crowd screams and whistles when I hit the floor and stalk toward the octagon cage in the middle. I notice everyone, yet I notice no one. All of it is flashes of color and movement. Music pounds through the speakers, and, in a moment of clarity, I recognize the song.

I glare at Jax and he's smiling like a damn hyena. "Sorry, couldn't help it. You scream Rocky." He slams a hand on my back. "Get a sense of humor. You're going to need it in there."

John and the ref exchange a few words before the ref motions to me. "Arms up."

I do as he asks, holding them straight out to my sides, then widen my feet. His hands skim my body, frisking me for foreign items. A quick scan checks my ears, that I'm wearing a cup and that my nails are trimmed and that the wraps haven't been tampered with.

When I'm cleared, John steps in front of me and offers my mouthpiece. I accept it and he moves his mouth as if talking while he applies a coat of Vaseline on my face. The noise in the room mixes together and nothing is clear or coherent. John looks me in the eye and says, "Got it?"

I nod. He glances at Jax and I don't miss the subtle shake of his head.

"Good luck and Godspeed," says John.

I walk up the three steps and enter the cage. Nervous adrenaline courses in my veins and I continue to work my muscles to keep the blood flowing. Matt stands on the opposite side of the cage with his back toward me.

The ref calls Matt over and the son of a bitch smiles when he sees me. "Have you pissed yourself yet?"

I smile right back. “Fuck you.”

“Guess we both fucked Haley, huh?”

A surge of anger rushes through me and I roll forward on the balls of my feet. The ref slams a hand into my chest and shouts, “Do we got the rules?”

“Got it.”

“Got it,” answers Matt.

“Keep it in line,” yells John and I silently curse myself for doing exactly what Haley had warned me about for months.

The ref claps his hands and slides out of the way. Matt and I extend our arms and bump fists. Haley talked about a peacefulness in the cage. All that surrounds me is chaos.

Haley

MY HEART POUNDS SO HARD I have no doubt people can see it past my skin. I fly through the doors of the convention center and a security guard blocks my way as I sprint toward the table.

"I'm a coach!" I skid to a halt. "Haley Williams. I'm with West Young."

"He's on now," says the security guard. The girl at the front flips through the paperwork and I will her fingers to move faster.

A wave of nausea causes tingling in my head. I grab on to the table to stay upright. "How long?"

"It's been a while. He's getting the hell beat out of him."

"Damn." I breathe out.

"Here!" The girl hands me the yellow pass, the security guard steps out of my way and I'm running again, carrying the badge up over my head, yelling at anyone who tries to stop me.

The crowd is on their feet, screaming at the two men thrashing it out in the center of the room. Most have taken to standing on their chairs, making it impossible for me to catch a glimpse as I push through to gain access to the front.

As I get closer, West holds his guard as Matt doles out a three-one combo. The power behind his punch is brutal, and West is able to throw a jab to push Matt back. West ducks out of the way from another assault and is able to gain enough space between them to hopefully create an offensive attack.

My feet continue to move underneath me, and, as I open my mouth to scream instructions to West, my body rams into something and I stumble back.

"Only fighters and coaches." Another security guard obstructs my path, not caring about the yellow badge I throw in his face.

"John!" I lean around him. "John!"

John keeps shouting instructions at West and Jax turns his head at the sound of my voice. He jumps off the platform outside the Octagon and points at me. "She's with us."

I latch on to Jax and he pulls me past the guard and into the inner circle. Sitting in the front row, Conner's eyes meet mine. With the glare I send him, he looks away first.

"How's West doing?" I ask.

"Not good." Jax hauls himself onto the platform and offers his hand to help me up. "He's blanked out and not listening to a word John says. West is moving, but he's getting the hell beat out of him in the process. There's no way he can last three rounds of this."

My fingers curl around the cage and my heart becomes sick. The skin around West's right eye swells and his lip is busted. His body droops forward and fatigue slows his movements, causing him to drop his guard. Sweat drips off his body like a faucet. "Tap him out."

"Thirty seconds left, Hays," says John. "He can do it."

But I don't want him to do it. "What round?"

"Second."

The metal wire cuts into my fingers. Dear God in heaven.

Matt mock throws a cross, West deflects it wrong and Matt lunges for his middle. "Get out of the way!"

The entire cage vibrates as their bodies slam onto the fence. In a smooth, fluid motion, Matt pins West and pounds him, hook after hook to West's guarded face. West's knees begin to buckle and if he falls to the floor it'll be over for good.

"Knees, West! Use your knees!"

West

"KNEES, WEST! USE YOUR KNEES!" It's the first clear voice in the chaos. A knee goes up, then another. A sharp hit into the ribs and Matt stumbles back. I push off the cage, my legs more Jell-O than muscle, but I've got to keep going. Three rounds. Three rounds for Haley.

The bell rings and the ref slides in between us. The world circles and I raise my arms over my head and press my forehead against the cage, fighting for each intake of air. Everything throbs and the exhaustion is enough to cause a loss of consciousness.

Then there's a face on the other side of the fence and I swear I'm fucking hallucinating.

"Where the hell is your guard?" she shouts.

Damn if she doesn't sound like Haley. "I'm tired."

"Do I look like I care? You're getting the hell pounded out of you. If you want to tap out, then tap out, but don't stand there and let him win."

I glance around as best as I can with my eye swelling. Does the world see me talking to the hallucination? Does no one give a fuck I'm losing my mind?

She's beautiful and strikingly real. "I love you."

Her fingers curl around the fence and touch mine. The coolness of her fingertips against my hot skin causes me to close my eyes. Fuck, she seems so real. "Open your eyes, West."

I do and those dark, gorgeous eyes dig deep into mine.

"John, we've got a problem."

There's commotion behind me and a hand goes on my arm. "Turn toward me, son."

The voice is John's, but I'm not interested. I'm only interested in what's in front of me...only interested in her touch. I'm fucking lost in my own mind, but I don't care. If I turn away, she'll be gone and I can't live through that again.

"West," she says calmly. "Let the doctor look at you."

"You'll go away," I answer. "I don't want you to go away."

She presses her nails into me, penetrating deep enough to cause pain. "I'm real."

The air slams out of my body and I lose my grip on the fence. "You're what?"

John slides in front of me. "What's your name?"

"West Young." I yank my head to the right to see Haley again. "She's here."

"She's here," he repeats.

Another man blocks my view of Haley and he takes my hands. "Look at me."

I do. He asks a few more questions and I answer while trying to shake the cobwebs out of my head.

"Can you fight?" he asks.

Haley holds on to the fence and stares at me like she's actually worried. Like she's actually in love with me. "Fuck yeah."

I swing around and face Matt again in the center of the ring with the ref between us. The son of a bitch glances over at Haley, and when he meets my eyes again, I smile. "You ain't got nothing."

"Clean fight, boys," says the ref.

"What the fuck did you say?" demands Matt.

I hold out my fist and Matt bumps it. "I said you ain't got nothing. No girl and no hit."

We break apart and I keep my arms at my sides. Haley spent months drilling it into my brain to keep my head on straight, to keep my emotions in check, because if I lost it, I'd lose the game plan and the fight. The same has to be true with the bastard across from me.

The yelling, the cheering, the world fades out and a sense of calm washes over me. Two things remain in my world: the asshole in the cage and Haley's voice. "Guard up, Young."

It'll go up—when I'm ready.

Matt and I dance around each other and I pump my fist into my chest. "You ain't got nothing."

Matt jerks with the statement and I throw my arms forward and back, begging for the hit. "Nothing. Hit me all damn day. You ain't got it."

Abandoning his form, Matt lunges and I allow the free shot to my head. I turn with the impact and jump back at the same time. Fire consumes his eyes when I smile at him. "Nothing."

His crew yells at him and I laugh because they see what Matt doesn't. I'm mentally taking the show, but Matt's lost in my words. I nod my chin for him to try again, but this time when he attacks, I pull up my guard, watch as he lowers his, then ram a two-one combination into his face.

Haley

"KICK SERIES! KICK SERIES!" I bang on the cage.

West has taken control and he solidly kicks Matt's side. Matt doubles over. Good God in heaven, West has struck a knee-bending blow. He could do this. He could stand for all three rounds.

The ref slides between Matt and West and checks Matt to make sure can continue. My eyes meet West's and I nod my approval. "Keep that guard up."

Matt waves the ref off and West refocuses on the fight. Matt's trained and he's experienced. He slipped into emotion and he won't allow the mistake again. He'll want retaliation and he'll want it on the floor. "Stay off the floor," I scream. "He wants the floor!"

Matt surges forward and West sidesteps the wrong way. Both of them slam to the ground and the cage vibrates with the impact. The crowd goes insane.

Matt tries to throw a knee over West to straddle. His elbow and forearm go after West's air passage and West scrambles to move away, but Matt's too trained to allow easy release.

"Kick your hips up! Get under his legs!"

West thrusts up and Matt crashes into him, sending him back down. He presses his forearm into West's windpipe.

"Kick your hips up!" I yell again. "Under his legs!"

But West panics with the loss of air and his hands shoot to Matt's arms. I bang against the fence. "Listen to me, Young!"

The reaction is instantaneous. He thrusts back up again and Matt's grip loosens. The crowd hollers their approval when West ducks and rolls out of the hold and brings the fight back to their feet.

Matt and West round each other. The crowd claps in unison, waiting for either to attack. I glance at the ticking clock. "Thirty seconds!"

Three rounds of three minutes each and the end is near. His first competition and I know he needs to finish it out. Both of them sway with exhaustion. Matt stomps forward and West reacts by jumping out of the way. Matt will go for the knees again.

We trained for this moment. I dragged West through the mud and back again. At this point, it has nothing to do with strength, but everything to do with heart.

"Kick series!" I rattle the cage. "Kick series."

West wipes at the sweat over his eyes and begins the dance on the floor. His legs switch as he searches for the right moment. Sensing an attack, Matt parallels, then strikes.

Matt throws a cross and West blocks and lands a front kick into his chest. Matt stumbles and I join the crowd cheering. West continues the attack, pinning Matt against the cage.

The entire arena stomps on the floor when the bell rings and the ref pulls West off Matt. West circles the cage, pounding his fist to his chest and the crowd eats it up.

With palms up against the cage, he leans into me. I wish

this was the movies. I wish I could rush the cage and wrap myself around him, but there are rules and there is respect and later I'll show him my love and gratitude. "You did it."

West sucks in air and latches on to my fingers that I weaved through the fence. "I didn't win."

"I don't care." The decision by the judges against him should be fast. Matt scored more punches. He dominated the fight, but West stood three rounds and he sent a message to everyone within earshot of the cage: West Young has heart and he never gives up. That, in the fighting world, makes him dangerous.

He rests his forehead against the cage and I press mine against the same spot. Our fingers touch and I close my eyes, wishing we were alone.

"You're worth it." West is black-and-blue and bloodied and swelling. His body has been hammered and brutalized and cut. "You are worth all of this."

"I love you," I whisper.

The ref approaches West from behind. "Decision's in."

West flashes me that same glorious smile as the first day we met. "I already won."

West

JAX ENTERS THE SMALL ROOM wearing a shit-eating grin. Since I walked out of the cage with my defeat set in stone, the kid's become my new best friend. He tosses another gallon bag of ice to John. "Haley's about to kick some ass if we don't let her in soon. How're you holding up?"

Sitting in a chair, I'm down to my briefs and John's adamant his granddaughter isn't witnessing me exposed. John's wrapped two bags of ice on my shoulder where something popped out, then repopped back into place during the fight. I hold a bag to my eye, and he sets another one on the knuckles of my right hand. "I'm fine."

"Remarkably, you are," says John. "But I can't start training you again until you heal. This swelling needs to go down."

I rub my jaw, then work it around. There's not a spot on my body that isn't pounding and the shock of John's statement is enough to numb the pain for a second. "Training?"

"Payment due on the first of the month and you're required to practice at least five days a week."

"Bullshit," coughs Jax. "He requires seven."

John checks the bag of ice on my shoulder. "You're not tapping out after your first fight, are you?"

It hurts to smile. "No, I'm not."

"Good."

A knock on the door sends Jax into a laughing fit. "I told you, Hays, you aren't seeing him until he's got..." Jax swings the door open and the words fade away.

He scratches the back of his neck and chances a glimpse at me. "It's some guy claiming to be your dad."

Denny or Dad? The thought floats before I can stop it. I nod and the door widens to reveal my father. He's out of place in a pair of jeans and a collared polo shirt.

"Come on, Jax." John stands. "Let's go keep Haley from starting a brawl."

The door shuts with a loud click and the only sound in the room is the ice shifting in the bags. I pop my neck to the side, finding myself too damned tired for a screaming match. "Whatever it is, can we argue about it later?"

Dad slips into a seat across from me. An hour ago, John sat in that same chair and offered me more fatherly advice than my own supposed father had my entire life. "I told your mother you're still alive."

"Thanks."

"Call her. She'll want to hear your voice."

"I will." I stretch my shoulder and wince. "Mind keeping me on your insurance for a little longer?"

Dad's face moves up as he smiles and I raise my eyebrows in response. What the hell?

"You're good at this," he says. "It was awful watching it, but at the same time, I smacked the guy next to me and told him you're my son."

I chuckle, because I got nothing to say. I take it back. I do know what to say. "Did you always know I wasn't yours?"

The smile slips off his face and I sort of regret my choice of words, yet, I don't. This conversation needs to be had and there's never going to be an appropriate time or place.

"Yes. Colleen had been sick for a long time and let's just say there was a breakdown in communication between me and your mother and I'm aware how babies are made."

I nod, the truth not making me feel much better. "Why did you stay with her? She cheated."

"I loved her. Denny loved her first and I stole her away from him and then when things got rough I abandoned her and Colleen. She needed comfort, and when I didn't give it, she ran to arms that were still open."

Fuck. I toss the bag I'd been holding to my eye into the trash. "You're real live and let live about this."

"I love her, West. She loves me. When you feel like that about someone, you find ways to make it work."

My heart aches—Haley. Was what I did to her different?

"You say you love her, but you wanted me to break up with Haley. You told me to trust you, that a girl would be my worst downfall. Is that how you see Mom? Do you really love her or has it all been a show this entire time?"

My dad ages ten years with each second that passes. He appears smaller, grayer and weary. "I loved your mother from the first time she poured a beer over my head because she'd heard my type of lines before."

My eyes widen and my lips twitch up and down. My mother poured a beer over Dad's head? My father used pickup lines on my mother? Who the fuck are these people and part of me is loving every second. Watching my reaction, Dad's mouth tilts up. "I think you can understand why your grandparents were less than thrilled with me."

Dad's parents are picture-perfect conservative and stuck-up. "Then why did you push me so hard on Haley?"

The happiness vanishes. "Because the road with your mother was difficult. From the moment we met, nothing was easy. Life threw everything it could at us and sometimes we won and other times we failed. But through it all, never doubt that I loved her and never doubt that she loved me. While that's true, my choice to be with your mother, her choice to be with me—it made life complicated and we suffered because of it. You have to understand, West, that when it comes to your children...you don't want hard. You don't want to see them hurt."

I readjust the ice bag on my shoulder, acting as if it's slipping, but I really need a break from the intense. There's a sadness within me and this happiness that has got me all screwed up. My parents love each other and that's...that's something to hold on to, but to know they've experienced pain, too... It somehow makes them human.

Dad leans forward and rests his combined hands in the gap between his knees. "What I said is true. You may not share my blood, but you are me through and through. Not just the stuff that drives me up a damn wall, but the stuff that makes you, you. Your sense of humor, your tenacity, how you love your family."

Dad lowers his head and I wipe at my eyes. I'm tired. It's why I'm emotional, but somewhere deep inside the young kid that followed this man around like he was a god rejoices.

There's an edge in his voice, a brokenness that doesn't

belong to a man who owns the world. "You may not want it, but you're my son. You have always been my son. You will always be my son and I love you."

I want to say I love him back, but there are still parts of me that need to heal—internal parts—unseen hurts that need space and air. "I can't come home. Not yet." If ever.

"I know. I knew it the moment you threw your first punch in that cage. You've found something, a direction, a path I'm not allowed on, but let me at least be a spectator. Give me the chance to meet you at the finish line."

My own voice cracks. "Okay."

"Okay. And so you know, I'm not abandoning you. Your room's still yours. So's your car and credit cards. I'll still give Haley the scholarship."

"I've got to do this on my own. The temptations you're scared about me returning to... They belong to the world at home. I'm a boy there and here..."

"You're a man." Dad squeezes the only nonbruised part of my body and repeats, "You're a man."

"Did it bother you?" I ask. "That I ended up working with Denny?" A pause. "That I'll still be working with Denny."

"Yes," he answers quickly. "It does. As far as I'm concerned, you're my son. Not his, but I understand your need to know him. Just...just at least consider offering me the same chance that you're giving him."

I nod, but he knows it's not really an answer. It's something I'll need to think about. Dad stands and I can't let him walk away like this. "Tell Mom I'll be there for family dinners."

The small smile on his face tells me I nailed the first

board into that bridge the two of us are trying to rebuild. "She'll like that. I'm proud of you, son."

With a shut door, I find myself alone. I sigh and rub my hand over my head. Six months ago, I thought I owned the world, but I really owned nothing. Now, in the eyes of the world, I've lost everything...

"West?"

My head snaps up and my heart stutters. I've lost absolutely nothing of any value. My lips slant up and, out of respect for her grandfather, I grab a towel and stick it over my lap.

Haley's laughter tickles over my skin. She tilts her head and that sexy, silky hair tumbles over her shoulder. "You're letting John get to you."

I wave at my body. "I'm not in the position to be taking on any more fights."

Her hips sway as she strolls over to me. "Don't worry. I have your back."

I crave for her to curl her body over mine, but instead she drags the chair Dad abandoned moments ago next to me. She sits in it and laces our fingers together. "I should kick your ass for what you did."

I chuckle. "Which particular event would the ass kicking be for?"

"Any of it, but mainly that you broke up with me so I could go to school for free."

Damn, Haley's always been direct. "I wanted you to have a chance at a future. I couldn't stand in the way of that. At least I thought I couldn't. By the time I understood my mistake, you were gone."

"I didn't come back for you," she says. "By taking the fight you sped up my timeline, but I came back for me. You and everyone else were right—I had lost my fight and I wasn't engaging. You tapped out on me, but I tapped out, too."

"It won't happen again," I say. "Me tapping out. I learned my lesson."

"Me, too," she responds.

I think about her words. That there could be another meaning. "If this is you trying to let me down easy, then be warned I plan on fighting for you."

Haley smiles and I like that her eyes lighten with it. "I'm not going anywhere, Young."

"We have a lot to talk about." Exhausted, my head settles back against the wall.

I want to know what helped change her mind and where she's going to be living now that she's home. I need to tell her about my dad, my biological dad, about her tuition to college, a ton of things, but I'm too damned tired.

"We can talk about whatever you want later." Haley rests her head on my shoulder. "Right now, I'm focusing on the whole happy you're alive. You scared the hell out of me when I first arrived. You weren't focused and Matt was pounding you to pieces."

"I was focused." I focused when I heard her beautiful voice. I turn my head, nuzzle my nose into her hair and inhale her sweet fragrance. She's here. She's honest to God here. "You mean everything to me, Haley."

"I love you," she whispers as her fingers squeeze mine. After a second, she rocks our joined hands. "Sometimes, after a fight, I wanted silence. Just time to clear my head."

Silence. I exhale. Silence would be nice. "Will you stay with me?"

"For as long as you want me."

"Then be prepared to stay for a long time." I close my eyes and enjoy the sensation of Haley's fingers tracing my arm.

Haley

THE BELL RINGS and both Mrs. Collins and I turn our heads to watch the flood of students fill the student parking lot. I requested a meeting with her this morning and she pulled me from last period to talk.

My lap is full of applications and pamphlets. I've applied for the athletic scholarship, but I have to be prepared to be solely responsible for paying for my college education. West's dad offered to uphold his end of the deal, but I can't accept it. That money is tainted.

There's only a few remaining days left to graduation—the sand in the hourglass has almost run out. I sigh heavily while fingering the top pamphlet in my hand. No one ever said fighting is easy.

"Community college is an excellent option," she says. "In fact, that's how I started."

Ha. Frames on her wall advertise the University of Louisville and Harvard. "Is this one of those moments where you tell me a lie to make me feel better about my choices?"

Her lips flinch into a smile. "No. This is where I tell you the truth. I couldn't afford college, so I went to a community college to fill my requirements while I worked a job that could help me afford school. When I graduated with my associate's, I transferred. I didn't turn out so bad, did I?"

Guess not. I shove the paperwork into my backpack. "Thanks."

Outside the window, I spot West, Kaden and Jax forming a semicircle as they wait for me. Living with my grandfather in his camper with Jax and Kaden is a bit like a chicken living in a factory farm, but it's the first time in a year and a half I have a sense of home. It could be because I'm training again. It could be because I'm taking back my life. But I think it's because I'm learning how to rely on the people I love.

"How's your mom and dad?" Mrs. Collins asks.

"Good." Another parent-teacher conference later and Mrs. Collins learned from John that Jax, Kaden and I are living with him. I respect her because CPS didn't show at the gym to drag any of us away. "Actually, they're doing very good."

Mom found work. Nothing spectacular, but something better than what she was doing here. Maggie's made friends at her new school and is being spoiled by my great-aunt, and my dad...

My dad joined a gym. I smile when I think of our conversation last night on the phone.

"I'm proud of you," he had said. "For staying home. For trying again."

"Thanks," I responded. "Is it true? Mom said you're fighting again?"

Dad laughed and that sweet sound healed wounds that were still open. "No tournaments in my future, but, yeah, I joined one. Your old man is slow and this body creaks more than it should, but it feels good to move. It feels good to be useful."

Dad's healing and it will probably be a while before he's totally on his feet. Being in the gym isn't a perfect solution, but it's the start of one.

"Is there anything else you'd like to discuss?" Mrs. Collins asks.

I fiddle with the straps of my backpack, smoothing them out on my lap to see if one is longer than the other. "My mom said once if you say something out loud that it takes the power away from it. Do you think that's true?"

Her features smooth out. "Yes. I one hundred percent agree with your mother."

Definitely food for thought. "Thanks again."

"If you ever need anything, Haley, I'm here."

I smile at her as I leave. If I had a dollar for every time she's said those words to me, I'd be a very rich girl. The May afternoon is definitely short weather and I've got some holey jeans screaming to be cut. After my shift at the pizza place, I'm finding a pair of scissors.

My heart warms when all three guys in my life laugh as Jax breaks down a sparring session he had yesterday, but I only have eyes for West. His bruises from the fight have faded and he's back to drop-dead, stop-my-heart gorgeous.

He has dinner with his family four to five times a week and pays Isaiah's foster parents fifty dollars a month to sleep on the couch in their basement. Last week, he watched his sister, Rachel, take her first steps. Since then he's been flying high.

I've been to dinner with West at his family's house a few times and it's a strange combination of people at the table between West's family, Rachel's boyfriend, Abby and then me.

It's awkward for all of us, except for Abby. Because of that, we all sit back and let her do the talking.

Heat curls in my belly when West flashes me a smile. "Took you long enough."

"I've got options," I tell him. "She gave me lots of options."

West kisses my forehead and runs his fingers through my hair. Tiny goose bumps form along my neck and I wish for the millionth time we could be alone.

Jax makes a gagging sound and I stick my tongue out at him.

"Real mature, Hays." Yet he sticks his out in return.

West rests an arm around my shoulder and tucks me close to him. We have a half hour before the city bus, so they resume their conversation. The side door to the building opens and Conner walks out with Matt behind him. My eyes lock with Matt's and I shiver from the coldness inside me.

He won, but he lost. It wasn't the beating he'd hoped for and, according to the rumors at school, it's driven him harder at the gym. It really is a waste. West and I have changed so much, learned so much and Matt is where he was before—in denial over his brother and over his own emotional instability.

"It's over," West whispers into my ear. "Everything between Matt and me is over."

They hate each other and I imagine they always will, but neither will street brawl. This will become a rivalry in the cage. Matt and I have digressed to these moments of him staring at me as he passes by and me quietly panicking.

"I know." But maybe I don't. I'm still drawn to look at him to make sure he's not stalking up to hurt me from behind.

"He's not going to hurt you, either," West says softly as he notices where my attention still lies. "I promise you—it's over."

I shift and West drops his arm. The three of them stop their conversation and survey me like I've grown antlers and a red nose. West takes my fingers and rubs his thumb over my hand. Typically that touch weakens my knees, but right now, I'm full of angst and panic and all I can think about is returning to the building. "I'll be back, okay?"

West glances at my family, then back at me. "Do you want me to come with you?"

"No," I say way too quickly. This is one of the things West hates—when I live inside my head. It's also one of the things that drove me away from my family. "I've got to talk to Mrs. Collins about something. Just...talk."

"All right." He squeezes my hand and lets me go.

I sprint into the building and down the hall. The teachers lock their doors behind them and I pray Mrs. Collins hasn't bolted. In the main office, one secretary is already gone and the other one holds her purse. "Can I help you?"

I don't say anything as I skid to a halt in the doorframe of Mrs. Collins's office. My heart pounds and my chest moves rapidly with my breaths. Mrs. Collins has her car keys in one hand and a bundle of folders in the other. She's leaving. I'm too late.

Her forehead furrows. "Did you forget something, Haley?"

I force out the words before I lose my courage. "My ex-boyfriend hit me."

I said it... I said the words. My vision becomes fuzzy as I wait for the world to implode...as I wait for her hate and judgment and then I realize I crave her belief.

"He hit me." Suddenly the words aren't as painful. "He hit me and it wasn't okay."

Mrs. Collins sets her files and keys on the side of her desk. "No, it wasn't okay. Why don't you shut the door behind you and take a seat?"

Before I can do either of those things, I desperately search her eyes to see if she'll tell me the truth. "Am I going to be okay?"

"What do you think?" she asks in a kind, thoughtful way. In a way that makes me think that I may already know the answer.

My mouth pops open and Mrs. Collins moves around me and gently shuts the door. She's quiet as she slides around me again and sits behind her desk. "You look okay. You sound okay. And you're here talking to me. How do you feel?"

I sink into the chair across from her and drop my book bag to the floor. "I'm tired of handling this on my own because—" I wave my hand in front of my heart "—keeping it inside isn't working out for me."

She nods like she understands…like really understands. And the sincerity in her eyes gives me a flash of hope. "How about we start at the beginning? When did you first meet him?"

West

HOLDING ON TO HER ELBOWS, Haley toes a rotted piece of floorboard in the corner of the living room. Isaiah gave Kaden and me a lead on the place. It turns out he lived here for a couple of months.

"What do you think Jax will do?" she asks. I glance away, unable to endure the worry lines on her forehead. Next week, Kaden, Haley and I are graduating. Haley's determined to stay in the camper and save her money for college and Jax... Jax is considering heading home.

"I don't know. He's worried about his mom and brothers."

Haley bites her bottom lip and assesses the walls.

"It'll look better once we get furniture," I say.

"The floor will fall through when you get furniture."

"Not true." I grab Haley's hand and guide her into the only bedroom. "See." I motion to the mattress and box springs I bought today. "Floorboards are still intact."

Haley claps her hands together and the pride radiating from her eyes causes me to grin. "You bought furniture!"

"Yep." And in one solid motion, I bend over, connect with

Haley at her knees and flip her onto the mattress. "And I'm bent on trying it out."

She giggles and I love the sight of her light brown hair sprawled all around her. The strap of Haley's pink tank top slips off her shoulder and my heart freezes at the sight. "You're beautiful."

Haley becomes serious as she raises her fingers to my face and traces an outline of where my eye had been swollen weeks before. "You fought for me."

"Yes." And I'll be fighting again. Not for her so much as for me. I'm staying amateur and will be in the cage again in the fall. Haley's deferred the training to John, but what I like is that she's training along with me, though Haley has yet to decide if she's returning to the tournament ring.

I yank my shirt off and lower my head to taste Haley's lips. Shock registers through my body when she presses a hand against my chest. "I have something to show you."

"What?"

A sexy smile tilts her lips. "Are you impatient or something?"

I prop my hands on either side of her head and kiss a trail from her renegade tank top strap to her neck, keeping my body from touching hers. "We haven't been alone in weeks, Haley, and I'll be living with your brother. How much alone time do you think he'll be giving us?"

We barely find enough alone time to kiss now and I don't foresee our opportunities improving with her brother sharing a room with me. But it's all worked out for the best. Haley's been talking with Mrs. Collins regularly, which means Haley's been dealing with some heavy shit. Because of that, we've been taking it slow. Doesn't matter. I've waited this long for the perfect girl. I don't mind waiting a little while longer for her to be ready.

A contented sigh escapes Haley's mouth when I part my lips and kiss her neck deeper and longer. Her hands wander to my biceps and begin a gentle massage that causes my head to spin.

"You don't fight fair," she breathes.

I chuckle against her sweet skin. "You're the one that taught me all about offensive attacks."

Before I can react, Haley twists her legs with mine and we roll without my consent, but how can I complain when I have such a beautiful creature lying on top?

She waggles her eyebrows. "Amateur."

"Give me a couple years and I'll be a pro."

Haley doesn't scoff at me like some of my old friends do when I tell them what I'm doing with my life. Instead, a twinkle in her eye says she believes in my dreams. It's a step-by-step process that will take years.

I'm allowing Dad to pay for my education at the University of Louisville. In return, I will work for him thirty hours a week during the summer and twenty during the school year. I work another five to ten for Denny at the bar and the two of us continue our fucked-up relationship of never mentioning he's my father.

The rest of the time, I spend at the gym training and helping others train. I'm going to see how far I can take this… how far I can go.

Haley reaches back and produces a letter from her back pocket. "It's my answer on the scholarship. The one we did the videos for."

"What did it say?" I wrap my arms around Haley and I sit up so that she's straddling me.

Haley and I discussed Dad's offer to pay for her education. I even brought her to the house and Dad talked to her as well as my mom. She won't accept our money. She's hard-headed and stubborn and I love her more than my own life.

Haley's enrolled both at the University of Louisville and the community college. This scholarship will answer where she'll spend at least the next year.

"Well?"

She loses her spark. "I don't know. I haven't opened it yet."

Adrenaline pours into my veins. I'm more nervous about this than she is. "Are you going to?"

Haley slides off me and I immediately miss her warmth. She and I are like two separate halves to a whole. Separate in that the two of us could live life apart and be successful, but when we are together—when we are whole—that's when the magic happens.

She tucks the letter into the crevice between the bed and the wall. "I'll tell you what. Kiss me and when we're done, I'll open it."

I know her. Haley doesn't think she won. I slip my hand around her waist and pull her back into me. My lips roam her neck and my fingers lift the soft material of her tank top. "No matter what, you'll be okay."

Haley melts into me. "I know."

She lays a hand over mine and I stop, giving her a moment to collect her thoughts. It's hard for her to not live in her head and the time to process those thoughts is all she really needs.

"I'm scared of the rejection, but more..." She inhales

deeply and I urge Haley onto my lap. With her head resting on my collarbone, she traces the spot on my chest where I had been bruised for weeks. “I want to be a sports trainer. Sort of like John, but not. I want to help athletes recovering from injury. Watching your sister learn how to walk again... personally learning how to battle through emotional injury... It’s what I want to help people do for life.”

I tip Haley’s chin so her eyes meet mine. “Okay.”

Her head shakes against my fingers. “No. I need someone to know this before I open that letter. When I applied for it, I was looking for money and I would have majored in kinesiology because that’s what I had money to go to school for. I need someone to know before I get my answer that I’m choosing this degree...that it’s not choosing me.”

Of all the people in the world, she knows I understand. I lower my lips to hers and kiss the soft part between. She presses back and her hands move along my chest—a tickle, a caress and it’s enough to set me on fire.

We roll and soon her tank joins my shirt on the floor. I explore her curves, enjoy the taste of her skin and memorize each hitch of breathing and soft sigh that escapes from her mouth. My mind reels when her body responds to me and the fierceness of the heat created.

Time loses meaning and the only thing left is her touch and her love. Soon we are gasping and holding and whispering words that will only be said between us. Then everything stills as colors burst into the world.

I edge Haley so that she’s lying beside me. Her hair tickles my chest and I rub her spine, half awake, half reliving kissing her in a dream.

A crinkle to my right causes my eyes to shoot open and

I snatch the letter held prisoner by the bed. I hand it to her and kiss her temple.

With her head resting on my arm, Haley stares at it for a moment before ripping the back seal open with her finger. The envelope falls away as she unfolds the letter. I search her face for any sign of frustration or hope. Every ounce of me tightens as I pray for a miracle.

With a short release of air from her lips, Haley refolds the letter and lets it drop to the floor. My head hits the back of the wall. Just fuck. How could they deny her?

I tighten my hold on her. "It's okay."

Haley runs a fingertip along my cheek and a smile forms on her lips. "Yeah, actually, it is. I won."

*****

ACKNOWLEDGMENTS

To God: NIV John 15:12–13—My command is this: Love each other as I have loved you. Greater love has no one than this: that he lay down his life for his friends.

For Dave: with your forever gentle patience, you always let me know that I was worth fighting for.

Thank you to…

Kevan Lyon—I am continually honored to have you in my corner.

Margo Lipschultz—you out of anyone understand how difficult this book was for me. I will never forget your support, the phone calls and the encouragement. You have no idea how grateful I am for you.

Everyone who touched my books at MIRA Ink, especially Natashya Wilson and Lisa Wray. Honestly, you are all truly amazing!

Eric Haycraft, Scottie Sawade and the other fantastic people at Real Fighters Gym. I can't thank you enough for welcoming me into your gym. I also especially thank you for your patience with me, the girl who had to always think for a second about which one was her cross and which one was her jab and yet you still let me stay. The talent in your gym is world-class and astounding.

Angela Annalaro-Murphy, Kristen Simmons, Colette Ballard, Kelly Creagh, Bethany Griffin, Kurt Hampe, Bill Wolfe and the Louisville Romance Writers: if it weren't for your continued support and love, this book never would have happened. Thank you from the deepest depths of my heart.

A huge thank you to all my readers and especially to Linda Marie Bofenkamp. It still amazes me to see my books for sale and I am forever humbled by my readers' love and support.

As always, to my parents, my sister, my Mount Washington family and my entire in-law family—I love you.

Katie McGarry and MIRA Ink
are thrilled to announce the next book in the
PUSHING THE LIMITS series!
Echo and Noah's story continues in

BREAKING THE RULES,

coming soon....

Echo shifts, and the cold rush of air against my skin causes my eyes to flash open. The Colorado State Park Ranger for the Great Sand Dunes wasn't kidding when he said temperatures drop overnight. I stretch the muscles in my back, then turn onto my side in order to touch Echo again. My palm melts into the curve of her waist.

She's curled in with her back toward me and she's tugged the blanket tight to her shoulder. Her tank top no longer provides protection against the elements. Last night was hot, in more ways than I can count, and the cover wasn't required for any of our activities—neither for the sleeping nor the kissing. Without a doubt, this has been the best damned summer of my life...

And look for the first book in Katie's brand-new series
set in the dangerous and exhilarating world of
motorcycle clubs, also coming soon!

PLAYLIST

Theme:
"Harder to Breathe," by Maroon 5
"Wild Ones," by Flo Rida (feat. Sia)
"Love Is a Battlefield," by Pat Benatar

West:
"Save a Horse (Ride a Cowboy)," by Big & Rich
"Come Over," by Kenny Chesney
"This Love," by Maroon 5
"Bitter Sweet Symphony," by The Verve

Haley:
"Fighter," by Christina Aguilera
"The House That Built Me," by Miranda Lambert
"Stronger (What Doesn't Kill You)," by Kelly Clarkson
"Roar" by Katy Perry

Songs for Specific Scenes:
The night West and Haley meet: "I Knew You Were Trouble," by Taylor Swift

West and Haley training in the gym:
“Good Feeling,” by Flo Rida
When Haley sneaks West into her room:
“Secrets,” by OneRepublic
The fight in the cage:
“Eye of the Tiger,” by Survivor

Songs that Represent Haley and West’s future:
“Price Tag,” by Jessie J (feat. B.o.B.)
“Heaven,” by Warrant

Read on for a bonus
PUSHING THE LIMITS novella,

CROSSING THE LINE

now in print for the first time!

Dear Lincoln,

I saw this card today and thought of you. I know that I wasn't who you came to meet, but I'm glad we had a chance to talk. Even though I was just his little sister's best friend, Aires still felt like a brother to me.

Between you and me, I keep smiling when I think of the look on your face when we decided to sneak out of the wake without being caught. That was a strange, messed-up night, and I'm grateful you were there to help me through it.

I know how I miss Aires, so I can only imagine how you miss Josh. Just remember that I'm thinking of you.

Can I write you again? Will you write back? I hope you do. I sort of feel like we were meant to meet.

~ Lila

Dear Lila,

Thank you for the card. I'm going to admit, I'm not much of a kitten guy, but I appreciate the thought. Mostly, I appreciate your note.

Yeah, I agree, the night of Aires's funeral was messed up, but messed up in a good way. Mom and Dad thought if we met Aires's family that it would help us with losing Josh. I thought Mom and Dad had it all jacked up, and in a way, they did. It wasn't meeting Aires's family that helped, it was talking to you—so thanks.

And no, I don't mind if you want to write me again. Even if you do it in one of those kitten-hanging-from-a-tree cards.

~ Lincoln

Lincoln

Is it weird that I feel close to you even though you're hundreds of miles away and we've only met once? I hope not. I'm glad that you're in my life.

~ Lila

ON THE COMPUTER SCREEN, the question "Why?" glares at me like the correct accusation it is. This dialogue between Lila and me, it breaks every unsaid rule about our relationship. We never plug in like this. Never. Not that part of me hasn't wanted a faster connection to her. A link beyond the letters, but there was something about the written word that made our relationship safe.

And now we're crossing lines. The one relationship I need, the one relationship I depend on...I've jacked it up. Fitting since I have a natural inclination toward destroying anything good. It's genetic, my sister tells me. Anyone sharing our bloodline is inherently doomed.

"You should have talked to me before buying it," my father shouts at my mother in the kitchen. "I made a budget."

My home is a volcano, a constant gurgle of hot lava on the verge of explosion. I try to ignore my parents, but it's difficult. We have one computer in the house, and it sits wide open in the family room. From the corner of my eye, I have a clear shot of how Dad's hands shake with anger and how Mom's frustration paints her cheeks a frightening scarlet.

"Why should I have to ask your permission for anything?" A chair slams into the wooden kitchen table and Mom's high heels stomp against the tile floor. "It's my money, too. And as for the budget—you never asked me what I wanted."

I asked you why. Lila's words appear on our direct message conversation.

I rub at the lines on my forehead, and a tense uneasiness paralyzes my fingers over the keyboard. I don't know why I did it. That's a lie, I do know, but I don't know how to tell her. I don't know how to salvage this.

I'm sorry, I reply.

I didn't ask for an apology, she rapid-fires back, I asked WHY!

Because I love you. It's as if someone places two hands around my heart and chokes it. I love her. I've fallen for a girl I met only once, a girl I've exchanged letters with for two years. There's no way she can feel the same about me. Those words would push her over the edge.

I want to keep her, but what do I say? What can I do?

Like the warning tremors before an eruption, my parents' argument becomes more heated. Mom turns on the blender to drown out Dad. In response, Dad yells louder and bangs his hand against the table, making the china clink against the water glasses. The baby who was sleeping moments before, my nephew, begins to cry. It's not a cry, it's a shriek—one that causes my skin to peel back from my bones.

The noises press against my skull, scattering my already screwed-up thought process into more of a mess. I can explain, I type. Though I'm not sure I can.

Then EXPLAIN! She's a fast typer. Too fast. My heart thumps in my ears. I mentally will the chaos around me to stop and pray that Lila will...what? What is it that I expect her to do?

"Where the hell is Meg?" my father roars. "That baby is her responsibility! I never agreed to be her babysitter." He never agreed to be a grandfather at forty-five, either.

My eyes dart to my father, dressed in his polo shirt and slacks in preparation for my graduation, to the baby dressed in a blue onesie pulling himself up in the playpen placed in the middle of the spacious living room. His entire face flushes red. Drool pours from his small gaping mouth. He wails again, the sound like a tornado siren.

"Meg's out," Mom screams over the blender still grinding away. Meg just turned seventeen and is gone—at eight in the morning, meaning she never came home last night. She left Junior with us. With me. I also never agreed to be a babysitter.

As if on cue, the front door clicks open. Impressive—my sister has returned before noon. Maybe today, she'll hold her son.

I don't acknowledge Meg. I don't even glance at her. Instead, I focus on the cursor blinking on the screen. I have seconds before I completely lose Lila. I made a mistake, I type. I—

The screen flashes to black. "What the hell!"

"I need this," Meg says as she straightens from resetting the computer. She tucks her freshly dyed chin-length blue hair behind her ear. "Get out of here."

The new guy, the one who isn't the baby daddy, the one who

hates kids, stands in the front doorway with his hands shoved in his sagging jeans.

"Meg!" Mom rushes in from the kitchen. Does she know she left the blender running? Does anyone notice the baby still howling? "Where have you been? Lincoln's graduation ceremony is in an hour—"

"What did you do?" I mutter as I press my fingertips against my head. Lila. I lost Lila. The only sane person in my life.

"Why should I have to go?" Meg throws her hands out to her sides, barely missing her own child's head. "It's not my graduation."

"What did you do?" I say louder. Anger gains traction in my bloodstream.

Dad knocks over a chair in his charge into the living room. "Pick up your baby! Pick him up! He's your responsibility."

Mom's voice is smothered by Meg shouting over and over again that she's not attending my graduation.

"What did you do?!" I yell above them all, and slam my hands onto the computer desk.

They fall silent: Mom, Dad, Meg. Everyone except the baby. "Someone pick him up!"

No one does. They all continue to watch me with wide eyes because they know I've cracked. I never yell. Not once in eighteen years have they witnessed me lose my temper. I'm the odd one, yeah, but I'm the steady one. The unemotional one. The one who didn't cry at my brother's funeral. The one who never demands more of anyone or anything—even from myself.

The cries reach a higher pitch. In a quick motion, I slide the kid out of his prison and he immediately places his head on my shoulder, his thumb stuck safely in his mouth. The sweet scent of formula and baby powder drifts from his tiny body. We must look ironic: fifteen pounds of premature warmth curled into six feet and a hundred and seventy-five pounds of rock-climbing muscle. Part of me hates that he'll calm down for me, because it makes him my burden. The other part...at least I can help someone feel better.

I glance over at the shut-down computer. Lila. My hand covers the baby's back as if I'm seeking his comfort. I lost Lila. There's no way she'll connect with me online now. No way I can wait long enough to see if she'd respond to my letter. To see if she will grant me another chance.

"Take your baby," I say to my sister. Her eyes widen as her head convulses in tiny shakes meaning no.

"Take—your—baby." I'm wrong. My house isn't a volcano—I am, and the past two years have created a dormant giant who no longer will tolerate being ignored. I'm tired of this. Tired of how everyone's become so obsessed with themselves, obsessed with the moment, that we've ceased caring what's going to happen next.

I'm just as guilty, and that downfall has led to hurting Lila. Soon, the same damn poor decisions will devastate this family. God, I'm a moron.

I work hard at keeping my voice gentle, because it's not this baby's fault that I dropped out of reality or that his mother is so jacked up she's never held him or that his grandparents are so concerned about winning a fight that they can't comprehend what's happening to their future.

"Mom." I motion with my eyes for her to take the now-sleeping infant.

She bustles over like the busy bird she is and slips him out of my grasp. How the hell do I fix all of the mistakes I've made in the past two years?

My family still stares at me like deer waiting for the gunshot. I should start with telling them the truth, but the words escape me. No, not escape... I just can't stop thinking about Lila.

If she can find a way to forgive me, then I can find a way to fix this.

Lila

No, it's not weird that you feel close to me. Honestly? Sometimes knowing that I'll be getting a letter from you is the only thing pushing me through my days.

~ Lincoln

THE MOMENT I OPEN THE DOOR, I immediately regret not heeding the advice on the yellow Post-it note clinging near the small round hole: *Lila, Always check the peephole before answering the door. You never know who's on the other side.*

Translation: serial killers knock before attacking. I watch *CSI.* It happens.

Standing before me isn't a serial killer but a different type of nightmare. Stephen, the guy I've dated on and off since sophomore year, tilts his head with a way too smug *I'm concerned* look on his face.

"Are you okay?" he asks.

I sniff and use a crumpled tissue to wipe my runny nose. Let's see: swollen, puffy red eyes with dark circles? No, I'm not okay—and now I'm worse because he thinks I'm crying over him. "I'm fine. What are you doing here?"

"Checking on you." His green eyes survey the empty living room behind me. "I know your parents and brothers left yesterday for vacation. I wanted to make sure you made it through your first night alone."

First night alone—ever. And it epically blew. I've got six more days of alone and then, come fall, the rest of my life. "I survived."

Stephen scrutinizes me with a cocked eyebrow that says he can tell I didn't sleep. Which I didn't because I was too busy being terrified. My imagination boarded a train south to crazyville and convinced me that someone was scratching on the windows.

A hot June evening breeze drifts into the house, bringing with it the scent of the sickly sweet gel he uses to force his brown hair into a styled mess.

"Can I come in?" he asks when I'm obviously not offering.

No. I sigh. "Sure."

Stephen enters and fingers the purple Post-it on the phone reminding me to check the caller ID. When I woke up yesterday morning, I found the peephole note, along with about a hundred other Post-its stuck to various objects around the house. All of them my mother's desperate attempts to teach me how to live on my own so I'm prepared when I head fourteen hours away from home to the University of Florida.

"You can call me if you're scared to be alone at night," he says. "I'll come over."

I snort. "I'm sure you will."

Stephen was my first...and last. When I gave him my virginity, I thought I loved him, and maybe I sort of did, but then everything became complicated. Not everything—me. I became complicated and I didn't want to have sex anymore. Stephen lacked sympathy.

And then there was Lincoln...

My lips tremble and a new pool of warm tears builds in my eyes.

Stephen turns toward me with his mouth popped open for his next witty suggestion. It snaps shut when he spots my face. "Whoa. Lila. It's okay."

It's not. My bones suddenly weigh too much for my body, and I collapse onto the couch. The tissue in my grasp balls into a rock. "I'm fine. Just tired." Just heartbroken. Lincoln lied to me this morning and then he cut me off. As if the past two years of letters meant nothing to him.

Letters—not emails, not texts—letters. It's what we promised each other when we met. Because somehow, letters made our relationship private...different...real.

I stare at the red-and-black amoeba patterns on the Oriental rug covering the hardwood floor. My stomach aches when I see the project that started or ended it all, depending on how I choose to view it, peeking out from underneath the cherry end table. The sturdy scrapbook paper represents hours of cutting and pasting and care meant to celebrate Lincoln's graduation from high school. The petals of the dried-out lilac-colored roses Lincoln sent me for my graduation last week create the border.

I'm so unbelievably stupid to have fallen for a guy I've met once. Stupid because nice guys only belong in the land of make-believe.

The other end of the couch shifts as Stephen half sits on the arm. How many times did my mother ask him *not* to do that? Stephen licks his thumb and rubs dirt off his new prized possession: the two-hundred-and-fifty-dollar athletic shoes he stood in line for overnight.

"Seriously, Lila." One more lick. One more rub. "I'll stay with you this week. No strings attached."

I blow out enough air that my hair moves. I'm not being fair.

Stephen's a good guy. It's my fault I fell for someone else. Someone who doesn't really exist. "I know, and thanks. But I've got to work this out for myself. How can I even imagine moving to Florida on my own if I can't stay the night in my house alone?"

Stephen scratches his chin, indicating I'm going to hate whatever gushes out of his mouth next. "Look, I know you better than anyone else and here's the thing...you're not as strong as you make everybody think you are."

"Oh. My. God." A combination of anger and hurt splits open my stomach as my shoulders roll back. "Did you really say that to me?"

"Just listen," he says in a rush. "Your mom told my mom that you haven't turned down the offer from the University of Louisville. You must be having second thoughts, so I'm not saying anything you aren't already thinking."

My throat tightens and I avoid eye contact, ashamed that I'm close to trashing a dream because of fear.

"Stay home." He softens his tone. "And you don't have to worry about being scared. Echo's staying. Grace and Natalie are staying." He pauses and glances at the floor. "I'll be here."

I suck in my lower lip—half mad, half emotional basket case. The University of Florida has always been my goal, but I'm frightened of leaving home. Scared of leaving everything and everyone I've ever known. But I'm also tired of everyone wearing me down with their 1,001 reasons why I shouldn't go.

When I don't respond, Stephen continues. "I know that's why you broke up with me last month. That you don't think we can handle the whole long-distance thing. So stay."

No, that's not why I broke up with him, but it is the reason I gave. Two months ago, Lincoln sent this amazing letter and it shook me to the core. Actually, every letter he sends is amazing, but it finally hit me why Stephen and I could never seem to get it together. It was because I had given my heart to Lincoln.

I didn't want to hurt Stephen then and I don't want to hurt him now. Especially since I realize what a fool I've been. My eyes shut as I digest what I have possibly thrown away with Stephen. "I don't know."

The defeat crushes me in such a way that the couch no longer feels steady enough to carry my weight. Maybe everyone is right. Maybe all my crazy dreams of moving away are stupid and insane. Maybe I just think I'm capable of being more than what I really am: not strong, but a homebody.

All my strength and energy flows out of me and right into Stephen. He jumps off the arm of the couch. "Go to college here, in Louisville, Lila. It'll be like high school. Chad's staying. So's Luke. All of us will be together, going to the same school, and then you and I can start again."

My head snaps up. *But I'm not in love with you.* The words catch in my mouth. His green eyes shine and his face completely lights up. What do I honestly know about love? Obviously nothing after what's happened with Lincoln. "I don't know."

Why is that the only phrase I seem capable of saying?

His fingers spread out as he raises his hands. "That's good enough. For now. Look, I've got to get to work, but I'm serious—if you get freaked staying by yourself, call. Mom and Dad won't care if I stay with you."

I suck in a breath to try to explain to him that I need to do this on my own, but before I can form the first word Stephen plants a kiss on my cheek and strides out the front door.

I blink a few times, trying to let my mind process the turn of events. "Crap."

In the span of minutes, Stephen managed to drag me back into high school. Wasn't this drama supposed to end when I received my diploma?

Three quick raps on the door and a surge of angry adrenaline pumps in my veins. Good. He's back. Now I can really tell him what I think about him staying the night and implying that I'm not strong. Forget the fact he's possibly right. No guy should ever call me a coward.

With a particularly hard yank, I throw open the front door and yell, "You really are a jerk, you know?"

All the air rushes out of my lungs in a fast hiss. It's not Stephen. No. Not at all. This guy has hair the color of midnight. He's tall, built like no guy I've ever dated before—in an *oh, hell yeah* sort of way—and possesses soft blue eyes that entice me to hold him already. And he's clutching a bouquet. Roses. Purple ones.

Something nags me from the back of my brain. Then I remember that I'm required to speak. "Can I help you?"

He shifts his footing, shoving one hand into his faded jeans. "It's me, Lila."

Me? "Sorry?"

"Lincoln."

I really should have taken my mother's advice on the peephole.

Lincoln

I know I should stop gushing about the card you sent for my birthday, but I can't. See, Stephen forgot about my birthday. It's cool. Really. He remembered eventually, and bought me roses, but I need to complain. I know I'm going to sound like a snot, but he got me red roses.

Red. Whenever I see red roses I think of my grandma's funeral, and then I want to cry. I've told Stephen that—twice.

I've dropped hint after hint that purple are my favorites. Of course, I told him that I loved his present and gushed about it, but what do I need to do? Tattoo it on my forehead? Purple!!!

Or at least not red.

Here's the reason why I don't care about Stephen forgetting: you made my birthday special. No one has ever made me a card before. So thanks, Lincoln. Sometimes I think you're my best friend.

~ Lila

SHE'S STUNNING. YEAH, SHE WAS drop-dead gorgeous two years ago, but now...

I'm staring and I need to stop, but seeing her inhibits brain function. Girls don't know it, but standing in the presence of beauty impairs guys. At least, it impairs me.

Screw it. It's Lila. Lila impairs me.

The ends of her golden hair curl near her shoulders. She cut it and I like the new style. A lot. When I first met Lila, she was between—not quite a girl, not really a woman. With those curves, she left between in the dust.

I was only a few inches taller than her then. I grew. She stayed the same height. Lila would fit perfectly under my arm, tucked close into my body. She let me hold her hand the night we met, and I never forgot how her skin felt like satin. I hope she'll let me touch her again.

That is, if she can forgive me.

Her bewildered sky-blue eyes travel along my face, over my arms and chest. Crimson stains her cheeks as she prevents herself from checking out anything lower. I clear my throat to disguise the chuckle.

I want to laugh because she looks so damned cute, but she wouldn't see it that way. She'd think I was belittling her. Lila can't tolerate guys who view women as beneath them. I received more than one letter from her with that rant.

Lila's house sits in the middle of nowhere. Its zip code exists in the city of Louisville, but acreage borders three sides of her house and across the street is a state park. The only beings watching me beg for her forgiveness on the wraparound front porch are the crickets and God.

It's better this way. I'm not a people person.

Her blessed pink lips pucker to form a *w* and then flatten. She repeats the cycle three more times until she finally decides on a word beginning with *h*. "How did you find me?"

"Google."

She gives me the you're-crazy stare.

"Maps." Very awkward pause. "I know your address by heart."

The worry lines on her forehead disappear as the lightbulb turns on. "But you live..."

"Ten hours away. Yeah, I know."

"Twelve, actually," she mutters.

My world blanks out for a second. Does that mean she calculated the distance between us, too? "I didn't exactly adhere to recommended motor vehicle regulations."

Her mouth twitches; she's well aware I've never been a fan of rules. "You sped."

"I bent suggested limits."

The blush fades, leaving her cheeks pale. "Is that how you view what you did to me?"

The hand grasping the roses begins to sweat. "I got these for you."

Silence.

"They're roses. Purple." Keep talking, man. You're losing her. "Your favorite."

Lila folds her hands over her chest and juts her hip out to the side.

Stupid, moronic idiot. The girl has eyes and an IQ. Didn't she score a twenty-seven on her ACT? She can think fast enough to figure out what I'm holding. "Anyway, you're right."

"What?" Her eyes scrunch together.

"You called me a jerk when you opened the door."

"Not you. Stephen was. Is." She closes her eyes, then reopens them. "I take that back. You are a jerk."

My head snaps to the side. Stephen? Her ex-boyfriend? The kid will not give up and, when it comes to Lila, he has a proven track record of winning. This is the third time they've broken up.

He groveled twice and both times she took him back. When we first started writing, it didn't bother me. Lila and I were friends. But then I fell for her and Stephen became a sharp rock wedged in my side.

I trash all the questions I have about Stephen and his appearance at her house and focus on what's important: Lila. "I'm sorry."

"You. Lied."

"I know." I run my hand through my damp hair. It's ninety degrees with the sun setting, though it could be her microscopic stare making me sweat. "I can explain."

Her head falls back. "God, Lincoln. If you had come here two days ago or last week or last month, I would have been ecstatic. But now? I thought I knew you."

I step forward as my heart surges out of my chest. "You do." She does. Better than anyone else. "Yes, I lied. But everything else is true."

The way she sucks in her lower lip as her head shakes no tells me that the odds are against me.

"I don't believe you," she says. "For all I know, you're the serial killer the Post-it note warned me about."

"What?" Never mind. It doesn't matter. "Lila, you are the one person who knows me. I swear it. I lied to you about one thing. One minor thing."

"Minor!" Her eyes redefine the term *frigid*.

I retreat a step. Bad choice in words. "*Minor* could be an understatement."

"Understatement!" she shrieks. "You didn't graduate from high school, Lincoln, and you had the balls to lie to me about it." Lila bursts forward and stabs my chest with her long pink fingernail.

Each poke a piercing reminder of my mistake. "I...was...depending...on...you."

"You still can. I'm going to fix this."

"Go to hell."

A gust of air hits my cheeks as she slams the front door in my face. My arm drops and the leaves rustle together as the roses slap the side of my thigh. A few petals float down to the wooden porch. With a heavy sigh, I sit on the steps. Not that I ever wanted to know, but this is what being set on fire must feel like—everything shrouded in agony.

If I feel this way, how must Lila feel?

I glance to the left, then to the right. Disoriented. Lost. Not knowing which way is home. But that's been the problem since the beginning. The root of all my evils.

Lila

So the guidance counselor asked me what I wanted to do with my life. I answered—rock climbing. He said it wasn't a profession and to get serious. That if I wanted to get into a decent college I needed to apply myself now.

I told him I was serious. That I loved rock climbing. He said that was a hobby and that I needed to become realistic about my "goals."

I told him it wasn't my damn fault he pissed away his life to make thirty grand a year and to drink cheap coffee. And then I asked him to kindly stop dumping on my dreams. He gave me two days' detention. Did I mention the guy's an asshole?

Do you know the last time I had detention? Never. I'm no saint, but I keep my mouth shut and head down. Rules suck. Society sucks.

Josh followed the rules and now he's dead. He liked riding horses. Maybe if he had looked that damn counselor in the eye and said, "I want to ride horses for the rest of my life," then my brother would still be alive today.

~ Lincoln

SITTING CROSS-LEGGED in the middle of my bed, I turn over Lincoln's letter. My fingers slide over the deep indentations of words obviously written in agitation. Words written so quickly,

I wouldn't have been able to decipher most of them if I wasn't already familiar with his handwriting.

He sent this one to me in the fall, a week after he started his senior year. Lincoln hated his guidance counselor. He was the one who convinced Lincoln's brother to join the Marines out of high school. It's because of that fateful decision that I met Lincoln.

"Lila," says Echo, her voice a bit disjointed from the speaker. "You still there?"

"Yeah," I say and glance at my phone lying on the bed next to me. My best friend is in freaking Iowa with the freaking love of her life on their way to freaking Colorado. Right now, I despise happy people. "How's Iowa?"

"Kansas," she corrects.

"Whatever, it's flat and they have tornadoes." I pick up one of the many stacks of letters from Lincoln cluttering my bed and easily find the one I'm searching for. The one that promised he'd come with me to Florida.

Cluttering isn't the right word. Nothing about me is cluttered. Each stack represents the month the letter was sent, and each letter is arranged by the date on the postmark. My favorite letters have a pink highlight marking the side.

My entire life is systemized like this. My books alphabetized by author on my cherry bookcase. Within the matching glass hutch, my Precious Moments figurines are organized by date received. My scrapbooking materials are boxed in color-coordinated Tupperware. I like plans and organization and not boys who promise to attend the University of Florida with me and then screw it all up by not graduating from high school.

"Lila?" says Echo. She pauses for way too long. "Did you give him a chance to explain?"

The envelope crunches in my hand. "He didn't graduate from high school, Echo, and he didn't tell me about it. Do you have any idea how I felt when I had to find out on my own that he lied?"

I found out only by accident, when I searched online at his local newspaper to print out the list of graduates to complete the scrapbook page I made for Lincoln's present. His name was not listed among the one hundred and fifty graduates. I should know. I checked—three times.

She sighs through the phone. "Maybe you should talk to him."

"You're biased," I snap. "You're on Lincoln's side because of Aires." Lincoln's older brother, Josh, and Echo's older brother, Aires, were part of the same military unit. No one knows the whole story, but they died two and a half years ago in Afghanistan, in a roadside bombing. I met Lincoln at Aires's funeral.

"If I remember correctly," Echo says with an attitude that has very rarely emerged over the past two years, "I'm the one who said you shouldn't be writing a stranger and I'm the one who said you needed to stop writing him because you were falling for him."

And I'm overwhelmed with the urge to punch something—hard, because... "I know. Sorry. That wasn't fair."

"No, it wasn't."

We're silent for a few moments. I crossed a line with her by throwing Aires into a fight. I pick at my thumbnail. We've been best friends since birth and we never stay mad for long, but I don't want to get off the phone with her angry at me. At least not tonight.

"Hotel, motel or tent?" I slur the last word as a curse. More silence, then a rustle of sheets. Please, please, please play along, Echo. I need my best friend.

"Motel. We slept in the tent for the past few nights," she says in a light tone that causes me to smile. Yeah, I hate happy people, but Echo deserves happy. "Noah's in the shower."

"So..." I draw out the word. "Have you had sex?"

"No." She chokes. Hand to God, she chokes. I giggle as she coughs.

"Well, if you do," I say when she recovers from her hacking fit, "don't let your first time be in a tent. That would be awful."

"I think a tent could be romantic."

"Traitor," I say. Echo used to be in the only-if-there-is-room-service camp, like me, but then she permitted the hot and mysterious Noah to sway her to the dark side. "Dirt and bugs and snakes, Echo. Just saying."

In the background, I hear Hot and Mysterious's deep voice. Echo fumbles with the phone while she answers him. I check out the clock on my nightstand. Midnight. My mouth dries out as I smooth back my hair. Another night by myself.

No moon tonight, so the entire world beyond my window is pitch-black. I don't want Echo to let me go because then I'll be alone again in this big, empty house.

Part of me hates Noah. If it wasn't for him, she wouldn't be in Iowa or Kansas or where the hell ever and would instead be staying the night with me. She wouldn't be spending all of her time with him and his friends: that scary guy with all the tattoos and Biker Chick Beth. Tattoo Boy and Biker Chick Beth also live with Noah's foster parents, and they were a year behind me and Echo at school. Echo says they aren't a couple, but I'd bet the new heels I received for graduation they are.

If it wasn't for Noah, she would need me more...she would still be insecure, she would still be obsessing over the scars on her arms. She possibly wouldn't have recovered her memory of the night she got them. If it wasn't for him, she wouldn't be moving on with her life. Damn him for being a great guy.

"Guess I should let you go." Yep, I said it in a way that indicated that is *so* not what I want to do.

"I'll stay on," she says. "We could keep our phones on all night. Just like we did in elementary school." Only then it was landlines. She would, because that's what best friends do.

I swear I hear Noah groan in agony. Guess he doesn't like BFF breaking in on make-out time.

"No. I'll be fine." It's a lie. I stare at the scrapbook page that I lugged back to my room earlier and wonder where Lincoln's sleeping tonight. I should think I could sleep tonight, but the exhaustion only increases my terror...and deepens my sadness over Lincoln. I should have heard him out. Why didn't I listen?

"I think you should talk to Lincoln," Echo says, reading my mind like always. "Maybe wait until you'll know he's back home, like tomorrow evening, and DM him again."

My thumbnail clicks as I mess with it. "I thought you wanted me to stay away from him."

"Yeah, well, you already fell for him. Now I don't want you to have regrets."

Regrets. The moment I slammed the door on him, I sort of regretted it, and then I fully regretted it when I heard his engine accelerate down the road.

I hate that he won't be in Florida in the fall. I hate that I'll be alone at a strange college, in a strange state, and not know a soul. I'll be a complete and utter outsider. But what I really hate is that I'll never get to figure out if Lincoln and I would ever have been more than just friends.

Even with the lie, what I don't hate is Lincoln.

Echo remains on the phone with me as I lock every single window and every single door. It's only when I reach the front door and peek out onto the porch that I finally let her go.

My heart does this funny little tumble. Lincoln left the roses and an envelope.

I should have kept Echo on the line, and I almost press Send to reconnect, but curse myself. If I can't open a door and grab flowers and a letter then I should kiss Florida goodbye.

I undo the lock with an audible click. Thoughts of every urban legend and horror movie I've ever heard or seen flood my brain. My hand hesitates over the doorknob and adrenaline pumps into my blood. Oh, my God, I'm such a wuss.

With disgust I wrench the door open and step out into the humid night. It's not an envelope but a piece of paper with the words: *I'm sorry. I haven't given up on Florida. I swear. Lincoln.* He listed his cell phone number under his name.

I drop to the top step and caress the roses. Even in the heat, the petals are silky and cool. Lincoln is the only guy who has ever bought me purple roses. Sure, guys have bought me plenty of red ones, but not purple. Not my favorite.

Is it possible that he does know me that well?

I jerk my head toward a rustle in the thick overgrowth next to the driveway. My entire body pulses. Part of me panics and begs to run back inside, but the frustrated part stubbornly stays planted on the wooden steps. I've sat here countless times by myself in the middle of the night. Granted, my parents were asleep inside at the time, but why should now be different?

I swallow and dig deep for courage, snickering at my patheticness. With a sigh, I press Lincoln's number into my cell. Yeah, it's midnight, but he's either driving home or asleep somewhere. Either way, I'll leave a message.

The phone rings once, but then all I hear is footsteps: the snap of rubber hitting blacktop. My hand lowers from my ear as my eyes strain to scrutinize the dark road. The sound becomes louder, indicating it's coming nearer. I stand, my hands shaking at my side. My heart misses beats as it drums in my chest.

And that's when I see it: a silhouette, a shadow...blackness in a form. Then there is breath. I scream.

Lincoln

...and we'll be about an hour from the beach and I think we should go there every weekend. Oh, Lincoln!!!! You're going to the University of Florida, too!!! This makes everything better.

I'll tell you something that I haven't told many people. Actually, only two other people: I was thinking of backing out of Florida. The thought of being away from home and knowing no one, it scared me. I don't have to be scared now. I have YOU!!!!!!!

~ Lila

EACH WORD FROM THE LETTER she sent to me this past fall is embedded in my brain. From the moment I left my entire family slack-mouthed and shocked in the living room, I've been trying to form a plan to fix all the mistakes that led to me not graduating. If I can clean up this mess and somehow go to Florida, then maybe Lila will forgive me.

The windshield acts as a recliner while my legs stretch out on the hood of my car. My clasped hands serve as a pillow. The air doesn't move. It's stagnant and strangles me like a twisted blanket. Sweat drips down my back as the cicadas celebrate the heat by chanting in the woods. From a few campsites over, children giggle near a crackling bonfire.

Josh, Meg and I used to laugh when we roasted marshmallows at a campfire. That was before Mom and Dad began arguing over money, before Josh left for the military, before Meg got pregnant, before I started ditching school.

Today was jacked up. I walked out on my family and drove ten hours for Lila to slam the door in my face. Lesson learned: I need to talk faster. Or type faster.

In general: just be faster.

My parents remain ignorant of the fact that I didn't graduate today and of my exact location. But I'm not that bad a son. I called, so at least they know I'm alive.

On the hood next to me, my cell brightens and vibrates. I peek over and practically slide off when I notice the area code. Lila! The hood makes a booming, popping noise as I grab for the phone. It slips from my grasp and falls to the ground with a thud. "Shit!"

The buzzing continues. I scramble over the side and search on my hands and knees through the dirt. A quick wave behind the tire and I snatch the cell, pressing Accept. "Lila, I'm sorry."

As I take a breath to tell her what happened and how I plan to fix everything, I hear a high-pitched scream.

Chills spread across my skin as ice enters my bloodstream. "LILA!"

She sobs, begging God to help her. My hands dig into my jeans pocket, yanking out my keys. "Talk to me!"

My engine growls and the people from the adjoining campsite shield their faces from the glare of my headlights. Rocks kick up and hit the belly of the car as I tear out of the camp. "Lila!"

A thump on Lila's end accompanied by tapping draws my attention back to her. She continues to cry. A rush of panic washes over me. Lila's alone. Her letter last week told me about her parents leaving and how she was terrified of an empty house.

And I abandoned her.

Then there's no noise. No tapping. No cries. Silence. A glance at my cell and my gut rips open. Call disconnected. The car shakes as it veers off the winding forest road. I jerk the steering wheel to the right. My eyes dart between the gravel and my desperate attempt to reconnect. Her phone continuously rings. Lila's cheerful voice fills the line. But it's a recording. A damn recording.

"Shit!" I slam my hand against the steering wheel. What the hell is wrong with me? I left her there—defenseless.

Near the exit to the campgrounds, a park ranger waves at me to stop. As he opens his mouth to explain campsite hours, I spit out, "Call the police! Call them now!"

Red and blue lights become a homing beacon. My fingers drum the steering wheel as I coast into her driveway. The fear recedes as I see no ambulance, but then my frayed nerves explode in terror. What if the ambulance already took her? What if she's dead?

Nausea spreads through me, making me dizzy. I can't lose someone else I love. I can't. Please, God, please let Lila be okay.

I dash out of the car, the memories of my parents breaking the news of Josh's death replaying in my mind like a sick movie. I never got past the front door. I just saw them there, my parents crumpled together in a heap on the living room floor. My father holding my mother. My mother holding my father. Both of their faces consumed by tears.

I knew in that moment my brother had died.

My chest tightens and a crazy panic causes my hands to shake and my feet to quicken their pace. Not Lila. Not Lila, too. A police officer spots me and turns his head as if he's going to say something, but I move faster—my feet pounding up the wooden stairs, my hand twisting the sun-baked knob, my shoulder forcing the door open.

My legs wobble when I see her standing in the middle of her living room, and if it weren't for the two police officers in the room, I'd fall to my knees.

She runs a trembling hand through her rumpled golden hair as she wraps her other arm around her stomach. Even with the warm summer air creeping into the air-conditioned living room, goose bumps form on her arms. She wears only a tank top and shorts.

"Lila," I say to expel the idea that I could be dreaming.

Both she and the police officer who speaks to her in a low, soothing tone glance at me. Relief smooths the lines on her forehead, and her arms drop to her sides. "Lincoln."

My name leaves her mouth in a relieved, airy rush, as if she's glad to see me. As if she wants to see me. And those gorgeous blue eyes stare at me like I'm her man. My heart squeezes.

"Are you okay?" I ask.

She bites her bottom lip while nodding.

Having no clue what to say, I scratch the back of my head. "I—"

And I don't finish. Lila half stumbles, half runs into my body. The fact that she's touching me, holding me, causes me to lose my balance. I quickly recover as her arms become steel bands around my waist.

I inhale, trying to figure out what to do. Ah, hell, she smells like her letters; like lavender. I press my cheek against her silky hair and ease one hand onto the small of her back while the other hugs her shoulders.

Lila falling into me is peaceful, like landing on a feather bed. She's warm and soft, all curves and gentleness—alive, fitting perfectly into my body. Just as I imagined.

"It would be best if Miss McCormick isn't alone tonight. Will you be staying with her, sir?" asks the police officer, but the way she tilts her head and smirks at her partner informs me she can guess my response.

"Yes," Lila answers for me as she burrows her forehead into my chest. Her grip on me tightens. "I know him. He'll stay."

Everything stills. I have never heard sweeter words. She knows me and she wants me to stay. I'm not a stranger to her. Not some guy she barely identifies with. She *knows* me.

"Sir?" the officer prompts.

"Yeah," I say. "I will." I slide my hand along the curve of Lila's spine. "Are you sure you're okay?"

Her nose moves against my chest as she nods. "Yes. Just freaked." She pauses. "I'm sorry for sending you away."

Lila peeks up at me and I give her a half smile. "I deserved it."

For a split second, light shines in her eyes. "You sort of did."

The police officer clears her throat and Lila steps away from me. My arms feel empty without her. It's crazy. I've dated more than a few girls and have never had this reaction.

"Are you okay now, Miss McCormick?" the officer asks.

"Yeah," she answers. "Thanks for coming."

The police officers inch toward the door and I block their path. "Whoa. Wait. You're leaving?"

"Lincoln..." Lila rubs her biceps. Her mouth scrunches to the right, calling my attention to her lips. "I...uh...was calling you... and I thought I saw someone...and I guess you answered right as

I screamed...and I, ah...dropped my phone...then it turned off... and then the police came and said you called them and...yeah."

And...yeah. Not buying it. "Blood. Curdling. Scream."

Her eyes dart to the police, then away. "Well, I thought I saw something, but I was probably wrong." Then she looks at me, her eyes pleading, begging for me to drop it.

The muscles in my neck tighten.

"We searched the property," says the officer with a pitying smile at Lila. "And we didn't find anyone. Miss McCormick knows she can call us if there's an issue."

They think it's her imagination, yet I heard her terror. That type of scream can't be created by a fear in your head. That's death hovering in front of you wielding a bloody ax.

Lila thanks the officers and shows them out. With a click, she shuts the front door, and for the first time in my life I'm completely alone in a room with the girl I've fallen in love with. What the hell do I do now?

I should immediately tell her what happened with school. I should tell her my plan to fix things, how when I return home I'll sign up for summer school. I should tell her that the thought of losing her paralyzes me. Instead, I follow my gut. "You saw somebody, didn't you?"

Lila collapses against the door and her face drains of all color. "Yes. No. I don't know."

Her head dips forward. "I can't prove it. The police think I'm crazy. And ninety percent of me thinks everything's okay because if there was somebody outside they would have hurt me. But ten percent of me is pretty positive that someone is messing with me."

I fold my arms over my chest, not liking the thought of anyone screwing with Lila. "What are you saying?"

She shrugs and smiles at the same time, making it clear she doesn't believe the words. "Maybe I have a stalker."

Maybe? Knowing what to do to help calm her nerves, I hold out my hand. "Start talking, because I'm not leaving until I know you're safe."

Lila

When Josh first died, my parents got close, but as time has worn on, they've grown apart. The worst moments are when my entire family is in the same room. With the people I should love the most surrounding me, I feel the most alone.

~ Lincoln

LINCOLN ASSESSES THE ORANGE Post-it note on the oven meant to remind me to turn it off as he stirs milk over the stove top. From the second he knotted my fingers with his in the living room and led me into the kitchen, I've found it impossible to tear my eyes away from him.

He grew—stunningly so. Taller. Thicker. His blue eyes are aged beyond his years, but when he smiles at me he becomes carefree and eighteen.

"That's it?" he asks.

"Yeah," I respond. I downloaded everything, except he's not humiliating me with condescending looks or a lecture about overactive imaginations. I spilled about the scratching on the windows last night, the sound of shoes against the pavement tonight, and the shadow walking toward me and the sound of his breath.

The police didn't take me seriously, but the way Lincoln's shoulder blades tense, I can tell he believes me. "Why?" I ask.

"Why what?" He empties the steaming liquid into a mug.

"Why do you believe me?"

Lincoln slides the mug into my hands. His finger accidentally skims mine. Electricity! A fantastic chill runs through me that reaches the tips of my toes.

"You don't like liars and you're not big into hypocrites," he answers.

Those were my words to him a few months ago, when my sort-of friend Grace tormented Echo. Lincoln and I share a knowing smile and stare into each other's eyes. The world fades away and it's just me and him and a fragrant cup of hot chocolate in the palm of my hand. Lincoln breaks the link and withdraws his fingers. I'd give anything for him to touch me again. But first...

"You have some explaining to do," I say. "As to why you didn't graduate."

He turns away and washes the pot in the sink. "Let's figure out your problem first. Then we'll handle mine." The water beats against the pot. "Are you still mad at me?"

My finger circles the rim of the mug. Hurt—yes. Angry—"No." How can I be mad at a guy who drove ten hours to see me and returned after I rejected him? "So you believe me? That someone was outside?"

"I heard you scream. No one's imagination works that well."

He grabs a dish towel and dries off the pot before placing it back on the hook on the wall. Lincoln's so efficient, especially for a guy who "bends rules." With a scrape against the tile floor, he pulls out the chair next to mine and angles it so he's facing me. "Just so we're clear, a stalker suggests multiple run-ins over a period of time. I think this is more of a prank."

The skin between my eyes squishes together. "A prank? Really?"

Lincoln relaxes into the chair, his long legs kicked out, an arm resting on the table. I feel like a dwarf next to him. He drums his fingers once against the table, causing me to focus on his hands. The skin is tough, rougher than the hands of most of the guys I've dated. It's not an imperfection, but a reminder of how he dangles from rock walls.

I wonder if he'd ever let me watch him climb or if he'd teach me. My stomach tickles as if fuzzy bunnies are jumping around. Would he catch me with those strong hands if I fell?

"You're the *CSI* dictionary," he answers. "Didn't an episode talk about how stalkers have patterns or some crap like that?"

"You started watching *CSI?*" I'm grinning from ear to ear, and his cheeks redden in response. The big, strong rock-climbing guy folds his hands across his chest and switches his gaze to the floor. It's my favorite show ever, and I've written a few letters to him detailing certain episodes.

He sloppily shrugs one shoulder. "I caught a few shows here and there."

I don't know why, but the fact that he showed interest in something I like creates giddiness. I swirl the hot chocolate in my mug and blow on it in order to hide the glee. "What makes you think it's a prank?"

"You said it yourself. If someone wanted to hurt you, you'd be hurt. Your parents are gone, and I'd bet someone thinks it would be funny to scare you."

My forehead furrows with the idea that anyone would want to freak me out. "Why?" I ask again.

"Because people can be stupid."

True. Tired of thinking about it, I change the subject. "Hot chocolate?"

"I made it for Meg every night after she found out she was pregnant. It seemed to help calm her down when she'd get all worked up."

Translation? He believes I'm about to crack. My heart beats a little faster when I replay the image of the shadow walking toward me. Maybe he's not wrong. "Has she held the baby yet?"

Lincoln subtly shakes his head. "I keep wondering how jacked up the kid will become because his mother can't get her shit together."

The way his blue eyes darken into hurt causes a sharp pain in my chest. I reach out and claim one of the hands resting against his crossed arms. Lincoln weaves his with mine and we hold hands on the table, both of us staring at our combined fingers. God, his hands are warm—strong—and I swallow as I imagine him caressing my face.

"How's Echo?" he asks.

"Good. She's in Kansas or Iowa or someplace." Not here with me, and that sucks. She no longer needs me now that she has... "She's with Noah."

"So she's moved on," he says almost as a whisper.

From me? Yes. But she hasn't moved on the way Lincoln suggests. Sadness envelops me like a cloud. I've witnessed Echo grieve for her brother. Hell, *I'm* still grieving for Aires. He was like my older brother, too. "She's living. Not forgetting."

Lincoln removes his hand to rub his face. I leave my hand on the table for a second, hoping he'll wrap his back around mine. When he lowers it into his lap instead, I curl my arm into my own body—hating the rejection, missing his warmth. But I'm not mad at him. I can see I've lost him to memory. Echo has done this mental retreat several times herself.

We lapse into silence, I guess both of us processing the past couple of hours. The silence feels comfortable, like an old quilt, and I revel in it. But then my eyes dart to him. What if he's not comfortable? What if the written connection in our letters is all we possess? What if we don't ignite a real life spark?

What does it matter since he lied to me? We need to talk about it, but not now. Not when I've barely slept in almost two days and my mind's a disoriented mess. He could explain basic addition and I'd drool like an idiot.

Sleep—I crave it, but can I have it? My thoughts shift back to the idea of someone pranking me. "Who would want to scare me?"

"You tell me." He kneads his eyes, and for the first time I notice the dark circles beneath them. He's tired, and as I sip the warm drink, I realize my exhaustion is contagious.

"I have no idea." And the unknown terrifies me.

Lincoln

It's crazy how you brought up feeling alone. I feel alone a lot. Oddly enough, I feel the most alone when I'm in a room full of people. Everyone I know is changing. Echo's distant. Grace wants new friends. Even Natalie is spreading her wings.

To be fair, I'm changing, too. At times I feel like my skin is too tight on me. All the time, I fight the urge to cut my hair and buy new clothes. I mean, who exactly am I going to change into? I'm still me, but not.

~ Lila

LILA'S FINGERNAIL TAPS repeatedly against the table, like a machine gun firing off multiple rounds. "I'm too tired to deal with this now." She slams her hand on the table, silencing any more discussion on her possible prankster.

She stands and I follow, wondering if the park ranger will allow me back into the camp. Otherwise, I'm screwed. "Can I come back in the morning?" Then I remember what time it is. "Late morning? Afternoon?"

Lila freezes the same way Meg does anytime she's near the baby. Hell, Lila hates me.

"Will you stay? I told the police you would. *You* told the police you would. If you leave that would be like breaking the law or something, so you have to stay."

I raise an eyebrow at her logic—or lack of logic—but there's no way I'm blowing this opportunity. "I'll stay."

"Good. Because you have to."

Lila leads me back into the living room and mumbles for me to stay put. Her footsteps are light down the hallway. The one-story house is the size of a mansion and decorated like one of Mom's *Better Homes and Gardens* magazines. Nice and breakable shit—everywhere. After several abrupt sounds that indicate Lila must have accepted a wrestling match with an alligator, she reappears with blankets and a pillow.

"Do you mind sleeping on the couch?" she asks.

I'd sleep on nails in order to be near her. "No."

She hands me the ingredients for a temporary bed.

"Thanks," I say.

"You're welcome." Lila's fingers draw toward the hem of her tank top, and I remind myself to breathe when I catch sight of the sun-kissed skin of her flat stomach. In seconds, she pulls at the hem and her belly button disappears.

"Well, good night," she says while tucking her golden hair behind her ear.

"Night," I respond. Should I hug her? Kiss her? Shake her hand? Get on my knees and start begging for forgiveness?

She shifts her footing but stays in place. "The bathroom is down the hall."

"All right."

"You can take a shower if you want."

"Thanks," I answer.

"You're welcome."

And we've already had this conversation. Lila sniffs as if her allergies bother her, and she lowers her head. I want to comfort her, but I have no clue how to tread on this territory. "Are you okay?"

"I don't want to be alone," she whispers. "Not even alone in a room. Isn't that pathetic?"

"You could never be pathetic," I say. Not the girl I've come to love from the letters. The girl who defended her best friend, even though taking that stand cost her other friendships. The girl who tells me exactly what she thinks of me, even when the truth hurts. The girl who dreams of being more—the girl who dreams of Florida.

Her lower lip trembles. "If you think that, then you don't know me very well."

I know her better than she realizes. I know the letters she writes to me late at night are more emotional than the ones written during the day, as if a lack of sleep inhibits reasoning. I ditch the blankets and pillow on the arm of the couch and plop myself onto the cushions. "Come here."

Her gaze switches from the space on the couch to me. "I don't understand."

I snatch the extrahuge pillow and drop it on my lap. "Sleep here."

Lila stretches the hem of her tank top over her hips as she moves toward me. When she sits, it's with her thigh melting against mine. Her heat radiates past my jeans to my skin. Every single cell within my body sizzles to life. *Play this right, Lincoln. She deserves a man, not a boy.*

Without saying a word, Lila rests her head on the pillow and extends her legs on the couch. I drape the blanket over her body, and I love how she flips to her side, knees curled up in the fetal position.

Her eyelids flutter as she talks. "I'm sorry I slammed the door in your face."

A lock of her hair strays onto her cheek. I shouldn't, but I do it anyhow. With the same care I use when handling my nephew, I sweep the silky strands behind her ear. I'd give my left arm to comb my fingers through her hair until she falls asleep. "I deserved it."

Her chest expands and she yawns. "Why didn't you graduate?"

"Because I was stupid." A nauseating pit forms in my gut. Stupid—it's what Lila must assume about me. A moron who can't put two words together to form a sentence, a moron who can't add, a moron who didn't graduate. But that's not what happened. I didn't graduate because I stopped caring.

Lila closes her eyes and lazily mumbles, "You're not stupid. I've read all your letters—several times. You're a good writer. And you got a twenty-nine on your ACT. That's hardly stupid." She pauses. "Not unless that was a lie, too."

"It wasn't," I say. "I only lied about graduating."

"What about getting in to the University of Florida?" she asks. "You told me you were accepted through early admission."

"I was," I answer. "But admittance was contingent on graduating." I struggle to find the right words. How do I prove to her that I'm not lying? "I'll send you my official ACT scores. I'll send you my acceptance letter. Whatever you need in order to believe me."

"I believe you." She's motionless long enough that I wonder if she's drifted to sleep. Then she pats my knee and whispers, "Tell me what happened."

Lila removes her hand, but my skin still burns from her touch.

She believes me. Maybe, someday, she'll trust me. I prop my elbow on the arm of the couch and lean my head against my fist. I should keep my other arm resting on the back of the couch. Instead, I cave to temptation and snake it around her body. She nuzzles closer to me in response. For a girl who is just my friend—just a pen pal—this feels incredibly right.

"Lincoln?" she urges.

"We should wait until morning," I say.

"It is morning. And I'm impatient."

I chuckle. She is. Lila informed me of her unhappiness anytime a letter from me ran a day later than she thought it should have. I take a deep breath and jump.

"I began skipping in the fall and then skipped more days than I should have. By the time I realized I hadn't earned enough classroom hours to graduate, I was already screwed."

Her eyes flicker open. "Did you skip because you missed Josh?"

Hearing his name on her lips causes my chest to jerk. The familiar, unwanted pain spreads from my heart to my brain. She'll never know him. Never meet him. "Yeah, Josh. And everything else."

I told her in several letters that I had skipped. That when I woke in the morning and felt the emptiness of Josh's death, the burden of feeding a baby, the anger of listening to my parents argue, I'd feel like I'd explode if I didn't break free. So I'd drive to the state park and climb until my fingers bled.

Her head rocks in my lap. "I should have seen it coming."

"Seen what coming?"

"That when you can't handle things, you run." She wrote the same criticism in her letters to me when I told her I had skipped school.

"I don't," I say.

Her only response is the rush of air blowing out of her mouth.

"I don't," I repeat with the stubbornness of a dog gripping a chewed-up slipper in its jaws.

Lila fiddles with the frayed corner of the blanket. "Today was your graduation day and you drove here to see me."

"So?"

She shrugs. "Only stating the evidence."

"I came here for you." The tension in my muscles begs me to shift, but if I do, I'll give Lila an excuse to move. "You were upset with me."

A nagging pang of guilt causes my spine to straighten. What I said, it's not a lie. I came here for Lila. But then I remember my mom and dad fighting, the way Meg panicked when I asked her to hold the baby, and the nausea when I considered telling my parents about my failure.

Then my mind redirects to how summer school starts in forty-eight hours—on Monday. I drove here with the intention of telling Lila that I was going to fix everything, but all I really wanted was to mend things between us. I rub a hand over my head. Is Lila right? Am I running from the real issues in my life?

"I'm not running," I say one more time. Even I notice the doubt in my voice.

"Whatever," she mumbles, exhaustion weighing down her words. "Why didn't you tell me?"

"Because..." Because she'd be disappointed in me. Because I was disappointed in myself. Because her dreams became my dreams and I failed us both. Because I was chicken shit.

Two years ago, Lila began writing about the University of Florida. She talked about it enough that I checked out the school. Way before I fell for Lila, I fell for the dream of heading to another state for school. To possibly gain my degree in forest resource and conservation; to work around rock walls for a living.

How the hell could I lose sight of my future?

My right leg begins to tingle and all I can think about is getting up, walking around, heading back to the campsite, exploring the trails—even in the dark—and finding a rock wall. Then I glance down at the beauty cuddled close to me.

Her breathing becomes light and she flinches in her sleep. The baby does the same thing when he enters REM sleep. I tuck the blanket around her and permit myself to touch her hair one more time.

No, I'm not a runner. Not this time. She'll have more hard questions, and I'm determined to answer them—standing right in front of her. It's time I start facing the problems in my life instead of avoiding them. It's time that I create a plan and follow it through. And hopefully, Lila will forgive me and be by my side as I go forward.

"I didn't want you to hate me," I whisper as I respond to her last question. "Because I've fallen in love with you."

Lila

I thought of you when I climbed today. You should try it sometime. I think you'd enjoy the rush.

~ Lincoln

MY ENTIRE BODY SEIZES at the sound of pounding. I jump, my hands flail, and then I finally crash onto the hardwood floor, a disheveled mess. That crack had to be my tailbone. "Ow."

I blink several times as I nurse my lower back. What am I doing in the living room?

"You okay?" The gravelly, sleep-deprived voice causes my heart to thump hard once. My eyes dart above me to the couch. Lincoln stretches his arms over his head. Absolutely amazing. He slept sitting up, holding me, the entire night.

"Morning," he says. His gorgeous eyes fall on me, and my cheeks warm when the corners of his mouth lift. Echo would make fun of me for the silly smile forming on my face.

Feeling suddenly shy and self-conscious, I comb my hair with my hand. Oh, hell, tangles. Why, why, why do I always wake up resembling a troll? "Hi."

The doorbell rings several times and the pounding resumes. Sunlight streams through the venetian blinds. The brightness definitely hints at more of a midday than a morning situation. "It's probably Stephen," I say.

Lincoln's head jerks. "Your ex?"

I'll admit it. I sort of like the alpha-male pissed-off stare he's got going on. I scramble off the floor and for once heed my mother's Post-it note advice by glancing through the peephole. Nope, not the ex. Which is good since Lincoln looks annoyed enough to chop the boy into deer steaks.

"Lila!" Grace yells. "Are you in there?"

"Yes!" I shout back to my former best friend. "Give me a sec, Grace."

I turn to explain to Lincoln that it's Grace and ram right into his chest. Both of his hands land on my shoulders to steady me. "I thought you two weren't on speaking terms after what happened with Echo."

"We aren't. Which is why I need to answer. The world must have collapsed into a zombie apocalypse if she's here."

His grip on my shoulders changes into a massage that causes me to close my eyes. He could touch me like that for the rest of my life and I'd never move. "Then answer," he says.

My stomach knots into a big ball of dread. Lincoln's appearance screams that he just rolled out of bed and I'm in my pj's and my parents are out of town and Grace is a huge gossip. "Crap!"

"I can hide," he says as if reading my mind. His hands slide off my shoulders and I have to fight the urge to pout. "But you'd have to explain my car."

I brighten for two point one seconds and then deflate. "I'm not that creative."

"I'll give you a few minutes alone with her. Maybe she won't notice the car." Lincoln starts down the hallway, then pauses to eye me in a way that suggests my clothes are riding up. "You look good right now. All rumpled and drowsy."

The back of my neck explodes with heat, and I immediately focus on the muscles of his biceps. Lincoln flashes a flirtatious grin, grabs an extra pair of jeans from his backpack, which leans against the door to my room, and disappears into the bathroom. Good Lord, he's hot.

Tangled thoughts of him and me muddle my groggy brain. He touches me and talks to me as if we've known each other forever. Is it possible he's into me, too? As more than friends?

Grace resumes her banging. I bat at the hair sticking on top of my head and open the front door. "Hey."

In a cargo skirt that grazes her knees and a white lace tank, Grace hitches her thumb toward the car. "Have a guest?" She takes in my clothes. "An overnight one?"

Not interested in playing her games anymore, I say, "Yes."

Shock and giddiness burst onto her face. "Really? Who?"

Once upon a time, I would have told her. She knew all of my secrets—including my writing relationship with Lincoln. That is, until she chose her new friends over Echo. Echo and I have always been a package deal. What sucks is that I miss Grace. "I'm guessing you want to come in."

She does and practically pees her pants when she sees the pillow and blanket on the couch. "You had a guy overnight!" she squeals.

I shush her while waving my hands for her to keep it down. Embarrassment creeps along my skin. Lincoln must be laughing his ass off. "How do you know? It could be a girl."

"Your girlfriends sleep in your room. So who is it?"

"It's..." And I can't think of anything believable, because the truth is unbelievable. "Lincoln. And you better keep it to yourself. This is private, Grace. I mean it."

She grabs my hand, not missing a beat, acting as if our friendship didn't disintegrate in a shower of flames months ago. "Lincoln? Pen pal Lincoln? Oh. My. God. That is so...so... Is he hot?"

This is what I miss about Grace: her passion, her enthusiasm. And when she decided to, she could be a great friend. I clasp her hand back. "Smoking."

And I have the urge to call Echo and Natalie and force the four of us to be what we used to be—inseparable.

"How long is he staying?" Grace asks.

My energy fades and I release her. "I don't know." Will Lincoln leave soon? Have I squandered the only time we may ever have together? Remembering last night's late conversation, I remind myself that leaving would be Lincoln's M.O.

Grace's cell phone chimes to indicate a text. She reads it, then shoves the phone into her purse. "I've got to bolt, but I have something to tell you. Which is why I came."

I circle my hand, motioning for her to continue.

"I overheard Stephen, Chad and Luke talking about how they've been showing up here at night, trying to scare you since your parents went on vacation."

My mouth gapes and I go completely numb long enough to tense when the rush of anger pummels my bloodstream. "Excuse me?"

"I know. Stupid, right? Stephen thinks if you get scared, you'll call him, and then you guys can work things out." Grace glances at the blanket on the couch. "Guess he didn't count on the dark horse pulling up late in the race."

Disoriented, I lean against the arm of the couch for support. Holy crap, I'm not crazy. Someone was pranking me. But the relief is short-lived.

I lost my virginity to Stephen. He's the first guy I ever said the words *I love you* to. And he's betraying me? He's trying to scare me? What has he become?

I feel my eyes dart, even though I'm honestly looking at nothing within the room. My mind rapidly tries to sort through the anger, the confusion and the weird emptiness. I'm mad at Stephen—all right, that's the understatement of the century. The next time I see him, I'll fry him like the catfish my brothers catch at the lake, but what I'm lacking is the epic sense of betrayal, the massive pang of hurt, the emotions I experienced last night because Lincoln lied to me. I mean, Stephen and I were together for two years. That should count for something, right?

"Lila?" Grace refocuses my attention on her. "Are you okay?"

"The bastard is going to hang from his toenails, but, yeah, I'm fine." Astonishingly so.

She fidgets with her class ring. "Don't let him find out I'm the one who told you, okay?"

"Yeah. Okay. Sure." Grace and Chad are an item. She's worked hard over the past year to claim him as her guy. "Why did you tell me, anyway?"

The fire that always consumes Grace dissolves. "Because I want us to be friends again. I made some really bad choices, and I'm sorry. You're leaving for Florida, and if we don't fix this now, it won't be fixed."

Just as things will never be fixed between her and Echo. She doesn't say it, but it's there, hanging in the air like the stench of rotten fish.

A lot of bad blood has been shed, but maybe people can change. As much as that thought makes me happy, it also saddens me. No matter what, the relationship between Grace and me will never be the same. "Thanks for the heads-up."

Grace stands there, looking like a damn puppy locked in a cage at the store. Unfortunately, I've got a soft spot for imprisoned animals. "Maybe we could go shopping together sometime."

She cracks a smile. "Yeah. That'd be great."

I close the door behind Grace and walk to my bedroom. Across the hall, water beats against the tub as Lincoln takes a shower. A black T-shirt pokes out from the backpack still resting against my bedroom door. I told him to store the pack in my room last night as he was warming the hot chocolate, but I didn't realize what he'd see: the stacks of letters still lying on my bed and the scrapbook page I made for his graduation.

I sink to the corner of my bed and stare into the room as if I've never seen it. Everything is changing. My relationships are changing, my future is changing, my feelings are changing. My life is one big constant state of flux. I grew up scared of spiders, bees and dark corners in dimly lit basements. But this foe... change...it terrorizes me like nothing before.

For the first time in my life, I wish I wasn't growing up.

Lincoln

A rush? Heights and rocks sound like a huge risk. But if you were there, I think I would consider climbing.

~Lila

THE HIGH-PITCH CREAKING of drawers being opened and closed greets me when I exit the bathroom. Across the hall, Lila yanks a manila file from her desk, flips through it, then dumps it onto the growing pile on the floor. The papers of the folder spill out, creating a fan.

"Lila?" I ask and step into her room. "What's going on?"

"I can't find it." She hammers the drawer shut and opens the bottom one with such force that it falls out of the desk. "I can't freaking find it!"

My letters to her still sit on her bed, stacked neatly. My chest squeezes again at the sight of them. I can't believe it. She kept all my letters—just like I kept all of hers.

The room represents Lila perfectly—order, discipline. Yeah, everything fits, except for the golden-haired pixie set on mass destruction. "Can't find what?"

"My acceptance package from the University of Louisville.

The one that has the paperwork for me to return. I put it in a file. I labeled it. I would have filed it in alphabetical order under Colleges, but it's not here."

She frantically searches through the files. Once. Twice. A third time. Lila slams her hands on the floor next to her. "Where is it?!"

I approach her slowly. The way I had to with Meg when she found out she was pregnant. I bend my knees to crouch in front of her. "Why do you need the file?"

Lila tilts her head as if she's noticing me for the first time. Her eyes are too wide for her delicate face. "I'm going to accept."

I blink. "Accept?" I suck in air to steady myself. It's as if the girl socked me in the stomach with a bat. "What about Florida?"

"Stephen's the one pranking me." The words tumble out as she clasps her hands over her chest. "He wanted to scare me, and it worked. I was terrified. Terrified! I can't do it." She chokes on a sob. "I can't go to Florida. Not by myself."

I bolt upright. Rage explodes through me—the eruption of the volcano complete. The bastard's dead. No question. "Tell me where he is."

Her eyebrows scrunch together. "Who?"

"The asshole who has you doubting yourself. The asshole who scared you. Stephen."

Lila jumps to her feet. "All he did was point out what he already knew. That I can't handle being on my own."

"That is bull." Unlike yesterday morning, I don't yell. This emotion burrowing through me, it's an eerie, deathly calm. Since Josh's death, I'm used to numb, and Lila's letters have been the only weapon strong enough to slip past that wall. Since realizing I could lose the connection with her, I've felt anger, despair, guilt, hope, love and now pure, unadulterated rage.

"Before the prank you were ready to head south," I say. "Your entire last letter was filled with what you wanted to do the moment you crossed the state line."

"But that was before!" She throws her arms out at her sides. "That was when I thought I had someone."

The anger dissipates—gone in a flash—leaving emptiness behind. "You have me."

"No, I don't." Her eyelashes become wet as they flutter. "You were supposed to be right there beside me, and now you're not. I thought I'd be able to convince Echo to come with me, but then she found Noah. I'm by myself now. I can't do it. I'm not capable of going to Florida alone."

I scratch at the stubble forming on my jaw as she wipes at a renegade tear streaming from the corner of her eye. She glances away and I feel sick.

Lila was depending on me and I jacked it up for her. For my family. For me.

An overwhelming urge bubbles inside me to head home—to talk to my family, the counselor at school, to fill out Florida's spring admissions paperwork, which the counselor gave me to motivate me to do well in summer school. Since Josh died all I've been doing is ignoring my life, my future—just like how Meg ignores her baby. Yeah, going home, it would be running, but not the kind I've been doing for two years. It would be running forward instead of away.

When I left home to find Lila, I felt the first spark of awareness that things needed to change, but seeing Lila doubt herself, seeing her backtrack, it clears up my vision of what I need to do to get my life in order.

My grandpa once told me never to provoke an injured bear, especially one nursing its wounds, but sometimes the bear needs to be poked. "Who's the runner now?"

A flash of fear shivers up my spine at the way her ice-cold blue eyes strike through me. "Excuse me?"

Hope I know what I'm doing. "I came here for you, Lila. For the girl who would never let anyone walk all over her. For the girl who wouldn't be feeling sorry for herself because someone pranked her. Maybe I'm not the only one who told a lie. Maybe you invented the girl in the letters."

Her mouth drops open; her cheeks redden as if I had physically slapped her. "You are a jerk!"

"You mad now?"

"Yes!"

"Good. Now stop focusing on what you can't control and start focusing on what you can." Like summer school, working toward college, applying for spring admissions and not on my parents, my sister, my nephew...my brother's death.

Lila shakes her head, as if she's waking from a dream. She leans against the desk for support and runs her hands through her hair. "You're right."

This is the girl I know: 100 percent in or out. No waffling. A girl who treats life like a missile with a locked-in course.

Her eyes roam over me and I'm confused by the slant of her lips.

"Lincoln?" she says as the silly smile grows.

"Yes?'

"You're not wearing a shirt."

Embarrassment heats my body and my hand darts to my chest, feeling the exposed skin. "Sorry."

Those blue eyes smolder. "I'm not. But you may want to get dressed for this."

Lila

...and on the rock climbing—I think you're underestimating yourself.

~ Lincoln

LINCOLN WALKS BESIDE ME through the open field toward the tree line. He has a wide gait and I struggle to appear casual as I attempt to match his stride. His shirt's back on, which is a sin. He could definitely give Echo's guy a run for his money in the abs department.

At the wooden shed, the combination lock whines as I spin it to the right, the left and then back to the right. With a click, I unlatch the lock and open the door. Sunlight streams in and dust particles dance in the beams.

"Want to tell me what we're doing out here?" Lincoln asks.

"Reclaiming my pride." Stupid Stephen and stupid me. The past six months of our relationship flip through my mind like a bad award show montage: how I told him I was going to Florida, how he balked and then started talking about how scared I'd be once I moved. He played me. He played me so well that I almost abandoned my dreams.

If I'm being deep-down honest, though, Stephen's prank was just the excuse I'd been searching for to drop Florida. And I could include my anxiety over Echo leaving and Lincoln not heading to Florida in the fall in the pathetic-excuse category. The truth is I've doubted going away to school because I've doubted me. I'm afraid of being alone.

I don't know how to fix my fear, but I do know how to fix Stephen.

Once my eyes adjust to the darkness of the shed, I walk in and grab my brothers' paintball guns. Lincoln was completely right. It's time to stop being scared and start being proactive. It's time someone turned the tables on the slimy little bastard.

I toss Lincoln one of the guns. He raises his eyebrows once he realizes what he holds in his hands.

"Shoot for their feet," I say. "Their shoes cost two hundred and fifty dollars and they'd be pissed if they got stained."

His wicked smile answers that he understands the plan and that he's on board. "Have you ever used one of these?"

"Yep." But it's nothing I've ever broadcast to the world. "Have you?"

"It's been a while."

Good. "We've got six hours until sunset, and then it's on."

Lincoln's eyes travel over my body, his gaze lingering on my curves. "I think I'm falling in love."

At the word *love,* my insides flutter. I tuck my hair behind my ear, trying to imagine how sexy I could possibly be while wearing a pair of ratty cutoff jeans and a T-shirt and cradling a paintball gun. And then I wonder what it would be like if he really was falling for me, because Lincoln in real life is a million times more intense than Lincoln in letters...and I'm seriously falling for him.

Lincoln

Will you go outside on the 28th and watch the meteor shower? I know what you're thinking: 3:00 a.m.? But I think it will be beautiful. Besides, it will be cool to know that you're watching the sky at the same exact time as me.

~ Lila

WITH A HIP COCKED in the doorframe of Lila's room, I watch as she towel-dries her hair. Earlier, I witnessed Lila hit bull's-eye after bull's-eye with that paintball gun. The girl ain't playing. Experiencing her Rambo side brought on some fear.

I chuckle to myself. It also turned me on.

The late-afternoon sun floats into her bedroom. We've got a few hours until nightfall. Being a natural climber, I called the high position in the trees. Lila plans to be at ground level.

She tosses the towel into a hamper and combs through her hair. "When will you have to leave?" she asks.

"I called my parents while you were in the shower. I told them I'd be home by Monday morning." I also told them to expect major changes when I finally did arrive home—that I was going to focus on my future, not on the past. They weren't happy I left so suddenly and that I didn't graduate, but they weren't irate.

She bites her lower lip and sinks to her bed. "So you'll be leaving tomorrow."

"Yeah."

"I'm glad you came," she says.

"Me, too." Our gazes meet, and it's the most comfortable I've ever felt staring into someone else's eyes. "Will you be okay by yourself?"

She nods. "I'll probably wake to every little sound, but I'll be fine."

"That's my girl." My eyes widen as I realize what I said. Lila's not my girl. I want her to be, but... "I mean—"

"No, I like what you said." Lila glances away, her hair swinging into her face.

Could she possibly feel what I feel? Lila and I were once strangers who met at a funeral. We became friends through letters, bonded by a shared dream of college in another state, and then I fell for her. Could she have also fallen for me?

In a handful of hours, I'm going to head home, and the one lesson I learned from Josh's death is that life has to be lived now; the future isn't always guaranteed. I have this one shot with her, and I'm going to take it. "This past fall you told me that you felt close to me even though we're hundreds of miles away."

Lila's eyes jump to mine, I guess in shock that I remembered.

"Well," I continue, "that's what it's been like for me, too. I've never shared my private thoughts with someone other than you, and I can't imagine sharing them with anyone else."

I pause, terrified to continue. If I'm wrong on this, I'll ruin the relationship Lila and I share. Lila fidgets with a strand of her wet hair and keeps those gorgeous innocent eyes locked on me. No, I've fallen for her and I'll regret walking away from this moment.

"I like you, Lila. As more than a friend. I wake up in the morning and I think of you. I go to bed at night and you're the last thought in my mind. I dream of you. The best days of the week are the ones when I get your letters."

She blinks once, her face frozen. My stomach sinks. "But if you don't feel the same way, it's okay. I swear—"

"Lincoln," she says before I can finish. "I feel that same way... for you."

I inhale as if it's the first breath I've ever taken. Lila cares for me. I step into her room and pause beside her. "Can I sit?" Because it's her bed and there's no way I'm assuming I've got permission for a place as sacred as that.

She scoots over, creating a space for me. I lower onto the bed and my heart picks up speed. I rub my hands against my jeans and release a slow, steady stream of air. "I'll be starting summer school on Monday."

Lila angles her body toward me, a sure sign I've got her attention.

"My guidance counselor said that I've got a good chance at spring admission to the University of Florida because of my ACT and SAT scores and my grades before this year. He thinks if I can focus on summer school and write a kick-ass essay on how I learned from my screwup, the admissions board will look past my mistakes.

"I'm going to admit, until I came here, I was still ignoring what needed to be done. I knew I wanted to fix us, but watching you tackle your fears has helped me realize that I've got to tackle mine. I've made mistakes and I'm going to make it right."

Her thin, delicate fingers rest on her knee. Two and a half years ago, Lila and I sat outside a funeral home and she had the courage to reach over to me when I described my relationship with my older brother. No, I didn't cry at Josh's funeral, but what I never told anyone was how I wept like a baby to a girl I had never met before...to Lila.

Channeling the same strength she showed that night, I place my hand over hers. Lila immediately laces her fingers with mine.

I continue. "I should have told you the truth about not graduating before, but I didn't want you to be disappointed in me—I didn't want to admit that I let you down. I know I'm going to be a semester late, but I'm coming to Florida, Lila, and I swear I won't let you down again."

A tender smile eases onto her lips. "And I'll be there—waiting."

My chest expands as I lean into her. Her lavender scent engulfs me, and those sky-blue eyes draw me in. "I like you," I whisper as I nuzzle the satin skin of her cheek. More than like, but I don't want to rush things.

Lila tilts her head and whispers against my lips, "I like you, too."

Her kiss is soft and warm—inviting. We both explore, a hesitant dance as we glide over lines neither one of us imagined crossing. I let go of her hand to push the damp hair away from her face. My fingers trace her cheekbone, then drift to the nape of her neck.

My skin vibrates when a feminine sigh escapes her lips—a sound of approval, a sound of longing. Lila shifts and I take advantage by wrapping an arm around her body. She weaves her fingers into my hair and pulls me closer. My blood heats and so does our kiss.

I suck in her lower lip and in our next breath our tongues slide against one another. Hands—my hands, her hands—roam. Over arms, over backs, memorizing curves, lingering near shirt hems.

We kiss and touch and continue to kiss. With hearts beating hard and breath difficult to catch, we press our lips together one final time, then break away.

Yeah, we've crossed lines today, but there are some borders neither one of us is eager to breach. Lila's eyes shining up at me confirm her approval of the new path we've chosen, and on this path we have time to explore, we have time to kiss, and we have all the time in the world to fall in love.

Lila

The entire sky erupted into hundreds of streaks of light. I never felt so alive. I wished that you were here with me or me with you. But I think you were. Call me crazy, but it was a moment, Lila, and I'm glad I shared it with you. Even if it was from a couple hundred miles away.

~ Lincoln

"I NEED A CODE NAME," Lincoln says over the walkie-talkie I confiscated from my youngest brother's room. It's midnight and the two of us have been hunkered in our positions since nine.

If I squint and stare long enough, I can decipher Lincoln's shadow fifteen feet in the air in the large oak tree near the front of the house. It almost looks as if the tree has a cancerous growth springing from it. For the first hour, I worried over how he dangled from the branch, but I soon discovered that Lincoln's as comfortable with heights as I am at a sale at Macy's.

"What do you have in mind?" I ask. Behind the row of bushes and up against the trunk of a weeping willow, I scan the midnight horizon. The sky's clear. Beautiful white stars twinkle down on us, but there's no moon tonight. A good thing, as Stephen and his traveling band of hyenas won't see us. A bad thing, as it makes it hard for us to spot them.

"Something dangerous, like Razor or Blade."

I hear the tease in his voice and accept the bait. "How about Abe? Or Honest? Those sound like perfect code names."

"Har, har. How about you lay a president joke I haven't heard before."

It's been like this for the past three hours—a comfortable steady stream of conversation. Earlier, Lincoln kissed me...and I kissed him back. Before coming out here, we spent a couple of hours wrapped in each other's arms on my bed, alternating between talking and kissing.

My heart aches when I think of him leaving in the morning, but we have a plan and both of us are sticking to it.

"When did you know?" I ask. "That you had feelings for me."

Static on the other side. Crap. Maybe I went too far.

"I don't know," he says. "It grew over time. I guess I first knew something was up when I wanted to scratch out Stephen's name from your letters."

I giggle, totally unashamed that I like that he was jealous.

"Honestly, though... You wrote me a letter back before school started and I took it with me on one of my climbing trips. At the top of the rock, I read your letter and realized you were the one person I wished I could share the view with."

My lips tilt up with his words.

"What was the letter about?"

He chuckles. "Nothing. That's the strange part. You've sent me letters about Echo and Stephen and Grace and your family and Florida, and I loved those letters. I knew you were sharing your soul with me. But this one letter, you talked about lying in your backyard and watching the leaves in the trees blow. When I was done reading, I found a four-leaf clover tucked into the envelope. I knew then that I wanted to share the big moments with you, but more important the small. I want to climb rocks with you, Lila, then spend quiet time at the top sharing the view with you."

Warmth curls around my heart. I want the same exact thing. "I sent you the clover so you'd have good luck with your admissions letter."

"It worked," he says. "And it'll work again."

"So I have to find you another clover?" I tease.

"Nope. I still have the first one tucked safely in my wallet. I like having something from you close to me."

Overwhelmed, I feel my throat swell a little. He kept a gift I gave him. In his wallet. That is unbelievably sweet.

"How about you?" he asks hesitantly. "When did you know?"

"The night of the meteor shower," I answer automatically. "And then the letter you sent after it." I think of the hundreds of lights dancing across the night sky. "I knew you were watching. I know it sounds stupid, but I felt you with me, and then when you sent that letter describing that night..." I drop off, unable to find the right words to explain the emotion.

Lincoln rescues me. "I know. Me, too."

We sit in silence for a few seconds, both of us absorbing the moment. Finally, I clear my throat and ask, "How many hours is the University of Florida from you again?" We're going to take turns driving back and forth to visit on the weekends and we'll talk on the phone and use Skype and, of course, write letters.

"About four if I stick to the recommended posted limits."

"It's the law," I remind him. "Like the get-a-ticket-if-you-break-it type of law."

"A suggestion," he responds.

Before I can compose my comeback, Lincoln breaks in through the radio. "Incoming."

My chest tightens. They're here. My eyes sweep the yard around my house and my pulse begins to beat in my ears.

I wipe my hands on the side of my jeans to dry them of sweat and lie flat on the ground. Movement out of the corner of my eye causes my breathing to hitch. Three forms skulk against the side of the house. One of them raises its hand in the air, waving for the other two to head toward the front porch.

The lone stray shadow creeps to my bedroom window. Asshole. This has to be Stephen.

I ready the paintball gun, the tank tucked into my shoulder. I align my sight and decide against the shoes, aiming for the heart. Let's see how he feels after I sink a couple of balls into it.

Lincoln's under strict instructions—he'll shoot only after I fire, and Stephen is mine.

After a few seconds, Stephen raises his hand and rakes his fingers down my window.

It is so not your night tonight, buddy. Last night, I was terrified. Now I feel empowered.

I pull the trigger. Pop, pop, pop, pop. The figure yelps and bends over as each ball pummels his body. Shouts from the front of the house tell me that Lincoln has hit his prey.

"They're on the move. On the move." Lincoln's voice crackles on the radio.

His silhouette swings down from the tree in effortless grace, and once on the ground he takes off for the front of the house. I refocus on Stephen. His head whips back and forth, looking for his attacker in the bushes. "Who's out there?"

I drift up from the ground. Still hidden by the rain of branches from the weeping willow, I plug two more balls into the ground, right near his feet.

"Hey!" he yells as he dances away from the paint.

With a snap, I flick on my flashlight and aim it at his face. He places his hand above his eyes in an effort to see who approaches. Paint smears his favorite shirt and jeans. Good. I aimed too low, though, and barely stained his two-hundred-and-fifty-dollar athletic shoes.

I toss the flashlight in his direction on the ground. He blinks twice when he recognizes me. "Lila?" Shock widens his eyes. "I can explain."

This time I aim directly at his shoes. Pop. Pop. Light blue bleeds over his ex-white sneakers. "I'm going to Florida, Stephen. Do you have a problem with that?"

Headlights flash near the driveway. "Stephen!" yells Luke from the driver's side. "Let's go."

When Stephen hesitates, Luke honks the horn and beats his hand against the door of his car. Stephen glances at me one more time. "Lila—"

"There're still some white spots on your shoes." I set my sight on his obsession again.

"I'll call when you've regained sanity," he huffs as he retreats to his moronic friends.

"I'm shooting you with a paintball gun at midnight," I shout after him. "I think we left sane behind a couple of days ago."

When the red taillights of Luke's car disappear, I drop the paintball gun to the ground, flop down beside it and rest my arms on my bent knees.

From the front of the house, a shadow emerges. Yesterday, I

would have lost it if I were outside in the dark with a large figure looming. In fact, yesterday I did just that. Funny how much can change in twenty-four hours.

"You okay?" asks Lincoln.

Let's see, my best friend has moved on, I've conquered my fear of moving away, I shot my pranking ex-boyfriend with a paintball gun and I'm alone with a guy who causes my heart to stutter. "Yeah, I'm great."

And I mean it. It's a small yet humongous realization: I'm always going to be scared of something—spiders, the dark, being on my own—but I don't have to let the fear be in control.

"...and when I came around the corner, he ran into the door of his car and slammed right onto the ground." Lincoln's shoulders move with his laughter as he recaps tonight's events, and I giggle along with him. We lie next to each other on my bed: me in my pj's of a tank top and shorts and Lincoln in a fresh pair of jeans and a T-shirt.

Our laughter fades and we both stare into the darkness. The chirping of the crickets from the other side of the window fills the silence. My muscles have that good, exhausted jellyfish feel. It's two in the morning and even though I'm definitely tired enough for sleep, I'm not ready to give up this precious time with Lincoln.

As if reading my mind, he turns his head toward me. "Are you tired?"

"No." I flip so that I'm facing him and traitorously yawn.

Lincoln chuckles and mirrors my position. He runs his fingers down my arm, starting at the edge of the strap of my tank and ending at the tip of my elbow. I shut my eyes with the exquisite tickle. I inch closer to him and happily sigh when he cups the curve of my waist. It's a heavy, warm weight that creates the sensation of protection.

"You should go to sleep, Lila." Good God, his voice is beautiful—deep and smooth.

I shake my head. "I can sleep tomorrow and the day after that. I only have you for a few more hours." My stomach sinks and I open my eyes. "But you should sleep. You've got a long drive in front of you."

"I should." Lincoln shifts his head so that his mouth is wickedly near mine. I lick my lips and inhale to steady my breathing. We've kissed three times since this afternoon. Each time he's hypnotized me, and I'm greedy to be captivated again.

I nod. "You should." But I really don't want him to—not yet. "Sleep."

His hand slips to the small of my back and presses so that our bodies now touch. A rush of air escapes my lungs. Holy hell, he's solid. I allow a hand to skim along his back, and Lincoln smiles with the caress.

"I will," he says. My skin tingles as his mouth whispers against mine. "Sleep. But not now."

"No?" I try to ask innocently.

"No." He brushes his nose along the curve of my neck, and I could almost moan in frustration. I want kisses, lots of kisses, but I also love the slow burn. Lincoln has talent, and my heart beats faster when I think of all the hundreds of ways we could spend our evenings.

He slowly creates a trail along my cheek, and just when I'm on the verge of begging, his lips finally come within butterfly-inducing distance of mine. This is one of my favorite moments:

the seconds before the kiss. It's like dangling on a ledge with gravity pulling me forward and the wind daring me to let go and fly.

Lincoln breathes out and I breathe in. A synchronized movement that causes my mind to disconnect and conscious thought to float away. A nudge forward on his part, a tilt of my head, and then we fall.

His mouth is hot against mine and my hands tangle in his hair in response. Our lips part and our tongues slide together, a delicious slow movement that makes me want to purr like a cat.

Earlier, we let our kisses be just what they needed to be: simple, a sign of trust, a sign of what's to come, but this feels like more. After the words we've said to each other tonight, I'm tempted by more, but I'm not ready to give up that slow burn.

Lincoln draws my lower lip between his, releases it and then lifts his head. The warmth and sincerity in his eyes tells me he's not ready to leave the slow burn, either. This is why I'm with him, because Lincoln gets me, understands me, possibly more than I understand myself.

"How about one more kiss?" he asks.

"How about more than one?" I counter. "Just a few."

"A few," he agrees. His body melts against me and our lips meet again—a warm, building kiss that causes me to arch into him. Beneath his massive body, I feel small, fragile and protected. I've never felt so feminine, so in tune with another.

Our movements are soft and deliberate. Fingers exploring skin, lips moving in time, feet rubbing against each other. Until it becomes time for one last kiss. One that will be singed into my memory and will carry over until I can be in his arms again.

Lincoln places his forehead on mine and caresses my cheek.

My fingers trace the hollow of his neck, and I enjoy the beat of his heart against my chest.

"We should sleep," he says.

Unable to speak, I nod. Lincoln rolls onto his back and pulls me so that I'm cradled against him. He kisses the top of my head and combs his fingers through my hair. "Thank you, Lila."

Words are still hard, but I find the energy to ask, "For what?"

"For helping me find me again."

I mold myself around him and wonder what our future will look like. Someday distance will no longer be an issue and we'll have more than just letters—we'll be together. Who knows...maybe forever.

"You were always in there. You just weren't looking in the right place." I pause. He's not the only one who rediscovered himself this weekend. "Neither one of us were."

"True," he agrees and gathers me closer. "But we figured it out."

I close my eyes and hug my body to his. Two years of letters, two years of redefining myself and two years of falling for my best friend. As I cuddle into Lincoln, I know that I would relive it all in order to experience this moment again.

Lincoln

I think sometimes things we don't like happen so we can appreciate the good. Like, can I really enjoy a sunrise if I didn't experience the darkness of night? Without her past, Echo would never have met Noah, and without her losing Aires, I would never have met you. So, yeah, I do mean what I said in the last letter. You are like a sunrise in my life.

~ Lila

STRETCHED OUT ON HER STOMACH with her face toward me, Lila sleeps. Her tousled hair falls over her shoulder, onto her cheek. I've been awake for an hour, watching her. She smiles when she dreams. Twice, little lines formed between her eyebrows and I had to stop myself from smoothing them out. She's too beautiful to wear worry. I'll do whatever it takes to ensure her happiness.

Birds begin to chirp outside Lila's window—a warning of the impending moment. Soon, I'll have to say goodbye.

I've got a long drive and a lot of work in front of me in order to catch up with Lila. After spending time with her, going back to letters will be difficult, but we also agreed to phone calls and Skype and weekend visits.

I skim my finger against the soft skin of her cheek, and her head angles toward my touch. Her eyes flutter open and her lips edge up when she sees me. "Hi."

"Hi," I respond.

Someday I'll teach her how to climb a rock wall, I'll introduce her to my parents, let her hold my nephew and I'll confess my love.

Lila reaches up and smooths the hair near my ear. "I feel like I've known you forever."

"Same here."

"I really like you," she says in a low, sexy tone. And I recognize it, the spark in her eyes. It's more than like, more than attraction.

"Me, too."

Her hand glides down to my chest and pauses over my heart. When our eyes meet, I know she notices the spark within me, too. I capture her hand and keep it against my chest as I lean in for a kiss.

"I still expect two letters a week," she whispers.

Our lips move against each other's, and in between breaths I say to her, "I'll send you three."

EPILOGUE

October
Lila

IN THE BACK OF AN auditorium lecture hall, my pencil taps repeatedly against my notebook and my eyes flash for the millionth time to my smartphone, willing it to light up. It's on silent, but I wish it was on foghorn.

A nudge at my foot draws my attention to my right. My friend Jenna nods at the clock and a rush of nervous adrenaline makes the pencil beat faster. Two minutes until class ends and the weekend begins.

Usually, I love Fridays. Lincoln and I chat over Skype before he goes to work, but I haven't heard from him—in four days. It's a record. A horrible, horror-show record. I've texted him twice. Called and left a message once. Checked the mailbox every day only to find nothing. Willed him telepathically to call me two million times. My pride's about to take a trip to hell and I'll call him again if he doesn't reach out to me soon.

The phone glows to life and the pencil falls out of my hand and drops to the floor, rolling down the step to the row in front of me. I don't care. My heart thuds as I swipe my finger across the screen and then...I sink down in my seat. Crap. Not Lincoln.

Jenna nudges my foot again. "Lincoln?" she mouths.

I shake my head and mouth back, "Echo."

My best friend is very happy with the twists and turns of her life. There's some drama right now with Noah's foster sister, Beth, and Echo's been pretty torn up about it. The one thing my relationship with Lincoln has taught me is that distance doesn't mean a friendship ends. It just means you have to make more of an effort.

I read through the latest news and text Echo back a few encouraging words. Her returned smiley face is enough to warm a small part of my heart. Unfortunately, only an acknowledgment from Lincoln can thaw out the rest.

"Have a great weekend!" Our professor claps his hands once and the auditorium is filled with the sounds of people shifting out of their seats and closing books. Jenna and I gather our stuff and leave.

Florida is hot. Not that Kentucky doesn't have its fair share of summer weather in October, but there are typically some cool days thrown into the mix. Not in Gainsville. It's hot every single day.

And I love it.

My body shivers when I leave the air-conditioning of the science building and head toward my dorm.

"Dinner tonight?" Jenna pulls out her keys. We shared the same orientation class and the same fear of not knowing a soul. She's a commuter, but practically lives in my dorm room.

"Sure." It's not like I expect to be talking with Lincoln or anything. My mind replays our last phone conversation, last Skype chat and letters, searching for whatever I said or did wrong that would make him keep his distance.

During a visit here in September, Lincoln took me to the beach; while we lay on a blanket staring at the stars, he told me that he loved me. And I said the words back. My heart swelled to the point of explosion that night. Now it feels as if it's going to collapse in on itself in heartbreak.

A thought freezes me in midstep and Jenna circles back around when she notices I stopped walking. "What?" she asks.

"What if he's hurt?" My eyes widen to the point I feel they'll pop out of my head. "What if he went to go climb and he fell and he's bleeding and he's alone and—"

Jenna tilts her head and the pity in her eyes makes me want to smack her. Instead, I begin walking again. Her sandals snap against the sidewalk as she catches up. "Sorry. You know I think he's great, but it's been four days and he hasn't responded at all. I mean, come on, how many long-distance relationships really last?"

I pause at the crosswalk where I turn left to head to the dorms and she turns right to head to her car. I blow out a rush of air. "I love him."

Jenna now sports a matching oh-how-sad-she-really-thought-this-was-going-to-work smile to highlight the pity-eyes. "We'll go out tonight. Have a good time. Make you forget him."

"It's only been four days," I answer. He'll call. He will. Lincoln loves me, and why do I want to cry?

"Hey, Lila!" I look behind me and quickly step out of the way to avoid being pummeled by Bryant on his skateboard. He stops less than a foot away from me and, in a smooth motion, kicks the skateboard up into his hand.

"Bring Melanie to my game tomorrow night." Bryant's a sophomore and plays a game meant only for men over two hundred pounds of muscle: rugby. The big, bad dude has a huge, bone-crunching crush on the tiny girl from a small town in Mississippi who shares my dorm room.

Jenna rolls her eyes. "Because Lila possesses the ability to breathe life into the dead."

"Stop it or I won't go out tonight," I tell her. Melanie's had a rough time transitioning to life in Florida. Jenna doesn't understand since she still lives at home. Homesickness...it can kill you if you let it, and Melanie is seriously close to coding.

Coding over being away from everyone you love—I get it. I came close to packing my bags a week in, but then Lincoln chatted with me for hours, while I hugged a pillow tight and cried hysterically. He told me I could do it, and I stayed, and he was right. I'm strong enough to live away from home and pursue my dreams.

Jenna backs away, all smiles. "Then I'm leaving before I say something else. See you tonight."

We both watch her leave, and then I watch as Bryant spins a wheel on his board.

"You okay?" I ask.

He shrugs. "I'm scared Melanie's going to go home."

I bite the inside of my lip. "Me, too." I like Melanie. A lot. And I really don't want her to give up, because she'll regret it. Just like I would have regretted staying in Kentucky or heading home after a week.

Bryant drops the board and places one foot on it. "Just bring her to the game, okay?"

I nod and he rolls away.

Melanie doesn't see it, and I was also oblivious until I made the decision to stay. Almost everyone on campus feels scared and alone when they move into the dorms. Each and every smile is forced and faked. Yeah, there's excitement, but there's fear of the unknown, too. I sort of wish I had a paintball gun in my dorm room. Maybe Melanie would feel better if she could pop a couple of paintballs into her fear.

A welcome wind blows through the trees, and I wipe at the sweat forming on my forehead. If everything is going to hell for me and Lincoln, at least he gave me a great memory and lesson to hold on to forever: I'm strong and I'm going to stay strong.

I shove my cell into the back pocket of my shorts and head to the dorms. A plan. I need a plan. Plans make everything better. I'll go out with Jenna tonight. Maybe drag Melanie. Homework tomorrow, then Bryant's game, kidnapping Melanie if I have to. Then Sunday, if there's still nothing from Lincoln...I'll call his home phone.

I enter my dorm and wave at a few girls hanging out in the lobby as I head to the mailboxes. Two I like, but one's a gossip who I hate. Unfortunately, some high school crap doesn't get left behind.

I stop breathing when I notice an envelope in the slot. My hand pulls at the ends of my hair, creating a little pain. It's from Lincoln. It has to be. No one else mails me anything.

All of a sudden all the fear and insecurity I've fought over the past couple of days slams into me and my hands begin to shake. It could be good news. It could be...or it could be bad.

I unlock the small door and slip the letter out of the slot. It's his handwriting. I stare at it. Deciding. Open it here or in my room? Here or in my room? Unable to wait, I slide my finger underneath the lid of the envelope, not caring about the stinging paper cut.

The envelope falls from my hand as I yank open the paper. I blink. Several times. And read the two words again: *Turn Around.*

I spin on my toes, the world rotating twice at the normal speed. My heart rockets up to my throat—it's Lincoln.

With his hands shoved into his jeans pockets and his thumbs sticking out, Lincoln leans back against the opposite wall and flashes a small, unsure smile. Oh, my God...he's here.

With three leaps, I throw myself at him, and because he's made of solid steel, Lincoln catches me without stumbling back. He wraps his arms around me and lifts me off the floor. I giggle as my feet sway back and forth.

"Why didn't you call?" I don't bother pulling away when he sets me back on the floor. Instead I cuddle my head into the curve of his neck and inhale to smell his dark scent. He's here, but then I flinch as if jolted with electricity. What if he's not here to see me...? What if...?

"I wanted to tell you in person," Lincoln says.

A little unsure, I draw back and hold on to him only because he holds on to me. *Please don't let go. Please, please don't let go. I love you.* "Tell me what?"

He lets me go and I wrap a hand around my stomach as nausea overcomes me. Lincoln withdraws a piece of paper from his back pocket and hands it to me. I stare at it and he motions with his chin for me to open it.

I do and the nausea takes a hike when I see the beautiful words addressed to Mr. Turner from the University of Florida. "You were accepted."

Lincoln flashes this unbelievably beautiful smile. "I knew I'd spill if I talked to you before then. I got in. As of next semester, I'll be here right beside you."

He's worked hard for this—spending an entire summer in school, then this semester in community college at home. With no scholarship, he worked a full-time second-shift job in a lumberyard to save money to pay Florida's tuition.

I touch his cheek, and he reaches up and grabs my hand, keeping it pressed close to his skin. Yep, Lincoln's running days are officially over, and as much as I hate that his path has been difficult, I'm sort of grateful. It taught him how to work toward a goal and it taught me how to stand on my own.

"I'm proud of you," I say.

His grip on my waist tightens as he brings me closer to him. "I told you I'd never let you down again. I love you, Lila."

"And I love you."